Kitane, Bull Jumper

Courting and Catastrophe in
the Bronze Age

Suramarti Saga #1

J. Oestreicher
&
D.R. Oestreicher

Omega Cat Press — California

Omega Cat Press, independent publishing since 1990

"For how I firmly am resolved you know;
That is, not to bestow my youngest daughter
Before I have a husband for the elder."
— Act I, Scene 1, The Taming of the Shrew
— William Shakespeare

Dedicated to our daughters

Also by J. Oestreicher & D. R. Oestreicher

Pandemic Mysteries:
Darwin's Paradox
Plague of Equals

J. and D. R. Oestreicher

Table of Contents

Authors' Foreword

The Minoan civilization was centered on what is today the island of Crete and flourished for about 1,500 years, starting around 4,500 years ago. During the height of their civilization, the Minoans were traders and artisans who left extraordinary architectural achievements, most notably Knossos, and artistic creations in the form of pottery, jewelry, and frescos.

The culture was believed to be matriarchal and peaceful. Around 3,500 years ago, a massive volcano destroyed the island colony of Thera (today known as Santorini). Around this time evidence indicates the peaceful, matriarchal society transitioned toward a patriarchal and militant society.

While archeologists have recovered written records, they have not been able to decipher the language (known as Linear A) or solve the mysteries of the rise and fall of this fascinating Bronze Age civilization.

This book imagines an answer to these historical mysteries.

At the end of the book, the reader can find a list of characters, a glossary and gazetteer, a discussion of bronze age astronomy, another about language, and a bibliography for further reading.

The authors also drew on Shakespeare's Taming of the Shrew with Kitane and Biaja standing in for the two women looking for husbands. One major difference is the setting within a matriarchal society, which changes the courtship dynamic significantly.

MAP I — KEFTIU

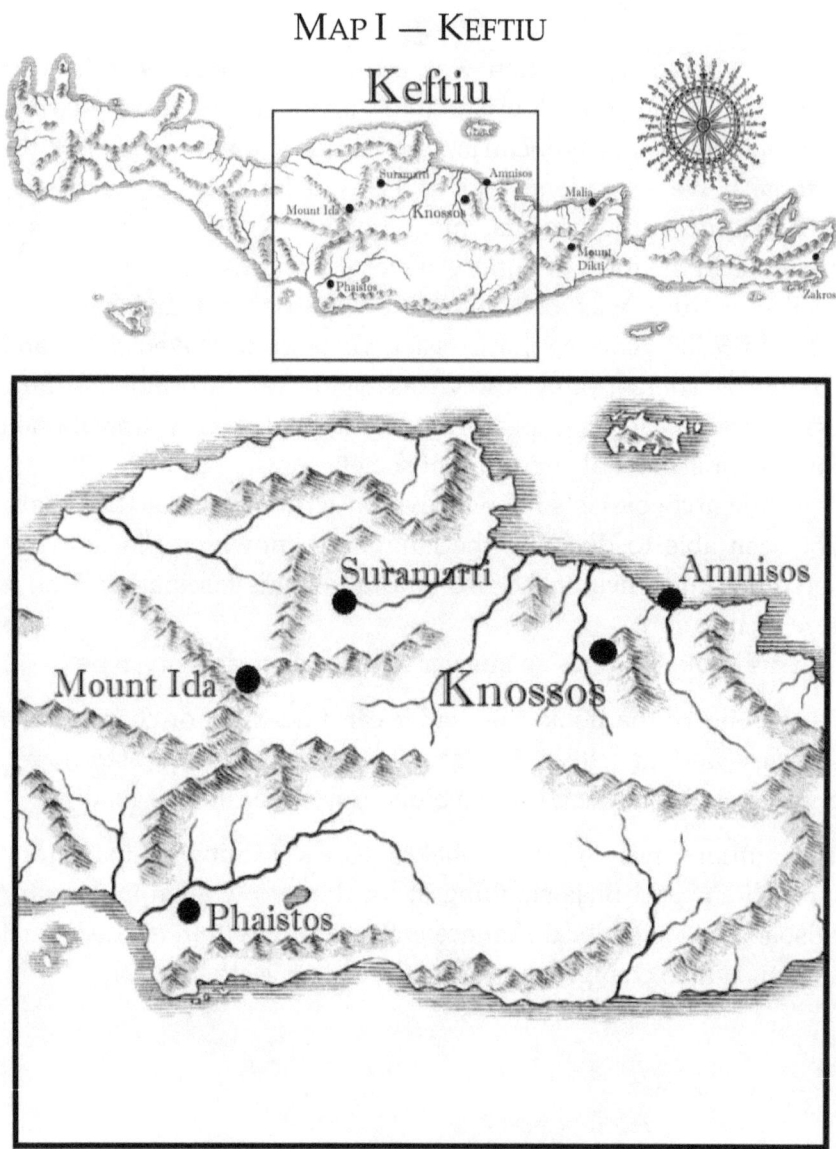

(Present day: Crete)

MAP II — THE MIDDLE SEA
(Present day: Mediterranean & Aegean Seas)

Hittite Empire

Arzawa

Hellene Territories

Thera

Archipelago

Keftiu

Alashiya

Middle Sea

Kmt

MAP III — THERA
(Present day: Santorini)

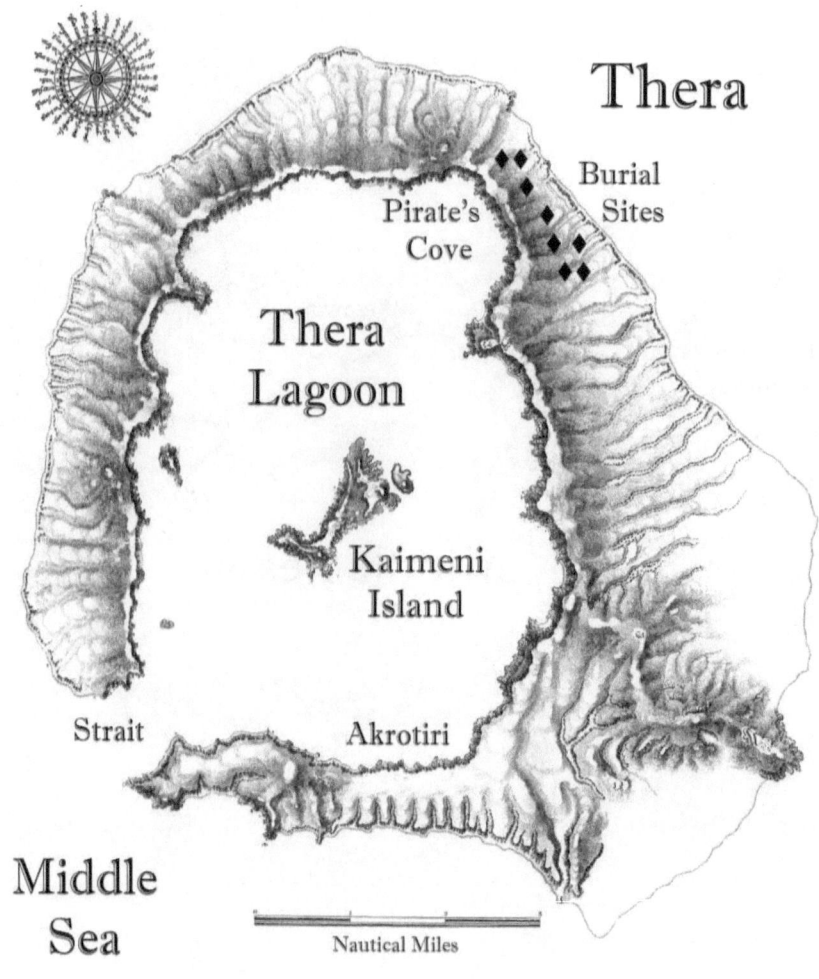

Thera

Burial
Sites

Pirate's
Cove

Thera
Lagoon

Kaimeni
Island

Strait

Akrotiri

Middle
Sea

Nautical Miles

PROLOGUE — DR. THERESA MARTIS AT ATHENS AND MT. IDA, PRESENT DAY

"There is no evidence for a priestess-led society, only for matrilineal family order and inheritance! That you continue to argue otherwise demonstrates to me—and to this entire committee—that you are incapable of objective analysis when it comes to Crete or, indeed, the Aegean entire!"

Dr. Whitten Stone's face was alarmingly red, and his eyes looked ready to pop out of his head. Dr. Theresa Martis, the object of his disparagement, waited a moment, composing her response. Just because the committee chair had gone off the rails did not mean she should follow him.

"There *is* evidence, it is simply ambiguous," she said. "I continue to believe there is a place in every discussion for open minds about the possibility of historical matriarchies. I believe it is wrong to decide *a priori* that Minoan society must have been patriarchal, simply because others at that time were."

And, she thought, in the absence of a decipherable written record, these men see the 3,500-year-old evidence through their privileged male view of power politics. *Why should an island between Greece and Egypt be anything but a kingdom and military power?*

Dr. Whitten made a disgusted face, then looked at his neighboring committee members. His expression changed to dismay as he realized he did not have the committee's support in this aspect of the disagreement.

"It is my intention to open and explore the remaining mountain sanctuaries and to utilize the latest ground-penetrating radar scans to locate and either clear or confirm the presence of other so-far-undiscovered sanctuaries and caches. Perhaps we might even find another Phaistos Disc."

"Wouldn't that be wonderful?" someone said.

"In undecipherable Linear A," grumped Dr. Whitten.

"But an excellent application for GPR," someone else added.

Several on the committee made comments on this, and Dr. Martis' only true ally amongst them, the American, Dr. Barbara Sanders of the University of Allentown, spoke up. "The more caches we find, the more likely we are to find our Rosetta Stone," she murmured.

Many agreed with this, including some voices in the audience.

"I call a vote," one of the committee men said.

Voting proceeded. Dr. Martis could only hope they would see fit to fund further exploration of Crete. That was more important than who would lead the expedition. Though it would be nice if it were she.

She hoped there would be financial backing for what she already was planning to do, on her own if need be. There was still a scant year's worth of support in the trust her parents had left her. Once that was gone, she supposed she would buy a goat and live off cheese and wild olives.

She listened as they tallied the committee's vote.

She had forgotten how hot and bright the Cretan sun could be. Fortunately, she had worn a long-sleeved shirt to protect her arms from the scrapes she often got on a dig. She'd worn a hat, to shade her face. But the Mediterranean sun burned her neck, along with the tops of her feet, except where her sandal straps had covered them.

Today she wore socks and shoes over the thick coat of aloe she'd put on her feet, and an aloe-soaked bandanna covered her neck. She wasn't going to take a day off for sunburn, she was so eager to find and make an opening into the Mt. Ida side-cavern.

Of course, several different archaeological teams had researched the big cave at the top of the mountain many times. But the GPR had discovered an adjacent cavern—one so far untouched by modern hands. The scan showed "things" inside the cavern.

She smiled to herself. GPR had paid off. Too much of Minoan archeology had been expended on Knossos with its 1,300 rooms and 24,000 square meters of space. With new tools, old ideas would be overturned.

She and her team members had looked carefully at all potential entrances to the "new" section. There was no outside entrance, and GPR showed no disturbances anywhere along the slopes leading to the main cave. A side tunnel from inside the main cavern had most likely accessed the undiscovered section. The tumble of rocks that blocked that access lay before her now.

She had the crew set up lights, so everyone could see what they were doing. A rough-excavation crew removed rocks—some of them truly great granite boulders—from the top of the opening. She wanted to climb up there and help them, throw rocks with her bare hands down to the floor of the main cavern, where laborers would load them into donkey carts and haul them outside for careful examination. She had not yet seen any signs of frescoes or other art on the walls of the main cavern, but who knew what the place had looked like before the cave-in?

The workers built a zig-zag path up to the top level where they had at last removed enough stones to peer into the new branch of the cave. Her foreman led her up the path, bright lights on his head and in their hands. She leaned gingerly against the stones at the top and looked down into the new section.

"Oh, my God. Oh, my God. There are stacks of stuff. I can make out pithoi, tablets, and piles of things covered in dust." She turned to the foreman, who was grinning as fiercely as she was. "When can I go in?" she asked.

Days, it took. Days to clear enough rocks to enter and make a path down the other side. She started moving rocks herself at the end of the second day, though what she wanted was to dive straight into the treasure trove.

At last she could descend. Her assistants, Dr. Jane Katsaros and almost-doctor Aeneas Sanna followed her down into the dark and dusty space.

It was huge.

It was full, the floor covered in goods.

Dr. Martis wiped the tears from her cheeks and got her assistants to set up work lights and help organize a marking grid. She had Sanna set up two computers for recording grid information and to categorize finds. Jane would be responsible for the manual recording as backup.

Outside, workers continued removing rocks, lowering the wall, and increasing access.

They emerged to discover they'd not only spent the day but most of the night working on their discovery. Sanna made phone calls, Dr. Katsaros wrote e-mails. They both sent out photos. Dr. Martis opened a bottle of wine, which they shared in celebration as they ate the stew their cook had prepared.

It would be good to get rid of the wall. They could set up a small space for food and drink well away from the workspace, which they must keep pristine and uncontaminated.

She worried about the lights, and what damage those might be doing, but they weren't going to have a choice about that. They could not work in the dark. She planned to bring in de-humidifiers the next day and get those set up with extension cords running over the wall. It was starting to be a capital-W Wall, it was such an obstruction.

Sunday, the work crew took off for church or family visits, or both. Aeneas Sanna drove down the mountain and west to spend the day in civilization in the charming city of Chania, where his girlfriend was staying. Dr. Martis and Dr. Katsaros went back into the find.

How could they stay away? Once Jane realized Dr. Martis was going, she insisted they go together. They left their lunch along the path down the Wall, bringing only their water, lights, and cataloging tools. Dr. Martis was intent on clearing a space in the center where they could stand. Each item removed must be photographed *in situ*, then in close-up, and then packaged for cleaning and removal to their study site in the main cavern.

They'd cleared a path about two feet long toward the center of the circular area when they paused and retrieved their lunch. They sat on the narrow shelf of the zig-zag path down the Wall, legs dangling, in the shadow of the lights directed at the floor of the cavern and the find.

"At least we don't have to worry about sunburn anymore," Jane said.

A rumble of the earth was her answer.

"Earthquake?" Dr. Martis wondered, abandoning lunch, and heading back down to the floor.

Jane joined her on shaky legs as the rumbling intensified.

"Rockfall?"

Both, they realized. First an earthquake, jerking and shaking everything around them. Next a rock fall, as the Wall closed up again, the ceiling above it collapsing with a thunderous roar. Rocks slid down the Wall, obliterating the path.

Dr. Martis wanted to throw herself over the piles of ancient Minoan goods to protect them, but what good would that do? She was not nearly big enough.

But the ceiling above the find held solid. Rocks tumbled down the Wall even after the quake had stopped shaking. A few stones fell in the back of the cavern well out of sight from where they stood. They could hear grinding and rumbling around them, even where the light did not show them what was falling.

At last there was silence.

Amazingly, the work lights remained lit. Dr. Martis turned one to light the Wall.

The path was gone, of course.

The opening was gone, as well. There was no way in or out.

"Well. They will know where we are," Jane said.

"Yes. Okay. That main cavern has withstood many centuries of quakes and the devastations of time," Dr. Martis cleared her throat. "There's no reason to think they won't be able to dig us out again, just like we found a way in in the first place. It may take a couple days, again though."

The fans of the de-humidifiers hummed, audible above the sound of a few more rocks clacking down in the distance.

"We have water. Do we need to be concerned about air?" Jane wondered.

A rumbling filled the air, then quieted, leaving them shaking. "Aftershock."

Jane nodded.

"I think air will not be a problem," Dr. Martis said, her eyes caught by a glint of daylight far above them, toward the back of the cavern. "It's not a reflection of our lights, it's an opening to outside."

"Maybe another way in."

"Possibly." Dr. Martis looked around. They had lights; they had room. They could do nothing about earthquakes or aftershocks. "Might as well work, I suppose."

Jane grunted, dusting off her computer. "No internet. But we can still catalog. I don't see the good camera, though."

Dr. Martis brushed dust off a stack of stone tablets. It was a bit of a miracle that none had been crushed by falling rock over the eons, if such quakes and rock falls were common.

She found a map of Crete incised on the reverse side of the top tablet she held. "Photo, please," she asked, and Jane complied, using the laptop's camera. "Highest quality setting?"

Jane nodded.

They recorded the map find and set it in the "discovered" stack. Dr. Martis picked up the next tablet in the stack. She looked it over, then quickly grabbed the next one in the stack. She stood holding them, the skin on her arms prickling, then going numb as she stared in disbelief. Beside her, she heard Jane gasp.

They stared, mesmerized.

"Holy shit," Jane said at last.

"Do you see what I see?"

"The Rosetta Stone for Linear A," Jane said, absolute certainty in her voice.

"It's an A to B and B to A dictionary."

"Unbelievable."

Dr. Martis sat down in the tiny space they'd cleared, holding the tablets against her lap like twin babies.

"Oh, my God," Jane said. "Photos and photos. Then, what if you read, and I'll type the definitions in?"

Goosebumps still covered her arms and legs. She was so stunned, it took a few moments for Dr. Martis to make sense of the first definition.

"Keftiu," she said. "The Minoan word for Crete, written out here in Linear A. And Linear B."

"Linear A first, suggests that was the primary, at the time?"

"Perhaps. We cannot jump to conclusions, but that would make sense. Linear B we know is Mycenean Greek."

"What's next?" Jane asked.

ACT I — LIFE OF A BULL JUMPER

Scene 1 — Kitane at Suramarti
Ϟℂⵊ

The bull whuffed then trotted toward Kitane. She reached her hand out and scritched the base of each ear. She had to stand on her toes to reach. Enosidas then tossed his head, ready to work out.

Kit gave his head a pat, then turned and trotted in a big circle, side by side with the bull. When they had good momentum built, she reversed, running the opposite direction, getting ready for her leap. Then she heard the roar and felt the shaking of another earthquake. She and the bull both stopped, waiting it out. Sometimes the quakes were quick; sometimes they kept going, as this one did. It felt like the ground beneath their feet was heaving, like some monster was trying to hatch out of it. Then it settled, the noise diminishing, the ground lying back down, still.

She heard the braying of donkeys and saw two animals running wildly toward them. She patted Enosidas' head, then ran toward the donkeys, arms waving. It would not do to have them spook the bull—he'd stayed calm so far. The donkeys' wide white eyes saw her. They changed direction, running down the hill toward the Tylissos fields.

"Which is probably where they belong, anyway," she muttered. Jura needed to get his animals under control. Weren't they supposed to be penned up?

Frowning as she thought about it, Kit moved downhill toward Tylissos. Jura's pack animals were kept in a pen with a good solid fence. Normally donkeys did not panic any more than any other animals. Was something wrong at Tylissos villa? She glanced back and saw Enosidas browsing on the sweet new grass coming up after the recent rains. He should be fine. She walked toward the neighboring villa, thinking about Jura.

He had been wooing her for months now. He compared well with her other suitors, except for his stiff disposition. The man seemed made of stone he was so rigid. She kept hoping she would catch him in a softer mood, but that hadn't happened yet. He was her mother's pick, and he would be a good match. But. She sighed. Was there always a "but?" Wasn't there one perfect man among her choices?

In truth, it wasn't only the choice of suitor that was the problem. The direst problem was the bulls. If she or Eno ever made a mistake and lost the competition, he would be sacrificed at the end of the "celebration."

She shuddered, just thinking about it.

This "tradition" was simply wrong. No trained bull should ever be slaughtered, no matter how badly they lost, how poorly they showed. She did not believe such a sacrifice could ever honor Jasasara, the Goddess of life whom they honored with the bull jumping.

At Tylissos, the steward directed a crew of atomai, bringing saws and axes to cut up the big tree that had fallen into the donkey pen. No wonder the animals had been terrified. One donkey lay pinned and squealing beneath the weight of the ancient plane tree that had crashed down upon it.

As she approached, Kit saw the steward bend down and cut its throat with a sharp bronze blade. The squealing stopped. Jura ran into the pen from the small Tylissos stable, a blade in his hand, a moment too late to do the deed. He and the steward conversed, then Jura spotted Kitane walking toward them down the hill.

"I am so sorry for your loss," Kit said, nodding toward both the tree and the donkey.

"Potidas is still so angry," Jura said.

"I am asking the Goddess to intervene," Kit said. "I am asking my sister for her blessing for all Keftiu. Whatever has angered Potidas, She may be able to intercede for Her people."

Jura nodded. "I honor Potidas each morning, in the traditional way."

"That is good, Jura. It is good." But is it enough? Kitane wondered, looking at the destruction.

The sun flowed warm over her shoulders as Kitane admired the new courtyard they'd built around the goddess tree. Her family had long intended to enclose the ancient tamarisk tree and create a small shrine here behind Suramarti villa. Now it was done. She stepped forward, under the tree.

The dappled sunlight the tree let through felt softer, as though the tree had gentled it, making it kind. She eyed the bench her cousin had carved from the dead goddess tree at Zakros. The costly wood had been smoothed and oiled and then left in its natural shape on a stone platform carved to hold the wood. Kit wandered over to look at it, and to compare the wood with the living bark of the tree that shaded it.

"Such a waste of resources," Jura said, walking into the courtyard on sandaled feet. "The money spent on that wood could have paid for the entire new wing of your home."

Kit eyed him over her shoulder with distaste. "Even if you think so, the living tree should still be honored with bare feet!"

Jura looked down at his sandals, retreated to the small gate, and slipped his footwear off, placing them outside the gate beside his dog, who had better manners than its master. Re-entering the courtyard in his now bare feet, he essayed a smile at her. "Sorry," he said, seeming to address Kit more than the Goddess with his apology.

Kitane continued to scowl, her peaceful enjoyment of the new enclosure now broken by this stone of a man. It wasn't as if Jura was poor, either, he just was a natural conservative when it came to spending—even when it was for the Goddess or the Temple. Or rather, his mother was, and Jura was too much a traditionalist to try to change that.

She could think of nothing to say to him. She looked back at the tree, brought her clenched hand to her forehead with respect, and backed out of the enclosure. She turned and walked rapidly toward the new wing of the Suramarti villa, abandoning Jura and the tree together.

Her mother's sister and family had recently fled from Akrotiri, which the priestesses said was no longer safe. The new wing had been built to house them here at Suramarti, and it had created another kind of courtyard, sheltered on three sides, filled with flowers and trees and a small fountain. The small rectangular garden was protected on one side by the new wing, on the other side by the old wing, and topped by the original cross-corridor with a shrine and a long wall pierced by doors and windows—the polythyron—for celebrating the Goddess.

With six sleeping rooms, three workshops, and a plumbed toilet per wing, the villa was now huge.

She walked through the corridor of the new wing into the dining hall where the family was gathered. Everyone was here except her brother Diwoki—at sea in his trade ship, and sister Sakusna—also at sea, with the trader Tros.

Halima, Diwoki's wife from Kmt, far to the south, and her two little children were a dark accent among the bronzy-skinned Keftiu. Kit reached out a hand and clasped Halima's slender one. As graceful and agile as she was, Kit always felt chunky next to the tall, slim Kmt woman. They embraced, and Kit explained how the ceremony would work for the benefit of her sister-in-law.

Kit's eldest sister, the Priestess Qazipatima, had come from the Knossos Temple to bless the villa's new wing. Kit smiled to see her little sister Biaja following Qazi rather like a little bald duckling waddling after its mama. Bee was an initiate at the Temple, learning what the school there had to teach.

Her mother, father, aunt, and cousins filled the space along with several neighboring telestai, including Jura. She nodded at Jura, then grasped her cousin and friend Isari's hand. The three young women, Halima, Kitane, and Isari, watched as Qazi and Bee walked around the room, making sure everything was in place for the ceremony.

"Everything looks so beautiful," Isari murmured.

"The rooms are lovely," Halima said, her accent clipped and charming.

"The Goddess has truly blessed us," Kit said softly.

They all filed through the lustral basin one by one, removing and stacking their sandals, and cleansing their bare feet with the herbs and leaves in the bottom of the basin. Kit had helped gather them that morning. The greens released a delicious aroma of bay and thyme and rosemary as they were crushed. Formally, each person saluted Qazipatima, fisted hand to forehead, as they entered the ceremony room on cleansed bare feet.

Qazipatima the priestess would transform into an incarnation of the Goddess before she made the blessing. Kit tried not to burst with false pride at the sight of her beautiful sister honoring the Goddess Jasasara and blessing their lovely villa. It was due to Jasasara, not to her mother or father or her sisters or any of the Suramarti families, that they had such a beautiful home. Kit knew that pride was one of her personal failings, and she worked on conquering it every day.

Beside her, Isari sighed and Halima stood a silent shadow. They faced the first door and window combination. One novice priestess who had come with Qazipatima oversaw opening the door and window shutters of the polythyron at the correct times. Another initiate, probably her sister Biaja, would light and extinguish the lamps, so that the appropriate sections of the frescoes would be illuminated as the ceremony proceeded from west to east. At peace, Kit smiled and prepared to celebrate Jasasara's blessing.

After the family and guests finished eating and the ceremony was complete, the younger people dispersed. Halima went to her rooms to care for her infant daughter and chase after her son who had just discovered running.

Kit invited Isari to come out to the field to watch her practice. Isari was suffering from displacement, loss of her regular routine after the abrupt move her family had made. Much had been left behind when they escaped Akrotiri. The earthquakes were so large that they had been felt on Keftiu. Priestesses at Thera had sent strong warnings to all their people on that island. Earthquakes and steam warned of the Goddess' anger. Now Isari was on Keftiu with nothing to do.

"Take Isari around with you," Okune, Kit's mother had said. Okune had welcomed the refugees, but expected them to help at Suramarti. "Let her see what is available here for her. She could set herself up in one of the new workshops, perhaps."

"What is she going to do for tools and supplies?" Kit asked.

"Her father should be here soon with all that he could carry on the last family boat," Okune said, frowning with concern. "Until then, I suppose she could borrow from us, or perhaps from Jura's family."

Kit automatically scowled at the mention of Jura.

Her mother went on, "She could follow you around until then, perhaps help groom Enosidas?" At Kit's even deeper scowl, she hurriedly added, "Or perhaps they could use help at the Temple; she can go with you to the ceremony at the end of the week."

"Yes, all right. I'm happy to have her with me. But no one touches Enosidas but me. He *is* a bull, mama, not a pet for all to play with!"

"Of course," Okune had said, lips quirking.

Still scowling, Kitane went to find her cousin.

"I don't understand," Isari said as they walked to Kit's practice field. "I don't have to marry until I find the perfect match. Is your family rule so different from ours?"

"You don't have three sisters," Kit said. "That's the difference. Mama made sure we all understood that a long time ago. By age seventeen we have to be married, or the estate passes along to the next youngest sister. Qazi and Sakusna both chose not to marry— Qazi for the Goddess, Sakusna for trade."

Isari shivered. "She sails with that pirate Tros."

"He's not a pirate!" Kit looked at her cousin in shock. How could Isari believe such nonsense? Perhaps her mother was feeding her stupid stories—or Kit's own mother was. "He's a powerful trader. And rich." She thought about Tros, his strong, angular face, his dark-lashed deep green eyes. "I have thought about choosing him."

Isari looked at her, disbelief clear in her features. *"Tros!?* Oh, Kitane. *Oh."*

Kit flinched. Now even her cousin was going to become involved in her choice of husband? It felt as if there was pressure coming from all sides. Then she thought of her father, who had said nothing at all about husbands or suitors or choices. She felt as if she had been hugged by the quiet, kind man. Perhaps she should spend more of her time with him, who did not pressure, did not judge her.

With a sigh, Kit turned and signaled Enosidas to catch up. The big animal had stopped to chew on his favorite snack bush. Kit watched carefully to make sure he did not get into the nearby oleander that made him so irritable. He—and she—needed to be perfect for the ceremony.

"Try to think of Tros as his own person, not as the wild man your mother has obviously described," she said. She hated to be short with Isari, but really. The prejudice she showed when she had never even met the man was a disgrace.

Isari shrugged. "Everyone says so, not just mother. But if you like him, I will try to also. He's probably better than Jura, who is just as big a statue as you said."

"Mother is looking at his wealth, his villa, his proximity. I don't think she's ever looked at the man himself. Oh! So rigid, so...umgh!"

Her cousin laughed.

"Oh! Remind me on the way home to show you where the best clay dig is."

"Yes, I want to get started, my hands are bored," Isari said with a smile.

They stopped walking at the top of a hill amidst wild grasses and small shrubs. This was Kit and Enosidas' practice field. From here they could see far down the slopes to the distant, blue Middle Sea, the jumble of stone and clay roofs of the Temple at Knossos, tiny so far away in the East and partly hidden by laurel and pine trees.

"I think it would be best if you sat here. I usually take him in a circle around this hillock. We won't run up here because of the stones, and they make a nice seat."

Isari nodded and lifted her pale blue linen robe up enough not to pull as she sat down. Kit tugged her own robe off over her head, leaving her torso and legs bare, just the tightly-woven wool loincloth covering her, held up by the wide firm belt that fitted around her waist. She took off her necklace with its seal on a leather thong and set it on top of her robe. Isari patted the robe and watched as Kit stretched out briefly, then asked Enosidas to begin trotting in a circle.

Kit moved alongside him for a bit, loosening up her muscles some more, then she paused, turned, and ran the other way so that she and the bull were on a collision course. As they neared one another, Eno lowered his head and sped up a bit. She leaped, placing her palms firmly on the broad plane of his forehead, letting the momentum of her leap carry her feet over her head and the bull's. She landed facing backward, the soles of her feet firm and flat on Eno's back. She pounced forward, still using the momentum from her first leap and the bull's speed, placing her palms on his rump as she flipped off his back onto the ground, momentum still propelling her forward in a trot away from Eno and then around to meet him again.

After a few leaps, Kit fed Eno a handful of the oats she kept stashed in a sack among the stones, then stretched out again, and let Eno rest between the practice runs.

Isari walked over to where Kit was catching her breath. "Wow cousin, I never saw bull jumping like that on Thera. Our jumpers always grabbed the bull's horns. The bull did all the work tossing the jumper to the animal's back. Your way looks harder, but more dramatic. Is it dangerous?"

"There are many styles of jumping. I found when I used the horns, I always over-jumped. I landed on Eno's rump without room to push off for my final flip. I imagine it has something to do with the jumper's size and the bull's strength."

20

Isari shook her head. "I thought all jumpers did the same tricks."

"No, the most dangerous part of bull jumping is the many falls and injuries while figuring out the best method for the team. It's one reason no one ever tries a different bull once the camaraderie between the jumper and bull develops."

Isari watched, eyes wide, as Kitane and Enosidas performed the maneuver over and over again. Two leaps, two flips, two landings. For the ceremony, with thousands of people watching and the terrible penalty for losing, they needed to be perfect.

SCENE 2 — JURA AT TYLISSOS

𐘃 𐘄

Jura relived his childhood as he walked through the ancient olive trees to the highest point of the Tylissos villa. He entered the sanctuary and could recall his father's voice.

"Young Jura, the goddess Jasasara planted this olive tree when she granted your mother's family this land." He had raised Jura to touch the double-axe. *"We call this a 'labrys' and it honors Jasasara."* Next to Jasasara's monument, the horns of consecration towered over young Jura. *"When you look up at the twin pylons, imagine the horns of the god Potidas' Bull."*

The horns of consecration no longer towered over him and these early memories filled Jura with gratitude to be living in this time of peace and prosperity. Even when his little brother Ukan was born and Jura felt abandoned, he could find solace in the sanctuary. Jura upheld the traditions of his mother, and his mother's mother, with pride and honor.

His assistants filled the bull's head rhyton with wine and placed two baskets of small terracotta cups at his feet. The preparations for the morning ritual were complete. The atomai, all given time off for the ceremony, lined up to receive their portion of wine to honor Potidas, god of earth, sea, and the underworld.

Before the ceremony began, the earth shuddered, the baskets of cups rattled, and the atomai fell to or sat down on the ground. Jura reached for the nearby horns of consecration for balance and stood strong as a third pylon. He never skipped an opportunity to praise the gods. "Do not be afraid. Get up, arise. Potidas protects you in his sanctuary." They followed his example, though arising cautiously.

Jura was a telestai, a landowner. As a child, he walked with his father and looked for broken bricks, crushed stones, and pottery shards.

"Father. Look at that! What is it?

"Jura, you know. That is from an earthquake that collapsed an old building. All our villas and temples rest on the ruins of previous ones. The telestai always rebuild bigger and better after earthquakes."

Jura did not fear earthquakes.

The line of people moved quickly, each picking up a cup and receiving the portion of wine Jura offered. After refilling the rhyton several times, fifty supplicants stood around the horns of consecration. Before the ceremony started, Jura addressed the gathering. "Welcome, atomai of Tylissos. Together we protect and bless Keftiu."

He raised his cup and turned to face the priestess along with the others.

A priestess originally from Mount Ida, dressed in a purple robe with a gold belt and matching gold circlet, pronounced the invocation. Each person took a sip of wine, anointed the horns with the remainder, and smashed their cup.

One more earth tremble, stronger than the rest, knocked over a basket of cups and ended the observance. Still, Jura had honored Potidas as custom required. He knew the God approved.

He drank one extra cup of wine and smashed it for the many telestai and atomai who neglected their responsibilities. The gods had inflicted the recent spate of earthquakes because the people of Keftiu had forsaken their traditions. Good times had brought lax observances of these important rituals.

Later in the day, he searched his family's storerooms for a gift to bring Okune, something appropriate for the mother of the woman he wished to marry. Today he selected a pitcher, painted with graceful blue dolphins. He knew that both Okune and her daughter Kitane favored dolphins, and the Keftiu artists had portrayed them so well they almost looked like they were alive and leaping in the waves.

He filled the pitcher with his special olive-blossom honey and sealed it with beeswax. He strapped it to his back for the short walk to the Suramarti villa. That family was the oldest and most revered in the area. Some said that they had settled here even before the gods chose Knossos for the temple site.

"Thank you for the lovely pitcher and your fine honey." Okune handed the round-bottom pitcher to a servant and took Jura's hand. "Walk with me and tell me what is on your mind."

Even though tradition said Kitane would make her own choice, everyone knew Okune was in charge. Okune had already broken tradition by demanding her daughters marry by seventeen or forgo their inheritance. Two daughters had already lost their chance. Jura had to please both Okune and Kitane if he wanted to marry Kitane, and Kitane's seventeenth birthday was closer every day.

They walked through the vineyard. He began, "Every day I come to visit Kitane, but she is always busy. Yesterday she rebuked me for not removing my shoes, then ran away. Before that, she sat with her ladies spinning. Another day she worked with her father, Radamitu, in his goldsmithing workshop."

When Okune didn't reply, he thought she didn't believe him. Then he recalled, "Once she was baking pita. She walked around the saj, constantly turning each piece of bread with a long wooden spatula. Each time a loud clang interrupted our conversation."

Okune kept walking in silence.

After waiting to see if she would respond, he continued. "Sometimes I think she is avoiding me. I can never get her alone to talk about us and our future. My father says I must talk to her uninterrupted."

Okune nodded. "Your father is correct. Even though I support the match, you know the ultimate decision is with Kit."

She said it was Kit's decision but without Okune's endorsement, his chances were small. He took her comment as an indication that while he was her choice, he was not Kit's.

Discouraged, he looked at the ground. "I don't know what to do. I have followed the Keftiu way. I am here every day. I bring gifts, some of which she accepts. Still whenever I am around, she is busy. My younger brother Ukan, who is in training at Knossos, just laughs at me. I am sure he talks to her sister Biaja in Knossos and they laugh together."

Her mother took a deep breath as if she felt talking to her future son-in-law was tedious. She let out the breath and spoke slowly, as if to a child. "Every morning she walks by herself to our sanctuary in the hills." Okune pointed toward a hill covered in olive trees, but he didn't look up. He knew the place well. He had lived next to the Suramarti villa all his life.

When Jura's first facial hair sprouted under his nose, his father walked with him up to the sanctuary. Under the ancient olive tree, he explained, "Your sister Eluwari will inherit Tylissos." He then put his arm around his son, "Radamitu and I expect you will marry Kitane and move to Suramarti."

Jura did not reply. Even at that immature age, he understood that such decisions belonged to the women.

He had never expected so many difficulties courting Kitane. He explained to Okune that custom demanded he honor Potidas each morning to help calm the earthquakes, something others were neglecting. "I'm certain that these critical ceremonies are getting smaller and fewer. I dare not stop now."

Okune nodded. "Good, thank you."

That short answer told Jura to try something else. "Thank you for your suggestion. For one day, I will have my steward organize the ceremony. I will be there tomorrow morning."

"Without your shoes," Okune said with a quirk of her lips.

Jura couldn't believe that these women kept complaining about his shoes when they had not fulfilled their responsibility of daily rituals to entreat Potidas to save Keftiu from the earthquakes. Of course, Kitane's extraordinary bull jumping also pleased Potidas and helped. Nothing at Suramarti was simple.

"Yes," Jura said. "Without my shoes."

SCENE 3 — BIAJA AT KNOSSOS
𐘾𐙝𐘂

Biaja rubbed at her scalp again. The barber had scraped a little too closely that morning, and cut her. She tried to rub it gently, so as to not start it bleeding again, but it stung and itched. Had he put something in it? She crept out of the prayer room on her hands and knees and went to the apothecary.

"A small pot of beeswax, please?"

"For what purpose, Initiate Biaja?"

Wordlessly, Bee turned her head and pointed at the cut.

"My, that is a bad scrape. Did you annoy the barber?" the woman said, turning toward a shelf on her right.

"I did not," she said. "Not that I know." Perhaps he was drunk the night before, she thought.

"Perhaps he was too rushed."

Biaja shrugged and accepted the tiny bowl.

"Chamomile flowers in that, for soothing. That should help."

"Thank you." She immediately scooped up some of the soft scented wax with her fingertips. She set the bowl down, pulled the back hair lock out of the way and spread on the ointment. Immediately, the sore patch on her head felt better. She gently spread another scoop over the area, then took the bowl and walked to her dormitory. She placed the beeswax on the little table of cosmetics on the wall opposite the six sleeping mats, where all the initiates had their hairbrushes and other personal things.

She stopped to admire one of the other girls' hairbrush, with bristles made from boar whiskers, or some such thing, that had come from very far away. It was made near the land of the stone circles, which her brother the trader had talked about. She wondered what other treasures they might have in that land, where such a wonderful brush was made. Such faraway places always sounded like intriguing mysteries to her. She sighed and set the hairbrush back down in its place.

She was stepping out into the hallway to head back to the prayer session when she saw the klawiphoros heading her way. She flinched, trying to hide when there was nowhere to hide.

How did they ever get initiates to stay and become priestesses when they were exposed to someone like this woman? The klawiphoros was in charge of the initiates; it was her job to keep track of the young women and ensure they exhibited proper behavior. But no one called her by her title. Everyone called her the Aurochs instead, even the Priestess Qazipatima, Biaja's eldest sister.

Biaja ducked her head as she passed the old woman, but she did not get away so easily. The Aurochs grabbed her by the upper arm and pulled so that Bee came to a stop sideways. Then the Aurochs leaned forward and spoke in her ear.

"This. Is. Prayer. Time," she said in a heavy whisper.

Bee bowed and kept silent, as was proper. Of course, she knew it was prayer time. But it did not honor the Goddess to have blood dripping everywhere from improperly shaved heads. She turned her face away from the Aurochs, to show the back of her scalp, now glistening with beeswax.

"Oh, such a deadly wound," the Aurochs said. "I see it has been treated. Get back to the business of prayer. One-mark extra service duty tomorrow morning."

Biaja bowed again, still silent. Inside, she seethed. This was not her fault. It was not her doing that the barber made a mess of her head! The unblessed *barber* should have to clean for an extra mark!

Nopine commiserated with Biaja over the extra work.

"She is so strict. I wonder if she is just unhappy?" Nopine said.

Bee set down Nopine's hairbrush and began braiding her friend's hair. "I don't know. I mentioned it to Qazipatima and she seemed surprised."

"You are so lucky your sister is here to watch over you."

"Actually, I believe that is part of the problem. Maybe the Aurochs thinks I expect special privileges or something."

"But you don't, Bee. I make a lot more mistakes than you do," Nopine said, handing Biaja the ribbons to tie off her braid. Bee wished she could have hair again. She would not be a full initiate for another half-year. Then she could let her hair grow out. Nopine's had been growing for two years now. It actually looked like hair, instead of one front and one back lock pasted on to a bare head.

Biaja shook out the ribbon strips of fine linen and aligned them to each other before tying them onto the ends of Nopine's heavy hair. Even after two years, Nopine's braids were frizzy from all different hair lengths—the ends escaping and looking rough.

"Qazi said, 'That is not the Goddess' Way.'" Biaja shook her head. "Then she said something about aching bones, and walked away. I really hope she doesn't talk to the Aurochs, or I'll be in even more trouble. I should never have said anything to her."

"It will be all right, Bee. I'm sure the priestesses keep an eye on things, to be certain they are fair."

"I am pretty sure this *is* the Aurochs being 'fair,'" Biaja said, sarcasm weighting her tone.

Nopine went on to the classroom where she was studying writing and reading and accounting.

Bee went and got a rough pitcher of warm water and a scrub brush. She put some lye from the pithos full of cleaning solution into her pitcher and took it into the Preparatory Room.

She'd worn her oldest robe, but now she tied the skirt up with her tight belt and got down on her bare knees. They'd heal better than the robe would. She scrubbed the floor of the lustral basin, thinking about robes. Qazi had been wearing a beautiful purple over-gown when they'd spoken the previous evening. For the ceremonies she had been doing all day as priestess, Qazi had tied on one of her two flounced long aprons and had worn a matching headdress. The colorful traditional outfit was the only thing Bee looked forward to—if she ever got that far in the Temple.

She dunked the scrub brush back into the pitcher of lye-softened water and scrubbed each stone of the steps with care.

Qazi was already so beautiful, and when she donned the formal clothing of a full priestess she became quite intimidating, both because of her position, and her beauty. It was no wonder the guasileus begged Qazi to attend when he must entertain foreign dignitaries. She was impressive and carried the Goddess in an aura of sheer feminine power. Her Presence helped all Keftiu.

Biaja sighed. Even Sakusna was prettier than she and Kit were. It was as if the Goddess had run out of beauty by the time she got to the two younger girls. Kitane was graceful and agile. Bee didn't know what she herself was yet. She liked to think she had lovely blue-black hair and interesting green eyes. But so far, no man had even looked at her, much less shown interest in courting—because Kitane must marry first. If she was going to at all.

Biaja shook her head. She could not make up her mind between wanting Kit to marry Jura so that she herself would not have to, and wanting Kit to not marry at all so she could inherit.

Owning and running an estate did not seem so bad. She liked the idea of having the resources of an entire villa at her disposal. But it would be at the cost of marrying Jura. She felt a fair amount of sympathy for her next-oldest sister. In truth, no one seemed to want to marry Jura. If Kit married him—which she must do soon or lose her right to inherit—then Bee could choose among the many other young men available. She went down the list geographically: closest to Suramarti was Tylissos where Jura lived, along with his younger brother Ukan. The younger brother was funny and kind—and well on his way to becoming the village drunk. He would not do for Biaja.

Then there was the young man from Amnisos, the port below Knossos. What was his name? He was cute, but foolish. Maybe he would improve with age.

She went and dumped the dirty water from her pitcher down the drain, made her way to the rainwater cistern by the kitchens and refilled it. She splashed lye into the water with a wooden scoop and used a stick of firewood to stir it. She returned to the

Preparatory Rooms and, turning the corner, ran full into the Aurochs. Sudsy, caustic lye-water splashed over both of them.

The Aurochs was speechless. Then the woman snatched Biaja's robe loose from her belt and used the skirt to wipe her own legs and feet dry. Biaja set down the pitcher and tried to help.

"Stop it, you stupid girl! You are only making things worse!"

Bee froze like a mouse in the shadow of a hawk.

When the older woman was dry enough not to drip, she glared at Biaja, then turned to walk out of the room. Just before she went through the door, she turned back, scowling, and said, "There is a load of goods that must be taken to the shrine at Mount Ida. That will be your job tomorrow. You may take one donkey to carry the goods. You will, yourself, walk. I expect you back before the end of the following day. Use this time to think about what you are doing, who you are becoming, initiate."

"But— " her hands flew up to cover her traitorous mouth too late to prevent the escape of the single word.

Eyebrow raised, the Aurochs went on, and "I expect you to help the priestesses there to store away the votive cups and tablets."

Biaja bowed. She stared at the Aurochs' back as the woman swept from the room.

So much for being able to join Nopine at the initiate's ceremony tomorrow.

SCENE 4 — TROS ON THE MIDDLE SEA

The open sky and bright midday sun provided no warning for the afternoon winds. The waves washed into Tros' ships, soaking the oarsmen. He could taste the salty sea foam that filled the air. He raised his triangular signal pennant and spun it around. "Left. Left! Turn left into the waves."

The oars on the left side, totaling three hands, rowed in reverse and the three hands of oars on the right side pulled forward.

"Archers, don't just stand there. Help them."

The archers squeezed in beside the oarsmen. The two smaller boats, with only a hand of oars on each side, followed his lead.

"Good. Now bail. The rest of you bail!"

The nighttime oarsmen, who had been sleeping amidst the cargo, jumped up, grabbing pottery and baskets, and bailed the ships. The bare-chested men, soaking wet and covered in salty spray, sweated and grunted as they battled against the sea.

Tros kept careful watch, for the ships threatened to sink into the angry water as the waves grew larger. "Bail! Faster!"

He took a mental inventory of the cargo in his care. The cheapest, heaviest cargo would go first. However, he was an experienced captain, the best sailor in the Middle Sea. This storm would not frighten him into foolish action. He knew his men. The danger gave them energy and strength.

He had the foresight to take on an extra load of bronze-gold. It didn't bring as great a profit as the scarcer bronze-silver, but the extra weight kept his ships stable in rough seas. Regardless, this would be the first to go, if the gods demanded a sacrifice.

With sunset, the winds exhausted themselves, and Tros had not needed to throw any cargo overboard. By dark, the wind had stopped and they were victorious. Tros had once again demonstrated his expertise as the ships' captain. The crew knew he was the best.

This reputation went beyond his home in the Hellene territories, all the way to the island of the major trading families—

Keftiu. Several months ago, one of the strongest trading groups had partnered with Tros. Their representative, Sakusna, now occupied the captain's tent at the front of the ship.

Tros hadn't wanted a woman on his ship, but in the end, he had made the family pay dearly for her passage. The fee had been enough to replace the worn woolen sails with shiny new linen ones. Only the best ships had linen sails, and this showed everyone that Tros was the best.

He smiled to himself when the Suramarti seal stamped the agreement. Beyond the prestigious partnership, he had bigger plans. He intended to marry Sakusna's sister, Kitane.

With the evening calm, Tros' little fleet returned to their easterly heading on the final portion of the many-months journey. They had visited the great island of Alashiya for bronze-silver which they had traded for cypress lumber from the Hittite empire on the eastern shore of the Middle Sea, and for gold, ebony, and ivory from the Pharaoh of Kmt. In Kmt, Sakusna also traded Keftiu palms for date palms. They completed the circle back to Alashiya for more bronze-silver, and on to Arzawa for resin before returning to the Archipelago.

This had been a profitable voyage. Now they headed back to Keftiu and the grand port of Amnisos. When Tros agreed to the voyage, his hope of a union with Kitane had prevented him from negotiating too hard. Tros could still feel the attraction of her athletic form, and her tantalizing odor, a combination of sweat, grass, and her bull.

During the long expedition, the situation changed. The gods expressed their displeasure with the Keftiu outpost on the island of Thera. The volcano at the center of Thera, known as Kaimeni Island, spit steam and ash. The god Potidas shook Thera, Keftiu, and the entire Archipelago. Everyone abandoned Thera. Others refused to even sail through the Archipelago. He was not afraid, and if Sakusna had not demanded her strange concept of fair trading practices, he could have made a good profit. He regretted his alliance, but the thought of the lithe Kitane kept him going. *If Sakusna had not been on board… If Kitane had not been so tempting…*

While it was still dark, Tros scanned the night sky for the big and little *Double Axes* **to locate the star of the** *Great Bull,* **the North Star.** Once he confirmed his ship's course, he looked to the east.

The *Triton* was rising in the east. Next would be the *Dolphin* with the sun. Tros had not slept. Even though the wind was calm and the sky cloudless, the god Potidas had stirred the sea all night. Tros had pointed the ships into the angry waves, but still the crew had not slept, bailing all night.

Tros was a young captain. He'd only lived four hands of summers. From an early age, he had sailed with his father, over his mother's objections. She kept him home during short days of the stormy season and prayed to Jasasara the rest of the time when heavy winds could interrupt even the nicest days. His parents fought over this constantly. In the end, Tros sailed during some winter storms and stayed home from some peaceful summer voyages.

Fate and his mother made him miss the journey that was hit by an unexpected summer tempest. His father's ship had not returned. His mother urged him to stay ashore and manage the family bronze-silver mines, but he demanded to sail in his father's memory. Now, also in his father's footsteps, he intended to marry a Keftiu girl and bring her to the Hellene territories.

The boy at the top of the single mast shouted, "Ship!" Tros wasn't a pirate, but every ship at sea was an opportunity for profit, profit he didn't have to share with Sakusna's organization. Information, trade, and salvage could all benefit the better crew and captain, and Tros was the best.

Tros curled his fingers into a small opening and peered through it to better view the target. It was a solitary ship, sailing the Middle Sea alone. No experienced captains went out with just a single ship. Small planks lashed together marked the ship as cheaply made. Tros sensed many possibilities.

"At stations, boys. Row hard. Approach with all speed. Archers take your places."

Tros rushed to the raised platform at the front to assess the situation. In the dim dawn light, he tripped into the captain's tent that shared the observation deck.

"Tros! Tros! Goddess curse you! What are you doing running around before the sun?"

That would be Sakusna. Tros had to remind himself that she was the Suramarti representative and Kitane's older sister. He put up with her imperiousness because her cooperation would help to convince the Suramarti matriarch that he was a suitable match for Kitane. More than once, he'd considered abandoning this annoying sister. As a last resort, he planned to have the lovely Kitane hide in the tent and sail away without her family's approval.

They neared the foundering ship, and an old woman shouted across the waves, "Greetings, we claim the right of the goddess for assistance at sea."

Sakusna immediately responded, "I am of the Suramarti family. Have no fear, the goddess brings you comfort and security."

Tros clenched his fists and assessed the situation. The approaching ship had oars totaling less than two hands on a side compared to his superior three hands of oars, plus his smaller boats. Their wool sail, which they should have furled in this weather, had been through too many storms. The rising sun shone through the tattered edges and holes eaten by rats. The ship held too many passengers and not enough cargo. It rocked precariously. Only the mercy of Potidas kept it afloat.

"Rowers, stow your oars." Tros looked away from the sad ship to Sakusna. He shook his fist, "Do not forget this is *my* ship. You are just a passenger. You do not speak for the captain."

She turned to Tros and replied in a steady voice, "I speak for the goddess."

He thought, *you and your goddess can join this sorry ship. Potidas can take you to his underwater home.*

SCENE 5 — PAIAN AT KNOSSOS SOUTH ENTRANCE
‡Ɏ⫟

Paian had traveled across the sea to Knossos, the grandest temple in all the world. He was born in a settlement far to the north dedicated to the Hellene goddess Athena. At first Knossos bewildered him with so many rooms and stairs. He thought the Keftiu who built it to be gods. Later he found the peaceful and orderly Keftiu society even more unbelievable than the Temple.

He could still hear his father, "Never venture outside our walls."

When he grew big enough to carry his own sword and shield, the advice changed, "Paian, always stay with your patrol group, never go off alone."

Still he could explore more than the girls, who were never to leave the village. Since he'd arrived in Keftiu, he'd not had an occasion to even unpack his sword or shield. Even without venturing beyond the temple walls, he observed and interviewed, writing a history of his visit to the exotic land of Keftiu, complete with sketches and a map.

Today he received shipments from the peaceful countryside. Men and women walked for days to deliver goods to the Temple with little concern for their own safety. The well-traveled paths presented negligible risk from man or beast. He waited in the south house. To pass the time, he took a piece of damp clay from a leather pouch that hung from his waist. He flattened it into a miniature tablet, inscribed a short poem, and hid it on a high shelf to dry.

Bull jumper of grace and agility
You inspire my admiration, my awe,
My love.

Due to today's festival, many people streamed over the ravine across the wide viaduct. Beyond the rolling hills to the south and west, he could see the sacred peaks of Mount Ida. He hoped someday to visit the holy sanctuary, but he still worried that such a journey would be dangerous without an armed escort.

Initiation Day, he thought. Groups of boys and groups of girls, all with shaved heads, walked through the South Entrance, chatting nervously. Most wore undyed wool, uncut cloth, wrapped around their youthful bodies and tied with coarse ropes. The rare robe dyed green or blue stood out in the mass of grey wool and olive skin. Many wore bracelets. Some girls wore small earrings and pendants with blue or green stones sparkling in the morning sun.

He searched the crowd for seal stones. Even in far-away Athens, he had heard of the Keftiu seals. For the entire world, seals indicated a people of organization. He tied his seal around his wrist with a leather cord. He had traveled to Knossos carrying a block of red marble, smaller than his fist, just for this purpose. Of course, he'd waited for his arrival to get it carved, as the most accomplished sculptors were in the Knossos workshops.

The seal stones marked the children of the telestai landowners or other important people, including scribes like himself. He silently thanked his mother for insisting he learn to read and write. Athens might be dangerous, but the people of Athens valued writing more than temples and gold. He thought proudly, *so many Athenians can read and write they do not need seals.*

The writing of his home differed from Knossos Temple writing, but there was enough in common and he picked it up quickly. Often, he wrote the same thing twice to keep in practice with both forms.

Behind the heads of the initiates, he spied a line of donkeys. He walked down the road to meet them, noting that none in this group wore a seal stone.

He greeted them with, "Welcome pilgrims. Blessings of the Goddess Jasasara upon you." Taxpayers would have been a more accurate salutation, but pilgrims sounded nicer, politer. Besides, he didn't know the Keftiu word for taxpayer.

The leader, no older than the boys and girls attending the festival, replied, "Blessings to you also, scribe Paian, from across the sea."

She recognized him. This was not the first delivery he received from her. He looked again and blushed in embarrassment at not recognizing her. "Goddess' greetings and blessings to you Maza, good friend."

She replied, "The Goddess may bring blessings, but the God Potidas shakes the ground terrifying the children and animals."

She added, "Do you have another poem you want delivered to the bull jumper?"

He worried that she remembered too much. "No poem today."

Paian felt nervous speaking to Maza. She belonged to the worker class, atomai. Since he could read and write, he was an elite on Keftiu where the atomai and telestai led separate lives. Back home all those living within the village walls were equal. They lived or died by the efforts of the group. This was something the Keftiu could learn from the people of Athens.

He thought of himself as an outsider in this strange place. He belonged with neither the atomai nor the telestai. He could read and write, but he didn't own land. Back home his mother had a school where all could learn their letters. Something else the Keftiu could learn. He found the situation awkward and confusing, but he tried to remain neutral, to be a friend to all.

He led Maza and the donkey train away from the initiates. "Because of a festival today, we cannot use the South Entrance. We must go around to the west."

She kicked a rock.

"I'll bring you as close as possible before we need to carry them..." He looked at the line of donkeys. They were laden with cloth sacks, so not olive oil, or wine. They could have brought ceramic clay, or wool for weaving, or plaster for frescos, or herbs for dying. Knossos required so much from the countryside.

It was none of those. The odor answered his question.

"...carry the onions to the storerooms."

She gave him a faint smile. "I trust you, Hellene Paian, to be fair."

They tied the donkey train in the west courtyard and carried the onions. Paian carried a sack on the first trip as a friendly gesture. Everyone else made several trips. As with all routes through Knossos, the halls turned many times, like a maze, until they reached the long repository corridor.

They emptied their sacks into waiting pithoi, the large ceramic storage jars which could easily have held a couple of those initiates marching to the festival.

Each time they filled a pithos, he secured it with a string and a wedge of clay from his pouch and imprinted the seal with his stone. He also made Maza a duplicate seal for her receipt.

She filled one sack with clay receipts and another with the empty sacks. He walked them out and watched until they disappeared at the bottom of the ravine where they'd water their animals for the return trip, to somewhere....

Back in the south house, he retrieved his poem. He wrapped it in a grape leaf and sealed it like a pithos. With Maza gone, he'd have to find another courier, but that was safer for the secrecy of his plan. He put it in his pouch along with his remaining supply of clay.

In the middle of the day, someone came to relieve him, and he went to the Central Court. The festival would certainly have food, and the seal stone around his wrist would gain him entrance and the privilege for a bowl of barley in olive oil with some bread or pistachios.

As he ate, he looked across the crowd for someone who could deliver his poem to the bull jumper, someone that lived or worked along the path to Mount Ida. He collected his courage and asked one of the initiates, "Do you go to Mount Ida often? Can you deliver my poem to the bull jumper who lives on that path?"

The girl ignored him and walked away. He turned to another and repeated his query adding, "Please. I am from across the Middle Sea and have never been out of the temple."

She looked at him. He gave her a crooked smile.

The girl pointed across the hall. "That is Biaja. She might help you."

"The one with the shiny black seal stone around her neck?" he asked.

"That's the one," she said and ran off to catch up with her friends.

When Paian left Athens, tears ran down his mother's face as she hugged him. She whispered in his ear, "You father wants to you learn Keftiu writing. He sees the days when we might go to war with one another, and we will benefit if we can intercept and read their orders."

He held his mother, "You know I am a good student. I will learn to read and write Keftiu. I will even write a story of my travels, twice, with both letters."

She did not let go, "You have not asked me what I want? Why do I let my son travel so far away?"

"What can I do for my mother?"

"You can bring home a Keftiu bride. They are the brightest and strongest. A Keftiu bride will be the best partner for you."

"Yes mother, so you've told me. I will not forget."

Paian searched for a Keftiu wife. His first choice was the graceful bull jumper. He watched the girl with the black stone as he walked around the large room, tightly grasping the small clay tablet wrapped in a grape leaf.

"Blessings of Jasasara, lovely Biaja."

She turned to him, first with a smile, but when she didn't recognize him, a small frown. "Who are you?"

He ignored her lack of return blessings. He thrust the package toward her, "Here. For the bull jumper that lives on the path to Mount Ida. Would you carry it there for me?"

She paused as if she would not take it, but finally did. She smiled as if there was some private joke here.

"Lucky for you, I am off to Mount Ida soon. I can carry the tablet, but I cannot assure she will read it."

He retreated, walking backward, embarrassed, but hoping the bull jumper would receive the tablet as he intended. Maza had delivered a couple of poems, but he'd not received any replies. Women of Athens loved poems; Keftiu women were different. He found this hard to understand.

The afternoon deliveries distracted him from his quest for a bride. The first shipment included many sacks of plaster. The plaster came from a nearby gypsum quarry. He knew some gypsum came in blocks of different shapes and sizes, but the quarriers cooked much of the gypsum to make plaster that the Keftiu used to cover their walls.

He directed the donkeys laden with plaster to the west courtyard. They had a longer trek to carry the plaster up two levels of stairs to the throne room. The new throne room had a beautifully carved throne made of gypsum. The walls were white. He watched the artists carve lines in the plaster. He could see plants and animals taking shape. Baskets of black, red, yellow, and blue pigments awaited the next step.

ᛉᚳᛂ

Kitane led the way as she and her mother walked toward the orchards and fields that were part of the Suramarti estate. The morning sun was hot on their heads and shoulders. The warm rain that had arrived at dawn had cleansed the air of dust and freshened the vineyards and olive groves. It was pleasant to be outdoors. She skipped like a small child, then remembered she walked with her mother. She stifled her exuberance and attempted a more adult mien.

"The brickyard is constantly engaged in production now," her mother said. "We used to have workers there for a week or two at a time when needed, but now the supply required is constant." Okune shaded her eyes, looking east toward Knossos for a moment, then back at the village they approached.

"Why?" Kit asked. "Is that because the village is growing?"

"Partly. And partly because earthquakes constantly damage the buildings." Okune sighed. "I wish we could afford to let the villagers build from stone, but we are so far from a quarry—it is an expense we cannot afford."

"The new wing in the villa cost a lot, then," Kit said, thinking of Jura's comment about the Goddess-tree wood.

"It did, indeed. Fortunately, harvests have been good these last few years. And our trading ventures have worked very well for us. Diwoki is a marvel at it."

"Sakusna?"

"She is less of a marvel. I still believe she has taken a huge risk in attempting to recruit Tros to our fleet."

Kit bit her lip. "He is a very good trader."

"He is, and yet he is also a very good Hellene," Okune said, twitching the skirt of her robe away from a puddle.

"You mean he does not care about Keftiu."

"Indeed."

Kit thought of Tros' deep green eyes, his smile that warmed her with his appreciation of her body, her movements. He seemed to care for her. Was he only thinking of himself, his own people? She frowned as she thought about his compliments—about her gold dragonfly necklace and her matching gold earrings that her father had made. About how lovely her new fine linen robe was.

Yet also, Tros seemed to appreciate Enosidas, and her bull jumping. It was perplexing. He had also suggested she would need to give that up if she became a wife and a mother. She was not willing to stop bull jumping yet. As the winner four years in a row, hopefully soon to be five, she had a good deal of influence at the Temple. She must see changes made in the bull sacrifice before she stepped down. She must save Enosidas, and the other jumpers' bulls from the sacrificial knife.

She glanced toward Knossos. How could the priestesses not see that killing the magnificent, trained animals was *not* honoring the Goddess? The Goddess was Life. How was she honored by the *deaths* of Her beasts? The jumpers and their bulls trained for years to be good enough to perform in the ceremony and honor Jasasara. It made no sense to sacrifice those animals to Her instead of offering a wild or untrained domestic one. That suggested to her that the sacrifice, despite the prayers and ceremonies for Jasasara, was actually for Potidas, who could be violent and cruel.

The priestesses considered themselves the last word when it came to honoring the Goddess. Sometimes Kit wondered if their rules were more about power and control than about the Goddess' wishes. She hugged herself and sighed deeply. She had a lot of work to do to prepare her arguments. She hoped to ask her mother for help.

They stopped walking at the top of the hill above the brickworks. Four men and a woman worked in the yard, slopping clay-rich mud into wooden drying forms.

"I've never been quite certain how they manage to keep the bricks from sticking to the ground as they dry," Okune said, obviously fascinated with the process.

Kitane dutifully turned her mind to the bricks and watched as another two workers shook finished dry bricks from the forms and stacked them on the platform for other workers to load onto donkeys. They would deliver the bricks where they were needed most—there was no tax on bricks, of course, because Knossos did not use them. Lumber and stone went to the Temple, but there were neither of those resources at Suramarti.

Thus, these bricks were available to Suramarti villagers and craftsmen for their own homes. A few also went to the workers at Tylissos—Jura's family estate, since their supply of clay—both the kind for pottery and that for building—was poor compared with Suramarti's. In exchange, Jura's family always sent honey, and sometimes a chunk of the ammoudha stone good for carving, which they mined from the hill below their villa.

Below, the foreman called out for a break, and the workers moved under a palm-thatched shelter to drink and rest. Okune watched them gather and chat, then she smiled at Kit and they moved on together toward the vineyard.

"Well, I am sure you know I did not invite you to join me to look at bricks, Kitane."

Kit groaned. "Suitors? Wedding?"

"Are you coming to any decisions?"

Kit thought about Jura, comparing him to Tros. Jura was a well-built man, with a face that was more attractive than many. But he definitely was not as handsome as Tros. And in behavior— Tros was a man who was sure of himself and moved rather like a bull jumper: he was smooth and agile, but a bit raw in his strength, and he commanded attention. By comparison, Jura was tame and uncertain, as if he did not believe in himself.

"Jura came to the shrine this morning to greet me with a bouquet of wildflowers."

"That was nice," her mother said.

"Yes. And no. He is so plodding. I think he has not had an original, creative thought in his head since he was born, Mama."

"Mmm. I think you might be surprised, if you gave him a chance."

"He's stiff, boring."

Her mother nodded. "All right. I can see that, but remember that his mother waited a long time before having children."

Kit thought about Jura's elderly mother and small family.

Okune stared off into the distance and whispered, "Jura's mother is closer to your grandmother's age. Her friends worried that she wouldn't have any children. 'What will happen to Tylissos?' they all wondered. The women celebrated when she became pregnant, but twice they were disappointed when she delivered a boy."

Kitane found this history interesting, but— "How does this recommend him as a partner? He does not have an adventurous spirit; he is old before he is old." Kit stared down at the bricks drying in the sun.

"Once he leaves Tylissos, he will be freed of the weight of his eldest child responsibilities. This may uncover hidden energy. Also—can you see that he could bring balance to your venturesome nature?" Kit looked up to see her mother's eyes steady upon her own. "Sometimes boring is good!" her mother went on. "He knows and loves this land. He honors tradition and all the things that make Keftiu strong."

"Papa is strong! Also, creative and funny. He honors tradition. Do you think he is also boring, mama? I don't."

"Sometimes. Because he gets so focused on his gold-crafting and little else. But he is a gentle man, and a kind one. As is Jura."

Kit made a face, wondering why she was so reluctant.

Was she just afraid to choose among her suitors? Afraid that her life would change, that *she* would change. That she would have to?

And that brought another thought. Was she simply unwilling to share her life with anyone else? Was she just as selfish as Biaja, after all?

Meanwhile her mother considered others. "What about the boy from Malia?"

Kitane could feel her insides flinch. "He is, as you say, a boy. Even our Zetis is more mature than he is. It would be like marrying a child. And it is very difficult to imagine what he will become, because he is not grown up yet."

"Mmm," her mother said. "Danqata, or whatever his name is? With the quarry at Mount Dikti?"

"We seem to have nothing to say to each other," Kit said. "And he is appalled that I am still bull jumping, 'at my age.'"

"Oh, that surprises me," her mother said. "Wasn't there someone from Zakros?"

"I am still thinking about him. It would help if we could meet again, spend some time together."

"Yes, he is rather far away." Okune looked across the vineyard, eyes distant. "Well, of course I am in favor of Jura, he was my suggestion. But if not him, then who?"

Kit took a deep breath. Then, "I am liking Tros."

Her mother was silent a moment. Kit kicked at a stone in the dusty path with the edge of her sandal.

"Well, he will be wealthy someday, I think," Okune said. "But I also think you would hate him trying to control you and all you do. The Hellenes are martial and patrilineal—at least all those I have met."

Kit thought about that. She thought it odd that her mother would view Tros' strength as a desire to control, at the same time she thought Jura's strength was following tradition. Strength was strength, wasn't it?

Her mother glanced at her face, then went on, "You and he would clash, my Kitane. I do not think fighting all the time is better than being a little bored sometimes." She cleared her throat, voice getting louder and harder. "Besides, what are *you* to contribute to a marriage, if not creativity and bold energy and quick intellect? Do you think *Tros* will appreciate those qualities? That Jura would not?"

Again, Kit was silent, thinking. She had realized some time ago that she kept changing her mind because none of her options was strongly pleasing. A decision seemed hopeless.

"Perhaps, Biaja should inherit," she blurted.

Okune shrugged. "She is young and selfish—flighty yet, but she might improve."

"What about Zetis? He is eager for power, and he is your favorite."

"That is exactly why your little brother is *wrong* as the head of Suramarti clan. We are not about power; we are about quiet cultivation, about growth and consistency. What he wants sits at Knossos. And he is not my favorite," Okune laughed. "Whatever makes you think so?"

"We all think so. You are almost always concerned with him and what he does, more than the rest of us."

Okune looked at her. "He requires the most attention, that is true. He is youngest. Like you, he is agile, energetic and smart." She looked off into the distance as she went on, "Unlike you, he has the traits of a spy: slyness, a chameleon-like ability to change, an interest in secrets. He could be helpful at Knossos. He would be a disaster as head of Suramarti."

That was a surprise. "Do you really think so?"

Okune nodded. "But I will not let that happen, Kitane. We have four excellent daughters. Before I gave the estate over to Zetis, I would pull Qazi from the Temple. Or I would insist Sakusna return from the trade routes. Even your cousin Isari is a possible fifth choice. But you and Biaja are still considering your options, and I am encouraging you. Zetis will not inherit."

Kit blinked. Her mother was so emphatic it caused her to rethink the family dynamics. She thought she could see what her mother meant about your youngest brother. But Qazi? Frowning, she said, "I did not think they released a full priestess from her vows."

"It can be done, though I would prefer to leave her where she is happy. She loves what she does, and she is good at it. Sakusna loves to travel, though she will tire of it eventually, perhaps." Again, her mother glanced at her, then away into the distance. "Do you truly have no interest in marrying? Do you have no preference of suitors?"

"I just can't choose." Another long silence. "Perhaps Tros," she murmured again.

Her mother looked sad. "Kit—" Okune took a deep breath. She did not look at Kitane as she went on, "You must let Tros know that if you marry him, *you will not inherit*. I will not hand over Suramarti to a foreigner, especially a greedy one. I suspect that will diminish his 'interest' in you rather quickly."

Kit stopped walking. A flash of rage swept through her, surprising her. "Oh? What happened to it being *my* choice?" She was yelling now, she could see workers in the vineyard looking at them curiously. The more she thought, the angrier she got. "*You* set this ridiculous date requirement. *You* chose your favorite suitor, you press for a decision, and now you inform me that I can choose and still will not inherit? Do you think Jura does not have his eyes on our holdings as much as Tros?"

Not intimidated at all by Kit's sudden anger, her mother blinked and calmly said, "Of course he does. But he knows how to run them, Kitane. His olive groves yield more per tree than even ours do! He would be a benefit to us. And he would be *here* with you to help run it, not off trading."

"Oh, yes, he would be here—he would never have the courage or the curiosity to be anywhere else! But our fields are only part of Suramarti. What does farmer Jura know about trading? About the other part of our holdings: our ships? Nothing!

"Tros is strong and decisive," she went on. "He's adventurous and successful. He would be as big a help to our trade ventures as Jura would be for our fields, which need no help at all, I might point out."

"I grant Tros knows about ships. But I also think he knows more about *taking* than he does about *trading*. In any case, Sakusna is assessing this very thing now. I do not want another daughter riding in ships away from Suramarti, which is where Tros would expect you to go."

"You want a husband for a telestai daughter, and you think that is me and Jura."

"I do, with some reason, Kit. You love Enosidas. You love the orchards and vineyards and grassy hills. You even love that stupid dog of Jura's that chases our cat. I think you are the family's best candidate for the conservator of the lands and creatures of Suramarti." Her mother gestured to the Middle Sea, turquoise and flashing in the sun to the north. "I think you would be very unhappy sailing around on a ship, with no home. How could you take Enosidas with you?"

"Oh! You will take home away from me, if I do not marry *your* choice on *your* schedule!" She shook her head and turned away from her mother. "A schedule you could change if you really wanted to give your daughters a choice, Mother. But you don't. Choices are dangerous! Choices are not predictable! I don't have a *choice* at all. You want your family to follow *your* plan, and nothing else!"

Kit could feel her heart threatening to burst from anger, from betrayal, from the attack that her mother had mounted against her. She turned and quickly walked away, before that anger pushed her to do something she would regret. She would be happy to leave Suramarti and her mother's plans, her mother's constant control!

If Tros had been there, down in the harbor at Amnisos, she would have fled to him at that moment, leaving everything and everyone else behind.

SCENE 7 — JURA AT SURAMARTI

⌐ ⌐

Jura set off early the next morning with Kano. The sleek dog, white with islands of brown, was the ideal companion, always happy to walk or hunt. She preferred to be with Jura rather than the hunting pack. He appreciated her company, except when she was too curious and got into trouble.

Her curled tail wagged as they cut through the fields between Tylissos and Suramarti. She zigged and zagged, checking out every hole and tree for something new and exciting. Jura arrived at the Suramarti sanctuary before Kitane. He sat on the wall, Kano resting at his feet, recalling Kitane and her mother.

"...without your shoes."

"...honored with bare feet."

He had removed his sandals. He waited. The monkeys chattered, and partridges cooed among the trees behind the sanctuary. His toes felt the dirt, soft from so many generations of feet.

When they were small barefoot children, he, Kitane and the others played hide and seek.

"One, two, three, four, FIVE. I will find you."

He found some children in the vineyards, and others had climbed a fig tree, but he couldn't find Kitane...until he looked in the sanctuary.

"Kit! Kit. You can't hide by the Goddess tree. I'm going to tell your mother."

The laughing girl ran out of the sanctuary, leaping over the old bench. "Don't tell. If you tell, I won't marry you."

Even at that early age, Jura loved the rules. Yesterday, he should have known better than to enter the sanctuary with his sandals on. He'd been so focused on Kitane, he had simply forgotten. It pained him that both Kitane and her mother knew he had done so.

Suramarti had the best views. To the south and east, he could see the sun rising across Keftiu. Knossos, with its white stone roof, shone like a pearl between the olive-colored valleys and the storm-colored sea. Behind him, the goddess Jasasara overlooked everything from high on Mount Ida.

When he saw Kitane walking up the path, he rose to his feet and waited. She stopped when she noticed him. He considered greeting her, but she was too far away, and he didn't want to dishonor the goddess by shouting. *I should run to meet her*, he considered. Instead, he stood in place, first with his hands behind his back, then at his side, later crossed, and behind his back again.

When she reached the sanctuary, she turned to him, "Good morning, and the blessings of the goddess to you."

Only then did he realized he'd been holding his breath. He took a quick breath and answered, "Morning blessings to you also."

"You are welcome to join me in the sanctuary for the new day ritual," she allowed.

Together they saluted, fist to the forehead, the labrys for Jasasara, and the horns of consecration for Potidas. When they stood in front of the horns, he recalled that his steward was performing the ceremony at his villa, with many in attendance.

"In times like this, with the ground trembling, honor for Jasasara and Potidas are important."

When she didn't reply, he continued. "I am proud you will be at the bull-jumping ceremony. Surely, your performance will please Potidas, and he will stop shaking the earth."

"Thank you."

He waited in silence and then added, "A few days ago, I noticed two yearling bulls wrangling. Kano separated them, and they are now isolated awaiting castration."

Kano, who had been resting quietly outside the sanctuary, perked up her ears when she heard her name.

"Intact bulls are the tastiest. If the priestesses choose to sacrifice Enosidas, I can bring one of these to the Temple for a replacement. I'd like to fatten the other for our wedding feast."

She took a deep breath, then turned away and left the sanctuary without a word.

He knew he would gain nothing by continuing to talk. He turned to the Goddess Jasasara's labrys, fist to his forehead. *Help me Goddess, please help me.*

Kitane's lithe form disappeared among the trees. Elusive. Like a slender deer. He ran after her. Kano did not follow until he abandoned his pursuit and turned toward Tylissos. When Kano caught up, he scratched her ears, "You understand her better than I do, don't you?"

Rather than going back to Tylissos, he changed direction again and headed to Suramarti, thinking he might meet Okune for some advice. It had been her idea to talk to Kitane in the morning.

Instead he met Radamitu, Kitane's father.

The two men saluted each other, left hand open, palm forward.

"Jura, blessings of the Goddess to you. Today is a blessed day. I was just thinking of you."

Jura thought, *I am glad someone at Suramarti is happy to see me.* "Blessings to you, Kitane's father, Radamitu. Always blessed to see you."

Kitane's father avoided the conflicts between Okune and her four daughters. Jura wondered why he wanted to see him. It felt like everyone at Suramarti was testing him. He expected her father wanted to know if he would be able to watch over the villa operation when Kitane inherited. Jura was certain of one thing, Radamitu didn't seek advice on goldsmithing. Kitane's father was the best goldsmith on Keftiu. *No*, he thought, *the best across the entire Middle Sea.*

Radamitu answered the unasked question, "Kitane's weaving ladies have asked for heavier loom weights."

"I am not surprised. My shearers told me that this year's wool is harder to work than usual."

His steward had been grumbling all shearing season, "I warned the shepherds. 'Look for fields of oats,' I told them. During drought years, the sheep eat too much barley. 'Find oats,' I told them."

Jura doubted that diet crimped the wool, despite what his steward believed. He blamed it on the heat, but they could not do anything about that.

He returned his attention to Radamitu, wondering why Kitane hadn't said anything to him about the loom weights. She directed spinning and weaving at Suramarti.

Jura and Radamitu walked over to the weaving area. Dozens of women worked with the spring fleeces. They washed the fibers, pulled the long strands into bundles, which they combed straight with wooden paddles fitted with overlapped swordfish bills. Most of the women were busy spinning the threads, which they then wound into balls. Jura could see the yarn balls were like the ones at home, thicker and bigger than usual. "Your yarn looks familiar. I regret, no one can spin fine yarn this year."

Radamitu smiled. "Only the Goddess can do that, but not even She, this year."

They watched the weavers. Each had a straight tree branch a cubit-or-more long attached to the wall with many warp strands hanging down and tied to loom weights hanging at the bottom. The weaver and her assistants threaded a ball of yarn through these strands, and another assistant on the other side tightened this new strand up against the completed section of cloth with her fingers while the threaders held the warp threads firm. With the curlier warp threads, the work was painfully slow. They repeated this process in the opposite direction. Back and forth, slowly, the finished cloth appeared.

Jura observed respectfully. The Suramarti weavers managed finer wool cloth than any he'd seen this year.

"You have the biggest pottery operation. The weavers have requested heavier loom weights." Radamitu pointed to the looms. Each time the assistant tightened a new horizontal strand, the loom weights bounced around and occasionally broke the thread.

Jura smiled. "Yes, I see."

"So, you can help? Kit thought you could."

Kitane did think of me. This encouraged him. "Yes, I will ask my potters to make some larger weights, so the strands will be held firmly. I will send a donkey load tomorrow."

Jura worried that if he didn't request something in trade, Radamitu might think him a poor steward, so he added, "Thank you for the excellent idea. I will also make similar weights for the weavers at Tylissos."

Jura went off with a smile. Her father had accepted his gift and he'd passed one more test. He saw Kitane and gave her an open-hand salute. She saluted in return. Jura felt confident that his well-run villa would win in the end. He'd tell his weavers about the new loom weights which would make their work easier and would please his sister who was taking over more and more of the duties of running Tylissos from their failing mother.

Jura thought proudly, *the telestai are good caretakers and all Keftiu benefits.*

SCENE 8 — TROS ON THE MIDDLE SEA

Tros stared at Sakusna, willing her to return to her tent. Instead, she stood with her legs spread and knees bent, prepared for rough seas or a fight. One hand held onto the tent for balance, but the other grasped the hilt of her obsidian dagger. Tros had noticed it before. She always had it at her hip. The gold hilt in the shape of the Goddess glimmered in the morning sun. Her dark blue eyes, the color of the sea, flicked back and forth between Tros and the refugees.

The old woman on the foundering ship interrupted their battle of wills. "We are the last to leave Thera. We have lost our way. We need food and water."

He quickly replied before Sakusna could intervene. "We have supplies. We can help you."

Everyone on all ships visibly relaxed. He made a fist and turned to his crew, giving them a frown and a hiss. The rowers backed away from the other ship, and the archers nocked their arrows.

"What do you have to trade for your rescue? Did you bring gold like the others leaving Thera? How much?"

Sakusna withdrew her dagger. "These people are lost at sea. You cannot take their gold."

The three closest crewmembers advanced toward the ship's bow where Sakusna and Tros stood close, but out of reach. Tros waved them off.

The head of the refugees spoke first. "Do not fight about our gold. We have no gold."

Tros shouted, "What do you have?"

"Tablets. We are the scribes of Thera. We have all the records, histories, and stories of Thera."

A man standing next to her added, "These tablets are more valuable than all the gold. The people of Thera live in these writings."

Tros couldn't believe what he was hearing. *No gold? Only tablets?* Potidas would surely take these crazy people to their underwater graves. The sooner he left them, the safer his crew and ships would be.

"Fools! They're fools. Rowers take us away."

Sakusna shouted, "No!" Tros turned around as she jumped at him, swinging her sharp knife. Surprised, he stepped back and lost his balance. He took hold of one of the lines holding the tent to regain his balance. Too late he found that the inviting rope was not what it appeared to be. Instead of offering him a firm hold, it slipped overboard with him.

He tumbled into the sea holding the line Sakusna had used to dry her laundry. In the few moments it took him to hit the water, he delivered his entire catalogs of evil epithets to Sakusna and her Suramarti family.

The crew sprang into action. The two smaller boats moved to rescue their captain. The rowers maneuvered to shield Tros from the rough seas. He removed his robe, so the wet fabric would not draw him down. While he swam to the closest oar and took hold, the other boat rescued his fine linen robe.

Four others surrounded Sakusna. Two grabbed her arms, and two seized the dagger with the gold hilt. Had she been a fellow crewmember and not from Suramarti, they would have surely cut her throat with her own blade. However, she was the elite passenger in the tent. They treated her as gently as possible under the circumstances.

She caught her breath, "Let go of me, or the wrath of Jasasara will curse you and your family for all time!"

The men released her, but kept the obsidian weapon and formed a wall between her and Tros, whom the crew had already retrieved from the water and transferred back to the lead ship.

Still dripping wet and angry, he shook his fist at her, "You dare attack me?"

"The Goddess would have you help these people!"

He growled, "You have some space left in your allotment. We can take six of them..." He flipped his hand toward the scribes. "Just six. And they ride in one of the small boats."

She spat on the deck, like a sailor. "In that case, I'll go to their ship, and you can bring seven back to Amnisos to tell the story."

"That is not possible. We will not return without you. Even if we need to bind you in ropes, you will return with us."

Sakusna didn't quit. She was headstrong like his Keftiu mother. Tros admired that and looked forward to having her sister for his wife. He understood why his father had chosen a Keftiu woman.

Sakusna kicked the sailor who held her dagger, hit him solidly between his legs. The weapon dropped, but she grabbed the hilt before it reached the deck. The sailor writhed on the deck, but no one approached her. She shook the dagger at Tros, "I order you to throw my share of the cargo overboard and rescue all the refugees. Surely without the weight of my goods, you can afford to carry them."

Tros laughed, "Silly. Silly. Those people do not weigh anything, but they eat and drink. We do not have enough water. We cannot drink from the sea of Potidas."

"With all of those..." He flipped his hand toward the other ship, "...scribes aboard we will all die while Potidas laughs at our folly." Tros had had enough talking. A good captain leads his crew with actions, not words, and Tros was the best. It was time for action.

He turned to the refugees. "Draw lots. Only six may board."

The frightened refugees talked among themselves.

"Rescue the tablets. We'll try our luck with the mercy of Potidas."

"Only six may board. Archers, if you see a tablet, shoot the carrier."

"No tablets?" Sakusna asked. "Tablets do not drink. You are just being mean...and stupid."

Tros smiled, "Say what you wish. That is to help you remember that I am still the captain."

Sakusna slashed her dagger through the captain's tent and entered through the new opening.

After more discussion among the scribes, six refugees lined up.

Tros looked back to the archers. "One for each finger on your hand. One more. After that, shoot them all if they try to board."

The archers pulled their bowstrings tight and aimed between the rowers who maneuvered a small boat beside the refugee ship.

Tros walked to the stern and back while the six boarded. He joked with the crew, accepted congratulations, and felt satisfied that he was still the best.

They set a southern course to Keftiu and the harbor at Amnisos.

During the day, the crew talked with the refugees, who seemed more concerned that Potidas would claim the tablets than about the family and friends they'd left behind.

"We all knew we might die, but we were going to rescue our history. It was a good trade."

"Now we are alive, and the tablets lost."

The crew talked about what happened on Thera, why everyone left.

"Earthquakes. Steam."

"The lagoon boiled."

"Now hot ash is raining down from the sky."

"Potidas is so angry. He will destroy all of Thera."

"The priestesses told us that the Goddess would not save us. We must save ourselves."

Tros met with the crew. "Thera is lost, but this can be good for us."

Someone asked, "How? All the people are gone."

Another crewmember added, "And they took all the gold with them."

Tros had a plan. He steered the discussion like a ship in the night. "You're not thinking. Thera was a rich colony of Keftiu."

Two of the crew protested, "Yes, but all the riches are gone. This last ship only had tablets."

The crew laughed, "Tablets and scribes."

Tros paused and waited for everyone to stop laughing. He shook his head at them, "Think. Think. What about the graves? Certainly, these nice people did not desecrate the graves of their parents and grandparents."

The crew finally understood. "But we are *not* nice."

Tros explained the plan. "We are not afraid of some hot ash. We will sail north and harvest all that gold before it is buried by the wrath of Potidas."

Sakusna, who'd heard everything from inside the tent, yelled, "I will not allow you to rob those graves. Besides, if you turn around you will not reach Amnisos on schedule." She paused for emphasis. "There *will* be penalties."

Tros turned to the crew. "Do we care about penalties?"

The crew shouted, "No! Never!"

Other crew shouted, "Gold! Dead people don't need gold!"

The three ships turned to the north, heading toward Thera. They passed the refugee ship again, leaving the scribes drifting with only a couple of oars in the water.

Sakusna shouted, "You are a liar and a cheat. You said we didn't have enough water and now you are extending our time at sea. You will never get more business from Suramarti...or any traders from Keftiu."

The rowers slowed their pace, looking toward Sakusna as if they considered her threat.

Tros did not wait to reply. "The time of Keftiu is ending. Your gods will destroy Thera, and Keftiu is next."

The oarsmen picked up the pace moving through choppy seas, rocking up and down over the waves radiating from the doomed island of Thera.

The six rescued scribes huddled together in one of the smaller boats. From her position of honor on the big ship, Sakusna called to them. "Have faith good scribes. Jasasara will protect you and destroy these pirates."

The scribes were not watching her. They pointed forward and shouted in fright.

Tros followed their extended arms to a village of whales, mothers and calves, swimming across the path of his ships. He would have preferred dolphins, known by all to bring good luck. Magnificent whales, the same size as ships, did not bring luck or danger…unless a hapless ship separated a mother from her baby.

Sakusna also saw the huge animals. "Be calm. Jasasara loves those whales. See that whale village? It has a wise woman in charge, just as the gods declare is proper."

The rowers continued, approaching the animals, and moving through them. The rescued scribes admired the noble animals, most bigger than their small boat.

Tros countered, "Jasasara does indeed love the whales, so she is sending them away from Thera and Keftiu. You and Suramarti will be no more."

Before Sakusna could reply, the rescued scribes panicked again, as an adult whale charged their boat. Too late all realized that the boat had come between the mother and her calf. The larger whale hit the boat and bounced it into the air, dumping the scribes and his rowers into the sea.

"See, Jasasara has attacked your scribes. I will save them this time, but the gods will obliterate the Keftiu in the end."

His other small boat rushed in to rescue the people in the water. The sailors knew to remove their heavy woolen robes and hold onto their capsized boat. Ropes and nets recovered the coughing, sputtering scribes.

One scribe, in his confusion, swam away from the others. Tros stripped off his clothes and jumped into the waves. When he reached the desperate scribe, the near-drowning man tried to climb atop his rescuer. Tros wasted no time. He dove under the water bringing his legs into the air and kicked the scribe in the head. The dazed man stopped struggling and Tros towed him back to the boat that his crew had righted with long ropes.

"Our boat is damaged."

Tros examined the place where the whale had impacted the hull. The master ship makers had built his ship of cypress planks from the Hittite empire. The builders had precisely carved the pieces to fit together, each joining to the next like a man and a woman. Wider and longer planks made stronger ships. His ship the widest and longest available. It was the best.

However, when it came to the smaller boats, they used the trees found in the hills of his home. They had bound the small boards together with willow branches and sealed them with wool and resin.

"We cannot make permanent repairs until we reach Thera. Until then smear the leaks with resin and bail. Give the scribes baskets. They can help save themselves."

He turned Sakusna. "The gods are after your people. You should be glad I'm here to rescue you."

She didn't have a reply.

"Everything will be better when we arrive on Thera," he bravely announced to the crew.

Potidas willing, it would still be there.

Scene 9 — Paian at Knossos Temple

‡Ɏ⯑

A rare and impressive sight greeted Paian for his final delivery of the day: donkeys stretching the full length of the viaduct, each with two blocks of ammoudha, a beautiful multicolor stone. The red, orange and yellow stripes sparkled in the setting sun. He greeted the telestai at the front of the line. "Goddess blessings to you."

With open palms, the telestai returned his greeting. "Jasasara's blessing to you also. Today's stones are for the new room on the upper level."

Paian had hoped for an easy delivery to the ground level workshops, but he knew where the new room was under construction. Knossos was like a living being, always growing. "I will take your donkeys as far as the Grand Staircase. After that, the blocks will need to be carried up by hand."

The telestai smiled. "I expected that. I have brought many strong men for the task."

Paian and the telestai talked while pairs of men carried blocks up the stairs.

"Where are these colorful stones from?"

"I have a quarry on Mount Dikti."

"Mount Dikti? Where is that?"

"I can see you are not Keftiu. How much do you know of our island?"

This touched on Paian's hobby. He reached into his pouch and unfolded a piece of papyrus. "I am from far north beyond the archipelago, but I am making a map of Keftiu."

The telestai examined the map as if he'd not seen one before. He turned it around and around and finally found an orientation he liked. "I see now. That is very clever."

"Can you show me where Mount Dikti is?"

The telestai pointed to the middle of the island, just south of Malia. "Over here. Will you add it to your map?"

"Yes, of course."

The telestai seemed pleased.

When the quarrier from Mount Dikti left, Paian took a detour before returning to his post to see the progress in the new throne room. This took him through a new section of the large temple.

He entered a space and realized it was for bathing. He'd heard rumors that important Keftiu washed indoors, instead of using a creek. He'd never seen anything like this. He paused to examine the uniquely Keftiu achievement. First, he removed a blue ceramic rod from its hole in the wall. Immediately, water poured into a large basin lined with a mosaic of intertwined sea stars.

He was so surprised he almost dropped the rod. Frightened the splashing noise would attract attention, he replaced the rod and the water stopped. He ran his hand through the water. It was warm!

He noticed another blue pole in the floor, carefully positioned amidst a circle of sea stars without touching any of them. He lifted it and the water rushed away. He replaced the rod hoping that there would be no lasting indication of his visit.

His previous explorations had shown him the Keftiu invention for personal waste, a plumbed toilet that could be flushed clean with a nearby pithos of water thus rinsing smelly output into the sewer system. The Goddess Incarnate and other priestesses needn't squat behind a bush. Some of the innovations seemed a bit silly—impractical and costly. But the Keftiu considered themselves very civilized, especially compared with his own *primitive* Hellenes.

When he reached the throne room, many artists and apprentices filled the area. The artists painted the lines carved into the plaster with delicate paintbrushes made from a single papyrus reed. Apprentices followed them with brushes made of reeds, feathers, or raw wool. For the large areas, they even painted with their hands.

Paian had never seen such a large crew all painting at once. "Why do you have so many painters?"

An artist with a seal stone hanging from his loincloth answered, "The best frescoes are painted before the plaster dries. This is the throne room for the Goddess Incarnate, so only the best will do. For such a large room, we need many workers to finish quickly enough."

Paian admired the scene of hills and grains and mystical animals that had the body of a lion and the head of a hawk. The artist explained that the previous day, the master artist had carved each scene into the damp plaster. Today a crowd of apprentices brought it to life with color. Paian tried to remember all the details. He wanted to describe fresco painting in his history along with a sketch.

Sunset marked the end of temple deliveries. Paian went looking for his telestai friend, Ukan. Rather than navigate through the maze, he exited the West Entrance and walked around the temple to the east side. Before he reached the workshops, he passed through the area reserved for fires. The priestesses banned them from inside the temple, too dangerous.

He'd heard a lot of stories.

"The Phaistos temple burned down."

"An earthquake destroyed the villa at Malia."

"Knossos has been destroyed three times."

No matter the story, they all ended the same. "The telestai rebuilt bigger and better."

Walking amongst the flames, he smelled bread baking, beer fermenting, a wild goat roasting, and a big three-footed cauldron of onion, leek, and garlic soup.

Beyond the cooking area, the good smells faded. The biggest ovens smelted bronze. Large slabs of bronze-gold, and the more valuable bronze-silver, heralded this area. Paian avoided it. The furnaces released noxious odors.

Once inside the workshop area, he knew where to find Ukan. He headed for the beer and wine.

"Paian! Over here!"

Ukan stood beside a pithos of fresh beer. The welcoming odor cleared Paian's nose of the bronze. Ukan held a small terracotta cup in each hand. He stretched his arm to offer a cup to Paian, except his arm wobbled and spilled the contents.

"Oh Ukan, you've had enough already. Give me the cup, I'll get my own."

"No, no, I'm fine. That was another of those earthquakes. Potidas is just grumbling again."

Paian laughed at this sorry excuse for spilling the beer and took his cup to the open pithos. He grabbed a plain rhyton to use as a makeshift pitcher and filled it with beer. Another pithos held cucumbers in saltwater and vinegar, flavored with fennel. Paian reached in for a sour, salty treat to accompany his beer. The two friends found a comfortable niche away from the crowds.

"Ukan, I don't understand the Keftiu. I met this girl delivering onions. I think she's intelligent. Why didn't she learn to read and write?"

"We telestai have taken care of the atomai since time began. We provide them with food and clothing and shelter. They have no need for letters."

"I see that all Keftiu lives in peace and harmony compared to back home, but I wonder if she would be happier if she could read?"

"You ask so many curious questions. Are customs so different where you come from? Most Keftiu sing and dance and enjoy the bull games. The Goddess blesses everyone, even those like that girl today."

"The Goddess? Yes, but this girl seemed angry with the God Potidas."

"Oh, I see. The earthquakes upset her. When they stop, she will be happy again. Just wait and see."

Paian refilled their cups from the rhyton and both boys drank more beer and shared the pickles.

"Can I ask you a question?"

"Certainly. Even though you're Hellene and I'm Keftiu, we are friends." He moved his arm to Paian and clinked their seal stones."

"There is this girl I like."

Ukan rolled on the ground and laughed. "Another burp from Potidas," he screamed, pretending an earthquake had knocked him over. "It is always a girl."

"I really like her. I write poems for her. I don't think she even knows who I am."

"Oh, poor Hellene. On Keftiu you must speak to her mother."

The mother? Paian thought, *Keftiu women were so powerful and owned so much land, but still they could not marry without consent of the mother? Why were they still treated like children when they were old enough to wed?*

Paian frowned and took a big bite from his pickle, spilling the tart juice on his robe. "She lives far away, and I don't even know if her mother can read."

"Silly scribe. These are not matters for reading and writing. You must visit the mother."

"But I've never left the temple. Isn't it dangerous beyond the viaduct?"

Ukan just laughed again, spilling beer on his loincloth. "Ah, now look. Potidas has cursed me and wet my pants."

More serious now, Ukan put his arm around his friend's shoulder. "Do you know where she lives? I will take you there."

Paian unfolded his papyrus map and pointed to a line starting at Knossos and going west. "They say she lives on this path to Mount Ida. The girl who delivered the onions this morning passes her home when she carries goods to Mount Ida. She has delivered poems for me."

"Perfect. The Goddess smiles on you. That's where I live too. Maybe I even know her mother."

This plan scared Paian, but he put on a brave face. "Perfect. We will go soon. All the way to Mount Ida even. My map will benefit from the journey." He silently added, *if I survive.*

Having emptied the rhyton, they both headed outside to find something for dinner and a place to sleep for the night.

The next morning Paian rolled over and noticed several others sleeping in the sheltered spot he'd found in the ravine. The evening weather had been pleasant; it was a good night to sleep outside. He found it agreeable to spend the night under the stars without fear of attack.

He rubbed the sleep out of his eyes and saw a familiar face staring at him. He thought he recognized the girl who had slept nearby. He blinked and blinked again. He did not want to make the same mistake as yesterday.

"Maza?"

The rising sun lit her face. She sat up and shielded her eyes. This time she smiled. "Paian? Is that you? Did we spend the night together?" She laughed at her joke.

Now he was embarrassed.

"Excuse me." She picked herself up and headed for the creek.

He did the same, but to be polite, he went in the opposite direction. When he could no longer hear footsteps, he went five more paces and relieved himself behind a bush.

He stepped into the creek to wash his feet. He knelt and put his face in the icy water, rinsing his mouth and taking a drink. After running his fingers through his hair, he went back to the campsite uncertain whether he wished for it to be vacant, or for Maza to still be there.

She was there.

He pointed up the hill to the temple. "Shall we get something to eat?"

She pointed to his wrist where his seal stone hung, and to hers, unadorned. "I cannot go with you."

Puzzled, he asked, "Why is that?"

"I can deliver food to the Temple, but I am not allowed to eat there. There are other places to feed the animals and people like me."

He shook his head. "Are you a slave?"

She frowned and moved away. "Of course not. I am atomai, free. There are no slaves on Keftiu."

"I thought…"

By now she was standing. "You didn't think. You're like the telestai."

He changed the subject, not wishing to upset her. "Please stay here. I need to ask you something." He wanted to touch her to encourage her to wait, but he didn't dare.

"Please, I will get some food and bring it here." He ran up the hill, hoping he'd get back before she left.

He had two bowls of cooked barley with a few dried grapes in each one. She was still there. He ran down the hill until he slipped on some wet leaves. He struggled not to spill the cereal and ended up sliding on his loincloth, both hands frantically working to maintain his dignity and the bowls of food.

He spilled hot water on his arms and legs, but came to a stop at her feet, just short of knocking her over.

Recalling last night, he made a joke. "Another earthquake. Potidas sneezing."

She might have smiled, but he didn't think so. Those jokes had been funny the night before when he and Ukan were drunk, but now he remembered that she did not find the earthquakes funny. He handed her the bowl with the most barley. He was grateful that she took it.

For the next while, they drank from the bowls and used their fingers to eat their morning meal.

He didn't know what to talk about, so he said, "I like this girl."

Maza asked, "Is this the bull jumper I took your poems to?"

"Yes, I write poems for her, and she ignores me."

"Do you even know if she can read?"

He laughed, "Of course she can read."

He recognized Maza's hurt face as she whispered, "I can't read."

He immediately knew he'd said the wrong thing, again, after he promised himself not to upset her anymore.

She stood up. "We have a saying: *Where do seal stones come from? Only two seal stones can have baby seal stones.*"

"But— "

She walked across the creek and up the other side. "You can ponder your fantasy romances, but people like me need to go to work."

He shouted, "I'll help you. I'll find a way to help you. I will."

She shook her bare wrists at him and continued out of the ravine, turning back for a moment to shout, "I don't need your help."

He promised himself, he'd do something, but what? Keftiu could be so confusing. Even without bands of brigands, it was still frightening.

He wondered if he could teach her to read and write. *What if she didn't care to learn*? He felt uncomfortable with a grown person who couldn't read at least a little, nor write her own name.

Scene 10 — Kitane at Suramarti

ᛉᏟᏗ

Kitane could see Isari's eyes widen as Kit approached. Her cousin had stopped talking to the villager selling votive figurines and just stood staring as Kit neared.

"What's wrong?" Isari ventured.

"My mother is an utterly unblessed demon," Kit managed. It was hard to breathe. She stood still beside her cousin and tried to take deep breaths. "She's tearing me apart," Kit said, realizing as she said it that was exactly how she felt. Torn, pulled, shredded. "She demands an answer at the same time she throws away my options."

"Oh," Isari said faintly, reaching toward Kit. Her cousin put her arm around Kit's shoulders. Kit bent into her embrace and burst into tears.

After a few moments, she backed away and took a shuddering breath. She lifted the skirt of her robe and wiped her eyes. "I'm sorry, Isari. None of this is your fault."

"What happened?"

"Well, you know I only have a couple weeks left before I must choose a husband or lose my chance to inherit."

Isari nodded.

"Now Mother has informed me if I choose Tros—the only decent option among them—she will still disinherit me. I'm damned either way."

"That's a surprise. Though...I guess I can understand she would want you to be here, and Tros would want you away with him."

They walked along the main path through the village.

"Now I may as well give up, which is what probably happened with Qazi and Sakusna. If Mother doesn't get what she wants, she closes every door."

She stopped talking at the same time she stopped walking. "Look," she said, "there's enough surplus fruit that our villagers can sell sour cherries."

A smiling woman sat on the ground behind a ragged cloth that held a pile of ripe yellow and red fruits. "Missy, would you or your friend like some today?"

"I would like to serve them at our dinner tomorrow," Kit said, trying to keep her voice under control. "I would need four dozen or so, do you have that many?"

The woman nodded.

"Thank you. Would you like a rhyton of olive oil in exchange? Or some wine?"

"The oil is always welcome, Missy."

Kit nodded and made arrangements for the exchange.

The girls wandered around. Another lady had some soaps laid out for trade and they went over to look at and smell them.

"Peppermint, honey, chamomile and olive scents this time, Missy."

"These are really nice. I cannot get my soap to come out so smooth," Kit admitted. "I think I will give up and just buy yours!" The woman laughed and waved a welcoming hand at her wares.

Isari smiled. "I tried a wedge of this last week, it was very smooth and gentle."

Kit considered. She would be receiving a payment for her participation in the bull-jumping ceremony at Knossos at the end of the week: several chips of bronze-silver. She should also again win the competition and the prize of a fat pig. She could afford to buy a big wedge of the soap for herself, and gift some to her sisters as well. That seemed a good plan.

Once they finished the negotiations, the girls left the village, taking the long way back to the villa.

"What about this new gentleman?" Isari asked. "The poet scribe?"

"I haven't even met him," Kit said. "He apparently has sent me several poems, only two of which have arrived so far. They are brief, complimentary and charming."

"That's...thoughtful," her cousin said.

They stepped off the path to let a laden donkey and driver go past.

"He's from Athens, where he intends to return."

Isari blinked. "Another foreigner. A poet."

"Well. He's creative," Kit said, and laughed.

Her cousin glanced at her in amusement, and soon they were both laughing. "That does have its appeal," Isari said.

But for all her laughter, Kitane's thoughts swirled warily in her head. Three, four, five very different men. Did she want to marry *any* of them? Did she really want to marry at all? She decided to trust Isari with her secret.

"It's not just that it's hard to choose. It's that I have a thing I must do before I wed and change my life."

"Oh. What is that?"

Kit faced her cousin, considering, then waved to a fallen plane tree trunk. They sat down on the natural bench, side by side.

"I believe this contest to select a sacrificial bull is wrong. I believe the sacrifice itself is wrong, that death does not honor the Goddess of Life."

Isari bit her lip and stared at her cousin's face.

"It did not use to be this way," Kit said. "Biaja researched it for me at the Temple. The bull sacrifice only began about twenty years ago. It used to be that just the bull jumping was the ceremony to honor the Goddess. There was no sacrifice at the end, there was no murder of the losing bull."

Isari nodded. "I remember, the first time they did it the new way at Akrotiri. They made the sacrifice of the loser. The bull jumpers were outraged, many of the people as well."

"Yes," Kit agreed. "Does the Goddess want her beautiful animals killed? How does that honor Her?"

"Kitane, animals have always been sacrificed to honor the Goddess."

"*Wild* animals, caught just for that, when there was a special purpose for the sacrifice. Not this regular murder of a trained, beloved beast." Kit felt a tremor of fear, along with the anger that roiled inside her. "Yesterday, Jura offered me a hand-raised bull to exchange for Enosidas, in case I lose. Even he doesn't think about catching wild ones."

"Well, that is…awkward." Isari twisted her lips while she thought. "I thought it was a way to save the hunters from being injured or killed catching a wild one."

"Then they should just pick animals from the herds, like they do the goats and sheep that are sacrificed to Potidas. Why is it only bulls who are chosen this way? Selected to die because they and their jumpers are less trained than others? Why should a less agile jumper have to make that sacrifice? How is it the bull's fault?"

Kit leaned forward, emphasizing her point. "And if it is the thinking that killing a trained beast is a bigger honor, why should it not be the *winner* of the jumping contest, and not the loser, who is sacrificed?"

Isari blinked. "I suppose it would be difficult to encourage jumpers to be excellent, in that case. They might try to do poorly, unless they could be made to see it as a rite of passage, an *honor* to themselves and their family that *their* bull would be chosen to die."

"It does not seem an honor to me. Nor to any of my friends. It is the destruction of something strong and beautiful that the Goddess has given us. It is *wrong*."

"I think it will be difficult to change this tradition," Isari said.

Kit grimaced. "It's not even a tradition. It is a new rule. I want to change it *back* to the traditional way. I think it will require me to use my influence, while I still have it, to persuade the Temple. We should return to the old ways. We should capture a wild bull. Those who are hurt or killed doing so would be honoring the Goddess, themselves. Or choose a less wild one from the herds. Or don't make a sacrifice to the Goddess of Life."

"Kitane— " her cousin reached out to her and put her hands on Kit's shoulders. "I can see that this troubles you. But I am not certain it is worth giving up your life, your plans, to do this thing." She sat back and let her hands drop into her own lap. "Jura will not wait forever. And your seventeenth birthday approaches. Please make a choice. Please do not force your mother to give up on you. I— " she took a deep, hiccupping breath, "I have been asked if I would be willing to take your place."

Kit sat in silence, letting the words echo in the space between them. Finally, she said, "Take my place?" She got to her feet, walked in a tight circle in front of her cousin.

"Your mother asked me, if you fail to choose Jura, if I would be willing to marry him, to take leadership of Suramarti, if...if none of you or your sisters do." She took a gasping breath. "Kit—I don't want to be asked, I don't want to do this. But if your mother dies before you choose— "

"What? *What did you say?*" numbness swept over Kitane. It was as if her arms, her legs, her heart had gone stiff and dead. "*Dies!?* What do you mean?"

Isari's fine dark eyes widened, then flooded with tears. "Oh. I wasn't supposed to— She said not to say— "

Kit bent and grabbed her cousin by the arms and shook her. "Say what? What are you hiding? She's dying?"

Isari shook her head, pulling away from Kit's grip. "I don't know! No one knows!"

"What? *What?*"

With gasping breaths, Isari said, "A prophecy. Your mother— " she shook her head.

Kit collapsed onto the road, a cloud of red-brown dust rising around her.

"That's why she had to set the deadline. I asked her if she could— " Isari waved a helpless arm, "if she would change it, give you more time. When she said no, I pushed her to explain, and my mother did also."

Kit looked up at her, speechless.

"She said Qazipatima had a vision, years ago, before she was even a priestess. Qazi said she saw a young woman in charge of the villa, Jura beside her, and your father, but your mother was not there. Your family was grieving. Your father placed a funerary urn on a grave."

"But— Why?"

Isari shrugged. "That is the difficulty with visions, there's often no explanations, no clarity. But Qazi was absolutely certain about what she saw, that scene was extraordinarily clear."

"No one knows why she will die? Are they certain she is dead, not just off somewhere?"

"The urn— "

"An urn is an urn. Maybe it is Sakusna's or Zetis'—or mine."

"Uhm," Isari's voice was shaky, "So...that is why Okune asked me if I would marry Jura, since I was there in the scene, too, maybe I was the one in charge. The vision didn't explain that, either. Asije, me, Jura, shaved-head Biaja, maybe you, Radamitu, Diwoki. No Okune."

"What makes her think there is a deadline?"

"Qazipatima, the Goddess speaking through her, said we were all young, all together, like now. My mother and I have arrived here now. We are *here*, as in the vision. It is almost summer, as in the vision. And if you don't marry Jura, she wants me to, so the succession is clear. But I don't want to, Kitane."

Kit stared at the row of laurel trees that separated the path from the fields ahead. A man and a donkey raised dust with each step in the road. She watched the dust slowly settle on the leaves, making the trees reddish brown on the path side, while they stayed shiny green on the field side. It was as if a blade was cutting the scene in two.

ACT II — TOO MANY SUITORS

Scene 1 — Biaja at Knossos

㋰

As she stepped out of the South Entrance, Biaja came to an abrupt stop, staring up at the grey, dusty sky. There was a pall across the sun. One of the men passing by pointed behind her. She turned around and looked down the pathway that ran along the western side of the temple complex. Far to the north, some distance across the Middle Sea, a thick plume of black smoke rose toward the clouds.

"What *is* that?"

A priestess and her accompanying workmen paused beside Biaja to say, "The anger of the Goddess."

"Is Thera on fire?"

The priestess shrugged, then passed into the propylaea with her workmen.

Bee stared a moment longer, then turned back and continued on her way south to the caravanserai. If she didn't start soon, she would never reach Mount Ida today.

At the caravanserai, she approached the steward, who stood talking to a group of men and women in a cluster around him. The man looked at Biaja, eyebrows raised in question.

"I need one donkey, to take to Mount Ida today."

"Payment?" the steward asked.

"The Temple," she said, and her heart sank as the people gathered around the steward mostly turned away. "I will make certain the animal is fed and watered properly," she said. How could she get the bundle of cups and stacks of tablets up to the shrine without an animal to carry them?

"I cannot just loan you an animal, child," the steward said. "You must hire a driver and pay them."

The Aurochs must have meant for Biaja to hire a driver as well as the donkey, hadn't she? "Yes, that is what I mean," she said.

"I will do it for three meals and the Goddess' blessing," a man said.

That seemed reasonable. The Aurochs would never notice the food vouchers. And Biaja thought Qazipatima would agree to include the man in the week's blessing, as a favor to her little sister, if nothing else.

"But I am next in line to get work," a young woman said. She gave Biaja a resentful look and moved in front of the man who had spoken.

"Oh, I thought you were not interested in Temple work, Maza," the steward said. Several of the other men and women waiting for assignments chuckled as Maza glared at him. "I would be willing to work for the three meals for me, and a sack of grain for my animal," she said.

"Without the Goddess' blessing?" the steward asked.

Maza scowled at him, and turned to face Biaja. "The priestesses at the Mount Ida shrine can bless as well as the Goddess Incarnation, can't they?"

Biaja wasn't certain if the question was addressed to her, but she nodded. "Anyone who climbs to the shrine may pray and receive a blessing."

She hoped the young woman would not accept. This was not a better deal for her. She wasn't sure where she would get the grain. The Goddess blessing had actually been easier to arrange, but that option seemed lost now.

"What is the load?" the girl Maza asked.

Biaja blinked, confused. Oh, perhaps she meant what would the donkey be carrying? "Tablets and votive offering cups and figurines."

"I will do this," Maza said, brushing her dusty bangs out of her eyes.

Bee nodded, thinking of how to arrange the payment. "Follow me, please." The meals were easy; vouchers were readily available even to pre-initiates. The grain—well, if she had to, she could take some from the Suramarti stores when they passed by her family's home. They had plenty of oats and barley stored from the previous year's bounty, and the family was well accustomed to gifting the Temple. A small sack of grain would be as nothing.

"I will see you tomorrow," Biaja said, as Nopine left to attend the beginning of the initiates' rites. They had both been looking forward to seeing young telestai and craftsmen's children turned into adults—each dedicated to a trade or the Temple. Now Nopine would enjoy it alone.

Her friend turned and gave her a quick hug. "The shrine is beautiful, I think you will enjoy it," Nopine said. She ran her palm over Biaja's shaved head. "Just a few more moons and it will be you in the ceremony."

Biaja shrugged. "Perhaps. Of course, I've been to the Mount Ida shrine many times, it is just up the mountain a short way from Suramarti."

But it was as if her friend had not heard her comment about Mount Ida at all. "Perhaps?" Nopine said, concern in her dark eyes.

"This was my mother's idea," Biaja said, waving a hand to mean the Temple, the initiate program.

Nopine bit her lip. "But, what else would you do?"

"Mother is certain Kitane is going to marry and inherit the Suramarti holdings," Bee said. "I am not so sure. I will not make the mistake of being stuck as a priestess if, instead, I might inherit. I would love to run our estate, and I would be good at it." She tried to keep the defensive tone from her voice.

"Do you hate it here so much?"

In answer, Biaja glanced at the bundles of goods she must take to the shrine. "I would hate leaving you here," she said. "But I know now that blind obedience to an already-established hierarchy is not for me. I would be years gaining respect and position.

"No, if I must, I am middling good at weaving," she said. "I could apprentice in our workshop, if Kit manages to get herself married in time. Otherwise, I would inherit one of the wealthiest and most powerful telestai holdings on Keftiu."

Biaja was truly hurt by the dubious frown on her friend's face.

"You think I cannot do it?"

"It's not that I think you will fail. I think your sister is sensible and smart, Bee. I think Kitane will choose a suitor and marry and become a telestai leader. Do you truly want to make cloth? As a priestess, everyone would look up to you."

"I don't care about that. But if the Aurochs makes me clean up one more mess, I am afraid I will do far worse than accidentally dousing her with wash water."

"Be careful, Bee. Some of the initiates and priestesses think you did that on purpose."

"What?" Biaja gritted her teeth, taking deep breaths. "Well. *That* is why I don't wish to stay," she said. "Gossip and petty jealousy. Retaliation is on their minds, so they think that is all I want, as well."

"No, I understand that isn't what you want. But, if you are this unhappy, I think you are right. Temple service is not for you."

Eyes filled with unfallen tears, Nopine gave her a fierce strong hug, then turned and left the room, hurrying off to the ceremony, leaving Biaja alone with her fear and frustration.

Was she really going to abandon the initiate program?

It was a boon for Nopine, whose atomai family had little beyond the roof over their heads. Nopine had learned to read; she received food and clothing and a space in the dormitory. She had already worked her way up among the initiates and seemed happy, unlike Biaja.

Bee could feel the decision become firm in her mind. She visualized herself back home, minding a loom in the sunny workrooms of the villa. No Aurochs yelling at her or assigning the most belittling chores. The sense of freedom she could almost grasp shook her with its intensity. The thought of returning to her mat on the floor of the initiates' dormitory was repellant.

Taking deep breaths to calm herself, she loaded one of the baskets of cups and offerings onto a small hand cart and made her way to the South Entrance where the atomai Maza was waiting with a donkey. Biaja made sure the meal vouchers were still tucked in her sash.

At one time, the caravanserai outside the temple had offered free food and lodging, but now the priestesses charged for it. She had been told it was because too many drivers had been bringing guests and extra animals and leaving them to be fed at the Temple's expense. Some of the drivers even seemed to be living there, which was quite against the rules.

Trying to think ahead, she had gotten two extra vouchers for the second day of the journey. Maza would need to be paid for the return trip, unless the priestesses at the Shrine had something to be carried back down, which Mt. Ida would pay for. But that was unlikely.

Bee stopped by the temple kitchens and picked up her own mid-day meal to eat on the road.

By the time she got back with the second bundle of baskets, Maza had the first lashed onto her donkey's back. The animal's load looked lopsided. The girl quickly took the second bundle from Biaja and balanced the weight on the donkey's back. Bee turned and made her way back to the hall and the last batch of baskets.

On her return, "Here," she said to Maza, handing her the three meal vouchers for this day, and pointing to the bundle. "That's the last of it. I'll meet you outside the caravanserai in an hour or so. Please enjoy a satisfying meal before we start out. Just leave the hand truck here against the wall."

The girl took the tiny tablets and put them carefully into the sack around her neck, then unloaded the hand truck.

Meanwhile, Biaja walked past the workshop area and across the big courtyard, looking for Ukan. He usually worked as a guard at the customs house at the North Entrance to the temple complex. On the small north courtyard, she passed a group of youngsters listening to their teacher. The teacher raised her head and smiled at Biaja. *Qazipatima*. Her sister, the priestess. Biaja gave her a weak smile in return, then looked away and hustled toward the guard post. What was she going to tell her sister, the one who had been a priestess for most of her life? Thank you, but no? I think what you are doing in life is stupid?

Unaware she growled aloud, Biaja was startled when two guards thumped the butts of their spears on the floor. She realized she had been moving at an aggressive speed, that she looked angry. She stopped and smiled at one guard, then the other. "I'm looking for Ukan," she said in a pleasant tone. "Do you know him?"

She arranged with her neighbor Ukan to meet her across the viaduct near the caravanserai entrance with his cart and donkey and a sack of grain she would repay him when they got to Suramarti. Jura's brother had been promising to accompany her back home before the bull-jumping ceremony, and Biaja was going to take advantage of that today. Why should she walk, when she had a friendly ride? She no longer cared what the Aurochs thought, anyway, did she?

Once again, she stared at the ash plume in the north while she waited for Maza and Ukan to show up. Then she remembered the poem the strange scribe from Athens had given her for her sister. She glanced around, and seeing no sign yet of either the donkey driver or her neighbor, she ran back into the temple.

She saw the Aurochs crossing an intersection of hallways ahead of her, and ducked into a light-well atrium just in time to avoid the woman's glance. She waited a beat then peeked out. The hallways were clear. She took a deep breath, noticing again how the air smelled like stone, here, not the freshness of trees or grasses or herbs like at home. She checked again for the Aurochs, then moved.

She made her way back to her sleeping room, trying to remember where she had put the tablet bearing the poem. The dormitory was empty as she walked quickly in and to her blanket. Yes, she had set it on the floor by the bay leaves that padded the floor beneath her sleeping mat. The poem lay near where she rested her head on a lumpy wool pillow. She picked it up and stuffed the cloth-wrapped poem into her carry sack. The old wool robe scrap was ready to fall apart. She smiled when she realized she might be able to weave herself a new one soon. She went to the table that held their personal items.

Biaja stared at her hairbrush, the beeswax scalp ointment, her kohl eye pot and brush, and her tiny bowl of the simple jewelry the Temple allowed its initiates. Barely breathing, she snatched up everything of hers from the table and stuffed it all into her sack. As she picked up the bowl of jewelry, she paused and used a finger to search for the ring in the shape of a leaping dolphin her father had made her of silver. She had let it tarnish, so it looked like tin and had passed the Aurochs' "not too fancy" inspection.

Heart thumping now, she gently set the ring on top of the things in Nopine's jewelry bowl. Then, pulling the ties of her carry sack tight, she tied it to her belt and left the dormitory.

Maza was waiting when she got back to the meeting point, but she couldn't see Ukan yet. Where was the man?

She thought about him, and his brother. And then about the poem in her sack. Another suitor for Kitane. This was going to be an interesting addition to her sister's marriage conundrum. Biaja hadn't been home enough to see how Ukan's brother Jura had been wooing Kit, but she could imagine it had been stiff and "according to tradition."

This poet was a foreigner, and not wealthy enough to impress the Suramarti family. But the poem might compliment Kit. Biaja opened her sack and withdrew the tablet with careful fingers. Without undoing the twine that tied it closed, she pulled a corner of the covering cloth back and peeked at what the scribe had written. She read to the line of the twine, then opened the wrapping from below and finished reading. It praised Kitane's bull jumping. Well, that was as expected. Who didn't like flattery? Kit was not ashamed of being a fine bull jumper.

But Biaja had to wonder how impressed her lively sister was going to be with a man who sent her bold paeans of love. That was not how things were done on Keftiu. Jewelry or a fine animal or quality cloth or other trade goods—those would impress Kitane —or any other marriage prospect. She thought about the foreigner's pale pinkish skin and light brown hair. His nose was slightly flattened and curved, a bit like a bird of prey. He even looked different from the Keftiu suitors.

Perhaps she should tell the Hellene man how to behave, so he could make a better proposal. Her sister should be offered only the best to choose from, yes?

SCENE 2 — KITANE AT SURAMARTI AND TYLISSOS
ϙⵤⵏ

To protect her cousin from censure for telling Kitane the prophecy, Kit pretended she did not know about it. Her mother seemed to know something had changed between them, but she did not say anything.

At breakfast, Zetis was being a complete brat, stealing his favorite foods from everyone else's plate, and sassing Okune. Kit finally snapped at him.

"How can you be so rude, Zetis? You were better behaved when you were three years old. Just stop it!" She swatted his hand when it darted toward her asparagus spears. He laughed and fled the room, dodging behind a column to snatch the last slices of bacon from the serving tray on his way out.

"Something needs to be done about him," Asije said. Kitane's aunt stared at her sister.

Okune groaned out a sigh and nodded. "I am leaving him at Knossos after the bull-jumping ceremony," she said.

"He won't stay," Kit predicted. "He'll just run away again."

"I warned the boy's klawiphoros. He is prepared to lock him in a cell and have other initiates escort him to classes and make sure he does his chores. I gave them authority to pound some sense into his foolish head."

"A very selfish foolish head," Kitane said, and her cousin nodded agreement.

Kit watched her mother help the kitchen workers clear the food trays away. "I'm off to the north vineyard," Okune then said. "We have some kind of infestation, the supervisor says."

"Better you than me," Asije said, laughing. "I get to spend the full day weaving." She disappeared into the kitchens, carrying the last tray and the soiled linens.

"I'm going to the pottery workshop," Isari said to Kit. "Papa brought my tools, so I'm setting up my work area. Do you want to come?"

Kit shook her head. "No, I've some things to do. Maybe I'll join you later, I need to catch up on my spinning allotment, and we can talk."

Her cousin smiled, a rueful expression on her face. "There's always spinning," she said.

Kit waved and headed toward the Goddess tree behind the villa.

After a brief morning devotion, Kit visited Enosidas in his field between the Suramarti olive groves and a row of fig trees. She found a couple dried figs still clinging to the branches and rolled them around in her hands, softening them as she walked. Eno loved the sweet bits.

He whuffed as she stood next to him, her hand open and flat with the fig nibbles on it. Eno's huge head eclipsed her arm as he delicately licked the treat up. She scritched around his ears, then he tossed his head up. The rumble of a small earthquake filled the little field. She stood with him, unafraid, patting his shoulder. The quakes were happening so often the bull was becoming accustomed to them, as was she. Beyond the head toss, he stood calmly.

"Today we rest, Eno. Tomorrow we practice once more, and then to Knossos and the ceremony."

Their eyes met, and she knew he understood the importance of gaining Jasasara's blessing. She hugged his massive head and felt tears well up as she thought about the possibility of losing. Were they getting too old? Had she decided to compete one year too many? One mistake at Knossos, and the priestesses would want to sacrifice him at the end of the ceremony. He would be dead.

She gasped and prayed for the Goddess' blessing: grace, agility, and speed would get them through. They had to. She patted Eno's forehead and picked a small piece of grass from his forelock.

He blinked and dropped his head to browse on the barley grass gone wild. They would plant grain in this field again next year. She would have to keep Enosidas somewhere else, assuming he was still alive. It was as if a hand grabbed her heart and froze it when she thought of him being slaughtered like a meat animal. For the Goddess. She shook her head. The Goddess she knew and understood could not want dead meat instead of the beautiful, strong animal that was Enosidas, alive.

She patted his shoulder again and walked back to Suramarti, meandering across the fields and through the orchards and vineyards, looking at the riches of the fields.

A small rabbit peered at her from behind a grapevine, nose wiggling.

"Hello, little one. I hope you are not eating our grapes." The rabbit did not answer, but hop-walked slowly toward the creek, nose wiggling, ears turning like leaves flipping in the breeze. She lost sight of it as she went down the bank and jumped across the narrow rill. Suramarti might have to conserve water this year, with so little rain. This little creek often disappeared in drier years, and it was low now, when it should have been full and rushing toward the sea.

Kit made her way to her father's workshop, at the end of the old wing of the Suramarti villa. She saw him talking to one of his apprentices, demonstrating something about the fine work they did. Radamitu was known all over Keftiu, even all the way to Kmt and Alashiya across the Middle Sea, for his fine gold work. He had perfected a way to make the gold form into miniscule balls to include in his design, making life-like texture, along with tiny strands that could look like hair or the stamens in flowers. He made golden petals that looked so like a real flower that people were amazed to see that they were only metal.

Kit's own dragonfly necklace was a composition of such delicate details. The shiny dragonfly wings seemed translucent, just like real dragonflies. She vowed to wear it to the dinner, to be sure he knew how much she loved it. It was not practical for bull jumping or other work, of course. All she usually wore of jewelry was a pair of tiny gold earrings that clung close to her earlobes, and her seal on a thong around her wrist or neck.

Finished talking to his apprentice, Radamitu glanced up and grinned, his face lighting up to see Kit. "How is my favorite daughter?"

Kit thought about what she had come to discuss, and her own smile faded. "Papa, I need to talk to you. Not here."

He glanced at the room with two apprentices and an assistant working. He took her hand in his and led the way out the back door, into the open space between the wings of the villa.

They walked to the bench Kit had had placed there in the shade of a rare jacaranda tree that was now so loaded with lavender blossoms that it didn't even look like a real tree, more like an artist's imaginary blossom-burst in a fantasy fresco. She sat down, and her father put one foot up on the bench beside her and leaned over his knee.

"What is so wrong?" he asked.

She glanced up at him. No one would ever say Radamitu was a handsome man. His nose was lumpy, his unusually fair skin was reddened from the heat of his workshop, his ears stuck out from his head like the handles of a clumsy jug. But his eyes were kind, deep golden brown, wreathed in wrinkles, and his hair was the normal blue-black of all Keftiu. He wore it pulled into a bun at the top of his head, out of the way of his gold works.

Kit just blurted out what she was thinking, all out of order from her planned talk.

"Did you know of the prophecy? That Qazi made about Mother? Did you know she was going to die when Aunt Asije and cousin Isari came here to live? Why did no one tell me? Why did I not know this? Why has this been a secret all these years?" By now, she could feel the tears streaming down her cheeks, and saw the concern in her father's eyes.

He sat down beside her and took her hands in his. "Your sister was twelve summers old when she had this vision. Yes, I knew. I was there when she ran crying into our sleep room having been awakened by this terrible dream-prophecy." He rubbed her fingers, his thumbs rough on hers.

"Why did no one tell me?"

"Kit— " He spent a moment looking down at their joined hands, then looked up, meeting her eyes. "For many years, we did not believe it *was* a prophecy. You weren't even born, yet you were in the dream. You, and Jura, Biaja and me and Asije and Isari. But not Sakusna. Not Zetis." He took a deep breath. "Now, Zetis not being there makes sense, since he wasn't born yet either. And we see now why Asije and Isari are here with Asije's husband also joining us, though Qazi did not see him in the vision, either."

"But Mother was not there."

"No, she was. She was there. She was dying, then she was dead, and Qazi saw me setting the funeral urn on her grave."

"From what? Why does she die?"

He shook his head. "Qazi could not see. It is the nature of these visions, that nothing is explained. And while she could 'see' you, she did not know your name, or Biaja's—it was just a couple of young women. Some things are very clear, and others are a complete mystery." He looked out toward the Goddess tree, gazing farther away than that.

He sighed, and went on, "We could not know if it was a true prophecy, or simply a bad dream." He swallowed and looked at her, eyes sad. "Then things came true. You were born and growing up, looking like the dream. Then Biaja came along. Zetis did not appear in the dream, so once again we wondered if what she had seen was a true prophecy, or why would he not be in it?"

Kit jumped to her feet, walking around in a small circle. "Then Asije and Isari came here."

He nodded, turning to follow her with his eyes as she circled in front of him. "And these earthquakes— "

"Promises of doom."

"Yes." He waved an arm. "And that is why she set the deadlines for you girls, trying to be sure an heir was named before— "

"Before we get to the time where she dies."

He nodded, his own eyes glistening now.

Jura's sister Eluwari had set a table up under the grape arbor behind Tylissos villa. She greeted Kitane and led her to the table, where fruits and bread were laid out, along with a rhyton of honeyed wine, two wooden stools beside.

"Thank you for joining me," Eluwari said as Kit sat down.

"It's lovely here," Kitane said, still trying to imagine why she had been invited to this late morning table.

Eluwari poured them both a cup of wine, three-quarters full as if she had measured it precisely ahead of time.

"You are probably wondering why I asked you to join me, as I have been more Biaja's friend than yours all these years," Eluwari began. "It is not a traditional thing I have done."

Kit sipped the wine, which had been loaded up with some of Jura's famous honey. It was almost too sweet. She met Elu's gaze and gave the young woman a gentle smile.

"You are known for your plain speaking, Kitane, so I will be blunt. I wish to know your intentions toward our Jura."

Despite the warning about bluntness, it was all Kit could do to not raise her eyebrows or let an eruption of astonishment escape her lips.

"Ah. So. I certainly do not mean to be cruel, Eluwari. I have had a great deal of difficulty finding a decision in my heart *or* in my mind. I feel this pressure to choose is making it even more difficult."

Eluwari took a deep breath, then leaned forward and fiercely tore a piece of bread off the loaf. She pulled the soft blonde center of the bread away from the crust and popped it into her mouth. She chewed and swallowed. "So, you are not set on him with any certainty?"

Kit shook her head. "I am sorry. He seems a good man, but there are other considerations, other circumstances that have made my decision...almost impossible."

Jura's sister cleared her throat. "It is not Tylissos' intention to make your decision more difficult, but— " she turned her head away and muttered something too low for Kit to hear.

Kit leaned forward and put her palm on Eluwari's knee. "What?" she whispered.

"Oh, please do not take offense!" Eluwari cried, "But Jura is not getting any younger, and he must take up his own place someday soon!"

Kit nodded. "Of course," she said.

"And I just wish to ask you— " Eluwari was almost breathless, her voice faint, "—if it would offend if Jura asked elsewhere."

Kitane leaned back on her stool, resting her elbows on the low stone wall behind them. "No, I would not be offended," she said. It was surprising that traditional, shy, Tylissos would even ask, but Kitane knew Jura had waited for her, and now he was beginning to be too old to still be living at home. Of course, his mother and sister were concerned. "Of course, you wish to see him settled. It is mostly my own fault I cannot make a decision, for there is something I wish to do first, and I do not know how long it will take. It would be cruel of me to ask Jura—or anyone— to wait."

"I had thought your mother had set a deadline, and we— we would...um, know by now."

Kit nodded. "A scant two weeks remain for me to choose and I cannot see that happening in time," she admitted. "I will eventually marry, but I suspect I will not be at Suramarti when I do. "

"Does Biaja have the same deadline?"

"No, of course she has more time if I fail to choose. But not much. I think you now know her better than I do, Elu. Do you think Bee would like Jura?"

"Maybe. Or Isari might."

Kit nodded, noting curiously that her cheeks were numb and there was a prickling in her fingers. What was happening to her? Why was this so disturbing? Perhaps she did not wish to give up on Jura just yet?

"There is a dinner tomorrow at Suramarti. It is supposed to honor me before the bull-jumping ceremony."

"Yes," Elu said. "We plan to attend."

"I had hoped to announce my acceptance of a suitor at that time." She threaded her fingers together and clenched her joined hands. "Now I think I must decline all offers formally until I have finished this thing I must do."

"Oh," Elu said.

"It is not fair to treat genuine suitors as if they have my full consideration and intent, when they do not."

"Oh," Elu said again.

"So, I will do my best to make that announcement. I am not spurning any suitor, so much as I am marriage at this time."

SCENE 3 — PAIAN ON PATH TO MOUNT IDA

Paian barely slept. Then as dawn approached, he overslept. Ukan had promised to take him to visit the bull jumper today. The rising sun glowed red. In the north, a black cloud filled the sky. Both bad omens for travel. Paian could not disappoint his one Keftiu friend. He grabbed his sword and shield and ran to the viaduct without any breakfast. He could not be late.

Instead of Ukan, he saw Maza. He ran to her. Out of breath, he panted, "Blessing of the Goddess to you, Maza."

Before she replied, she calmed her donkey, patting her withers, and whispering into her ear. Only then did she turn to him, "Blessings to you also Paian. Is something wrong? Clanging your weapons unnerved my donkey."

While he caught his breath, she added, "Why are you carrying a sword? And what is the big round thing that is ringing like a bell each time your sword hits it?"

He held up his shield. "This is my shield. When I fight with my sword, this protects me."

Maza shook her head. "Is this a joke? Do all Hellenes carry these things?"

"Of course. We must defend ourselves if we leave the village."

"How long have you been here?"

He tried to remember. "I am not sure. Several moons."

Now she laughed. "And how many people have you seen carrying a sword and that round bell thing?"

He smiled at her, a little embarrassed, and a little happy, "So I don't need a sword and a shield to go to Mount Ida?"

"Of course not. Go put that away before you scare people."

He ran back to the temple, now self-conscious, trying not to make so much noise. Without his sword and shield, he felt like he was missing something. He looked around his bed and reached underneath for his map. Certainly, for his first trip outside the temple, he should bring his map to make notes of the countryside.

When he returned, Maza still stood alone. He wondered why she stood at the viaduct instead of Ukan. *Had he come to the wrong place? Had Ukan also observed the evil sunrise and decided not to travel?*

Without thinking, he asked, "Why are you here?" Even before she responded, her downcast face let him know that was the wrong question.

"Why am I here? Why am I anywhere?" She kicked a rock. It flew off the viaduct, splashing in the creek below.

He stood frozen as she continued. "A telestai contracted with me to be here...prepared to go all the way to Mount Ida."

She kicked another rock. "Of course, I *am* grateful. If someone doesn't send me somewhere, I don't eat."

"I am also going to Mount Ida. Let's travel together."

"Depends on my telestai."

He pondered, "I guess I am in the same situation."

"Why are you going to Mount Ida? Is this about that bull jumper and the poems?"

Paian pulled two small tablets from his pouch. He hadn't wrapped and sealed them, but Maza couldn't read so it didn't matter. He held them up with a half-smile, "Yes."

She laughed. "Maybe you're right. I should learn my letters. Can you teach me? I may not always be an atomai."

He took a piece of flatbread from his pouch and tore it in half. He gave Maza a piece and they both sat in the shade of the donkey eating their delayed breakfast, while he told her of his mother's school.

They had finished the bread and a handful of raisins Maza shared, when he spied a donkey pulling a cart with two laughing passengers. He jumped up. Maza took hold of her donkey's halter.

The sight of his friend Ukan encouraged Paian. He reassured himself, *I'm in the right place and not late.* Ukan turned to the girl in the cart. Paian thought she might be Biaja, but she wasn't wearing the shiny black seal stone around her neck, so he wasn't sure.

Ukan spoke, "Goddess blessings to you, friend Paian."

He turned to the girl sitting beside him, "This is my friend, Paian. I am taking him to deliver some love poems."

Ukan and the girl laughed. Paian felt embarrassed but was unsure why.

The girl he thought might be Biaja pointed toward Maza. "I have to take these supplies to Mount Ida. Let's get started." She leaned over the front of the cart and slapped the donkey. Maza fed hers a handful of grass.

Thus, Paian embarked on his first journey over the viaduct into the wilds of Keftiu. He took up a position at the end of their small parade, with Biaja, if that was Biaja, and Ukan leading in their cart, followed by Maza walking with her donkey that carried the cargo bound for Mount Ida. He couldn't help being nervous without his sword.

Halfway across the viaduct, Maza stopped to greet a group of donkeys hauling sacks of revithia, the beans that reminded Paian of home. At home, his family added whole revithia to stews and soups. Here in Keftiu, the cooks ground the beans into a paste and ate it with bread and a little olive oil. The Keftiu added olive oil to everything.

Maza laughed and joked with these people. The cart with Ukan and the girl didn't stop, opening a distance between the two groups.

This friendly interlude ended abruptly when Ukan turned around and shouted to the donkey line, "Enough. Those sacks are already late. Time to get moving." The donkey line resumed the final part of their trek to Knossos, and Maza moved on as well.

Paian wondered what his friend had to do with a donkey line carrying beans to Knossos. Besides being a telestai and liking beer, Paian knew little about his friend.

Maza nodded to the departing people as they moved away. All those donkey feet beat a sad tune on the surface of the bridge.

He asked Maza, "Maza, what happened? Why were they late?"

Maza pointed to his seal stone, "You can never understand."

"I think it is you that refuse to understand. You never see through someone else's eyes."

She laughed, "You have it backward. You are concerned with differences...Athens and Keftiu...telestai and atomai. You do not see how people are the same everywhere."

He considered her accusation, and once again admired her intuition. He couldn't help wondering if she'd be happier if she read stories of being someone else, somewhere else. It was those stories of travelers that inspired Paian to visit Keftiu.

"The people on the donkey line are my friends. They are afraid to go to Knossos. Prophecy foretells of a coming cataclysm that will destroy the buildings and kill all the people inside."

Paian wanted to rest, but he didn't want to be the one to suggest they stop. After the long walk, his sandals were uncomfortable. He noticed Maza was barefooted, so sat down to remove his sandals and take the opportunity to wipe the sweat from his forehead and cheeks.

The couple in the cart turned around. They didn't yell at him, as they had several times before when Maza stopped to rest.

The telestai girl cleared her throat. "We are close to a watering place for the donkeys. It's time for them to rest."

At the water's edge, everyone took the opportunity to drink and rinse the sweat from their brows. Paian wanted to help Maza, but she did not seem to need or want help. She led both donkeys to the water and expertly held them while drinking and rinsing her face. He thought, *she has done this many times before*.

He had never seen telestai and workers together before. The distinction made him uncomfortable. He could see both sides, but didn't know what to say. He thought that someday he'd write a story about this. He looked around at the large trees, some covered with vines. He unrolled his map, and drew some large circles to remind him of the trees.

After he put the map away, he had an idea to start a discussion that might bring some cooperation among the Keftiu. He took the two tablets from his pouch. "These are for the girl I hope to marry."

Everyone laughed at him.

The girl turned to Ukan, "He's your friend and a visitor to Keftiu. It is your responsibility to assist him. Advise him of the best way to impress this girl." She laughed again.

Ukan seemed embarrassed for Paian. "I told you we had to speak to her mother. I said I'd help, but you need to listen and stop this crazy talk."

The girl smiled. "It's a good idea for Ukan to speak to her mother."

Maza jumped in, "He is right. You're in Keftiu now. I don't know about where you came from, but Keftiu girls are not wishing for tablets of poems."

He put his tablets away. The two in the cart could read and he didn't want them to see his words, especially after their disdainful responses.

The telestai girl touched her pouch. He thought she might be checking that she still had the poem he'd entrusted to her. Then, he saw that distinctive black seal stone hanging off her wrist. This *was* Biaja! And with this second look, he realized she'd chosen rare and difficult-to-carve obsidian for her seal stone. *She must be very rich to own such an exotic seal.*

He smiled because he'd found one topic where all Keftiu could agree. He feared that he'd not find a wife, for he'd never understand these strange people. Before they started fighting with each other again, he asked, "What do Keftiu girls want?"

Ukan sighed, "I keep telling you. Forget the girl. Think about her mother. My brother gave the mother of his girl a beautiful pitcher filled with honey. That is the way courting works here."

Biaja laughed and said to Ukan: "Maybe you can get a jar of honey for your friend."

Ukan agreed, "Clever idea. When we get to my house, I will do that."

Biaja seemed to disagree with her own advice, "You and your brother are so old-fashioned. I'd be happy for some new jewelry.

My sister is a priestess. She has a gold pendant shaped like a lotus blossom. I would like one of those…even though initiates are not allowed to wear such fancy jewelry."

She thought for a moment, "Or maybe a pair of nice earrings with labrys charms. I am not greedy. If not gold, silver would be fine. Just no bronze. Bronze makes my skin turn green and taste funny."

Ukan shook his head, "Who tells you your skin tastes funny? Does your mother know someone is *tasting* your skin?"

Biaja blushed and went silent.

Maza spoke softly, "Telestai girls might want gold and silver, but I would be very pleased with a few bronze needles or a nice piece of linen to wear at my wedding."

Ukan smiled at Maza and added, "I agree with Maza. Telestai girls can be very demanding."

Biaja snapped back, "You do not need to worry, Ukan. No telestai would be interested in you anyway. You could learn something from your brother."

Paian thought Biaja to be selfish and greedy, until she added, "Gifts do not have to be expensive. Flowers are nice. They are pretty when fresh, and can be dried to make soap and lotion afterward."

Paian interjected to bring some peace, "So you all agree: no poems?"

Ukan and Maza nodded in agreement, but Biaja demurred, "I'm not sure. Under the right circumstances, a poem, or two, could be very sweet."

This last comment encouraged Paian. If the bull jumper didn't like Paian and his poems, perhaps Biaja or someone like her would. He also looked at Maza and remembered his mother recounting her life before Athens.

"I worked in the weaving room at the temple in Phaistos. I remember the first time I saw your father. I could tell he was different."

Little Paian always asked, "Tell me mother. How was he different?"

His mother would look far away. All the way over the Middle Sea to Keftiu, little Paian imagined. Her voice would get very gentle. "He glowed with kindness."

Paian had never seen his father glow, but he'd never known his mother to lie. He'd put his head in her lap. "Did you get married right away?"

She got a big smile, "No it took me some time to convince him."

Paian just then realized that his mother was an atomai. Maza was also atomai. Was he making a mistake trying to woo a telestai girl?

That tenuous peace lasted until they met an old lady with a basket of pears at the side of the road. Biaja picked up two pears. "I do not have anything to trade today, but I will tell the donkey line from Suramarti to give you something the next time they pass this way. The women saluted Biaja with two open palms and bowed her head.

As the cart moved on, Paian thought the old lady looked sad. Maza also looked sad.

Paian could almost taste the pears as the two in the cart took juicy bites. He moved toward the pear lady, but Maza pulled him back. "We do not have anything to give her. *Your friends* have already taken two pears. She has little enough to feed her family tonight. Let her be."

SCENE 4 — TROS ARRIVES AT THERA

Thera announced herself with a column of black smoke and ash reaching to the clouds. Tros went to Sakusna. "We have arrived safely. Now, where are the graves?"

She replied in a loud voice for all to hear over the roar of the crashing waves, "Listen, all. The Goddess is against you. It is not too late. You haven't desecrated any graves yet. Do not die on this cursed isle. Return to Amnisos now."

"I'm tired of arguing with you." He turned to the smaller boat carrying the scribes, "I rescued you from the whales. I've delivered you to land. Tell me. Where are the burial grounds?"

Sakusna interjected, "Don't tell him anything. He hasn't saved you. He returned you to the place the priestesses have warned you to leave. He plans to desecrate the graves of your ancestors."

However, annoying he found them, he could not help but admire the women of Keftiu. Like his mother, they were strong, smart, and persistent. "Scribes, listen carefully."

They stopped bailing. The oarsmen brought the boats closer to Tros' ship.

"Here's my offer. If you cooperate, you can re-consecrate the graves and your ancestors might rest with the Goddess. If not, your ancestors will wander lost in this black cloud for all time."

Tros waited while they looked to Sakusna for direction. She crossed her arms and stood silent. The wind pushed them to the south, away from land. Tros needed to do something. "Your other choice is I'll leave you here in that damaged boat. Either way I will have the gold from those graves."

"He wouldn't dare. Don't tell him anything."

Tros now crossed his arms. He scowled at Sakusna before turning back to the disabled vessel. "Abandon ship!" he called to his crew.

The crew from the scribes' boat scrambled up nets and onto the bigger ship. The scribes drifted away.

Sakusna raised her hands. "Stop! The graves are in the northeast. That side of Thera has abundant Middle Sea beaches where you can repair the boat."

He turned to the crew. "We must now all work together. There is little time left. We sail around Thera. Quickly now!"

She spoke to the scribes. "Fill rhytons, cups, whatever you can find with olive oil for the rituals. We can't carry those enormous pithoi around the Thera burial grounds.

As they passed along the hills of Thera's south shore, the winds became violent. Under a cloudless sky, the rowers sweated so much the oars slipped out of their hands. The frenzied scribes bailed their leaking boat, barely keeping ahead of the waves blowing over the bow. The white salty foam gave an eerily wintery appearance to the hot work.

Tros silently prayed for the tempest to abate as it usually did in the evening. The cloud of ash rising from Thera grew thicker offering some relief from the hot sun as the ships turned north around the outside of Thera. Sakusna raised her arms and her voice. "Jasasara, mother of us all, shelter and protect us."

The north winds instead increased with the setting sun. Tros knew that once they left the shadow of Thera they would not survive in the open sea. This worst type of summer tempest buffeted the ships, just like the one that took his father. Sakusna's worried face made her look like his mother, and brought back the sad feelings of waiting, futilely, for his father's return. Their only hope was the sanctuary within Thera's circle of hills.

"Turn around. We must seek protection within the lagoon."

The exhausted crew reversed and headed for the strait, their entryway to the sheltered interior of Thera. As if the gods wanted to remind the crew of the urgency of Tros' order, the winds increased and stirred the sea into a dangerous maelstrom. The flotilla seemed small and defenseless as they rushed for the channel.

Sakusna walked over to Tros. "Do you now see that we need to support each other? The gods do not have favorites."

In the last light of day, dark shadow lines crisscrossed her face. Her hair blew in the wind. He almost hugged her and said, *mother*. Instead, he peered deep into her eyes, "Yes, we must help each other."

The sailors and scribes bemoaned their fate.

"No! We are going to die."

"Jasasara, Potidas, save us!"

"Don't let me die at sea."

When the ship rounded the promontory and entered the narrow strait, the base of the dark cloud was visible. Kaimeni Island illuminated the starless night. The column of ash glowed red and orange. The roar seemed to foretell the end of the world. The oarsmen stopped rowing. The scribes stopped bailing. Everyone put their heads to the deck and prayed.

"Do not quit now. We cannot remain here! Everyone back to your stations."

No one listened to Tros. Flaming rocks traced orange arcs through the air, ending with a hiss and explosion as they hit the sea. Even Tros was tired and discouraged. He could only think of his father. *Is this what it was like when my father died?*

Without waiting for orders, the crew turned the ships around. They left the lagoon, daring the stormy open sea, rather than the fires of Kaimeni.

"This is a doomed mission."

"The gods are against us."

"Give Tros a boat and let him enter on his own."

Tros stood up. He circled his signaling pennant. "Turn back! *Return!*" He banged the staff on the deck, but an explosion on Kaimeni overpowered his feeble actions. A huge burning rock curved over the lagoon and landed between the boats with a boiling eruption of the sea. It was as if Potidas had taken command. Ignoring their captain, the crew rushed away from the angry volcano. Tros ran between the rowers, pummeling the crew to no avail. They would not return to the exploding inferno. He sat at the stern and buried his face in his hands bemoaning, "Who am I against the wrath of Potidas?"

Then Sakusna took his hand and walked him to the bow. She raised her arms. The volcano and the sea seemed to quiet to hear her speak. "Sailors. Scribes. We have come so far together. We must help each other. The gods have blessed our mission. Do not forget your faith and ideals."

The peace continued. One by one oars reversed toward the lagoon the way they had recently fled, and baskets bailed out the water. They would brave the danger.

In the dark, the ships moved forward. Twice, small boats, and once, the big ship collided with submerged rocks. By the time they cleared the strait, the treacherous passage had damaged all three. Fortunately, the seas calmed within the encircled lagoon.

As on previous journeys to Thera, the crew turned east toward the city of Akrotiri. Tros immediately realized their error. The north winds had buried Akrotiri in ash. Only the flat roofs appeared over the dunes of ash; black debris filled the market squares. The plume had even buried the water under a layer of destruction. "Not this trip. We must go the other way around the lagoon."

Kaimeni continued to roar, the ash blew away from the intrepid travelers and the lagoon reflected the fires in its eerily smooth surface. The rowing and bailing achieved a calm rhythm, almost musical. Tros stood next to Sakusna and they both smiled.

She whispered, "You and I must work together."

Tros agreed, "Yes, and we need the protection of the Goddess to save ourselves. Thank you for not panicking like the others."

She touched his shoulder, "We share the same fate."

Tros thought, *there is more to this Suramarti lady than I imagined*, and echoed, "Shared fate. More than you know."

She looked at him with a puzzled look.

"My mother. My mother is from Malia, she is Keftiu."

Everyone recognized the need to stay far from the center of the lagoon where Kaimeni raged in threat. Most of the shore around Thera Lagoon was steep cliffs, taller than many men, many hands of hands. In the dim light, the crew pushed the ships forward, avoiding the certain death from the rocky wall to the left and the exploding kiln to the right. In a few places, the water had undermined the cliffs, which collapsed forming rough beaches. The ship circled the lagoon heading toward a black-sand beach well known to traders who needed a place to hide. The good people of Akrotiri called it Pirate's Cove.

The oars moved like a school of fish attacked by sharks, terrified and coordinated, with speed and energy, back and forth, up and down, sometimes together, sometimes crashing into each other. Tempers flared. Only the imperative to keep moving, keep rowing, prevented fights. The flurry of activity worked, and the ships raced through the calm lagoon, leaving a line of waves in their wake.

The fiery arcs of hot rocks were no longer so frightening. As each one exploded from the center isle, the sailors and the scribes looked up to enjoy the show. Sakusna and Tros sat down. Tros closed his eyes and must have fallen asleep, because he hadn't noticed the orange trail of sparks falling out of the darkness until the scribes screamed, "No. No! Potidas no." The sailors responded with cries of, "Abandon ship. Overboard. All go overboard."

Tros opened his eyes as the flaming missile landed in a small boat and exploded. The boat burst into flames. Flames spread everywhere and floated on the water.

Tros shouted, "Swim! Dive down. Dive!" The fire had hit some supplies of resin. Tros cursed the gods. *Why not land on the ore?* Bronze-silver and bronze-gold don't burn. Even the valuable cypress lumber from the Hittites didn't burn like resin.

Now that the gods had dumped the scribes into the sea a second time, they were better prepared. They followed the sailors' examples and stripped off their robes. Once unencumbered by wet clothes, they found they could swim, or at least float. They were not as swift as the crew, but they made steady progress away from the burning boat.

The other boats moved in to rescue the survivors until the burning resin unexpectedly reached several pithoi of olive oil. The result lit up the night like the midday sun. Worse yet, the burning mixture splattered and inundated several sailors.

The cries of dying men and the unforgettable, terrifying, acrid smell of burning flesh filled the air. Some men put their hands on their ears, others chose their mouths and noses. No one had enough hands or foolish courage to move closer to the struggling survivors until the floating flames died down.

As the bright light faded, the crew pulled the naked swimmers from the water and covered them with blankets to warm them up. Others jumped into the sea to cradle burned sailors in the cooling water until their pain abated. One sailor lost fingers and another his toes. Several had patches of hair burned from their heads or beards. Blisters covered many of them. Those were the lucky ones. The unlucky ones sank to the bottom of the lagoon covered with a mixture of burning oil and resin that the lagoon waters did not quench.

Sakusna moved among the injured, treating burns with a poultice she made from dittany leaves which she always carried. She bandaged the ones who had lost fingers and toes. The others, she just applied the salve and advised them to sleep sitting up.

Tros counted the survivors. Miraculously all the scribes survived, and just two sailors had drowned. He said, mostly to himself, "All the scribes are here. The goddess Jasasara saved them."

SCENE 5 — BIAJA ON THE ROAD TO MT. IDA
太ᛰ日

Biaja caught herself about to rub her rump in front of two men. Such manners! Had she been around too many foreigners? Her bottom was numb, but instead of rubbing it, she walked up and down the road a bit. The cart was not all that comfortable. She decided she would walk when they started back up the road. She took her small rough wool lunch sack out of the cart and walked to sit on the ground beside the foreign scribe. When Ukan returned from behind the bushes, he joined them, pulling a wrapped bundle from beneath his shirt.

They shared out their food, ignoring Maza who fed the donkeys some of the grain Ukan had brought, then let them graze on what they could find at the edge of the road.

Ukan pointed across the road, to the dark plume of smoke in the northern sky.

"It is still smoking. Is Akrotiri burning down?"

Biaja brushed a flake of ash from the edge of her cup of revithia, herbs and olive oil from the temple's kitchens. "I don't know. There have been no boats from Thera lately, have there?"

Ukan popped a small handful of olives into his mouth and shook his head. Chewing, he glanced to where Maza had taken a small packet from her donkey's load. Biaja looked also. The girl had used her food vouchers to buy prepared caravanserai meals. She was eating, also. Good. Biaja looked away.

"We should be at Tylissos before nightfall, Ukan."

"Yes. I am certain my mother will want to serve us a good dinner."

"Will Eluwari be there?" Biaja asked.

"Should be," Ukan said.

"And Jura?"

"Yes."

Good, Biaja thought. It was going to be interesting to see how two of her sister's suitors behaved when faced with one another. And she hadn't seen her friend Elu for weeks. They had missed each other the last time Biaja had been home, for the blessing of the new Suramarti villa wing. Elu was shy but observant. It would be fun to hear what she had to say about Paian, Ukan, and Jura.

And then on to Suramarti, where Kit would be confronted by two suitors at once. Biaja grinned, then finished her revithia and delicately accepted a piece of Paian's cheese.

Biaja noticed the sudden increase of smoke in the north the same time Maza's donkeys did. The animals snorted and moved restlessly, even after Maza comforted them. Biaja could smell the smoke as well as see it, close on the horizon.

"That's not Thera," she said.

Ukan got up and looked also. Abrupt flames showed in the near distance, black smoke billowing above them. A building was ablaze. She could see people running every direction like a flock of crazed geese. No one seemed to be putting out the fire.

Biaja grabbed her sandals and slid them on, then ran toward the fire. She could hear Ukan following, heavy steps on the narrow dirt track, and farther back lighter steps, either Maza or Paian, she did not look back to see.

The smoke became very heavy and black, thick coils from what must be the kitchen of a small villa or big farmhold. A man with no shoes was fumbling at the gate where several donkeys milled, eyes white and wild. She shouted, trying to warn him, but her voice was lost in the roar of the fire and the braying of the donkeys. As soon as the wooden gate was open, the animals bolted, knocking down the man who had foolishly stood there in the way. Now twice stunned, he just sat there in the dirt.

Paian passed her and ran to the man, helping him up. Biaja saw a young girl at the well pond, trying to fill pithoi with water, but the huge jugs were too heavy for her to manage.

"Ukan! Help her!" Biaja shouted, pointing at the girl. He ran over and lifted a filled pithos from the pond. By then Biaja had grabbed and sent several more men over to help. Soon there was a small relay going, and a few men were dumping pithoi filled with water on the fire, or carrying them back to be refilled. Biaja gathered a few more good-sized men to help and soon there was an actual effect on the fire, diminishing it.

She could hear someone calling for help. Was the cook or her helper trapped inside the kitchen? She ran around to the back side of the building where a middle-aged woman was darting in toward the fire, but the heat of the flames forced her back. Unaware her robe was on fire, the woman tried again to brave the fire. Biaja grabbed her, made her stop running back and forth, and poured handfuls of dirt on the woman's burning clothes. The woman sat or fell down, and Biaja got the fire out on her clothing.

"Children inside!" she gasped.

"Go get wet," Biaja said. "Just jump in the pond."

The woman nodded, got up and wobbled toward the well.

There was a loud crack and rumble, and Biaja backed up as the brick walls of the kitchen, their wooden supports burned away, collapsed. A thick cloud of dust, smoke, and ash billowed out. The water-bearers had the flames almost out, now, but the cries of whoever was trapped had turned to screams, then whimpers.

"You, you, and you," Biaja pointed to three young men who had run from behind the main house. "Go get wet in the pond, then come back here and help."

She saw a teenage boy digging at the ruined wall, and ran over to stop him. "No, not like that! You'll collapse the rest of it onto whoever's inside!"

He looked at her, eyes wide and white as the donkey's had been.

"Start from out here, clear a path through these fallen bricks to reach them from this side," she said, demonstrating with her foot.

"Papa," a child's voice said from under the rubble. "Papa, sister's not moving."

"Sit quietly, sweet child. We will be there to help soon," Biaja said. The last thing she wanted was for him to try and dig his way out. A mostly-burnt beam seemed to be holding the bricks away from him—so far. One of the other walls teetered in a precarious balance. Bee directed a couple of the water-carriers to gently push it, so it fell outward, away from the trapped people. Gradually the wet young men worked their way in. A small tear-stained face looked up at her from within a tiny bubble of safety in an angle of the beams and the stone ovens. Bee pointed to the top of the pile and two of the men moved those bricks away from the child.

Soon enough, Biaja reached down and took the boy into her arms. She turned and handed him off to one of the women who had joined them in moving the rubble away. She could see a slender bare leg still next to the ovens, but when they cleared away enough of the bricks and beam remnants, she could also see that the girl's head was smashed. A woman's wail went up behind her. She stepped out of the way as the mother gathered up the dead child and made her way out into the yard away from the destroyed kitchen.

Using what little she had learned at the Temple, Biaja knelt, fist to forehead, and said the blessing for the dead. The Aurochs had actually taught her something useful—for the ritual, the words to the Goddess, served to calm the people. They gathered in the yard, soot- and mud-stained, bloody and broken and sad—they gathered to make themselves whole again. They joined in saying the chorus, asking Jasasara to take the girls' *anima*, to let it rest, to bless those that remained with sweet memories of the child's life.

When she finished, Bee rose to her feet, turned, and found Ukan and Paian in the crowd. She made her way to them.

"Thank you, Missy," the people said. And, "Blessings upon you." "You saved my boy."

"*We* saved your boy," Biaja said softly. "All of us. I'm sorry we could not save the daughter, as well."

"Thank you, Missy."

Biaja looked at the now muddy and ash-covered water in the well pond. "Get your drinking water from somewhere clean for a few days," she said to the men standing near the pond. One nodded. Bee bent and cupped a handful of water to wash her face and hands, drying them on her filthy robe. She nodded to the people, then led the way back to the road to Tylissos.

SCENE 6 — JURA AT TYLISSOS

|ᵀ ↳

Potidas greeted the Tylissos villa with a frightening pillar of angry black clouds. Everyone lined up for the morning ritual. Jura proudly observed how the group had grown. This morning almost a hundred supplicants gathered around the horns of consecration. He had delayed a shipment to Knossos until after the ceremony, so more could attend.

While his steward poured wine into terracotta cups, Jura walked up to the horns and used the hem of his robe to clean off the layer of fine ash that had accumulated overnight.

When the steward had served everyone, he signaled the priestess from Mount Ida. Her gold circlet glowed in the sunrise and she pronounced the invocation as she did every morning. Each person took a sip of wine, anointed the horns with the remainder, and smashed their cup. This large group encouraged Jura. People were returning to the traditions.

The steward shouted, "They're gone! They're gone!" interrupting Jura's lunch of pita, ground revithia, and a few chunks of leftover roast lamb. The steward ran through the vineyard. As he came closer, Jura could see he was waving several donkey halters.

Where did he find those halters? Jura wondered. With the bull-jumping ceremony in a few days, Tylissos had sent festival supplies to Knossos. Jura had personally checked the sacks of olives, almonds, pears, and pistachios. He'd even included a sack of dates that he'd received in trade from Kmt. The donkey line was supposed to have left after the morning ritual.

The appearance of the black clouds in the north emphasized the importance of the bull-jumping ceremony. Of course, he also had his personal reasons. He wanted Kitane to see his support. She seemed to think he was just a clumsy oaf. This would demonstrate his effective organization, an important trait for telestai.

Finally, the steward was close enough, "Where did you get those halters?"

"I found them in the paddock. Just thrown on a pile in the dirt."

"Do you mean they took the donkeys to Knossos without halters? That's crazy."

The steward stammered and waved his hands. "They... The... Missing..."

Jura handed his steward a piece of bread dipped in olive oil. "Eat this. The olive oil will help you calm down."

The steward obediently chewed.

Jura's father kept a pithos of olive oil in his sheep-shearing shed. "Remember Jura, olive oil cures spider bites, sticky bronze shears, sunburn, stinging nettle, lots of things. Boiled nettle served with olive oil increases stamina." In recent years, he'd given his son a sly grin and added, "Remember that when you're married."

The steward swallowed, and Jura tried again. "There. Now start from the beginning. What happened?"

"Donkeys? The donkeys are in the pasture. I counted them. Seventeen. They are all there. In the— "

"Do you mean they didn't go to Knossos? They were going to leave after the ritual for Potidas!"

The steward replied softly, "The donkeys are here, so they didn't go to Knossos."

They had not followed the plan. This surprised and disappointed Jura. "Go to the donkey line and tell them they can still deliver the shipment on time."

The steward backed away. "The workers are *missing*!"

"Missing?"

"Yes. Also, all the supplies...missing. The pears, pistachios— "

"I know what we had."

Jura walked around the villa trying to think of the next step. Kano followed, sensing something wrong and sniffing every corner for clues. He went to the stables. They were exactly as his steward had reported. The potters were making loom weights. The jewelers were polishing red chalcedony stones Kitane's sister Sakusna had found on a trading voyage to the east. At the main house, he met his sister.

He gave her an open palm salute. "Blessings of the Goddess Eluwari." Kano wagged her tail.

"Blessings to you too, brother."

"Have you heard about the delivery of supplies for the bull jumping?"

Eluwari looked away and stopped walking. "Yes. This is so unexpected." She turned to a small girl hiding behind her, "Come here child. Tell him what you know."

The young girl stood with her face hidden in Elu's robe. She said something, but Jura couldn't understand. The bull-jumping ceremony was important to Keftiu...and Kitane. Jura kneeled down, "No need to hide. Speak up, please."

His sister put her hand on the girl's shoulder, pushed her forward, and whispered words of encouragement. "Do not be afraid. Just tell what you know."

Tears ran down the girl's face. She tied her rough wool robe in knots. Kano licked her hands. She looked down at the dog and said, "I am scared. The black cloud has frightened everyone. They ran away. The prophecy. The prophecy..."

At that point, she started bawling and again buried her face against Eluwari.

"Sister, you spend more time with these people. Do know what's she's trying to say?"

Elu frowned. "I can't believe this. I've heard rumors of angry gods, gods that will collapse the buildings, rumors that only those living in the forests, like long ago, will survive."

Jura thought, *this is what happens when the telestai ignore the traditions. Chaos.* He was so disappointed at the donkey drivers for running away, at the telestai for not following the traditions. Most of all, discouraged with himself for seeing something like this coming and not being able to prevent it.

He turned to his sister. "The telestai and the priestesses are here to prevent such superstitions. How could they believe such a silly children's story?"

"I agree. I never thought much about it. It was so childish."

The girl balled her fists. "It is real." She stamped her bare foot. "Real! The black cloud is a sign, a sign from the prophecy."

Eluwari gave the girl a hug, "Where is everyone? Did the black cloud take them?"

The girl wiped her eyes on her arm. "Just like you said, they have moved into the woods to wait."

Eluwari turned to Jura. "The Temple and Kitane expect you to deliver those supplies. Do something about this."

Jura wondered if he caused this. *Did the morning ceremonies terrify the atomai?* Frustrated, he went to do what telestai do, solve the problems, even problems they created themselves.

Jura found his steward. "The girl said they are hiding in the wild."

The steward asked, "But why didn't they take the donkeys?"

Jura guessed, "Donkeys are no use in the deep forest."

The steward still struggled to understand this unexpected disappearance. "Why did they wait until daylight?"

Again, this made sense to Jura. "With the black cloud, the night is too dark to safely travel through the woods, especially with children. Lions hunt at night and everyone knows they can see in the dark."

The steward added, "And since they were expected to have started for Knossos today, no one would be looking for them. I only discovered them gone because I took a shortcut through the paddock. Otherwise, it could have been days before they were missed."

Jura had had enough talk. "Get two groups, one to take the path toward Knossos and the other to go toward Suramarti. Ask every telestai you pass to send help. We must search the wilds and find these people before they scare atomai at other villas."

The steward ran off.

Jura thought a little and added. "Hurry. If you're fast enough, we can reclaim the supplies and get them to Knossos in time for the bull jumping."

Jura didn't finish his lunch. What started out as such a good day, had quickly gone bad.

After the little girl's funeral, Maza's concerns about the coming calamity and Paian's about his tablets of poetry both seemed petty. Paian thought that everyone looked at Biaja with more respect as she walked at the front of their little caravan holding the halter of the donkey pulling an empty riding cart. When Biaja abandoned the cart, Ukan followed her lead.

Biaja, as if realizing she was in charge like during the fire, stopped, and turned to the group. "Up ahead is Potidas' Trial, the steepest section until we get Mount Ida. We'll take a short rest here. Fresh water is available down there."

She pointed to a narrow track, almost hidden by the growth of round-leaved plants covered with white fuzz. Paian did not recognize the plant, so he reached out to touch the soft-looking leaves.

"Don't touch!" Biaja called. "That plant is dittany. The Goddess Jasasara has given it to us for medicine and scent. In return, we treat the plant with respect until it is needed." She gently held the delicate leaves aside for the others to get to the water. Maza walked each donkey down the trail. The donkeys—that usually tried to eat every green plant—ignored Jasasara's dittany.

Potidas' Trial challenged both people and donkeys. The climb was steep with loose rocks and unsure footings.

Halfway up, it happened. A basket of terracotta cups fell with a crash. Paian froze. He looked to Biaja, wondering what to do. She stopped long enough see the basket on the ground and shake her head. Without comment, though Paian was sure everyone knew there was a problem, she returned to guiding the donkey cart up the rocky trail.

Ukan rushed over to Maza and the basket. She was uncharacteristically quiet as Ukan helped her to unpack the basket to assess the damage.

After Biaja had advanced far up the hill, Maza began to softly sob. "The gods hate me. One donkey is not enough for this load.

Biaja should have taken the cups in the cart. Nothing falls out of a cart. It's empty, isn't it?"

Maza separated the intact cups from the cracked ones. She saved the soft grass that the Temple helpers had used to protect the cups. When she found a broken cup, she picked up the shards, threw them against a rock.

Ukan put his arm around her shoulder, "Let's check the basket and discard the broken cups together."

Maza threw another handful of shards. "The priestesses at Mount Ida will punish me for every damaged cup."

Ukan gave her a hug before she threw more shards. Her hand relaxed and she dropped the pieces to the ground instead of throwing them. "There are not many broken," he said. "We'll pack up the good ones and perhaps they won't notice."

Paian couldn't believe that Ukan was so helpful. Maza should have checked the ropes holding the baskets when they stopped at the bottom of the climb. He tried to see both sides, but this time had been Maza's own fault.

Paian, never one to hold a grudge, helped repack the cups and secure everything to the donkey. There were a few more baskets than they could safely attach to the animal, so Paian and Ukan each carried one up the hill.

At the top of the hill, a small group of men, out of breath and sweating, greeted them. "Ukan! Biaja! We are so glad to see you. Something terrible has happened."

Paian stood back and listened.

Ukan saluted the speaker with an open palm. "Tylissos steward, what are you doing so far away?"

The steward bent over, placing his hands on his knees. After a few deep breaths, he told his story. "The workers at Tylissos have run away. Not only that, they have taken the provisions for the bull jumping at Knossos."

Paian cut his eyes to Maza. She had a tight smile, as if she was both happy and scared. She moved behind her donkey.

Ukan pointed to a boy wearing only a loincloth of light wool held by a thin rope. "You, run back and let them know we are coming. My mother will be glad to hear that news. You can also tell everyone that Biaja is with me."

The boy took off running. He quickly went around a curve in the path and disappeared. Late spring growth had thickened the foliage. Only the well-traveled Mount Ida path remained free of green leaves and colorful flowers.

Ukan turned to Paian, "Do not worry. This happens, but we always find them, and everything returns to normal."

Maza emerged from behind the animals. Her tight smile turned into a frown.

Ukan continued. "I'd hoped we'd have a nice dinner after our long walk, but with the so many atomai gone into the wild, the dinner selection might be limited."

First the fire, then the broken cups, and now this. Paian feared the gods opposed this journey. He covered his concerns with some cheerful encouragement. "I am sure everything will be wonderful."

Biaja added, "I can guarantee we'll have an interesting time."

Paian didn't know what to think. After a single day out of the temple, he had seen more conflict than his entire time inside it. He'd also seen bravery by Biaja at the fire, empathy by Ukan helping Maza, and friendship between Maza and her friends along the path. This was a momentous journey, certainly comparable to the sagas he'd read at home, and tomorrow he'd meet the bull jumper face to face.

Scene 8 — Jura at Tylissos

ﾚﾛ ﾚﾐ

A young boy came running into the courtyard of the Tylissos villa, "Mistress! Mistress! They are coming!"

Jura's mother, who had been speaking to his sister, turned around. "Who's coming? Have they found the missing people? Have they returned?"

The boy hiked up his loincloth. "Ukan. And he has Missy Biaja with him. And some others."

She turned to Eluwari and Jura, "Did you know your brother and your friend were coming? How are we to have a proper feast with so little notice?"

This was just like his brother to show up unannounced. Even worse, Ukan had invited Biaja. Now his mother and sister had to organize a banquet for a representative of Suramarti.

His brother must have known this would embarrass everyone at Tylissos. He wondered if Ukan had been drinking again. *He cares more about beer than the family.*

Jura offered some support. "We have had good harvests. We have plenty of provisions, even after those ungrateful workers stole the sacks prepared for the bull-jumping ceremony at Knossos."

His attempted reassurance did not work. His mother chided him, "Jura, were you listening? Biaja will be here."

Eluwari added in that tone she used when she thought her older brother to be a fool. "Do you still want to marry Kitane from Suramarti? Did you forget Biaja is also from Suramarti? We cannot serve boiled barley and smashed beans. Even adding pistachios and olive oil will not suffice."

Jura hated it when the women ganged up on him, but understood fancy dinners belonged to them, and Suramarti would always intimidate Tylissos...until his wedding anyway. He hoped. He thought, *could it be that marrying a Suramarti is not a promising idea?*

His mother took charge, surprising both Eluwari and Jura with her sudden show of strength.

"Jura, we will celebrate our visitors in the courtyard. You assemble the food that we don't need to prepare. Wine. Olives. Pickled radishes. Dried fruit: quince and figs. Nuts: pistachios and almonds."

He suggested, "We have some nice fresh pears. I'll get those also."

"Good. Also, bring the best bowls, and the good chairs from the house. Thank Jasasara the weather is fine today."

Eluwari, always happy to give her brother orders added, "It's too late to roast a goat. My friend Bee likes octopus. I know we have a good supply of dried octopus. Jura, start a fire and fill the big cauldron with water, the pretty bronze one with the carved bull jumpers."

She turned to the atomai girl who was always at her side. "Octopus stew. Select the best vegetables, and fennel, sesame, coriander, and cress. I'll fetch the octopus."

His mother turned to Jura, "Be sure to make the fire big enough for the saj, the large bronze one with incised seashell designs. Eluwari, get your weaving women to prepare pita. Stew is always better with fresh bread. They can cook during the meal, so everyone has hot pita with their stew."

Jura and his sister stood on either side of his mother, each holding an arm to support her. He had wanted to bring a chair, but his mother had protested that it would not be proper to greet guests while sitting. They all waited at the Tylissos stone gate, modeled after the Suramarti one, which was quite famous. Like the Suramarti gate, it had a double-axe labrys carved on each side and the horns of consecration displayed above the lintel.

When Ukan appeared, his mother raised both hands in an open palm salute. "Welcome. Greetings and blessings of the Goddess Jasasara to all travelers."

When her hands dropped, Jura and Kano ran to greet his brother. Eluwari welcomed her friend Biaja.

Following his brother and Biaja were a boy, a girl, and a donkey carrying baskets. Jura assumed Mount Ida to be their destination. He guessed the girl to be the donkey driver, he thought he had seen her before, at the caravanserai at Knossos. He pointed to the boy, who didn't look Keftiu, but had a seal stone around his wrist. "Ukan, who is this?"

"This is my friend, Paian. I am taking him to deliver love poems to a girl that lives along the path to Mount Ida."

Jura laughed, "Love poems? I thought he looked like a foreigner. I wish him luck with his love poems."

Biaja laughed, "We've been telling him that. Your brother has been trying to help him, but the Hellene is so proud of his poems! He is a scribe, in love with reading and writing."

Jura turned to the donkey driver and pointed to the corral, where the Tylissos donkeys waited without their drivers. "You can take the donkeys to the stables. There is plenty of room for you to spend the night there. You will find food for you and the animals. Water is available in the creek behind the stalls."

When the girl didn't move, he added, "Don't worry. There is no charge if you could just feed all the donkeys tonight and tomorrow morning."

She grabbed the halters of both donkeys and escorted them to the corral.

With the donkey girl out of the way, Jura led the guests to the villa. Biaja would spend the night with Eluwari, and the strange scribe would sleep with Ukan.

Jura's mother invited everyone to dinner "at sunset in the courtyard." Jura could tell she wore a brave face hiding her discomfort from the sudden visitors and no roasted goat or boar.

Biaja raised a cup of wine. "Jasasara's blessing to Tylissos. Tomorrow, Suramarti." Everyone sipped the wine. Jura noted that his brother had found a large cup and took advantage to drink more than the others. After a couple of cups of wine, Ukan suggested inviting the donkey girl to join them. Jura simply scowled at him, and Ukan took the hint, for once, and shut up.

Jura looked to the north in the last light before sunset. The ominous black column of smoke had grown during the day. He wondered what evil this predicted. *Were the atomai right?*

Biaja raised her cup again. Ukan smiled and refilled his cup. She tapped her cup against the foreigner's. She handed a tablet, strangely wrapped in a grape leaf and sealed, to "Pijan," Jura thought that might be his name.

Biaja raised her cup higher, "Paian our friend, you may take your poem back. Tomorrow you can deliver it to my sister yourself."

All three, Paian, Ukan, and Jura said, *"Your sister?"*

Jura's mother echoed the three boys, *"Sister?* What are you saying Biaja?"

Biaja smiled sweetly, "I thought everyone knew this Hellene scribe has been sending love poems to Kitane."

Jura couldn't believe what he was hearing. He waited for his mother to say something more, or for his sister to respond to her friend. When they were silent, he didn't think it was his place to chastise Biaja.

However, his brother was a fair target. "This is just like you. Drunk and bringing someone to court the girl I'm to marry. How could you do this to me? How could you humiliate your mother like this?" As if to emphasize the point, his mother collapsed into her chair.

Jura grabbed the large cup from his brother's hand. He threw the little remaining wine in Ukan's face, who responded by spewing his dinner of octopus stew and stumbling to his knees in the mess. "Ukan, I am ashamed to call you brother."

Jura helped his brother stagger to his feet, then pointed him toward the villa. "That's right. Stagger to your room. Nobody wants to see you anymore tonight."

Jura then turned to the foreigner, Pijan, or Palin, or Paian, but whatever-his-name-was was already retreating to the stables.

Biaja pointed to the departing scribe. "Don't be mad at him. He didn't know anything. He's just a sweet guy trying to do his best and keep peace."

Jura found he had no response to that. It seemed Biaja was complicit in this game of competing suitors, but how could Tylissos admonish Suramarti? He could say nothing, but he seethed. Things were difficult enough between Kitane and himself. Now this.

Biaja and Eluwari walked into the villa. He relaxed as they disappeared. Two troublesome girls: Eluwari, who so enjoyed teasing her big brother; Biaja, who brought that foreigner to write love poems for Kitane. In his dark mood, he recalled Kit and her mother, so concerned with his sandals.

The evening had ended, not even as well as it had begun.

He pulled one of the good chairs closer to the fire, which had died down. He reconsidered the last few days. He looked down to the bright red coals and up to the dull black sky. Light below and dark above. All the world seemed upside-down.

Kano rested her head on his lap. Why did he struggle and fail each time he met with Kitane? Why had those Tylissos workers run away? Why had Potidas added smoke to the earthquakes? He wondered if the Keftiu and their traditions had become too weak and old. Was Keftiu failing?

Someone approached out of the dark. He pulled over another chair and joined Jura beside the dying fire. The stranger recognized Jura. "Thank you for your hospitality to a foreigner."

Paian picked up a pottery shard and threw it into the fire. Sparks jumped up to challenge the dark sky. "There is so much I don't understand about Keftiu. Why do I see pottery shards everywhere? Do you throw cups and bowls at each other?"

Jura first thought to explain the morning rituals and the smashed cups at the horns of consecration. Instead, he told the other story. "Over and over earthquakes have come to flatten Keftiu. Each time we rebuild in the same place, on top of the ruins. Those shards are the ruins."

"How wonderful to have such a long history."

Jura smiled with some pride. It was true Keftiu had survived many disasters. He also picked up a pottery shard and exploded sparks into the sky. The telestai would rise again. This disaster on Thera had delivered a refugee family to Suramarti, with a daughter who was talented with ceramics. New pottery to replace the old. Tomorrow he would meet her.

The next morning everyone prepared for the short journey to Suramarti. Jura could see that yesterday's activities had exhausted his mother. She was past the age when her daughter should have taken over. It had taken her a long time to have a daughter, so Eluwari was still young. Nevertheless, Jura's mother bravely took charge, distributing gifts for Suramarti. Biaja and Eluwari received fresh flowers still covered with the morning dew. She directed the two atomai to fetch sealed rhytons of wine for Jura and his father to carry. She handed Ukan a large basket of perfect pears.

She whispered something to Biaja, and Biaja spoke to Maza. "I am not able to accompany you to Mount Ida. You know the way."

Maza looked disappointed, but not surprised. "I understand."

Biaja added, "If you go directly to Mount Ida, you can return to Knossos in time for the bull jumping."

Jura's mother started walking. It was time to go.

Biaja went to the old woman. "We have a cart. Would you like to ride?"

Jura knew his mother held two walking sticks with delicate gold handles formed into seashells that fit her hands perfectly. "Thank you, but my sore hips can better endure walking than to be bounced in a cart."

Maza prodded her donkey. Jura's mother stopped until Maza was out of hearing range.

Before the group started again, Ukan handed the pears to Paian. "Here, take these to Suramarti. I'm going to accompany Maza. My brother and I need some space between us." He ran to catch up with her.

Jura would have preferred if they had also banished rival suitor Paian to Mount Ida, but at least he didn't have to see his traitorous brother.

SCENE 9 — KITANE AT SURAMARTI

ⵟⵛⵉ

Kit gave up on her hair the third time she dropped her comb, as it jerked from her fingers when she tried to pull it through the knots. Her sleep had been disturbed, and her tossing had put deep tangles into the long strands. Exasperated, she left it hanging loose and snarled, and picked up her comb, tossed it on her dressing table.

Her sister-in-law passed by in the hallway, then returned. "Can I help you please, Kitane?"

"I am falling apart, Halima. I cannot comb my own hair!"

Halima laughed, her soft burred voice making a song of it. "I have such days," she said. "Let me help."

Kit let her, knowing Diwoki's wife often felt useless at Suramarti.

The Kmt people did not allow their upper-class young women to perform "commoner's work" such as weaving or pottery, so Halima had no such skills. And of course, running an estate was considered a man's job in Kmt. There, women of good family were expected to sit around and look pretty to catch a mate, then have babies, which of course, Halima had done. The family joked that Halima's children would be spaced by the times Diwoki was home.

At least Halima could read and write. And she knew a great deal about the leading families of Kmt, who helped the Pharaoh rule. In fact...Kit thought of another way the young woman could perhaps help her.

"Halima, can you tell me about the priests and priestesses at Kmt temples? About how much or how little power they have, and what they do?"

"Oh, my. Such a complex question." Halima's hands paused, comb poised at the top of Kitane's head. "I should say first that the power and duties change depending upon how powerful the Pharaoh is. When there is a Queen, for example, they view her as weaker than a male Pharaoh, and the Priests seize more power. If

125

a strong King or sometimes such a Queen rises, they might dismiss a powerful Priest if they see him make trouble for them. Other times the priesthood coerces the ruler into granting them more dispensations, more riches, more power. Then later, a powerful ruler might take back those privileges unto himself."

"Are Queens always seen as weak?"

"Not always. But the general belief is that men are stronger Pharaohs."

"Do you think they see Keftiu as weak, since our priestesses are more powerful than our king?"

"I would say yes. But they have not been able to turn this into a trading advantage, so how weak can you be?"

Kit noticed the "you." It was clear Halima did not see herself as part of Keftiu. Perhaps she never would. "Do you think your own family's position has weakened since you joined us here?"

"Oh! Me? No, Kitane. This marriage was— Oh, I always find myself speaking so bluntly with you," she laughed, but looked worried. "My own place is happy. My family prospers, the Keftiu goods have given us wealth and status we would not have otherwise. And I love my Diwoki," she said, voice firm. As if she must confirm her contentment to Kit. As if she was afraid she would be forced to leave Suramarti if she was not fully happy?

"I hope you would tell me if anything about living here is unsatisfactory for you, Halima," Kit said, turning to meet the other woman's eyes.

The Kmt woman nodded, a serious expression on her face. "But it is true," she said. "While I find your customs strange sometimes, I do not miss the infighting and backstabbing I hear of at the Kmt court. I might have been forced to move to Avaris or Thebes, depending on what Kmt man I might have married. Tanis is a bit of a backwater, but it was blessedly quiet. Therefore, I love it here, where it is also quiet, and very beautiful."

Kit hoped it was not fear she saw in the shadows of Halima's eyes. The woman's beauty was solemn, rather than the lively look usually appreciated in Keftiu. Diwoki was unusual, being so enthralled with Halima's serene countenance and behavior.

"So, if there is something your Priests are doing that the people do not like, what happens? Is there any recourse?"

"If enough of the nobles complain, there might be changes. Of course, the priesthood is jealous of their power. The Pharaoh might step in and insist on a change to please his nobles, or himself. But there is always a bit of a battle going on between these three points of power: Pharaoh, Priests, Nobles."

Kit nodded her understanding, comparing it to Keftiu. Here, the priestesses definitely were at the top of the power tree. Below them, the more powerful telestai, who were perhaps on the same level as the guasileus. Below that, the lesser telestai and the smaller farmholds and craftsmen, including scribes and teachers, such as the klawiphoros. Then the atomai and lesser craftsmen. And below all, the few slaves the Keftiu kept, mostly captives from pirate attacks that they had repelled, or gifts given by other leaders. Theoretically, anyone could rise to a position of power among the priestesses. In reality, those with the gift of Goddess incarnation or prophecy were most likely to rise.

Of course, the guasileus was a hereditary position, so that he would be like the Pharaoh and male rulers of other nations Keftiu must treat with. But his power, or lack of it, was different than Kmt or Alashiya, the Hittites or the Hellene.

"I am glad you are here with us, Halima," Kit said. "And thank you for taming my hair. I had no patience for it this morning."

Halima laughed, then turned as the atomai crèche-worker appeared in the doorway holding her little girl. Seeing her mama now suddenly reminded the little one that her mother had been absent, and she began to cry.

"She cannot be hungry again, can she?" Halima murmured, accepting the wrapped bundle.

Kit watched in fascination as Halima cradled the infant, bared her breast, and offered it. The darling latched on as if she was starving, and the three women chuckled.

"Of course, she is," Halima said, smiling with a mother's tender smile down at her child.

Someday, perhaps, Kit thought. Someday I will have such a child. But who would be the father?

Kit rubbed her fingers on her robe, cleaning off some of the oily wool residue so she could grip her spindle better. She watched her two best weavers set up the linen loom in preparation for the warp threads. Meanwhile another pair of atomai measured out the warp on the wall hooks. Instead of ordinary Suramarti weaving, this week she had had them begin making the clothes for her own wedding.

Even if she somehow failed to decide before her deadline, she knew her little sister Biaja would need wedding clothes. It would be for one or the other of them. Once the garments were complete, she would supervise the dying and bleaching of the linen: blue and white. Dolphins would be embroidered around the finished hem of the robe and short wedding apron, as she and Bee both liked them.

She still wasn't certain if she hoped it was her costume or her sister's. She had read again the two poems from the Athenian scribe. They were flattering and sweet. But since she still had not even met the man, how could she imagine choosing him?

She replaced her filled spindle with an empty one, leaving the rewinding onto a weaving spool to one of the apprentices. She and her workers had spent so much time on the linen over the previous weeks, they had fallen well behind on their usual wool output. Whatever she could spin this morning would help them catch back up.

In her mind, the only choices she had were Tros, Jura and possibly this new scribe from Athens. She thought about that a moment. Two out of three were foreigners. Was there some secret reason for that lurking in her heart? Did she dislike telestai—her own people and class—so much that she searched elsewhere?

She did not think so. It was simply that the telestai choices were so limited. She had met the Zakros candidate only once. Perhaps if they met again, she could see virtue in him, but Zakros was so far away, it was impractical in the time she had left. The boy from Malia she had eliminated as hopelessly immature. The telestai with the quarry was completely out of the question—he had no respect for bull jumping, nor therefore, for Kitane.

Her aunt Asije came into the workshop and smiled to see Kit already at work on the wool spinning. Asije set up her own loom with fine linen thread, one of the atomai they'd brought along from Akrotiri helping her. *For Isari's wedding clothes*, Kit realized, feeling her spirits knot up with stress...and perhaps, with regret...for Jura?

Oh, how could she be so confused that she was jealous of her cousin about someone she herself had rejected?

She threw her spindle down so hard the thread snapped, and she had to stop and blend the downy wool back together, blinking back tears of fury.

Okune asked Kitane to help choose the menu for her dinner, and Kit wept internally. This might be the last thing she and her mother did together. How could she pretend she did not know about the prophecy? How could she pretend things were normal?

"You said you ordered fresh cherries. Do you think we should have figs as well?"

"There are none ripe," Kit said in a choked voice "We could put some dried ones out along with the nuts."

"Yes, something besides pistachios would look nice on that green papyrus plate."

"Mother— "

Kit could say nothing more. She took the two steps separating them and put her arms around her mother and burst into tears.

Okune stood stiffly for a moment, then, as if she was ice melting, put her arms around Kit and patted her shoulders with cool, gentle hands. They stood so for several minutes as Kitane attempted to get her weeping under control.

"When did you find out?" her mother asked.

"A day ago," Kit said.

Okune sighed deeply. "I wanted this whole thing not to affect your decision, but of course you could sense something was— "

"Things didn't make sense. Something was wrong." Kit hiccupped, then managed to ask, "How accurate are these old prophecies?"

Her mother stepped back to look at Kit's face. "All of them have inaccuracies of interpretation," she said. "And some just never occur at all. But many are true, and, as you know, especially those Spoken by Qazipatima."

Kit's sigh was shuddery. She reached for her mother's hands and met her gaze. Dark gold eyes looked into deep brown ones. "Are you ill?"

Okune shook her head. "No, we do not think it is disease, or old age, nor any infirmity. Qazi's *feeling* is that it was due to an injury. That is all we know."

"If I do not choose, does Biaja even still have time?" She flinched internally as she realized she was asking her mother to predict her own death date.

Okune shrugged. "This is not known."

"I have yet several days to decide," Kit said. "Unless you wished the *wedding* to be done by the date of my birth."

"I would love to give you all the time you need, and Bee as well, but as you know, there is no way to get exactness from a Seeing. I will be happy if you are settled with someone decent and Suramarti is well cared for." Okune sighed. Kit looked down at their clasped hands, old and young, pale and tan. "If you are crazy about this young man Tros, then you should go with him and be happy, Kit. Other arrangements can be made for Suramarti."

Kit shook her head, fighting back tears again. "I don't know."

"We have Bee and Isari, either of whom could be excellent administrators, though I think neither of them will ever love this land as you do."

"Oh! I am trying to save the bulls, and am losing my home instead," Kit wailed, tears dripping down her cheeks and splashing onto their joined hands. She felt as if she had spent this last week in tears, when normally she was not one to cry at all.

"Bulls?"

"I need to stop this sacrifice of bull jumpers' bulls," Kit said, realizing she had never spoken of this to her mother—only to her father, who was proud that his athletic daughter cared so much about her own beast and others'. "Why would I ever want to see Enosidas murdered before my eyes? Why would the Goddess ever be *pleased* by such a thing?"

"This is what you are waiting for?" Okune said. She shook her head, looking very worried. "I had no idea, my daughter. No idea. But I think you will not be successful in trying to change temple rituals."

"Not the ritual. Only the source of the sacrifice—back to the way it used to be, mama. Where they capture a wild bull." Frustrated with the way her voice burbled from crying, she stopped, gulped, and took a breath. "You know as soon as I marry, I must put aside bull jumping and any influence I might have to change things."

Okune hugged her again. "I am so sorry we kept the reason for the choosing date hidden from you Kitane. We should have announced the prophecy when we announced the deadline. I had no idea that you would have plans of your own this could interfere with. That is my mistake, and I am ashamed. I have not given you enough credit for your own plans."

"I think I could make a good decision if I didn't feel so pressured." She grimaced and looked at her feet, bare toes curling on the stone floor. "I really like the *idea* of Tros, but perhaps would hate the reality. I do think Jura probably is the best match for me. Just—just not yet."

"Yes, I see."

"Now this black cloud rising above Thera and bleeding over all the Middle Sea...your oncoming doom...my bull—this is not an auspicious time to choose a husband, mama."

"Not at all, and yet— "

"Yet it must happen. I know."

Okune stepped back, eyes on her daughter. "And still, we must have this dinner to honor our famous bull jumper."

Kit nodded. "Yes." She looked at the room once again, hoping she hadn't missed anything, sniffling up the moisture that again threatened to drip from her nose. "Is Biaja able to get away from the Temple? Will she be here, do you know?"

"She is on her way from Tylissos as we speak. She will be here before the others to speak with me and prepare to honor you." Okune pressed her lips together, then said, "She is leaving the Temple service permanently, I believe."

"So, she is available to marry."

"Yes."

"Good."

Kit looked at the beautiful room again, trying to imagine what life would be like to never see it again. It was her home. She could not imagine living anywhere else. That was going to be a very important factor in her choice of what to do, she realized.

Could she live on a boat, traveling from port to port with Tros? Could she leave Keftiu to go to Athens with the crazy poet she hadn't even met yet?

She knew her heart yearned to be here, at Suramarti. That could only happen if she married Jura, and soon.

SCENE 10 — TROS EXPLORES THERA

ПᵇꞀ

The men rowed and bailed in silence at a somber pace. The sun had not cleared the hills of Thera when the black-sand beach of Pirate's Cove appeared ahead. As with Akrotiri, ash covered everything. Since there were no buildings, Tros had difficulty estimating how much ash had accumulated until he spied a patch of rockroses. The hardy plants grew through the ash and several pink and purple blooms bravely searched for sunlight despite the dark sky.

Once the ship scraped the sand hidden below the ash-coated water, Tros sent archers to wade ashore with long landing ropes. As they pulled the ships into shallower water, the scratching sounds became louder and more men jumped into the surf to assist. Finally, they rolled the small boat onto the beach, its cargo all tumbled together. They wedged the larger ship, still upright, into the sand, just enough to allow for repairs.

Tros gave orders. "All rowers, day and night crews, now is the time to repair the damage from those rocks in the strait."

Fortunately, they knew their roles, because Tros did not plan on staying to supervise. He and the archers would find the graves and retrieve the gold. The two rowing lieutenants organized the repairs.

"Unload. Everyone helps with unloading, except for the carpenters. Carpenters up the hill. Harvest lumber to repair the ship."

The carpenters grabbed their bronze axes and ran up the stone steps to the fields high above the beach.

Once the rowers unloaded, they would begin the repairs.

Sakusna and the scribes scrambled ashore, each holding a rhyton or cup of oil. She looked at the steep ascent up from the beach. The ancient steps went back and forth—left and right—dug into the steep incline. The rock steps were smooth from wear and covered with a slippery mixture of sea spray, fog, and ash. She turned to Tros, "We can climb that, but you need to bring the oil up for us." The scribes searched the beach for driftwood to use for walking sticks.

Tros walked to one scribe and grabbed his jar of oil. He pushed it into the ash and sand, burying it up to its rim. "Just leave this here. You can retrieve it when we're done."

Sakusna gave Tros a stern look, picked up the jar, and handed it to one of the archers. The archer held the jar away from his body like it would poison him. He looked to Tros seeming to ask, *what should I do with this?*

Tros balled his fists and walked toward Sakusna. She stood firm. "This is a big island, and no one knows how much longer Potidas will wait before He destroys it. Do you want help finding the graves?" She pointed to the terror across the lagoon. "Or do you want to be burned to dust when Thera is destroyed?" She picked up a handful of ash and scattered it in the air.

Tros could not deny her reasoning. He kicked the ash on the beach raising a big black cloud. He turned to the archers. "Each of you take a jar or rhyton of oil up the cliff. We do not have time to waste."

Out of admiration or respect, or a tinge of fear, he offered her his hand to assist her up the stairs. She shook him off and led the ascent two stairs at a time. *Never underestimate Suramarti*, he reminded himself. He wondered if any woman could compare to Sakusna. At that moment, she seemed smarter and stronger than even his mother. Kitane was childish in comparison.

Before anyone followed her up the path, the carpenters returned.

A rowing lieutenant ran over to meet them. "Why have you returned so soon, and without any planks?"

The carpenters all spoke at once. "No trees."

"Bushes. Ash."

"Lots of ash, but no trees."

One of the scribes stepped forward. "For many full moons, we built ships to escape Thera. We harvested every tree we could find."

Another scribe added, "You saw the poor ship we stitched together with the remaining scraps. That was the last lumber on Thera."

Tros remembered those cypress planks lost when the small boat burned in the lagoon. That was all the lumber in his cargo. For a moment, he wondered about a bronze patch. They had plenty of bronze-silver and bronze-gold, but no metal workers, and no tools, and no forge. He tried to imagine a bronze ship, but bronze was too heavy to float.

One of the carpenters asked, "We bailed enough to get here. Can we make it to Amnisos?"

Sakusna suggested, "We can abandon some of the Suramarti cargo if that would help. Those date palms I received in Kmt can go."

Tros just wished they would all be quiet, so he could think. "No, no, no. Amnisos is too far and the seas have been too violent to embark on damaged ships."

He had resin and wool, but he'd never get across the Middle Sea to Amnisos without lumber. He considered Sakusna's date palms, but the palm wood was too porous. She was right. They should be dumped. They might even grow on Thera if the cursed island survived.

Everyone looked to him. He turned to the carpenters. "Take apart the small boat and use those boards to repair the big ship. Better one strong ship than two damaged ones."

With that decided, everyone went to work.

At the top, Tros looked across the field of sage growing through the layer of fine ash. He saw a few tree stumps, but no apparent paths or buildings.

"You and your precious oil are here. Where are the graves?"

Sakusna looked around. "I usually come from Akrotiri."

She talked with the scribes. "They have never come up this way. We are lost."

Tros demanded action. If no one knew which way to go, he'd decide. "Follow me." He picked a direction and walked with determination. Sakusna and the scribes followed.

Tros had no idea what he was looking for, but was certain they wouldn't find anything if they stayed in one place. The ash covered everyone's ankles. As they walked they stirred up a black fog. Soon everyone was choking and coughing.

Sakusna raised her hand in an open palm salute, "Everyone stop!" Tros watched as she tore the hem from her long robe. He thought it was slowing her down as it dragged through the ash. But then she tore the long strip into squares.

She approached Tros. She moved very close to him. They were face-to-face. Any closer, he could have kissed her. He realized she was just as tall as he was. He pursed his lips and scrunched his eyes, not to kiss, but to signal, "What are you doing?"

She soaked one square in her jar of olive oil and handed the dripping cloth to him. "Here, hold this over your mouth and nose. It will help you breathe."

He did as she instructed and soon was breathing easier.

She gave oil-drenched squares to all the archers and scribes. She still hadn't fulfilled her bargain to help find the graves, but she was being helpful. He turned to the group. "Let me know if we are moving too fast. Archers, please help the scribes if the oil jars are too heavy." He laughed. "These scribes usually spend their day sitting at tablets. They are not prepared for this."

The group marched single file, carving a straight line through the desolate landscape. Every now and then a tree stump or a patch of rockroses interrupted the monotony of sage. Tros knew the sage had a pleasant odor, but he'd smelled nothing today with the air choked by the wrath of Potidas and his face covered with an oil-soaked rag.

They had walked so far that the cliff disappeared into the black fog they'd stirred up. Then one of the scribes started crying. "Those are my wife's grandmother's rockroses. See the eyes at the center. She is looking at us."

Just as he'd said, the rockroses had a black spot on each petal.

Tros was dubious. "Those flowers are everywhere."

The man wailed, "Please don't disturb her grave. I also buried my wife here. Please don't do it."

Tros repeated, "Those flowers are everywhere. How are you so sure?"

The man pointed to an arrangement of small bumps in the ash. "See those statues? I made those effigies. That is my family, my children, my cousins, their children."

Tros looked again. Now he could recognize a grave. What previously just looked like ash-covered rocks, marked a grave.

Tros turned to Sakusna. "Please take him away. He doesn't need to watch this."

She put her arm around his shoulder and led him away.

"Archers, over here. Find the graves."

The archers scrambled. They were on their hands and knees scattering dust, searching for graves marked with ceramic figurines.

"Found one!"

"Found another!"

"Over here."

The archers threw the grave decorations all over and began to dig. Tros watched as they found additional graves. Through the dust, he could see pottery, cups that once held wine, and plates that had the remains of a final meal of bread and meat.

Sakusna collected the scribes in a circle. He could hear her. "This is only pottery and ceramics. Grave robbers always find the graves. When they stop, we will anoint the grave with oil and chant the sacraments. We will bring peace back to the burial."

A few of the scribes were in tears, especially the men. She consoled them, "Be strong. The Goddess is with us."

Meanwhile, the archers were celebrating.

"Gold!"

"I have a ring."

"Look at this mask."

"This must have been a rich lady. Gold pendants and bracelets."

When they had collected the gold, Tros announced. "We know how to find the graves now. We can find more." He pointed to two archers. "Take this gold back to the ship and return as fast as you can."

He walked in another direction. "The rest of you come with me."

"Not so fast. You must help us rebury the remains and rededicate the graves."

Tros looked at Sakusna wondering what made her imagine he'd stay here after they had the gold. "That is *your* job, you and the scribes. These graves are not far apart. Catch up with us when you're done."

As they moved around the plateau finding the more graves, he could hear the Sakusna chanting as the scribes filled the graves with ash and dirt and sprinkled olive oil.

They searched and harvested gold. Sakusna and the scribes never caught up with them. They tore open the graves faster than Sakusna could put them back together. The area of open holes and scattered pottery grew and grew. There was a steady stream of archers delivering gold back to the ship.

After two days of this, Potidas interrupted with an explosion in the center of the lagoon. Tros wondered whether the desecration of the burials angered the God, or he was simply ready to destroy Thera. Either way, Tros knew it was time to go.

He went over to Sakusna. Her white linen robe was black. Everyone had worked hard for the previous two days. He saluted her, "Blessing of Jasasara to you. The ground has been rumbling. We are out of time. We must leave."

"No! We are not done." She paused for a moment. "Help us repair the graves and we'll finish sooner."

"We are out of time," he repeated.

Sakusna pulled out her knife. "We have done our part, you can't leave us here."

Tros never understood his next action. He put his arms around her and this time he did kiss her. "Sakusna, if we survive, will you marry me? Please?"

She did not break away from his hug, or draw her knife, as he feared. "I don't know. Maybe. Ask me again if we survive."

He kissed her again.

Tros turned around. He and the archers prepared to carry the last of the gold down to the ship, but first he turned to Sakusna. "The ship is repaired and in deeper water. We must leave."

She did not move. "We will finish our work. Tell my family what happened and how we served the Goddess to the end."

Ominously, the conflagration on Kaimeni Island had stopped. Tros found the silence terrifying. He looked at her shoulders, relaxed, and at her eyes, firm and unblinking. He didn't want to leave her. Still, he couldn't imagine what else to do.

Sakusna looked away. Tros followed her eyes to the scribes. They weren't young, but they weren't old either. He could imagine her appraising her team, like he considered his crew before a battle.

"We can do it." She explained her plan. "Send your carpenters up here to build us a bonfire of sage. A big fire to light the night."

She turned to the scribes. "We will toil all night to fill and re-dedicate the remaining graves."

Everyone watched her. Tros wondered what she could be thinking. He couldn't stay the night to wait for her. He had to leave Pirate's Cove tonight to be at the strait for the first light of day. He wouldn't risk another nighttime passage through the strait, but he also would not risk waiting any longer than sunrise. This silent calm would not last long.

She continued, "When the sun returns, we can run to the coast south of Akrotiri. We'll be there before the sun is halfway to the top of the sky."

Tros couldn't believe it. She had a good plan, one he hadn't thought of. "Agreed. We will be through the strait and meet you on the Middle Sea. I will wait for you."

Tros called down to the carpenters to build the bonfire and to the rowers to prepare to leave.

Scene 11 — Kitane at Suramarti

ⴲⵏⵉ

The floors and benches and chairs in the dining area were spotless, but Kitane looked them over again. She rearranged the seating mats for no good reason, adding a couple more cushions for those that preferred to sit on the floor. She likewise inspected the low serving table, ensuring their best rhytons were placed ready, including the lovely dolphin one that Jura had gifted to Okune.

She made certain that everything was clean, with no noticeable chips. The cone-shaped drinking cups were spread in a row in their holder rings, ready for wine. A small vase of flowers brightened both ends of the table.

She ran the menu over in her mind, ensuring there were enough serving dishes ready.

If everyone came, there would be fifteen, including herself. She counted seating for twelve. She asked the head housekeeper, an atomai who had been with the family for years, to dust off and bring out two or three nice chairs and add another mat. Kit wanted to be sure everyone had comfortable choices and that people could move around to change discussion groups as they ate. The goal was to have enough open space to allow private conversations, yet also enough seating if everyone wanted to be together on the floor, on benches, on chairs.

She looked around the room again, remembering the story Diwoki had once told about a fancy dinner at Tanis, a port in Kmt. Apparently, everyone had been seated at a single, giant table.

"I was just stuck there, between two people I didn't know and didn't much care for, for the entire meal," he'd said. She remembered her mother laughed as though that was the strangest thing the Kmt did, out of all the strange things they'd heard about. Kit sighed. Diwoki had come away from that dinner with an invitation to meet Halima, whom he had wooed and wed and brought home to Suramarti. Okune had been delighted—not only with the trading possibilities but also with Halima herself. And now there were grandchildren.

Kit rubbed her forehead.

Every time her mind neared thoughts of her mother, it darted away again, like a rabbit shying from a fox. She could not think about her mother dying, yet she must.

She returned to the room she shared with Biaja when her sister was home, and dressed for the dinner. Her best robe had been woven of threads dyed sunshine gold, with rusty papyrus stalks embroidered in a band above the hem. She put on her gold dragonfly necklace and earrings, then pulled her hair back into a loose knot at the base of her neck, rather like a married woman's knot, tying it with a braided strip of fine golden-dyed threads.

She checked the polished bronze mirror and decided not to redo her kohl-outlined eyes. It did not look good when applied too heavily, in her opinion. Of course, Biaja thought the opposite, layering on cosmetics until she resembled the black-eyed sheep they raised in western Keftiu.

She walked outdoors and down the road to the Suramarti entrance gate. The gate—too grand in Kit's opinion—had been her great-grandmother's addition to the estate. She'd had thin marble slabs imported from the Archipelago to face the columns and lintel. She had had grapevines carved into the columns and a bronze strand of grapevine with bronzy leaves made to drape from the top of the lintel. Her daughter, Kit's own grandmother, had added stone benches to either side of the gate.

Okune's contribution to the estate was, of course, the new wing housing her sister's family from Thera. What would Kitane contribute? She sat on the left-hand bench, looking down the road, waiting for her guests to appear. She thought she might add a stable and fenced corral for her bull and others to follow. There was not always a bull jumper at Suramarti, but even so, they carefully bred and raised fine bulls, work oxen, and milk cows. It was time to provide better housing for their animals. Of course, she would not have the choice of what to add if she didn't accept a husband in time.

She saw distant motion on the road and jumped to her feet. A small group of figures approached. It was Biaja, with Jura and his parents and sister Eluwari. And a stranger. But no Ukan. Kit frowned. She had been counting on Ukan to lighten the mood with his jokes and silliness. She could hope he was joining them late, rather than not at all.

She heard rapid footsteps behind her, and turned to find Isari trotting up to join her. What was her cousin doing here? It was a dinner in Kitane's honor: Isari had no place in greeting guests.

"I am sorry, Kit. My mother insisted I join you, no matter how improper."

Kit blinked, feeling as if her world was spinning too fast. What was Asije trying to do? She and her family were guests here themselves, weren't they? Yet Asije had thrust Isari into this position. Whether her cousin was a proper match for Jura or not, the pleasant chore of greeting guests was not part of that, and was none of their business.

Deciding her own mother must have invited Asije to act as co-hostess, Kit brushed a strand of hair back from her cousin's face, gave her a quick hug, then turned to greet her guests. To make a fuss now was even worse manners than the breach of sending Isari in the first place.

Kitane stepped forward as their guests approached, palms facing them, a genuinely happy smile on her face.

"Blessings of the Goddess upon you, my friends and my family. Welcome to Suramarti."

Beside her, Isari also stood in the welcoming pose, palms out and a small smile on her lips. But at least her cousin didn't say anything.

Their guests might still feel that it was Kitane's party, alone.

Everyone had been served wine and had a chance to taste the dried fruits and nuts, the olives and herbed cheese, when Okune signaled the servers to bring in the meal. Roast lamb fragrant with rosemary, tender carrots roasted in honey—Tylissos honey, in honor of their guests—cumin and coriander flavored revithia, almond-crusted mashed quince, roast partridge stuffed with raisins and barley, and plain and spicy herbed pita. Besides wine and minted water, they offered chilled mint tea for those who wished not to over-indulge in wine.

"The atomai are frightened," Eluwari was saying.

"Some foolishness about black clouds and evil prophecies," Jura grumbled.

"Yes, we have had to reassure our workers as well," Kit said. "Thera is casting a pall over Keftiu."

Halima said, "This cloud is a bad omen."

"That is harsh, to blame our home for the Goddesses' doings," Asije said, sounding offended.

Kit saw Halima's eyes widen. She stepped in. "It was not my intention to cast blame at all," she said, hoping Halima realized that Asije's crisp rebuke had been leveled at Kit, not her foreign sister-in-law. "I was just *observing* what it is that the atomai are afraid of."

Looking irritated, Asije walked away. What was wrong with the woman? She had been close to outright rudeness. Kit smiled at Halima, trying to take away the sting of her aunt's words.

"I did not mean—perhaps I should simply hold my tongue," Diwoki's wife murmured.

"You have every right to speak. Asije chose the worst interpretation of what I said."

"Nevertheless... "

"You said nothing wrong, my sister," Kit said.

Halima smiled faintly and went to sit by Okune.

The space she left seemed to encourage the Athenian to join them. Paian was the poet who had sent her the interesting poems. "I hoped to honor you," he said, "with another poem or two tonight."

Biaja laughed and joined them, saying, "Pi doesn't understand that he should not woo you directly." Bee tossed her head, making her two tiny tails of hair bounce. "We keep telling him to talk to Mother, but he does not listen." She smiled at her sister, then at the Athenian.

It was clear to Kit that Bee had had a hand in bringing these two of her suitors together tonight, face to face at Kitane's dinner. It may not have been her doing, but she had not stopped the Athenian from joining them. Jura was grumpy about the presence of a competitor. And of course, also angry that the foreigner did not follow tradition in trying to woo a bride.

"Lovely as the willowy tree above the silvered pond
Is Kitane the bull jumper of great renown."

Paian cleared his throat. "It rhymes in my language, of course."

Maybe it did. Certainly, Kitane did not know, nor to be honest, much care.

"Thank you for your thoughtfulness in honoring me this way," she said. There was no reason to be rude to the man. She had a tough time imagining how poetry was going to improve life at Suramarti. Wasn't being a suitor an opportunity to show what he could contribute? "Perhaps I can hang the poem tablets in a pattern," she said. "A collection of thoughts on my wall, in the shape of a lily. Or perhaps a bull."

Paian smiled, looking pleased at her response.

"More useful to create a Goddess blessing," Jura said, from just behind Kit.

She turned to smile at him. "Ah, yes! It could help with the atomai fears," she agreed.

Jura's smile was faint, but it was there.

"Paian can create many more things than poems," Bee said, sounding mischievous. "Drawings, building plans, maps."

"Maps?" Kit asked. Diwoki had once shown her a Middle Sea map drawn by the navigator on his ship. Learning of her interest, Sakusna had promised to get a copy made of Tros' map for her. It was an even better map than his own, Diwoki had claimed. Where Tros had gotten the thing, no one knew, but many speculated.

"I have been preparing one of Keftiu for the priestesses at Knossos," Paian said.

"Pi is their favorite scribe!" Biaja gushed. She turned to face the Athenian. "You don't mind if I call you Pi, do you? It doesn't mean anything bad, does it?"

Paian laughed. "It would surprise my mother, but no, it doesn't mean anything bad, if that is what you would like to say. I notice many Keftiu shorten their names, as Kitane is called Kit, and you are called Bee."

Biaja nodded and walked along with Paian as he returned to the table for more roast lamb.

Kit turned back to Eluwari and Jura who remained standing beside her.

"Have you decided, Kitane? Are you to become my sister by marriage?" Elu asked.

The blunt question took Kit aback. She had no response, but finally just smiled at Eluwari, then turned to Jura. "Did your atomai return to Tylissos, Jura?" She realized that might sound critical, when she had only meant to change the subject. "I fear some of ours are so frightened they may flee also."

"They have not returned," Jura said, his face stiff, his eyes showing his frustration.

"I am sorry to hear that."

"We have prayed and done proper honor to Potidas and to the Goddess. It is difficult to understand why that does not reassure the atomai."

"I think the earthquakes and smoke cloud are working against you, against all of us," Kit said. She saw Eluwari nod in agreement.

Beyond Jura's shoulder, she saw Radamitu and Okune sitting with Jura's parents and Halima. Her father glanced up and smiled at her, then gave her a heavy wink, trying to show his support.

"I am hoping the bull-jumping ceremony will appease the goddess and Potidas," she murmured.

"Blessings upon you, Kitane, and upon Enosidas, upon whom so much depends," Eluwari said.

"Depends upon what?" Paian said, rejoining them. Kit moved away to the serving table, letting her suitors argue it out. She wanted a taste of the partridge before it disappeared. She took the last piece, and some quince, then walked to a mat that had no one seated on it. She sat down and ate a few bites, then Bee and Elu joined her, and a moment later, Isari.

"That partridge was lovely," Isari said, and everyone nodded agreement. Then Kit's little brother Zetis came over. Zetis squatted, rather than sitting on the floor. He took no notice of either sister's glare to sit properly. When Jura joined them, he bumped Zetis just enough that the boy lost his balance and plopped to the floor. Everyone laughed, and he sniffed, jumped up and stalked off to eat by himself as Jura sat in his space.

"Pardon my brother's manners," Kit said.

"Mother's sending him off to the Temple. All Suramarti hopes they will manage to set some manners upon him." Bee grinned. "Like one of the spells the Kmt believe in." She made floaty rainfall-like motions with the long fingers of her hands.

"Spells are nonsense," Paian announced.

Everyone looked at him and smiled tolerantly. He was a foreigner. Some grace needed to be allowed him.

"Everyone should know that," the Athenian went on. "If your people were all educated, as we are in Athens, you would not be so superstitious."

"Well that is offensive to say," Jura said. "Telestai do not believe such silly stories. It is just the atomai who do."

"Just so," Paian argued. "If the atomai were educated, as you are," he waved a hand around in a circle, meaning everyone nearby him, "they would not be cowering in the forest because of a black cloud."

"Perhaps they are smart to be out in the forest," Eluwari said. "They have seen plenty of buildings fall down, but trees rarely fall."

"That may be," Paian said sounding very sure of himself, "but think how much safer we all would be if we had facts instead of rumors to go by."

"Shall we have all scholars then, and no workers?" Biaja said loudly.

"There is nothing wrong with an educated atomai," Pi said.

"While they are reading and writing they are not weaving and spinning," Kitane put in.

"That's right," Jura said. "They're not making pots or planting grain. Do you plan to eat tablets with writing on them, rather than bread?"

"With tablets about how to plant grain and winnow it and harvest it and grind it—everyone could learn to make bread."

"We do that by letting our head farmers teach their children," Jura said. "You do not need tablets for that. Tradition exists for a reason."

"That is true. But why do you say that, Jura? Why do you always say the old ways are best?" Kit looked at him, genuinely interested in knowing if Jura was so stuck in his ways he would not ever consider a new idea.

"Now I have said something wrong again."

"No more than Paian has," Biaja laughed.

Suddenly Kitane realized their little group was surrounded by adults: Okune, Radamitu, Asije, and Jura's parents.

She stood up and smiled at each of them in turn.

"Is there a decision to be heard, Kitane?" Okune met her eyes, gave her a tiny smile.

"I would prefer to delay my decision until after the bull jumping," Kit said, wishing she had drunk another cup of wine before she had to do this.

"However, if I must announce a name, I will name Tros." There were murmurs and whispers at this. "Only Tros has done nothing improper. Only he has not pressed me for a decision or caused my heart to ache because I have not yet announced my choice."

"Tros has done nothing wrong, because Tros is not here!" Jura's voice was harsh.

"We can all see that Tros is not here, Jura."

"There is no pleasing you!" Jura said.

"Perhaps you are right," Kit responded, feeling sad. "But perhaps that is why Tros is so appealing, you see: *he does not judge everything I say and do.*"

Jura's mouth opened, but nothing came out. Paian's face was pale, and his lips were pressed tight together.

Isari and Eluwari and the parents all stood in silence, disapproval plain on their faces.

"Oh, look!" Zetis yelled, clapping his hands. "Dessert!"

ACT III — BULL-JUMPING CEREMONY

SCENE 1 — BIAJA AT THE CENTRAL COURT, KNOSSOS
太竹日

Family filled the viewing station toward the south end of the Central Court set aside for Suramarti: Biaja, her parents, her brother, and her aunt and uncle. Her father and mother seemed so proud, standing in the sunlight of the Suramarti viewing station, talking with everyone.

This time of day, the Suramarti area was in full sun, but within an hour or so, they would have shade from the upper floors of the West side of the temple. The line of shadow already crept across the courtyard toward them. Bee glanced at the smaller nearby Tylissos viewing area, where Isari had joined Jura to celebrate the day.

But her own pleasure was much diminished by her little brother. Zetis had invited five of his friends into the station—*five!*—so that Bee had to squeeze up against the band of grubby, giggling boys in order to fit her own guests in. Nopine held her hand as they squeezed past the others. Paian smiled at her over the bobbing heads of Bee's brother, his little cousin and the other four boys. Fortunately, her mother was in no mood to put up with foolishness.

"Boys, you may sit in front by the rail, if you are still." She gave them a stern look. "If you wish to dance around, please take it to one of the outside or empty stations."

Biaja was relieved when Zetis and his friends came to some silent agreement and galloped off, laughing and rowdy, as usual.

"Thank the Goddess," she said, and unfolded her stool and sat down. Paian did likewise, beside her now. Nopine, having no stool, stood beside them, shading her eyes against the sun.

Bee felt a thread of guilt for whatever role she had played in advancing her cousin's case over her own sister's, but she had to admit Jura seemed quite delighted with Isari, so far. Though perhaps Kitane's sharp tongue had done the job of turning him away rather than anything Bee had done. No one seemed convinced Kit actually planned to marry Tros the Trader—*trader, hah!*—but she had definitely discouraged Jura.

Meanwhile, it seemed Paian the Hellene had turned his poetic attention to Biaja. He had been delighted when she invited him to watch the bull jumping with her. Certainly, Kit had given the man no encouragement—though she hadn't turned him down flat, either. Bee had a chance with the fascinating stranger. This was her opportunity to shine.

She smiled at the man, noticing that however foreign he looked otherwise, his eyes were dark warm brown. He smiled back, his unusually even white teeth making his smile seem to glow. But his nose! Every time she looked at him, she was reminded of an owl.

"Biaja, I am wondering how the winner is decided?" Paian asked. "I know Kitane has won several years in a row, but how is she chosen?"

"The people watching help the Priestesses decide. They cheer loudly and applaud the best jumps. But it isn't just about the crowd's favorite. The Priestesses also look at how powerful and imperial the bull looks, how well he behaves, and how graceful the jumper is."

"I see," Paian said. "Then I will cheer loudly for Kitane and Enosidas."

Biaja smiled at him, but flinched internally. Was he still focused on Kit, then?

Bee patted her sister's dragonfly necklace where it gleamed against the smooth skin of her throat. Two small dragonflies flanked the big one—a hand's width in size—which all depended from a fine golden chain. It was Kitane's, and Bee had snuck it from her sister's carved ivory jewelry box without asking this morning when they'd left Suramarti for the journey down to Knossos.

She wore it to honor Kit and as a good luck charm, even though her sister surely did not need luck in the bull-jumping contest. But to be honest, she also wore it because it went well with the deep blue and pale gold of her new linen robe. Her own necklace, a ruby, rose and pale pink lotus blossom, was another of her father's fabulous creations, but it did not go so well with her robe. She felt she glowed like a Pharaoh's daughter, in blue and cream and pale wheaten gold, with lapis and gold filigree glinting at her neck and ears. If only her hair was grown out full and lush as it used to be. She scowled and bit her lip, thinking about her shaved head.

She still needed to tell her mother she was leaving temple training. In her own mind, she had already left. She was not certain what her reluctance to tell Okune meant; she only knew that she would not spend another moment hiding in fright from the Aurochs. It was not fitting that a daughter of a telestai family should be terrorized by an old atomai woman no matter how many years she had faithfully served the Temple.

Beside her, Nopine stirred and pointed as a mighty black bull and its rider, a slender young man, entered the court. The crowd roared.

The Aurochs' voice rose, introducing him. Bee felt it was terribly bad luck that the klawiphoros should introduce anyone, much less a new rider like Waro. But the young man and his fine bull proudly trotted into the court, followed by nearly every eye in the crowd. Bee could see Zetis and his friends laughing and pointing at something in the dirt by their feet at the end of the courtyard. Of course, it would be Zetis not paying attention. It was hard to believe that her brother and the serious young bull jumper named Waro were the same age.

Biaja's excitement rose as Waro began his first leap. The bull was steady and had a nice smooth trot. Bee had a tendency to watch the animals more than the jumpers—she had learned a lot about bulls from Kitane and from hearing about the breeding of their own animals. This was an outstanding beast, and it looked as if Waro had trained it well. The audience went silent as the boy turned and ran head-on toward the bull. He leaped, placing his small hands on the animal's horns in the traditional way. The flip, the push off the withers into another flip, and the landing, still running, perfectly done. The audience shouted and applauded in approval.

Usually the jumper would do a full circle trotting beside his animal for a round before beginning the second jump, but Waro did something different. Instead of turning and running alongside his animal before reversing direction, he and the bull continued on their separate trajectories, around a semi-circle away from each other, then facing each other again as they each completed the arc.

Even before the young man started his leap, Biaja could see something was off. She could not identify the flaw exactly; perhaps Waro's pace was too slow? But she heard the audience gasp at the same time she took a breath and held it.

He went up and over, but did not complete a full rotation on his flip onto the animal's back. He landed short, tried to save it by tucking and rolling off the bull's rump, but did not have enough momentum. He landed awkwardly and instead of running forward to meet the bull again, he stumbled and came to a limping halt. His bull continued its turn and ran toward him, picking up speed as though expecting a normal jump.

Whispers murmured through the crowd. *Oh no! Is he charging?* The audience was on its feet, yelling warnings and prayers as the huge animal ran toward the boy. *Jasasara save him!*

Bee was still holding her breath when the bull came to an abrupt, dusty stop beside its rider. The huge animal had impressive speed, it had raced fast toward the injured boy—and then it just stopped. The bull lowered its head, wide horns threatening further injury. But the bull sniffed the injured ankle, and Biaja could see its dark tongue lick Waro's wounded leg. The audience applauded in wild approval. Biaja sat back down just as Zetis and his five friends ran back into the viewing station.

"Did you see that?"

"Wow!"

"I'm telling my parents I want a bull like that!" the smallest of the boys said.

The boys milled around, gesturing and managing to step on everyone's feet. They bumped into the adults with knees and elbows until Okune yelled, "Out!" and they left again.

The audience applauded the efforts of Waro and his bull, then another priestess introduced the next jumper. It was not Kitane, of course, she would go last, as the reigning champion. Bee stirred and felt her bare wrist against the skirt of her robe.

Bare? Heart leaping to her throat, she realized her seal stone on its bracelet of blue linen ribbon was missing. She jumped up and looked on the ground for it. She was still standing there, staring into the dirt when Jura and Isari walked over from the Tylissos station.

"Blessings upon you, Biaja. Is something wrong?"

"My seal stone is missing!" She clapped her hand to her chest and realized that was not all that was gone. The necklace— Kitane's golden dragonfly necklace—was not there! Bee felt dizzy, as if she would faint. Which was ridiculous—Suramarti women did not flutter and faint. Nevertheless, she took a firm grip on Paian's arm and met Jura's worried gaze. "The dragonfly necklace is also gone," she said in a small, scared voice. She sounded like a frightened little girl, not like a strong heir to the wealth and security of Suramarti. Beside her, Nopine gasped.

Jura scowled, said, "Kitane's dragonfly necklace?"

"Yes. I wore it...for—for luck," she said. "And now it is gone!"

"How could it be missing?" Paian said. "We have been only here, not out in the crowd!"

She met Pi's gaze and had the same realization he did. "Zetis and his brats!" she said.

She saw Jura's face darken even further.

"Can you find them, Jura?"

"I will find them," he said, abandoning Isari as he ran out of the station.

Paian was likewise scowling. "Would he do such a thing to his own sister?" he wondered.

"I don't know. Maybe. Maybe his stupid friends thought it a fine joke."

"Or maybe a fine treasure," Paian said. "I think a buyer of stolen goods might be quick to hide these things or disguise them. Melt them down."

"Dear Goddess, not my father's magnificent work! Would it not be worth ever so much more, whole?"

Paian shrugged. "We Hellenes do not have such fine jewelry," he murmured.

"Paian, do you know any people who would do such a thing? Buy a stolen piece?"

Paian bit his lip, eyes distant. "Maybe," he said.

"Oh, please, can you look?" Bee whispered, hoping her mother and aunt did not become aware something was wrong. Bee turned away, so her mother would not see her face—or her bare throat. "Can you go ask them? I would not know where to begin."

"Of course," Paian said.

"Thank you. I will stay here, in case they come back with it."

Paian nodded and left, moving down the narrow aisle between stations toward the workshop area of the temple grounds.

"Goddess, Biaja. How awful," Nopine said.

Bee felt tears spring into her eyes. She blinked them away, glanced over her shoulder at Okune and Asije. The mothers were talking to Isari about the bull jumping. So far, they seemed oblivious to the theft and Bee's panic. She calmed herself, evening out her breathing, and ordering her face to look serene.

She gestured to Paian's empty stool. "You might as well sit, Nopine," and the girl smiled and sat down. In the Temple, all were supposed to be equal; out here, the atomai girl's poverty became apparent in her rougher dress, her ignorance of the tradition of bringing a stool to sit on. She could have borrowed one from the Temple—if she had realized that everyone sat in the telestai viewing areas. Bee chided herself for not advising her friend. This seemed to be a day marking her thoughtlessness. How could she imagine she was mature enough to capture one of Kit's suitors for herself? She bit her lip, suddenly glad her head was shaved so she looked like a youngster. She was certainly behaving like one.

Though not as stupid and greedy as Zetis and his friends. How *could* they?

The crowd cheered for the current bull jumper's stunt. The red bull trotted past the Suramarti station, raising dust. The thud of its feet matched the thud of Biaja's heart.

What could she possibly say to Kitane—or her father—if the necklace was lost?

Jura's scowling expression and words: *"Kitane's dragonfly necklace?"* repeated over and over in her mind as she pretended to watch the red bull and its rider.

How could she have been so foolish?

SCENE 2 — JURA AT KNOSSOS

ｌⲁ Ｌ⊆

Jura vaulted the rail fencing the Suramarti viewing area. He pushed up a bit harder than necessary and landed with a bounce. The excitement of the bull jumping energized everyone. He considered how bull jumping was one of the few activities where men could compete with the women. Even though he would never appear before the crowd, he felt pride watching young Waro. Unfortunately, Waro's inferior performance might cause some people to renew the argument that men did not have the required grace and agility to be great bull jumpers.

On the other hand, he was willing to bet that the boy was more sensible than Suramarti's youngest daughter. Why, by the Goddess, had Bee taken Kitane's famous necklace? And now it was stolen. If he ever married into the clan, he would take the even more foolish Zetis aside and talk some sense into him.

Still invigorated with crowd's energy, he bounded up the stairs to the next level of the temple. Zetis and his friends would be easier to spot from above. Though old enough to wander independently, they were still small as children. Girls his age had grown into tall women, but the boys took a few more years. Yet more reasons why boys needed supervision.

"Excuse me," he said. "Can I get through please?"

Some of the people standing on the upper level noticed his fine robe and made room for him. He smiled and tried to be as polite as possible. As he approached the balustrade, a woman blocked his way. Jura stopped before he bumped into her.

"Who are you? I've been up since dawn to get this spot."

Telestai women wore elaborate, tailored garments. Atomai women, like the one in front of him, had plainer clothes. Her rough woolen robe smelled of sheep and goats. She stood firm, with an ornately carved staff held in front of her. Her muscular arms indicated that the stick was more of a weapon than a walking aid. He looked at her hands, dirt everywhere, under her fingernails, and in every crease. He guessed she was a shepherd.

She pushed the staff forward and moved very close to him. He could smell beer and garlic. She challenged him, "What are you doing up here anyway?"

Jura saluted her with open palms and moved to the right, not wanting a confrontation. A short way away, someone let him squeeze into a space overlooking the Central Court.

He scanned the crowd below. Sure enough, he sighted several groups of short boys, but none of them were Zetis and his friends. They must have left the Central Court. One last time he checked the Suramarti viewing station. There were Biaja, Isari, and Nopine in the cool shade, laughing and enjoying the ceremony, but the boys had not returned.

As he retreated through the crowd, the shepherd lady tapped him with her staff. "You better quit running around. Kitane of Suramarti will be jumping soon. You don't want to miss her. She is the best."

He proudly said to himself, *my Kitane*, but quickly remembered that she seemed to be more interested in that pirate Tros. He considered Isari. Even though Biaja seemed to think her cousin was nice, Jura didn't like her strange ideas from Akrotiri. If Akrotiri had stayed with the traditions, Potidas would not have felt it necessary to destroy it.

When Jura returned to the Suramarti viewing area, the three ladies were discussing the missing atomai.

Without interrupting, Jura shook his head at Biaja, letting her know he had not found her brother or his friends. Her expression was panicked for a moment, then she licked her lips and looked at the ground.

Nopine, who came from an atomai family, said, "We can stay in the wild for a long time."

Biaja, now composed, looked up and asked, "Won't they return to their home when they get hungry?"

Nopine laughed, "It's already summer. There is plenty of food. My family often spent weeks in the wild after they finished planting the crops. I can still smell the wild goat my father roasted over an open fire."

Isari seemed confused. "Do the atomai simply disappear into the wild?"

Jura joined the discussion, "Many of my atomai have vanished."

"Well nothing like that ever happens on Thera. Our island is too small. There is no wild."

No wild? Jura thought. *The wild taught the Keftiu the majesty of Jasasara's creation. That might explain why the people on Thera strayed and Potidas is destroying them.* He asked Nopine, "Where do they go?"

"My family had a camping area they visited every year, far from the villages and paths, but furnished with abundant water and food."

Nopine closed her eyes, as if in a dream, "I remember getting up early and gathering berries moist with the morning dew."

Isari patted Nopine's shoulder. "Now see, you've made me hungry! Let's go find something to eat."

Nopine laughed, and they headed out of the courtyard toward the various food stalls set up for ceremony days.

When they were out of sight, Biaja took Jura's hand and led him to a quiet corner away from her parents. "Thank you for looking, Jura. The boys will turn up eventually, don't you think? "

"I would assume so," he said. He hesitated, then blurted, "This whole problem would not exist if you had not taken your sister's necklace."

"I know. I am sure she would have been happy to give me permission if I had thought to ask. I was thoughtless this morning."

He forbore saying he thought she was always thoughtless; she appeared to be trying to apologize and be reasonable.

She met his gaze. "What do you think of Isari? My cousin's pretty, isn't she?"

As he thought about a way to tell Biaja that he wasn't interested in her cousin, or anyone from the cursed island of Thera, the Central Court went dark. A thick black cloud moved over from the north. The shocked crowd went quiet.

Jura thought, *I can forget about getting married, or finding the missing atomai. It seems Potidas intends to destroy Keftiu along with Thera.*

Beside him, he could hear Bee's breathing. She gasped and said, more to herself than aloud to him, "Don't be afraid. Kitane's jumps will so please the gods, we have nothing to fear." She had reached out and taken his hand as she spoke.

In a way, she might be right, he realized. Kitane might be the only one honoring the traditions. Would that be enough? He could pray so. Jura wished that Kit was holding his hand instead of Biaja.

From the Central Court, a priestess announced the next bull jumper. A girl from Malia on the northern coast, east of Knossos, ran into the courtyard with a dizzying series of handsprings, right on the ground without any assist from her bull. The black-and-white bull stood in the center of the courtyard, turning his head to follow her.

The crowd completely ignored the clouds when the bull pawed the ground and ran toward the girl who was upside-down standing on her hands. In a move never seen before, the bull charged and just as he reached her, using only her arms, she popped into the air, flipped over and landed straddling his neck. He had lowered his head just as he reached her; she landed lightly, legs pulled up tight to either side of his muscular neck. She then grabbed his horns and they raced in a large circle while the crowd cheered. Jura almost believed that the sun found its way through the black cloud.

Biaja pulled on his robe and pointed to the upper level. There were Zetis and his friends eating expensive sweets. Even from this distance, Jura could see dates from Kmt and a fancy pastry made of nuts and honey layered between layers of thin pita.

The elders of Suramarti also noticed this group. Radamitu asked, "How did they pay for those sweets?" Jura could see Zetis' bare toes peeked under the railing. "Didn't he wear his best sandals today? What about the other boys?"

Jura looked at Biaja, but she didn't say anything. The boys were standing where he had just been, by the dirty shepherd. No one seemed to be moving to do anything about it.

"Shall I go and bring them here?" he asked.

Okune shook her head. "No need to chase after them. Zetis will return home soon enough. I will deal with him appropriately."

No one thought to interrogate Okune on her plans, and the boys had already disappeared into the crowd, so Jura shrugged and gave up.

He hoped for Kitane's sake that Zetis had only traded his sandals for the treats and the boy hadn't sunk so low as to steal from his own family merely to indulge himself.

Nopine and Isari returned with cups of warm pistachio nuts that had been soaked in sea-water, fried in olive oil, and dusted with spices. The girls passed the cups out, so everyone had some. Jura stuffed a handful of mint and sesame flavored nuts in his mouth and imagined how the clouds would clear after Kitane's performance. If anyone's performance could please the Goddess, hers could. Maybe that would be enough to convince Potidas as well.

Scene 3 — Tros Leaving Thera

Tros opened the captain's tent to make room for the extra people on his remaining ship. The crew discarded the straw intended to go between the pithoi. The extra space held the cargo from the scavenged boat. They exchanged bronze-gold, abandoned on the black sand, for real gold, stolen from the graves. A double crew pulled on the oars, crowded close together, but grateful for a place to sit.

Tros inspected the ship repairs. Unfortunately, he had no trouble seeing the repairs. The planks scavenged from the damaged boat were miniature compared to the originals. He frowned at the ugly patches. The ship's carpenters had done their best, but the result was small pieces, lashed together with leather straps, packed with wool, and smeared with resin. The repairs were unsightly, but hopefully sufficient to carry them to Amnisos where better materials would be available.

He pushed on the patches with the end of an oar and hit them with a bronze hammer. The work appeared good, but experience had taught him that he would not know until it was too late.

In the dark night, the brightest light shone atop the bluffs where Sakusna and her scribes were still awake, pouring oil on the hastily re-covered graves and chanting prayers. As he had several times that night, he considered waiting for them before departing. An explosive report from Kaimeni followed by a resounding echo against the cliffs overwhelmed his feelings for Sakusna. *She is a strong woman of Suramarti. The morning will see us reunited on the shore of the Middle Sea.*

Like a blind man, Tros felt his way around the lagoon, turning left each time the oars found the rocky cliffs. The strait announced itself with a whistle of wind rushing into the Middle Sea. The sun appeared dimly through the smoky sky. He raised his linen sail and the morning breeze eased the ship into the larger sea. Now in the open water, Tros revisited the hull patches.

Happily, they had held and were dry as a hot saj. The men sped in the direction of the safe harbor to the south.

"Easy. Slow down. Turn east. We have an appointment and passengers to collect."

The rowers decreased the tempo, but the heading was unchanged.

Behind them, Kaimeni roared. Boulders the size of sheep and goats rained from the sky. One as big as an adult bull landed close by with a huge splash that rocked the ship. The crew murmured to each other.

"We are going to die."

"Potidas is angry, very angry."

"We must leave as soon as possible."

Tros knew this was a critical time. He picked up the bronze hammer he had used to test the repairs. Walking down the right side of the ship, he hit each oar with a bang.

"Pull!"

"Be Strong!"

"Now!"

At the front of the ship, he pushed the lead rower aside and took a seat. He grabbed the front oar and shouted, "On my count!"

In double time, he counted, "One finger, two fingers, three fingers, four fingers, HAND."

The ship turned, and the crew forgot their fears. Soon they were heading toward the southern shore of Thera to rescue Sakusna.

He would have her as his wife. A choice that would please his mother and the memory of his father.

He relinquished the oar and jumped up to the bow. He curled his fingers to make a small viewing hole. Through the tiny opening, he could make out deer and goats on the crest of the hills scrambling away from the volcano. The birds had evacuated long ago leaving the sky to the black ash. Still no sign of Sakusna. She had said she would arrive later, but he hoped that she might be early.

Tros sent the boy up the mast to get a better view. The rain of boulders still rocked the sea, but the men looked to Tros and waited. He felt safe separated from Kaimeni by Thera. He searched the wall of mountains for Sakusna, eager to rescue her. He prayed to the gods, *one more kiss, just one more kiss.*

"I see them! Over there! There!" The boy pointed straight ahead. First one, then two more, then all of them appeared over the crest. *They are early.* He celebrated in his thoughts. *That woman can perform miracles. I will love her for my entire life.*

Tros didn't need to say anything, the crew aimed the ship at the Thera shore. All understood the urgency. He reached toward the land, as if he could grasp her and bring her to him. He saw Sakusna in the lead. He gasped when she tripped and rolled down the hill.

He turned to the crew. "Row! Faster! Harder!"

He looked back to shore. She had gotten up and was running again. He relaxed. *Just a bit more.* He smiled. He waved as if she was much closer and could see him.

The rocks stopped falling.

Ominously, Kaimeni went silent again.

A breeze cleared some of the ash, and a beam of sunlight lit the way for Sakusna and the scribes as they ran and tumbled down toward the beach.

Then it was as if Kaimeni had taken a deep breath and exhaled all the wild energy of fire and earth: the biggest explosion blasted through the sky. It sounded like Potidas burst through the earth from the underworld.

The men dropped their oars to cover their ears. Tros knelt on the deck, massaging his ringing ears. Through the strait, all could see Kaimeni Island racing toward them. Potidas had turned the land into hot rock and ash that raged across the lagoon.

No one moved.

Kaimeni Island had become an enormous wave of fire. No amount of water mattered. The steaming pulverized earth pushed through the strait into the Middle Sea.

Then smiles appeared throughout the ship. Thera had shielded them. They picked up their oars and rowed toward the protecting hills to rescue the people on the shore. Tros thanked the merciful gods.

The boy, holding tight to his perch at the top of the mast throughout all of this, was the first to realize their folly. "Stop, stop! No! NO!"

Hissing filled the air. First steam boiled over the crest of Thera's hills, immediately followed by dust, ash, and rocks. The plants burst into flames before the onslaught buried them.

Tros watched waves of fire roll down the hills toward Sakusna and the scribes on the beach. Helplessly, he saw them strip off their robes and dive into the water. They fought through the waves and frantically swam away from the oncoming horror.

Tros could not turn away as the terror burned and swept Sakusna under the sea. Like the onslaught through the strait, the flow continued over the water as if it was solid land.

The oars reversed, and the ship moved backward away from what remained of Thera and the wave of destruction that was still roaring toward them. Tros smelled burning flesh for the second time. The odor split his head and filled his eyes with tears. He collapsed on the deck. *Why was she so stubborn? Why didn't she come with me last night?*

The next day Tros had still not left his corner of the captain's tent. Everything reminded him of Sakusna. Her clothes. Her smell. Even the slash she'd cut using her obsidian knife with the golden handle in the shape of the Goddess.

"Captain, the scribes..."

Tros shook his head and blinked his eyes. *Scribes? Is this another bad dream?* He looked through the hole in his tent.

There were the scribes. The other ones. The ones he'd abandoned. He never expected to see them again, but there they were. Their boat, built with the final scraps of wood from Thera, still floated. *Potidas had destroyed Thera…and those few scribes…and Sakusna*. But not these.

He slowly got to his feet, staring. He should greet these Thera survivors.

Their leader spoke first, "Captain Tros. Blessings of Jasasara to you. We apologize for needing your help again. We still have no gold." The lady who spoke trembled visibly. The other passengers littered the deck, shivering and red with sunburn.

Tros could not let any more people from Thera die. "Archers, each of you find a rhyton and fill it with fresh water. Board their boat and wet their lips until they drink. Wet their robes with sea water to cool them down."

Tros' ship carried extra people and additional cargo from the lost boats. Nothing had a place, they had stacked everything wherever it fit. The archers scrambled, but could not find the rhytons.

"Forget rhytons. Use jars, or cups, or bowls. These people are dying. Do something!"

Some scribes shivered, others lay like asleep.

"This one is dead."

Tros went over to the refugee boat. The man was cold to touch. Tros listened for a breath. Silence. He ripped open the man's robe and pressed his ear over the man's heart. Silence again.

He shouted, "Save as many as you can. We will patch their ship… escort them to Amnisos…and rescue their tablets."

For the remainder of the day, Tros moved among the scribes directing their care. The men kept the feverish people cool using robes wet with sea-water. They wrapped blankets around the shivering ones. In all cases, they fed them water, dripped on their blistered lips, poured into their throats.

A few coughed and seemed to improve. Others did not respond.

A sailor whispered, "Another death."

Two more died and Tros wondered, "*Can't we save any of them?*"

Around sunset, one of the scribes stood up. Tros looked at her. "Would you like something to eat? What happened? Who are you?" He handed her some water and honey.

"I am a Hellene from the lands to the west."

"Hellene? You are not Keftiu? What were you doing on that cursed ship?"

She backed away and answered softly. "I am but a child." She held up two hands with her fingers spread. "This old." She looked at the deck. "My parents were poor and sold me to Akrotiri."

Tros shook his head.

The girl backed away and stood behind the archer who had cared for her. "They treated me well," she whispered.

He replied to himself, "The gods saved you because you're not Keftiu. They are determined to destroy them."

He turned to the sailors. "Is anyone else going to survive?"

At first no one answered. Then a few shook their heads. Then some more responded.

"Mine is already dead."

"This one too."

It was clear. Only the girl, the Hellene, survived. He moved her to his ship. He repeated a few Keftiu words that he remembered Sakusna saying and poured an entire pithos of olive oil over the bodies. He set the ship on fire and watched it float away.

"Farewell to Keftiu. Your gods have abandoned you."

He turned to his crew. "Forget them. Keftiu is no more. Their gods have abandoned them. Their Potidas, god of the earth and sea, will destroy them."

The setting sun shone across the water, sneaking under the clouds of ash. Tros pointed to the beam of light. "The Kmt sun god Ra is now supreme. We will empty the warehouses and the temples of Amnisos before Potidas covers them with fire and drowns them in the sea...just like that ship."

He paused.

"Potidas has spoken."

The men looked puzzled.

"Our new trading partner will be Kmt, honoring their victorious God. Our cargo will be even more valuable when we arrive in Tanis, the city by the great river."

The men, more interested in gold than gods, smiled and the ship picked up speed.

The one thing he didn't tell them was his plan to marry Kitane, his darling Kit. He'd steal her from her angry gods and rescue her from her dying land. He would have his Keftiu wife—perhaps the last one in the world.

SCENE 4 — PAIAN AT BULL JUMPING
𐘿𐘓𐘈

Paian headed for the outdoor theater area where traders congregated to exchange goods and offer their wares to the festival crowds. He navigated the maze of hallways through the temple with confidence. With each turn, the noise of the bull-jumping crowd diminished.

The more he learned about Keftiu women, the more he despaired he'd ever find a wife here. There was one possibility. Everywhere he went, Maza showed up. Maza made deliveries to Knossos. Maza went to Suramarti and Mount Ida. She was always happy to see him and interested in what he had to say.

He could imagine her shape as she loaded her donkeys, and her smile when he made a joke.

Stop!

The thought of bringing her home reminded him that his mother would never approve of a girl who could not read. After she had worked so hard for him to learn his letters, he would not let her down by returning with someone who didn't know theirs.

He cheered himself recalling that all Suramarti women could both read and write, but who from Suramarti might be interested in him? The Keftiu laughed at poets and writers. He might have a seal stone, but he wasn't a telestai.

Shouts from a group of youngsters interrupted his reverie. *Could that be Zetis' little gang?* he wondered. *But, where were they?* The beautiful frescoes decorating the walls of Knossos created a problem. Hard walls meant echoes. He found it impossible to tell if the laughter came from the hallway with papyrus plants and nesting birds, or another passage with dolphins and fish.

Kitane loved the dolphins, so he searched down that corridor. He followed the sounds, entering one room after another. These were personal rooms with wooden beds, colorfully woven blankets, and chests for the storage of fine garments. Everyone was attending the bull jumping, so this might have been a good place for mischievous boys, but the laughing sounds soon abated.

After a few wrong turns, he found the corridor with the young-women-bathing fresco, which led to the outdoor theater.

Paian walked among the traders and crafters. Some had their offerings spread on woolen blankets in the center of the theater. Paian ignored them. Goldsmiths and stone carvers were his target. They would be around the edge where the stone floor bordered on dirt pathways and eventually fields of grass. This is where they would be, in a place where they could have their animals.

Goldsmiths had crucibles made of clay and used to melt the metals they worked. Stone carvers had bronze tools to smooth and shape small pieces like seal stones and large ones like rhytons and even pithoi. These were too heavy to move without the help of donkeys.

Paian spied a craftsman working a small piece covered with cloth. *Why was the stone covered up? Because it was hiding Biaja's seal stone?* He ran to him and pulled the cloth away.

"Curse you!" the man shouted in Hellene, the language of Paian's home. Several men in adjacent work areas stood and moved toward Paian. By this time, he realized that he'd made a mistake. The man had been working on a seal stone, but it was red, not black like Biaja's. Someone might have stolen it, but that was not Paian's concern.

"My apologies. My mistake," Paian quickly replied in Hellene. His use of the man's language seemed to calm the situation. Several others joined a discussion of life across the Hellene territories. After some friendly conversation, Paian explained his quest.

Everyone listened politely. As the story of the naughty telestai boys continued, a crowd gathered and Paian embellished just a bit as everyone seemed to enjoy a tale of someone else's woes. When he got to the part describing the beautiful Biaja and her valuable obsidian seal stone, there was a commotion in the back, and a stoneworker ran away into the field behind the temple. The others pointed at him and yelled, "Him! Get him."

Paian took off. Soon enough he reached the steep bank of the creek and slowed. Paian leaped at him and the pair rolled down the embankment. He pried the obsidian from the stonecutter's fist. The man gave up, lying flat on his back.

"Where is the necklace?" Pi yelled.

The man scrambled back, crab-walking on his hands and feet, scrabbling away from Paian, terrified.

"Where is the necklace that was stolen with this?" Paian asked again, in a calmer voice.

Eyes wide, the man shook his head. "That is all. The boy brought only the fine obsidian. He said he found it."

"There wasn't anything else?"

"No, sir. Just the stone."

Paian grunted, then clambered back up toward Knossos and away from the theater area. He had no interest in seeing this Hellene punished. The fault was with Zetis, not this stoneworker. It was unlikely the boys would have tried to sell a mere stonecutter a necklace of pure gold and lapis, in any event.

He entered at the Grand Staircase and ran triumphantly toward the Suramarti station.

"I found the seal stone. Here it is." He handed the stone to Biaja. Instead of congratulations, everyone just stared at him.

Okune spoke first, "What is going on? Biaja, why does that Hellene have your seal stone?"

Paian felt sorry for Biaja as she explained to her mother about the missing seal, now returned, and how she also had lost Kitane's dragonfly necklace. When she explained Zetis' role, her mother interrupted her.

"I don't care about Zetis. He is a small boy. You are an almost grown woman of Suramarti. What are *you* going to do now?"

Biaja was silent. No one dared to face down Okune, matriarch of Suramarti. Paian thought that Okune was wrong to let Zetis' part in the theft just go by—that was no doubt part of the problem with the boy. He never had to take responsibility for his actions.

Though, Biaja ought not to have taken her sister's necklace without asking either.

Paian studied the group. Jura, suitor for Biaja's sister, looked to Biaja. Her cousin from Akrotiri, Isari, looked to her own mother, Okune's sister. That sister stood by Okune but had nothing to contribute. Even Biaja's father, Radamitu, creator of the dragonfly necklace, just waited.

Paian spoke up. "If Zetis sold the stone to the traders outside the temple, probably the dragonfly necklace is there also."

Still no response. Paian felt Biaja's fate rested with him.

"Let's go back to the theater and find the necklace before it's melted down."

Jura now joined in, "Come Biaja, let's hurry."

Without waiting for Okune's consent, they left. They ran through Knossos' passageways, passing down the corridor of young women bathing, followed by Jura's steward and several other men from Tylissos.

Paian realized that a crowd of telestai asking questions would upset the Hellene traders. "We should search in ones or twos. We can see more if we break up."

They all spread out, but Biaja stayed with Paian.

"Thank you for speaking up," she murmured, clasping his hand in her own dainty one. "My mother means well, but she scares most people." She smiled at Paian, "You were brave," she squeezed his hand, "and smart."

"Thank you," he said. "We should find Kitane's necklace." He walked over to an area populated with jewelers' tables. Biaja followed. He found a stoneworker with grey hair and wrinkled skin. They talked in Hellene. "Greetings old man. Where are you from?"

The man looked at his seal stone and the telestai woman with him. "Where did *you* learn to speak Hellene?"

"I am from the city dedicated to the Goddess Athena far north within the Hellene territories."

The man was also from the north and had heard of Paian's mother. After they shared stories of home, the man became sad and said, "I fear I will not return home in this lifetime. I will never see my grandchildren."

"I am returning home soon. I will tell them I spoke with you."

The man hugged Paian and cried. Paian introduced the man to Biaja and translated as she told him the story of the dragonfly necklace.

The man knew who had the necklace. "It is so beautiful. You must be so proud of your father. They would not melt it and destroy such an elegant piece. They simply would not dare."

In the center of the theater, Biaja collected everyone together, whispering she knew where the necklace was. If they made an accusation and were wrong that would give the real thieves the chance to disappear. As a cover, they bargained for pitas filled with fried revithia. Biaja gave the vendor her tiny woven copper ring to pay for several servings of the filled pitas.

She said, "Everyone eat, otherwise such a large group of telestai will raise suspicions." She took a bite and looked around as she chewed. Paian and the others also ate and watched the crowd, then the gold jewelers, then the crowd again. Biaja lowered her voice, "Look over my left shoulder. Do you see the gold merchant with long red braids?"

Everyone ate their pitas and nodded.

"He has two assistants. Paian's friend says he has the dragonfly necklace."

Jura smiled, "That is good to hear."

She explained the rest of the plan.

While Paian spoke to the gold trader, Jura grabbed one assistant, and the steward grabbed the other.

Paian spoke, "You have a necklace belonging to a powerful telestai from Suramarti."

The man just said, "Suramarti? Not Suramarti!"

Paian prepared to be rough with the man—after all he was a Hellene and accustomed to violence. But that was not necessary.

When the goldsmith saw the two men holding his assistants, he told one apprentice to get the necklace.

The boy dug into a well-used crucible, cold today, and filled with rags. He returned with the necklace, dirty, but undamaged.

Paian could see tears in Biaja's eyes as the boy tipped the dragonflies into her outstretched hands. She made no accusations. The man and his apprentices obviously knew Zetis had stolen the necklace. They were not the ones who had pilfered it. Biaja nodded to the man, who said, "I planned to return it to Radamitu, Missy. It is clearly of his making."

"My thanks," Bee said.

Paian and the others pretended to believe him, whether he spoke the truth or not, and they all headed back to the bull jumping.

When they re-entered the corridor of young women bathing, Paian heard a familiar voice. Biaja shouted, "Oh! That's my sister Qazipatima. She's announcing Kitane!"

Everyone ran.

ᛉᏟᛮ

Enosidas snorted and skipped about like a silly kitten when Kit asked him to enter the Central Court. He knew it was time to compete. His feet seemed weightless as he danced his way forward with Kit perched on his shoulders. He seemed to love the adoration of the crowd, and their appreciation of the skill of his rider and himself. Kitane laughed and patted his shoulder. Qazipatima stood at the north edge of the courtyard, ready to announce them, a bright smile on her lovely face.

From so high on Eno's shoulders, Kit could see the rest of her family in the audience; they filled the Suramarti station, waving and smiling. She knew she was letting pride suffuse her; she would banish it before her jumps. For the moment, she enjoyed being the center of attention, drawing admiring stares and cheers from the entire audience.

Soon she would have to give this up, so for her own sake as well as Eno's she was determined to enjoy this last time.

"Kitane, riding Enosidas, from Suramarti," Qazi said, and the crowd roared.

Eno trotted forward, and Kit stood up tall and graceful on his back, waving to the Keftiu filling the edges of Central Court at Knossos. As she approached the south end of the court and her family's station, she could hear the cheering get louder. Biaja was waving at her in excitement, and Kit could see her own dragonfly necklace around her sister's neck. Bee touched it with the hand that was not waving, then put her hand palm out greeting Kit and Enosidas, then both palms out, to honor the Goddess. Kit smiled. It would have been nice if Bee had asked to borrow the necklace, but Kit knew her sister had worn it to honor the family, to bring extra luck for her big sister's jumps.

She did not feel she needed luck, but it was also true that the sky was dark and ominous with clouds. Rather than believe that meant doom for her or her bull or Knossos, Kit believed the darkness was instead a warning to the Keftiu—and to Kitane herself—to be not too proud.

"For the Goddess," she said.

She patted Eno's shoulders as she slid lightly down to the ground. The entire audience went still. She signaled the bull with a flick of her wrist and they started their trot. She ran beside Eno, heading back toward the center of the court, and arcing their path into an ellipse. She felt as light and free as the fluffy dust that rose from their feet. She broke away from Enosidas, turning the opposite direction and picturing in her mind their comparative gaits, the distance to their curving turn back toward each other, feeling the smooth flow of their path.

They both picked up speed, and then he was there before her and Kit leaped, flying over his horns, landing with a spring in her wrists and elbows upon his withers. Her flip that immediately followed was very high above Eno's back. She landed lightly on his hindquarters and flipped again, to the ground. Focused on her jump, she was barely aware of the roar of the crowd. She trotted beside Enosidas back to the center of the court, reversed direction, and soon her path curved back to face him.

Her second jump was even better than the first. For her final jump, she felt confident to perform something never seen. She signaled Eno and ran faster than the previous jumps. Jasasara powered her swift approach. As practiced, Eno ducked his head extra low, almost touching the ground. At the last moment, she sprang into the air and flipped onto his back without even touching his head. The crowd went wild.

She realized one truth as she and Enosidas bowed to the four sides of the court and again to the Goddess: she did not have to stop jumping just because she stopped competing. She and Eno could continue to work together as long as they were both physically able. She ran her fingers through the small mop of curly dark golden hair on his forehead and kissed his nose, to the delight of the applauding crowd.

After a short break, the priestesses unwound their conference circle and stood in a long straight line facing the audience. Kitane signaled the other bull jumpers, who rode out from the stables area where they had quietly waited for the vote. Kit had warned them she was going to interrupt the awards ceremony with a plea for the bulls. No one had argued with her; it was not a breach of tradition, so much as a plea to return to the old ways. And they all knew it might be their own bull next time....

Of course, as expected, the priestesses announced Kitane and Enosidas as the winners. And Waro lost, and his bull was to be the sacrifice. The audience groaned, having found appreciation for the bull that acknowledged his rider's injury.

Kitane could see the bonfire where the Temple workers would roast the sacrifice. Her stomach turned at the thought of murdering and eating one of the competition bulls.

Not again, she swore. Never again!

Kitane jumped onto Enosidas' back and stood with her arms wide.

"Hear me!" she yelled.

The commotion among the audience, and notably, among the priestesses, stilled. The noise diminished.

"Hear me!" Kit called again. "I speak for the bulls!" She set her palms toward the priestesses, to honor them and the Goddess, despite how her words might sound.

There was a little noise among the crowd at that, but the priestesses remained still, faces set. Even Qazipatima looked at Kitane as if she knew her little sister was up to something, as if she was some kind of traitor.

"Once we *honored* our riders and our bulls at this ceremony. But now— " Kit took a deep breath, " —now we slaughter them!" She could hear the audience rumble. She spread her arms theatrically and knelt on Eno's broad back. "I beg you to tell me why? Why kill the bull whose rider makes a small mistake?" The audience muttered; she could not tell from the sound whether they were with her yet or not. But she could see the Aurochs' hard face, and her sister's. "How does this honor our Goddess Jasasara, the *Giver of Life*?" At this the audience roared in agreement. "Does she deliver these fine animals unto us so that we can *murder* them?"

"No!" yelled the crowd.

"No!" Kit yelled back. "She helps us train them in Her honor! She watches us jump—in Her honor!"

She tapped Eno's left shoulder with her toes, signaling him to turn and move. They trotted across the front of the line of competition bulls. "Are these tame oxen?" She called.

"No!" she yelled, with the audience.

"These are bulls! They are in competition with one another! In the wild they would be fighting, yet the Goddess gives them the grace to stand here, next to one another, competing but not attacking one another!" *Fewer words, Kit. Stronger.* "See how special they are! They are Hers!" she cried. "They are not meat animals, they are the Goddess' special beasts!"

She had said enough, she felt. Now she must make her plea. She dismounted and knelt before the line of priestesses. As she stood back up, a wide shaft of light broke through the heavy, smoky clouds above, as if promising rescue from Thera's doom. The light lit the courtyard, and the bulls, and Kitane, and she knew that was her moment, given by the Goddess.

"Please do not sacrifice the Goddess' trained bulls!"

Most of the audience knelt as Kit again knelt, facing the priestesses, palms out to honor the Goddess. She could hear the priestesses murmuring; she continued to kneel, even as there was a stir to the north end of the court, and she glanced up to see Jura entering, leading one of the bulls he had shown her as being available for sacrifice. His steward held a rope on the other side. She immediately wondered if the two men were enough to keep the animal under control, as it snorted and tossed its head. It was not a trained bull.

"So that there might be a *return to the old ways*," Jura called loudly, addressing the priestesses, "I offer this animal in sacrifice as a replacement. In every way a fine bull," he said, "but not an animal trained for years to honor the Goddess as one of Her bull jumpers' beasts."

This bull was clearly not trained, and snorted and dug his hooves into the earth by Jura's feet upon seeing the row of bulls facing him. Everyone realized at once this could be trouble—the audience rose to its feet almost as one, the priestesses clustered together, and each of the bull jumpers spent a few moments calming and reassuring their own beasts, as Jura pulled the lead rope, putting some distance between his animal and the others.

The Goddess' hand was at work in this, Kit was certain, as Jura's animal obediently followed the two men. Qazipatima took in the situation and nodded at something one of the other priestesses said.

"This is not tradition," one priestess called out, challenging Jura.

"What is the point of the competition, if not to choose the sacrifice?" called the Aurochs.

Then, as if a river had flooded, the priestesses were all shouting, condemning the substitution of a sacrifice. "Is this a bull trained to honor the Goddess?" one asked, pointing to Jura's bull.

"How can we claim to honor Her with lowly substitutions?" Another said. "Shall we offer a stone instead of a goat, next?"

The shouting continued, with both sides yelling and not listening to one another, for several minutes.

Then a gong sounded, reverberating across the Central Court, and stilling the priestesses, bull jumpers and audience alike.

There was a tendency to ignore the guasileus at Knossos. The priestesses' power had grown to the point where his position was honorary. The priestesses trotted him out to speak to the representatives of their allies and trading partners, many of whom refused outright to deal with a woman. Beyond that, and his right to live in the palatial quarters of Knossos, the priestesses and the telestai ignored him.

But now: The gong was his.

The honor guard that flanked him and his beautiful Kmt wife was his.

And now he seized his right to speak, and the audience was his. Kitane watched in astonishment as this man spoke out.

"It is foolish to destroy these animals, this wonder of the Keftiu that all nations bordering the Middle Sea revere and marvel at." His voice was surprisingly strong, carrying even to those at the far end of the Central Court.

Kitane blinked, as if seeing him for the first time. He was an old man, but he had a powerful set of lungs on him.

"I speak now as your Guasileus, honored among our trading partners. Keftiu loses status among our allies each time these kings hear that we have slaughtered another of our wondrous bulls. This is a matter for all Keftiu, not merely the Temple. I must report that *all our allies* question our way and our Goddess.

"It does not appear to me or to any guasileus of any nation that the Goddess Jasasara is honored more—*or less*—by which bull we kill in her name."

He stepped forward from his covered viewing station, out into the court. He faced Jura and the Tylissos steward, still holding their bull.

"*I* will accept your offering as a sacrifice in place of Waro's beast," he said. He thumped his ceremonial staff of office into the dirt at his feet three times, as if he was the pharaoh of Kmt. Then he nodded and stepped back.

Kit found she had been holding her breath. She had hoped for support from the people. She had never imagined the guasileus would have an opinion.

Jura and his steward bowed to the king as much as their grips on the lead rope would allow them. Then Jura turned and faced Qazipatima. He offered her the rope. With a fierce glance, first at Kitane, then the guasileus, she scowled at Jura and stepped forward.

The audience burst into cheers and wild applause, and really, there was nothing Qazi could do but accept the bull as sacrifice. Several priestesses joined her in grasping the lead rope. Jura's steward continued to hold the other rope, helping to lead the bull toward the North Entrance and the altar.

Kit bowed to Jura and honored him, palms out. "Thank you," she mouthed, and he nodded and smiled back at her.

"This gift Honors the Goddess," Qazi called out, and the dark clouds above them seemed to thin and brighten.

This resolution delighted the audience, but they seemed not of one mind about how to show it. Half the people knelt, palms out, to honor the Goddess Jasasara, and the other half applauded loudly—for Kit, or Jura, or the guasileus or priestesses who had made the decision and carried it out.

Kit stood beside Enosidas and wiped the tears from her cheeks onto the fur of his shoulder, then turned and smiled at the other bull jumpers. She got Eno back in line, signaled, and all the bulls ducked their heads, then began leaving the court, filing out in reverse order of achievement. Waro and his animal went first, then the others, one at a time until Kitane and Enosidas trotted off last.

Kit leaped aboard Eno and stood palms out as she and her animal left the field, and the audience broke up into groups, talking, cheering, and hugging. It would soon be time to drink and feast—all to honor Jasasara. As Enosidas trotted past the priestesses clustered around Jura's sacrificial bull, one of them looked up and caught Kit's eye.

It was Qazipatima.

Her sister gave her such a look of fury that Kit could not take her eyes away. She stared in disbelief as she passed by, trying to imagine she had seen something or someone else. But no, it was her sister's gaze, eyes filled with hatred like a spear aimed at Kit.

No one seemed to notice the clouds closing in overhead making the sky dark again as Jura's gift was sacrificed: the bull's blood spilled into the waiting rhyton as Kitane rode away.

SCENE 6 — TROS AT SEA

The crowded ship sailed low in the water, but Tros was encouraged that they were out of sight of the cursed Thera and still afloat. The crew looked forward to the riches of Amnisos and the protection of the Kmt sun god Ra. Whenever the crew emptied a pithos of water, they turned it on its side and rolled it overboard to make more room.

With no place to lie down, the sailors stood in groups, squeezed between the ballast and the cargo. They retold stories of their bravery in the face of Potidas. With each telling, the challenges grew, and their valor increased to match.

"Potidas threw burning boulders at us the size of houses."

"I swam through waves bigger than our ship to rescue the people in the water."

"Potidas will have to send something bigger than the island of Kaimeni to frighten us."

"I extinguished the burning swimmers by hugging them with my wet body."

A sailor still wearing a bandage Sakusna had applied to his fingerless hand, shook it like a fist, "We sail with Tros and *nothing* scares us!"

The boy safely nestled against the raised sail stood up and shouted, "Land. I see land. We are saved."

They were nowhere near land, yet a rocky shoreline appeared in front of them. The more experienced sailors shouted.

"It can't be."

"Potidas has sent another island to destroy us."

"This voyage is cursed, *cursed!*"

Tros thought, *how quickly their mood changes*. He realized the black land undulated like the waves. "Fear not. Keep rowing. It is not what it appears to be."

Some of the oarsmen held their oars aloft. Others kept rowing. Arguments broke out amongst the double rowers sharing a single oar.

"Stop! That evil island will be the death of us."

"Tros says, 'row,' so we row."

Quickly they hit the land, and with a rattle of small clatters, they slid through the apparent island. Some sailors laughed, others were still frightened.

"First burning rock, now floating rocks!"

"We are doomed."

The braver men reached over the gunwales and picked up the mysterious objects.

"Foam! Nothing but foam."

"Hard, black foam."

One sailor brought a piece to Tros. Tros handled it with care, having seen these volcanic rocks many years ago when sailing as a child with his father.

"Be careful. These rocks might be light like foam, but they are hard and sharp. They can cut you."

Several sailors dropped their play toys and looked at their bloody palms.

"Curses."

"These are from the explosion and can do us no harm. On to Amnisos!"

With the rocks no longer a threat, a couple of archers cast their nets overboard to collect a supply of foam rocks. Like a berry bush, it was nothing to fear, if treated with care and respected. Ever looking for a profitable opportunity, they filled several pithoi with this surprising bounty from the sea. It might fetch a decent price in Kmt.

The oarsmen dusted off their palms and resumed rowing, slicing through the flotilla of rocks accompanied by the gentle rumble against their ship drumming them toward the attack on Amnisos. After they left Amnisos for the last time, they would be on to Tanis and wealth.

With the decision to sack Amnisos, Tros flew a black pennant from the mast.

"Ships. Three ships to the west," shouted the boy on the mast.

"Turn to the west," Tros ordered.

Tros curled his fingers and peered through the small opening. "Small ships. Only a hand of rowers on each side. No archers."

With that news, his rowers increased their tempo and the archers took their positions. Everyone talked of good fortune.

"First, all that gold on Thera."

"And we escaped from the eruption."

"Now what treasure will these ships offer us?"

When they pulled alongside the three small ships, they saw that they were even smaller than expected.

The other captain spoke first in the language of the Keftiu, "We are peaceful traders bound for Malia with a cargo of resin."

Tros replied, "Where do you sail from? Are you Keftiu or Hellene?"

"Hellene."

The captain of the smaller ships noticed to the black pennant, smiled, and switched to the Hellene language. "Why do you fly the black flag?"

Tros replied, also in Hellene, "Thera is dead. We were there. We saw it ourselves." He described the eruption of Kaimeni Island, the land chasing them across the sea, and the rain of boulders. He gave all the details except the death of Sakusna and the scribes. "The gods will next destroy Keftiu. We go to sack Amnisos and then on to Kmt to form a new alliance."

The other captain thought for a while, looking at the black cloud of ash visible even though Thera was far away. "We will join you in exchange for the city of Malia as our share of the spoils."

Tros slapped his side and turned to his men, "He doesn't understand, does he?" The men guffawed.

Tros pretended to scold them, "Not his fault. He wasn't there. I'll explain it to him again."

"Kaimeni is gone. Akrotiri is gone. Thera is gone. The Gods have obliterated them. There will be no spoils. The gods will destroy Keftiu."

"What should we do?"

As usual, Tros had a plan.

"You sail with us and bring your best fighters. Send the other ships to the east and west to alert the Hellene traders to join us at Amnisos. Spread the *Call to Arms* across the Archipelago."

The other captain turned to his people. "Raise the black pennants. You've heard your orders."

Before the ships moved apart Tros added, "Quickly. In a few days, just as with Thera, the gods will claim the warehouses and smother them in ash and fire. Let's empty them before then."

ACT IV — BATTLE AT AMNISOS

SCENE 1 — TROS ARRIVING AT AMNISOS

ᘓᘈᖮ

Tros didn't want to announce his intentions, so he ordered a boy to lower the black pennant when he sighted Sail Rock. The distinctive structure, taller than any ship's mast, balanced on a narrow foot. On hot days, the harbor seals sought refuge in the shade of the overhang. A long arm of sand connected Sail Rock to the coast.

Amnisos was typical of many harbors. The sandy promontory between Sail Rock and the beach offered a protection from the winds. Depending on the wind direction, captains would anchor on one side or the other. Also, they could beach their vessels on the sand for repairs, as he intended to do.

In addition to protection from variable winds, the traders preferred these sandy capes to isolate their ships from the mainland. The captains contracted with the locals to construct a sturdy wall where the promontory met the beach. At Amnisos the wall exhibited the same precision ashlar stonework that had made Knossos famous around the Middle Sea. This elegant masonry protected the ships' cargo and crew from both curious and malicious visitors. All ships contributed a few crewmembers to monitor the gate and maintain fires throughout the night at each end of the wall.

Amnisos was special because it had an unusually broad beach where the Keftiu had built three rows of warehouses. The shoreline reminded Tros of a ship's hull as it gently curved around a wide bay. The cape formed the mast reaching out into the bay from the center of the ship with Sail Rock positioned as its pennant.

As Tros approached the harbor, a crowd of Keftiu workers gathered. He worried that someone had warned them of his nefarious intentions, but they weren't armed, so he proceeded. In a soft voice, he warned the archers, "Be alert, but not threatening. Be prepared for anything."

188

He looked beyond the coast wall. The beach was empty. Beyond the beach, the warehouse buildings were unguarded. He stared into the dark interiors searching for signs of soldiers. He saw none. The crowd greeting his arrival was welcoming, but that was no assurance that they hadn't heard of his plans and prepared a surprise attack.

He signaled the oarsmen to throw the landing ropes. At the same time, he whispered to his carpenters, "Take your axes to the emergency retreat positions in case we need to cut and run."

Prepared for any response, Tros stepped forward and raised his open palm. "Blessings of the Goddess to you."

The foreman returned the greeting.

Tros handed him a papyrus bearing a Suramarti stamp. "We've had a hard voyage. We lost two boats, and now need repairs and supplies."

The foreman examined the papyrus. Tros doubted he could read, but all dockworkers were familiar with the Suramarti seal.

"We are in a rush." Tros pointed to the column of darkness on the horizon and the dark clouds above. The harbor had filled with floating rocks. The clicking of rocks against rocks competed with the braying of the harbor seals. "We saw Potidas destroy Thera. The dark sky and tide of rocks are evil omens. How soon can we be ready to continue our journey?"

The foreman laughed. "Tonight, you can leave tonight. For sure."

Tros looked puzzled.

The foreman's assistant spoke, "We thought you knew. You sail under the Suramarti seal." She continued, "Tomorrow is the bull-jumping ceremony! We expect Kitane of Suramarti to win. Everyone is here today because we will all go to Knossos tomorrow."

That fit Tros' plan perfectly. Truly the gods had stopped protecting the Keftiu lands and peoples.

All day the crew and dockworkers never stopped working. Before they rolled the large ship onto the beach for repairs, they needed to unload the heavy cargo. They stacked the talents of bronze-gold and bronze-silver on the beach "to be left for Keftiu metalworkers," and lined up rows of pithoi, some from the ship and more from the warehouses. After the repairs were complete, the dockworkers would reload the pithoi and fill them with fresh water, wine, or olive oil.

Tros' carpenters went ashore to search the warehouses for the best cypress planks for repairs. They knotted ropes, measuring the damage to know the size of the most appropriate replacement boards. In the meantime, archers with bronze hammers removed the old patches and cut away the resin with knives.

By the evening everything was ready. The Keftiu headed up the hill for the next day's bull jumping. Tros prepared to capture Amnisos and fill his cargo spaces with a bounty of Keftiu treasures. Gold jewelry. Painted ceramics. Artworks on papyrus. Linen garments. Bronze fishing hooks and tools.

Overnight the clouds of ash got darker and the sea of floating rocks louder. Tros felt the same urgency he'd experienced on Thera. He looked north and spotted three masts flying black pennants. *The reinforcements.* He had escaped Thera with gold and would do even better here.

Before dawn, he roused the archers, oarsmen, everyone. "It's time. We attack."

He formed the men into small groups, three or four men each, with a few teams having as many as a full hand. They spread across the shoreline, one group at each warehouse. On Tros' signal, they attacked the warehouses. With most Keftiu gone for the bull jumping, they easily captured the remainder. The captives, mostly dockworkers, included one priestess and a couple of women. They even rounded up a few children under the age of two hands. The shoreline wall and the sea imprisoned the hostages on the promontory.

By midday, the pirates included six ships and controlled Amnisos while the Keftiu celebrated the bull-jumping ceremony unaware of the pirate victories. The warehouses were open and streams of men carried Keftiu treasures to their cargo spaces.

That night more ships arrived; the *Call to Arms* had been successful. The space along the cape filled up and a couple of ships had no choice but to dock along the unprotected beach. Tros was unconcerned as he now controlled the entire beach. He made plans to loot Knossos the next morning.

Throughout the night, Tros heard splashing. In a half-sleep between exhaustion from yesterday's battle and his anticipation of the attack the next day, he wondered about the unexpected commotion. He knew the seals hunted for octopus at night. *The seals are feasting from Sail Rock to the shore and back. Or an incoming tide of floating rocks. Or waves all the way from Thera.* The noise eventually stopped, and he returned to a deep sleep.

In the morning, he understood the splashing when he noticed that his prisoners were cheering and shouting. Looking closer, he realized that the children were missing. During the night, the children had swum around the wall and alerted some Keftiu.

Those few Keftiu, armed with farming tools, rocks, and firebrands, stretched out in front of the rows of warehouses. Tros looked at the line along the beach and laughed, "Farmers."

Tros had his boy wave the signal pennant. "All fighting men assemble."

These farmers did not worry Tros. Each small group defended their own warehouse, so he decided to send his men to attack the warehouses left to right until he'd recaptured them all.

"Secure the remaining prisoners."

The pirates moved along the sandy peninsula, forcing the prisoners against the water and opening a corridor to the gate. Tros led the main force through the gate to the beach.

Before they advanced, the farmers attacked. They rushed his forces. In the process, the width of their line narrowed and strengthened with the increased depth. The farmers overran the two unfortunate ships anchored on the beach and set them ablaze.

The defeated sailors desperately swam for the promontory and safety behind the wall.

From the front of the pirate line, Tros ran toward the farmers yelling, "Attack! Attack."

The pirates formed two lines, a short defensive line at the wall, and a wider attack line championed by Tros, challenging the farmers, and stretching across the beach.

The melee pitted sailors armed with fists and a few knives against farmers armed with rakes and hoes, a surprisingly even match. Tros watched in frustration as his attack line alternated between pushing toward the warehouses and receding back to the sea. He had stationed archers on the wall, but they were little use because the melee made it impossible for them to distinguish friends from foes.

The battle was a standoff. Both sides were brawling with more bruising than blood. This could have continued until nightfall, when fighting would stop, had not more pirate ships arrived. Tros said a silent prayer of thanks for fair winds and the *Call to Arms*.

The newcomers anchored on the beach on both sides of the peninsula beside the burning hulls. Their fighters rushed ashore at the ends of the battle line. Tros recognized the tactical flanking advantage he now had. He directed the center of the line to follow him back to the defensive wall creating an opening for the farmers to stream through. Once the farmers took the bait, moving toward the center of the battlefield, the men on the flanks moved around to encircle them. The pirates drove the farmers into the sea or took them prisoner within the sandy enclosure.

Tros had not fooled one group. Instead of rushing into in the claws of the trap, they retreated to a strong position on the warehouse roofs, the row closest to the Knossos road. Tros surrounded that line of warehouses. He had them isolated and out of the way. He was free to loot the remaining two rows of warehouses and march on to Knossos.

He had just one more concern. *How can I find Kitane? She should be here to celebrate with me.*

SCENE 2 — KITANE IN KNOSSOS & AMNISOS
⍦ᘉⵊ

Still puzzling over Qazipatima's hateful look, Kitane rejoined her family for the bull jumpers' feast. She had intended to ask her sister about it, but Qazi was not there.

She hugged Biaja, who offered her back her dragonfly necklace. Kit shook her head. "It looks better with your robe today."

"I'm sorry I did not ask to borrow it," Bee said.

Kit cocked her head and stared at her sister. Was something wrong? Kit tried to make light of it, "You've 'forgotten' to ask to borrow my things many times, Bee. I do appreciate being asked, but it's all right."

"It does look magnificent with this robe, doesn't it?" Bee asked, a smile dancing on her lips and in her eyes.

Kit just smiled.

She moved to where Jura was standing, wanting to thank him for his offering. He was talking to his brother, chiding Ukan about something. Kit moved forward, interrupting the brothers' conversation.

"Jura, you saved the day! Thank you so much for thinking about the bull sacrifice, and for bringing your fine animal."

"I— He was to be sacrificed for the feast," Jura said. "Though to be honest, the bulls aren't the best meat; a younger castrate is more tender."

"Nevertheless, you offered an alternative, just when I needed one. I am thankful."

Jura met her eyes and smiled. "I am glad I was able to help," he said. "I noticed your family sent one from your herds to help with the feast also," he said, ever fair and honest.

Behind them, on the feasting grounds, a sistrum rattled, and a dance rhythm began; a conch-shell trumpet called for dancers to come. Soon she could hear the auloi's smooth notes rise along with the thump of drums and the pat of bare feet as celebrants joined in the dancing.

She smiled at Jura, hoping he'd invite her to dance. When he did not, she looked at the darkening night sky. There was no moon tonight. The black column from Thera combined with the ash-darkened sky above to hide the stars. It was a dark night, indeed.

The smoke and clouds still covered the sky in the morning. Kit washed and dressed for the second day of ceremonies and celebration, removing her lavender linen robe from her wooden box. It was a little too lightweight for the gloomy day, but it was what she had brought, so she stuck with it.

After dressing and putting her hair into a neat braid down her back, she joined her family in the big open guest dining room. Jura joined her, along with Biaja and Isari.

In the corner, Paian plucked and strummed gentle music on his people's version of the forminx. He called it a *lyre*. She nodded at him, thinking how multi-talented the young man was. Really, she should have given him more consideration as a suitor—but she had simply run out of time.

She had just finished her bowl of revithia and yogurt when she saw Qazipatima approaching. Her sister wore her finest flounced skirt and top worked with embroidery, the front of which was covered by the short apron. This apron had been embellished with semi-precious stones, thin slices of lapis and amber and malachite enriching the color of the flowers and vines embroidered over it, laid-work of black fine-twisted wool in spiral patterns completing the effect.

Qazi's face was not so beautiful, however.

"Do you know, you just undid two decades of Temple work! To save your silly bulls, you may have sacrificed all that the priestesses have worked for."

"What?"

Kit saw Jura bite his lip and back away. The volume of Qazi's words attracted the attention of the rest of the Suramarti family, who took Jura's place, then gradually surrounded the sisters.

"We have been trying for years to keep the guasileus *out* of Temple affairs, and now you have invited him back into one of the most important ceremonies of all!"

"What?" Kit said again, even more confused. "I did nothing except what you saw. I asked the *people* to help save the bulls. I asked for a return to the traditional form of sacrifice!"

"You opened the way for the guasileus to stick his fingers back into our affairs. This ceremony is none of his business!"

"I did nothing *with* the guasileus, Qazi! But even he could see that killing bull jumpers' bulls is not right."

"I don't care about the stupid bulls. I care about whose authority it is to make that decision. It is not yours! It is not the people's! It is not the guasileus'! It is for the priestesses to decide!" She added in an exasperated tone: "Why did you not bring the matter to me?"

Now Kit was feeling her fury rise. It was obvious Qazi didn't care about the bulls, stupid or not. She never had. She only cared about her own power!

"I *did* bring the matter to you, Qazi," Kit said in a low, dangerous tone. "You patted me on the head and said the Temple 'might consider the issue when you had time.'" Kit took a step toward her sister, crowding her. "Obviously, you were *never* going to have time! Your party dresses are more important than the bulls you sacrifice with such trivial concern!"

Qazipatima's face expressed outrage and fury in equal measure. Kit's heart sank. How could her own sister believe Kit would undermine her authority? It *was* about the bulls no matter what Qazi thought.

"Dresses? Don't be absurd. But if you must know, Kit, the entire Temple is outraged, all the priestesses."

"*You?* What about the bull jumpers, oh Queen of the Priestesses? We who work to please the Goddess, and Potidas, and *you!* What will *you* decide next? Are you going to start sacrificing the bull jumpers too? *Am I to have my throat slit?*"

Their mother gasped and reached a hand out, putting her arm between the sisters. "This needs to wait for cooler tempers," Okune said, and beside her Radamitu nodded.

What might have happened between them would never be known, because at that moment the big disc gong at the temple's distant Customs House sounded, quelling all other sound, announcing an attack. The *"bong!"* reverberated throughout the temple grounds.

Then, "Attack! Pirates at Amnisos!" a man's voice bellowed.

Still seething with anger, Kit ran to the stalls where the bulls were housed. Each animal had its own small room, stocked with fresh hay and special treats. She kicked a brush she'd left on the floor after grooming Eno and hopped a moment, holding her toes and cursing.

Enosidas eyed her uneasily, his mouth full of grain. She stood beside him as he crunched and chewed, while she regained some composure. How dare Qazi treat this as an assault on the Temple? Kitane had never spoken to the guasileus in her entire life. Though the man obviously knew her family, he did not know Kit. He could not have said anything that would have given Qazi the idea they'd colluded. Why had her sister jumped to that conclusion? What was wrong with her?

She sighed and gripped the edge of the food box.

Attack. At Amnisos. That must be her priority now, no matter how much she wanted things settled with the all-powerful Temple and its priestesses.

She put one of her old training belly bands around Eno and tied it off. She could tuck her feet under it. It would help her stay aboard if they got into the fighting. She looked around for a weapon. The only thing in sight was a wooden hayfork. It didn't even have a bronze head. But it was a size she could manage and might do some damage. At least she could push pirates away from Eno's sides. His hooves would take care of the before- and aft- dangers to himself.

She pulled off her lavender robe and tossed it over the wall. She tightened her loincloth and mounted Enosidas.

As she kicked him forward away from the stable stalls, several of the other bull jumpers joined her. Were the pirates going to loot only the warehouses at the port, or would they head toward Knossos?

"We will hold the road. No one must get past us to come here," she called out, and the other riders nodded and shouted, waggling makeshift weapons, or patting their animals. Now all the jumpers led their bulls out of their rooms. They headed out of the stable, the hooves of ten fine bulls rumbling on the stone pavement of the road. North to the waters of the Middle Sea. To Amnisos.

Wishing Tros had come back in time for the bull-jumping ceremony as he'd promised, Kit thought about how much help his sailors could have been in fending off these pirates. The guasileus had a guard to help protect Knossos. She could see a few soldiers with spears and the big Keftiu double-circle shields setting out toward Amnisos while others set up barricades in front of the stairways into Knossos. So few trained soldiers. Would they be enough?

As they trotted down the road toward the port town, others enlisted in the brigade. Some atomai, mostly unarmed, ran up to join them, then paused now and then to pick up rocks for their slings or just to throw. Others grasped various tools, like her own rake.

As they passed the last buildings of Knossos, a group of telestai on donkeys strengthened the force. Jura waved to her from among them, a heavy-looking staff in his big hand. She tried to call to him, but the thunder of bull's hooves and trotting donkeys made it impossible. She kneed Eno to turn him, and worked her way through the cloud of dust over to where Jura rode among various telestai, some still in their fancy bull-jumping ceremony clothing, others stripped to their loincloths. All bore arms of one sort or another, though Kit wasn't sure anyone knew how to fight. The mounted telestai were outpacing those on foot, jostling past the runners and joining the bulls.

"Are any more soldiers coming?" she called to Jura.

He shook his head. "I believe they are setting up to defend Knossos. The palace and temple guards are closing and locking gates and preparing slings and spears. Archers on the roofs."

"So, no one to help us?"

"These," Jura said, waving his arms at the mixed groups around them.

Kit nodded. "Well, we can slow them down, perhaps."

As they rounded the last curve in the road, Kit got her first view of the Amnisos fight.

A few atomai stood on warehouse rooftops, throwing anything they could get their hands on down onto the pirates below. She saw boards and rocks and broken marble go flying. A few workers and guards had fishing spears and were holding off the pirate attackers at the side of one string of warehouses. In most other places, the pirates were pushing the defenders back. There were pirates between Kit's mob and the other two warehouse rows.

So, should they give up on the warehouses, and just focus on defending the road? She could not see much of the beach or the docks at the peninsula, but given what she could see, there did not seem much of a chance to regain the warehouses, not without reinforcements. They'd have to make a stand here.

"Form a line!" she called to the bull riders, waving an arm to show what she meant. Across the road, where a steep hill on their right and a boggy estuary on their left would force the attackers onto the road to face them. "We hold this spot!"

Some of the fighters on the beach closest to them saw what they were doing. They fled the enemy, running toward the bulls and away from the pirates. That left the group fighting at the untaken warehouse surrounded by the enemy. Those defenders were going to die or be taken prisoner.

She scowled. Diwoki would know what to do: he had studied war tactics in Kmt and Arzawa. She had no idea what she could do for the lost guards at the third warehouse.

Behind her, she heard laughter and the sounds of a scuffle. Scowling, she turned and saw Zetis and his pals coming toward her. They seemed to think the battle was an adventure: excitement lit their eyes, and they jumped and fooled around like always.

"Zetis! I need your help!"

He laughed aloud, ran toward her, and leaped aboard Enosidas, who grunted and tossed his head. She patted Eno's shoulder, adjusting her seat so that she could look her little brother in the eye.

"See the third warehouse?"

He nodded, a more serious expression falling over his face.

"Do you think you and your boys could clear an escape route for them to get safely to us? Don't fight, don't engage the enemy, just sabotage their footing or distract them so our people can get away."

"We will clear a path!"

"Also, if you can find the leader of these attackers, tell them I want to meet."

He nodded again.

"Zetis— "

"Don't worry. I won't get dead."

"Your friends either," she said. She held back her hand from ruffling his hair with a conscious will. She needed him to feel capable, not like a little boy.

"We will do it. We will be careful."

"Good." She cleared her throat. "It will make up a bit for yesterday."

He didn't say anything, just paused for a moment, then nodded, slipping down from Eno's rump, and vanishing into the crowd. She could see a ripple among those behind the line of bulls as Zetis gathered his friends and moved toward the third warehouse.

𐄂𐄁𐄀

Biaja helped her mother pack up the Suramarti things, including Kitane's belongings, to be sent home from Knossos. Their villa should be safe at its distance from the shore, and Biaja wanted her mother away from the temple and any fighting. Also sent to safety were Halima's small children, the family's young handmaids and old steward, and Bee and Zetis' ancient crèche mother.

Halima seemed excited by the fighting. Bee was concerned that her sister-in-law was jealous of Isari—her cousin had gone with Kitane and Jura to form some sort of resistance to the pirates, hopefully holding them off long enough for Knossos to prepare a defense.

"Will we fight here, do you think?" the Kmt woman asked, her dark face lit oddly by the shadows and light beams of the guest room.

"I hope not," Bee answered. "Are you certain you do not want to retreat to Suramarti? Your children will need you."

"I will flee there if it must be so, but for now, I owe it to all of you to help protect your temple, don't you think?"

Bee grimaced internally. "*Your temple*" meant that Halima still felt like an outsider.

Then Bee had a horrible thought: Were the pirates *Kmt*? Did Halima know her people had sent this attack? She did not want to believe that of her sister-in-law, but Halima consistently held herself apart from the Keftiu. In little ways, but ways that showed she did not fit, did not feel a part of Suramarti or Keftiu, despite her obvious love for Diwoki and their children.

"I think my brother would be horrified if you were not sent to safety at Suramarti."

"But *you* are staying to fight," Halima said.

Bee shook her head. "I hope I do not have to, but think, love: I don't have children. I don't even have a husband. Of course, I will be defending our home. You— "

"You will come with us, Halima," Asije said, waving a hand to indicate whom she meant by "us."

What was her aunt doing? Biaja felt resentment rise that Asije thought she had a right to tell *any* Suramarti what to do. And given her aunt's position—or lack of one—in the house, shouldn't *Asije* be staying to help fight? "Mother will want your help, Halima. Please go with her, she needs you, as do your children."

Asije scowled, grasping Diwoki's wife's hand. "Yes. Now help us pack, please," she said with an irritated glance at her niece.

Bee's mother looked at the three women and shook her head. "We need to leave," she said. "Halima, I want you with us, please."

Halima's eyes flashed at Bee as she turned to join the other women. But she went, and that was good.

It was Bee's day to catch women's anger. Next was The Aurochs who burst into the Suramarti guest rooms, her round face red with exertion. Or anger. Her eyes targeted Biaja.

"Where have you *been*? You are supposed to helping the Temple, initiate!"

"I— " *haven't told you or my sister I am leaving the training*, Bee realized.

"Indeed, we don't need your help, Biaja," Asije said.

Even Okune seemed annoyed by this. Her head jerked up and she said, "Asije! Sister, this is not your concern." She faced the klawiphoros, not at all afraid of the woman as far as Bee could see. "Of course, my daughter is helping those who came for the bull jumping to get safely back home. You cannot deny her that time, priestess."

The Aurochs' mouth opened and closed, then she nodded once and turned back to Bee. "Please join us as soon as Suramarti is on its way. There are Temple things to attend to."

Bee made a small bow. "I will."

As the Aurochs left the room, Bee turned back toward her mother just in time to see Okune roll her eyes. "She's just as grumpy as I remember," her mother said.

Already in trouble, Bee decided not to say anything at all.

They were loading donkeys with the Suramarti belongings just inside the South Entrance to the temple grounds, when the now-guarded South House admitted a runner. The runner was a young girl, her eyes wide and her whole demeanor speaking of fright.

"That does not look good," Radamitu said. "I need to get down there to help the defenders—our daughter, our neighbors."

Okune stood a moment, staring at her husband. Then she nodded, taking the reins of the lead donkey. Halima lifted her daughter onto the second donkey's back, fitting her little legs into a basket and propping her up with a blanket. The girl wasn't walking yet, and her mother would only be able to carry her for part of the journey. The little one seemed delighted with her perch, and giggled, oblivious to the tension of the adults.

Okune smiled. "Let us depart. Be safe, my husband."

Radamitu leaned forward and planted a kiss on his wife's cheek. "And you as well," he said.

Biaja made sure their youngest handmaid was in the group. The child had only seen ten summers, yet had wanted to stay and fight. Bee had finally *ordered* her to go, since none of her logical arguments had made an impression on the girl. The older youths and strong adults would be fighting, not the children and old ones. Okune led them off. Halima walked beside her daughter's donkey, holding her son's hand as he toddled beside her. She darted one last angry flash of her eyes at Biaja as they walked off.

Radamitu and one of their atomai men headed off to the Knossos armory. Her father would be permitted to take one of the good soldier's spears, and maybe get extras for their atomai as well.

The small caravan had reached the dip in the road when Bee heard Qazi's voice yell behind her. The priestess ran up, panting. "I missed them."

"They're on their way to safety," Biaja said.

Qazi grabbed Bee's shoulder. "I need your help!"

"All right. I was going to find you. You need me to wait here or go fight?"

"Others can fight. I need you for something else."

"What?" Bee said, thinking of Kit and Qazi's earlier argument. Hopefully, this wasn't something about the bulls or the guasileus. Bee didn't like to see her sisters fight. More, she didn't like to see how much Qazi's great power had gone to her sister's head.

"These attackers could reach Knossos. We need to send a caravan to the Mount Ida sanctuary to bring some very important things to safety, and some of the elder priestesses as well."

"Ah," Bee said, heart sinking. Another caravan up the mountain. It seemed she couldn't avoid the place. "Is there no one else who could go? The clerics?"

"The clerics are packing. Then they will arm themselves and defend Knossos. I want the younger initiates to get to safety. I sent the two youngest home. I need to get the oldest priestesses, and the treasures and important tablets away from here. I need a telestai in charge." She made a face. "I'm sorry, Bee. It's a matter of trust. There will be at least four donkeys, so get some help. I was thinking Nopine? I will send one guard with you as far as Suramarti; maybe he or she can return with some of the villa atomai to help fight or guard the temple. The Hellene can join you. They all have fighting experience."

Bee sighed and nodded, looking at Qazi's gold-threaded headdress and gem-encrusted apron. Weren't those treasures, too?

As if reading her mind, Qazi tore off the headdress, untied the apron and thrust them at her sister. "These, and anything else you can think of from the initiate's area and nearby. Meet me back here before mid-day with whatever you can find!"

Bee nodded again, already running. They'd want to take the gold work, jewelry, idols, fancy robes and ceremonial valuables. She entered the guest room where Suramarti had stayed; there had been a gold, gem-encrusted idol by the small altar she should take.

A noise behind startled her. "Nopine!"

Her friend turned, holding up Kitane's dragonfly necklace, wide-eyed. "It slipped behind the sleeping mats, Bee."

"Oh, Goddess! All I need is to lose it again! Thank you!" She took it, then not having a sack or pockets at hand, simply put it on around her neck.

Nopine nodded, heading for the door.

"No, wait, I need you!" Bee explained about the caravan, and needing guards, and help to manage the donkeys. "Come with me, I need to find more helpers, and gather anything of value."

Biaja stood on her toes as they left Knossos, trying to see if she could see anything of the battle at Amnisos as they left. Beside her, Nopine, Paian, and Ukan likewise looked. While they were watching, a bull and bull rider raised dust heading up the road toward them. Even from here, they could see blood, dark against the bull's shoulder. The rider held one arm against his chest.

Nopine ran toward him and Bee joined her, hoping for word of the fight.

It was Waro, the young man whose bull Kit had saved. His face was pale, they could see as he slowed the bull down to a walk. Bee could see a huge bruise and swelling above the injured wrist.

"How goes it?" Biaja called.

"I'm coming for help," he said. "We're badly outnumbered."

"We will send what help we can find on our way to Mt. Ida," Bee said. "But we must move on."

Waro nodded, then continued toward Knossos and whatever help he could glean from the Temple and the guasileus. Since those were frantically preparing for a siege, Bee didn't think Waro would get many fighters to help.

Bee turned and ran also, back to the caravan, which had continued moving up the road. Maza was at the lead, Ukan, with a spear and long double-circle shield as tall as him, beside her. They'd added a donkey at the end for the oldest priestess to ride, along with one for one of the old scribes who had been at the Temple forever. The two women growled at each other—some history between them Bee did not know, but they managed to keep their donkeys moving at the same pace as the rest of the caravan.

Bee rejoined Paian, who also carried a shield, the small round one of his people, along with his short sword. They walked at the rear, behind the priestess and scribe's donkeys.

Things were not going well for the Keftiu at Amnisos. Earlier, Maza had seen ships burning, and groups of men and women fighting on the beach. She had not said one word of complaint about taking a caravan to Mount Ida. Bee sighed. They hadn't taken time to bring any food. They'd have to stop at Tylissos or Suramarti before the last long uphill to the sanctuary.

SCENE 4 — JURA'S MISSION

╟ ╘

Jura had never seen a battle before. Telestai leadership had always maintained peace across Keftiu, and he never imagined outsiders jeopardizing their relationships with the powerful trading families who controlled most of the commerce across the Middle Sea. At first, he found the action exhilarating. Like the others, he grabbed the first shepherd's staff he saw for a weapon and jumped on a donkey from the west courtyard. He rushed to join the fracas.

When they'd reached the beach, he'd charged ahead. His first few hits knocked down a couple of pirates, but when he swung his staff back to target a third, a couple of unseen pirates hit him and knocked him to the ground. The sand was soft enough, but one blow bruised his arm and the other his opposite hip. He couldn't swing his staff, instead he used it as a crutch to limp back from the front line.

His donkey stood by calmly, but Kano ran in circles, first advancing toward the commotion, and then looking back to Jura for encouragement. When none was forthcoming, she retreated to the safety of his side. She barked loudly, but Jura doubted she'd frighten anyone as her curled tail wagged frantically. Like Jura, Kano was eager to join the battle, but did not know how.

Kitane had no such hesitation. She stood atop her bull, shouted orders, chased pirates if they broke through the line, and directed the atomai. The atomai proved to be valiant soldiers, throwing stones with their slings, and fighting with spears. When they were close enough, they struck the pirates with their fists and wrestled them to the ground. Even young Zetis had a mission. Jura knew exactly how to run a villa, but was uncertain how to contribute to a battle. He knew he could do more than throw rocks and wrestle on the beach, but what?

Jura struggled back atop his donkey and pulled the reins to get out of the way as two bull jumpers sped after a group of pirates. He stopped at a large boulder. Kano bounded to the top for a better vantage point from which to chastise the pirates. Jura struggled up to the top.

He reviewed the scene, looking for inspiration. The pirates held the center of the beach and had split the Keftiu into three groups. The first group was imprisoned behind the wall on the promontory. The second group, led by Kitane and the other bull jumpers, defended the path to Knossos. The pirates had the third group trapped on top of some warehouses. That group seemed to need the most help. Jura had no idea how to rescue them. The small groups fighting each other were evenly matched, and the bulls charged wherever they saw a need. More people arrived from Knossos, but not fast enough to tip the balance.

That was the greatest need: Jura would recruit more fighters.

He slid back down to the road. His sore hip had recovered, but his arm was still weak. He managed to mount, then rode his donkey toward Enosidas to let Kit know his plan.

Kit sat tall astride Enosidas. She had trained her bull for the jumping ceremonies, not combat. After so many generations of peace, the Keftiu taught their children practical skills, not warfare. Keftiu atomai learned farming, weaving, and cooking. Those with special aptitude could apprentice to make jewelry, pottery, or frescoes. Telestai like Jura learned to administer a villa or a trading ship. No one studied warfare.

He admired Kit as she rode Eno through the crowd knocking down and kicking pirates, and protecting the Keftiu. She performed on the battlefield with the same grace as she did in the Central Court of Knossos. He arrived at Kitane's position at the same time as a shepherd. He recognized her staff—she was the shepherd he'd encountered at the bull-jumping ceremony.

She jumped in front Eno. "Kitane! Kitane! I love watching you jump with Enosidas. I followed you. You'll show these pirates, won't you?"

Kit and Enosidas came to a sudden stop and threw sand in the air as they changed direction to avoid hitting the shepherd.

Jura couldn't believe she had interrupted Kit's action against the pirates. He looked at the shepherd, meeting her eyes. She recognized him and gave him an open palm salute. He frowned at her, but still returned the salute barely raising his hand above his waist, his injured arm stiff and unresponsive. Kitane continued her attack.

The shepherd again ran toward Kitane shouting praise and admiration. Kitane noticed Jura and gave him that look that let him know she'd had enough of this distraction.

Jura took immediate action. "Kitane, this shepherd and I will go to recruit reinforcements."

The shepherd banged her staff on a rock and shouted, "I have friends. We'll show these pirates."

Kitane turned to Jura with a smile, "Yes, a timely suggestion. Take her away."

He doubted her sincerity until she gave him an appreciative tilt of her head that previously had only been for Enosidas. She further encouraged him with, "Be quick. They could have more ships coming."

Jura went off, followed by his steward and the shepherd. He'd prove the value of dependable organization. He had his mission.

"Move quickly. Follow me." Jura led group organized by his steward up the road away from the beach. He intended to take the trail to Mount Ida and recruit reinforcements at each villa. He knew every villa between Mount Ida and Knossos.

As they approached Knossos, the shepherd shouted. "Kitane was right! More pirates. Lots more pirates."

Jura already regretted bringing her along, but he couldn't have left her interfering with Kit.

"Oh Potidas. Oh Jasasara! So many pirates."

Jura stopped to see what had set her off. Sure enough, from their position up the hill, they could see three pirate ships approaching the beach. They all flew black flags. Jura thought there might be more on the horizon, though they were too far asea to be sure.

He turned to the shepherd, "I see them. Let's go. We have no time to spare." He turned right at the Mount Ida path and headed toward Tylissos and Suramarti.

When the shepherd stopped talking, he heard another group ahead of them, so turned to his steward, "Run ahead and see who is there. Approach with care, in case they are not friendly."

A short while later the steward returned, "It was Biaja. They await us." When the two groups met, Jura told of the battle and the flotilla of pirate ships coming.

"We better warn Kitane."

Biaja turned to her friend, "Nopine, can you run to the Amnisos road and warn my sister about the other pirate ships?"

Jura jumped to the ground, "Here, you can take my donkey."

Nopine nodded and took off back toward Knossos and Amnisos.

Biaja turned to Maza, "We should keep moving. We don't want to lose the tablets."

Maza slapped the lead donkey, "I've heard rumors that the Thera tablets were lost."

Jura watched them move away wondering if the tablets were more important than stopping the pirates. He shouted to his brother, "Ukan! Get additional fighters from Tylissos, and Suramarti, and send them to Amnisos."

Ukan waved his hand in agreement and took up a position at the rear to help Maza, who assisted the two old women on the last donkeys.

As the donkey train disappeared around a bend, the shepherd came back to life. "Let's go." She uncovered a narrow path into the wild. "The atomai have moved into the forest to avoid the coming earthquakes. They don't know about the attack on Amnisos."

She pushed the brush aside with her staff. "Hurry up. We have no time to waste."

Jura thought, *maybe she can help after all*. Before he was ready to follow her, he asked, "How are we going to find them?"

"I live around here. I know where the summer camps are."

He considered hugging her, but decided against it. "Blessing of Jasasara to you." He and his steward followed.

Scene 5 — Kitane at Amnisos

꟒ᘯ𐊏

The chaos on the beach seemed impenetrable. How did military commanders make sense of such swarming battles? Kitane wasn't even certain who was an attacker and who fought for Keftiu in many of the skirmishes. A constant low roar numbed her ears, and a cloud of dust and smoke hazed her eyes.

Then, with a suddenness that was breathtaking, the enemy who had been attacking them all withdrew.

She glanced at the broad column of smoke visible across the sea at Thera, where fiery destruction held reign over that doomed island, over the sea, over this beach. It was a terrible omen. Then she noticed movement on the beach below, as a wedge of sailors formed up, the point moving toward her and the others on the road.

Here it came: the attack that would destroy them.

She gritted her teeth, pushing away tears of sorrow. Zetis still had not returned, so she had doomed him as well as herself, the bulls and jumpers and others that fought beside her.

But she was wrong; the wedge did not attack.

The sailors held their arms out to their sides, demonstrating they did not have weapons in their hands, as they slowly walked forward. Their leader waved a white signal flag. *Could the man in front be their leader? Was he coming to parley?* Indeed, she could make out a swarm of shorter figures—Zetis and his friends, she hoped—who ran like a pack of puppies around the neat column of pirates. *Had her little brother had managed a truce?*

Quiet fell. She could hear the crunch of feet moving in step across the gritty sand as they approached.

She could make out faces now.

She could see that the lead pirate was Tros.

Tros!

A surge of numbness swept over her as he approached, questions flooding her mind, awareness of her misjudgment washing over her like a wave.

Then she got angry.

"You!" She thrust her hayfork at him as if she would impale him upon the wooden tines. He was smiling. His handsome face showed no awe of the bulls, no fear of her. He looked happy to see her, which infuriated her further.

"Kitane!"

"What are you doing? What are you doing here, Tros? Why do you attack us?"

"I'm not attacking," he said in a mild tone. "I'm just protecting myself and my sailors. We are rescuing the goods from the warehouses before Potidas destroys Keftiu like Thera. I came to save you! Come with me, Kit."

Kit could hear the Keftiu beside her muttering at these words.

"Where is Sakusna? Where is my sister?"

Tros' face lost its pleasant expression. His eyes looked sad. His mouth turned down. "I am sorry, Kitane. Mistress Sakusna is dead."

"Dead. Yet you live."

"The volcano killed her," Tros said in a bland tone.

"And yet, you live," Kit repeated.

He shook his head. "She insisted on staying ashore. She refused to leave, though I begged her! The volcano— " his eyes were wide, an expression of awe that made him look very young. "The volcano blew up! It sent waves of fire and ash and stone over us, over all Thera. We were on our ship; I begged her to come!"

Why would her sister have gone ashore to Thera? There was something odd about this.

"Why were you at Thera at all? There is no one there; there is nothing to trade."

"We were— " he broke off and scowled. "We encountered an overloaded boat of clerics. We went to look for other survivors."

"And my sister? Why was she ashore, and no one else?"

"It was dangerous! She had others, clerics helping her, but— " he shook his head. "The wave of fire overwhelmed them." She saw actual tears in his eyes. "There was nothing we could do.

They could not outrun it. They died before our eyes. It was terrible."

"And yet, *you live!*" she screamed.

He stepped back as she leaned over him from Enosidas' back.

"How can you protect me, protect anything, if you could not even save my sister?" She kicked Eno's flanks, and he lunged forward, nearly trampling Tros and the sailors to his left and right sides. Eno kept going. Tros stumbled, was pulled back to his feet by his right-hand man, who grasped his arm, dragging him away from the bull and the angry young woman atop it.

"Kit, I am sorry. I see the end here for Keftiu. The gods have marked your land for destruction. Please join me. We can be safe, we can be happy together."

"You say this when you are killing my people, stealing our trade goods so *you* can be wealthy! Why would I ever join you?"

He moved closer to her again. Eno pawed the earth, eyes on Tros.

"Come to me at dawn. We will leave, *all* my friends will leave your people to die in peace. You and I can be happy and safe and rich *together*, my Kitane."

"They follow you, these thieves and murderers?"

He shook the white flag he held on a smoothly crafted pole. "I am their captain only for now. The coalition will break apart once we depart."

So, he couldn't even guarantee Keftiu's safety if she did go with him to save her people. Once Tros was gone, the other pirates were free to do as they wished—if they weren't already. How good were *pirates* at following a leader?

Then she noticed the man next to Tros wore a wide gold wristband. She felt deep fury wash through her as she recognized some of her father's work. She remembered the piece. He had made it for a friend, a man from Thera.

These pirates hadn't gone to Akrotiri to save anyone. They had gone there just as they had come here: to steal and murder!

In such a rage she could not speak, she screeched without words, kicking Eno forward again. This time the pirates turned and fled back down the road and on to the beach. Kit stopped before she and her bull got too far from safety.

"I will *not* marry you!" she yelled at Tros' back.

Then she turned and flew back uphill, back to her friends in the ruddy sunset light.

How dare he say Keftiu was fallen? How dare he come to rob them, instead of to help!?

The only good news that day was that Zetis had indeed returned, with some dozen or so Keftiu that had been trapped at the third warehouse and on the beach. Kit calmed herself and listened to her little brother brag about their exploits. He was, indeed, a braggart and a mischief-maker. But he had a right to be proud—he was saving people.

Unlike her supposed betrothed. Oh, how could she have chosen Tros? She was as stupid as he was to imagine such a match could have worked!

The bull jumpers led the way to a spot Kitane had chosen for them to rest during the night. From the road, she watched as a line of bonfires came to life on the beach. At least the pirates were civilized enough to hold truce during the night.

Nevertheless, she asked a couple of atomai she did not know to keep an eye on the pirates, promising to send replacements for the watchers as soon as some of the others had had time to eat and rest. They obeyed without question, which gave her pause. How had she become the leader?

The line of helpers from the temple was still arriving, bringing food for the fighters, and someone had even thought to send grain and some quickly-cut grass and herbs for the bulls and donkeys.

Kit made her way to the spot where some priestesses were working on wounded fighters. Others built up a bonfire to burn their dead, at least those they had been able to recover. Kit knew there were bodies lying on the beach that the Keftiu could not reach. *Yet. Perhaps tomorrow....*

The thump of hooves along the packed dirt road captured everyone's attention. "Kitane!" the rider called, slowing her mount.

"I am here," she said, stepping forward.

It was Bee's friend, Nopine. "I was with the caravan your sister takes to Mount Ida," Nopine said. Behind her, Kit could hear the priestesses murmuring at the novitiate's words. "From the road, where it has an unobstructed view of the sea and the port, we saw many more ships arriving. Ships with black sails or black flags."

"More pirates?" Kit asked.

"It seems so," Nopine said.

"Thank you for bringing this warning." Kit thought about Tros' promise to leave with all his "friends" if she would join him. Of course, she could not trust him. He'd lied about Thera. Now he'd lied about leaving in the morning.

Even if he had been truthful, she had to wonder how willing the other pirates would be to follow Tros if it meant leaving behind treasure when they had come all the way from who knew where for the promise of plunder. Surely, they would not be pleased to abandon treasure just because Tros asked them to.

Nopine took the donkey she had ridden over to the area where the other animals were eating. A few were grazing on the scant grass among the rocks of the hill around their camp. The amazing bulls were resting peacefully, one next to the other. Some were lying down, others standing with one cocked hoof resting, the other three legs taking the weight.

Kit walked back to the infirmary area. She was no healer, but she could hold bandages and help pack poultices. She noticed one of the healers was the Priestess Qazipatima. Her sister heard someone approaching and turned.

Kitane did not know what to expect from her sister. They had parted in anger. Now everyone knew that Kit's suitor, Tros, led the attackers. She had betrayed her people—all unwittingly, it was true, but she still felt like a traitor. She had brought this upon them.

Qazi's face was unreadable at first. Her eyes were sad.

"Is there something I can do to help?" Kit offered. *Besides jumping off a cliff,* she thought. But it was too late for that. She must stay alive, stay here and try to fix what she had begun, as well as she could.

"Help me set this man's leg," Qazi said.

Together they straightened the swollen leg. At least no bone showed through, though the shin was clearly crooked and wrong. Someone had given the man an herbal tea mixed with kuzbarah, to help numb pain. He still groaned and clenched his fists as they worked, but they got the limb straight and wrapped firmly to a flat-planed board. It looked like one of the ones Diwoki would use to build or mend his ships. Kit was glad someone from the family could provide some useful help to these people who were innocent and tireless in the defense of their home. Diwoki and Qazi and even Bee helped.

Sakusna was dead. Kit would probably be dead soon as well. Suramarti had made a poor choice in supporting Tros. And it was all Kit's fault.

"You should eat," Qazi said when they were done with the broken leg.

"I had some barley stew," Kit said, thinking of how the cooks had added herbs and a few vegetables to give it some flavor while stretching it as far as they could to feed the many fighters. How much better such a stew tasted when it was made in her mother's kitchen.

She stood up and faced her sister. "Sakusna is dead."

Qazi blinked, then Kit saw tears fill her sister's eyes, and dribble down her perfect cheeks.

Abruptly Kit was also weeping, tears flooding her own eyes and her nose running, deep sadness filling her at their family's loss, and for the attack, and for all that was wrong at Thera and now Keftiu.

And then she was held safe in Qazipatima's arms, her sister's embrace a remembrance of all things good, a promise of all that *could* be, not the sadness that was, but the hope of the future.

Suramarti was strong. Keftiu was strong. Jasasara held them in Her arms.

SCENE 6 — PAIAN SEEING THE WORLD
ǂ¥₸

The sun had left the Keftiu hills and climbed into the sky before Paian awoke. Everyone had been up late the night before preparing for the battle at Amnisos. Runners spread the word through nearby villas. No one had any experience organizing so many people. In the morning volunteers started arriving, but they were not equipped or prepared for battle. Paian had to repeatedly explain the need for supplies and arms.

It was dark by the time each fighter had a ration of barley and some dried fruit. Much of the confusion involved arming the defenders. After much discussion, the men from the fields grabbed rakes and shovels. Some women had slings and loom weights, which made excellent missiles. Potters carried pieces of broken pottery to use as knives or to throw. Paian helped locate weapons, confident with the familiar task of preparing for combat. He carried his short sword and round shield even though he wasn't joining the brigade going to Amnisos. Finally, late in the night, they marched off and Paian finally went to sleep.

The next morning he splashed the sleep from his face and met the Biaja's group in the Suramarti courtyard. Her mother Okune and her aunt Asije had put out a nice breakfast in honor of the delivery of tablets and treasures to the Mount Ida sanctuary. After a breakfast of pita stuffed with revithia, washed down with berry tea, Paian was ready to continue their journey.

Yesterday's travel from Knossos to Suramarti had been warm, too warm. He had hoped to get an early start before the sun was high in the sky, but it had been too late for that. Even with the black clouds, the sun had warmed the day. Paian's skin was lighter than the Keftiu and his neck, shoulders, and arms had turned a bright red. Today, he vowed to wear his hooded robe regardless of the heat.

Biaja strolled around the serving table. She filled her basket with cut peaches and pears, strawberries, and raspberries. The Keftiu, especially the telestai, ate more fruit than his family back home. When Bee reclined on a blanket and casually ate her berries one at a time, Paian realized that when Okune served breakfast, all were expected to be respectful. There would be no hasty exit.

Biaja took a bite of her pear, wiped her chin with her robe, and pondered aloud. "Why is Jura so upset by the attack? Nothing can defeat the bull jumpers. I think he is just trying to impress Kitane."

Ukan nodded. "You may be right. My brother wants to show that he can be as brave as that pirate Tros."

Maza fed herself small bites of cooked barley with her fingers, reminding Paian of a mother bird feeding her baby chicks. "Jura is a strong leader. The atomai will follow him."

Okune handed Ukan a small basket of berries. "My daughter and your brother will stop the pirates. They made a big mistake when they attacked Amnisos."

"For sure, when this is all over, my sister and your brother will both be celebrated as heroes."

Impatiently, Paian prodded them to leave. "Agreed. Meanwhile, we should get started."

Even though the old women from Knossos decided to stay at Suramarti, the continuing group included too many people and donkeys to get a quick start. The telestai further delayed the departure passing around a basin of water to rinse fruit juice from their faces and hands. Just as they were ready, Okune and Asije came running with packages of pistachios, pita, dried boar, and some small pithoi of wine. Like mothers all over the world, they worried their children would starve as soon as they were out of sight. The group dutifully tied the packages to the donkeys and embarked with the sun still at their backs.

Paian thought about his map, but the path was like yesterday. He didn't need to make additional notes. Upon leaving Suramarti, they followed a river bubbling with chilly water. However, when the sun reached to the top of the sky, the group turned and headed south toward Mount Ida, which he could see in the distance, still covered with snow even in the summer.

As they moved away from the Middle Sea, the trail narrowed and became steeper. Paian felt out of place when the Keftiu, with their darker complexions, removed their outer garments and hiked in their loincloths. The exertion of the climb prevented much talk and the midday heat left his hair and robe soaked in sweat. His skin burning from yesterday reminded him to keep his robe around his shoulders and neck. He regretted not soaking it in the refreshing water when they were along the river.

Biaja and Ukan maintained a steady pace. Maza drove the donkeys. He could no longer see the river when they reached a small lake. Maza spoke first. "We usually stop here to water the animals." *Now I see why everyone was pushing ahead. This was the objective.* He was glad for the chance to rest and cool off. He took off his robe and jumped into the lake. The water was so cold that he couldn't breathe. Ukan laughed and pointed to the snow on Mount Ida. "Colder than it looks, isn't it?"

Biaja didn't laugh, but instead gave him a small smile and wrapped him in his sun-warmed robe. Paian appreciated her support. At least it felt like support after Ukan laughed at him. The warm wool rejuvenated him. After he dried, he took out his map. Except for the few trees around the lake, the hillside consisted of low bushes, reminding Paian of the hillsides back home. He marked his map with small circles for the bushes, different from the large circles he had used to show the trees along the path from Knossos to Suramarti. He drew in the tiny outline of the lake.

The air chilled as they climbed higher. The cooler air and a slower pace made the trip more relaxed and pleasurable. In the silence, his thoughts returned to courting in this foreign land. His mind wandered, and he considered the possibility of returning home without a bride. He imagined his mother's disappointment.

In the late afternoon, the party stopped again. On top of a small hill, they opened the packages Okune and Asije had given them. The summer sun had moved to the west, but was still high in the sky. To the south, white ashlar walls shone, accentuating the precision masonry the Keftiu were famous for. They had reached the sanctuary at the base of Mount Ida. The three-story temple stood tall on the stark mountainside, a smaller version of Knossos, which had five stories and a far larger expanse. From their vantage point, he recognized a ceremonial courtyard, aligned in a north-south direction. He took out his map and marked a square to show the location of the temple.

To the north, Thera glowed orange like the inside of a kiln. Black surrounded the remains of the island. The sea and the sky were black and connected by a thick column of ash still rising from the ruined island.

He turned to Biaja. "Isn't that a frightening sight?"

Biaja glanced across the sea. "My aunt Asije had a villa outside Akrotiri, but the priestesses' prophecy warned them, and they left in plenty of time."

"Couldn't Jasasara have just stopped the destruction of Thera?"

"Paian, you don't understand," Ukan explained. "Jasasara doesn't control Potidas, she can only warn the Keftiu. Asije's family evacuated in plenty of time. They are all at Suramarti now. Safe."

Everyone turned back to the south to admire the sanctuary, signaling to Paian that they did not want to talk about Jasasara and Thera. Courtship still occupied Paian's thoughts. "She really doesn't care about poetry, does she?"

Ukan squinted at him. "Are you still thinking about Jasasara, or are you back to Kitane?"

"Uh? Yes. Kit. Kitane."

"I don't understand why you are so interested in writing. Here on Keftiu practical things are more important."

"I am practical." Paian unrolled his map.

Ukan gave a small chuckle. "That's your map? Right? Why would anyone need a map on land? You've never been to Mount Ida, but you had no trouble following the path from Knossos."

Maza added, "I agree with Ukan. I drive donkey trains all over Keftiu and I've never wanted a map."

Biaja pointed to the square he had just added. "Is that drawing of a box the Mount Ida sanctuary? Is that where we are now?"

He smiled. "Yes, and see how the mountainside beyond the temple is covered with pine trees? I am going to add some triangles to signify that forest."

"Clever idea. We will go through that forest to reach the sacred cave where we will store these tablets. The cave is safer than the temple."

They went down the south side of the hill, and arrived at the sanctuary. Several priestesses met them at the Grand Staircase. "Greetings Biaja of Suramarti, novitiate from Knossos."

Paian noticed that she cringed, but couldn't figure out why. Her response didn't give a clue. "Greetings to you. We've had a long journey from Knossos and tomorrow we still must go to the sacred cavern to complete our assignment."

"The hospitality of the sanctuary is open to you."

One priestess turned to Maza. "Welcome back, Maza. Your presence honors us. You know where to stable your animals. They must want to rest."

Maza led the donkeys away.

"We saw a column of smoke from Amnisos. Was there another eruption?"

"Not an eruption. Pirates have attacked Amnisos."

The priestesses all looked surprised, and some looked worried. "Pirates?" they asked as if they didn't believe that was possible.

"But don't worry, my sister and the bull jumpers will take care of them."

The priestesses whispered among themselves.

"Was that the prophecy? Pirates?"

"That isn't right. What should we do?"

"They must talk to the high priestess up at the cave."

A priestess turned to Biaja. "We heard a prophecy of a threat to Amnisos."

Another jumped in. "Something very bad will happen there."

"You must immediately go to the cave and speak to the high priestess. She said nothing about pirates."

"Go now." That priestess ran to Maza shouting, "Don't unload them. Come back. Now."

"Biaja and Ukan, you must leave right away. You can still get to the cave before nightfall."

"What? Why now? Why the rush? I told you we've had a long journey. It is time to rest."

"Don't worry about Amnisos. My brother is there also, and we sent a group of atomai from the villas around Suramarti to help."

Maza returned with the donkeys. "Why are we going right away?" She led the animals to a water trough. "They must drink before we leave. It has been a sweltering day for them. It will not take long."

Beyond the need for urgency, the priestesses did not know any more. In a short while the tired travelers were in the pine forest climbing an even steeper path.

Biaja and Ukan walked in silence, stomping their feet. Paian entertained himself by studying the forest. It had a sweeter smell than the trees on the coast. The sound of songbirds cheered the hike. Biaja and Ukan eventually stopped stomping. Maza sang a happy song about a bobcat that played with its food.

I catch the mouse and let it go, let it go.

It runs away but I am faster, I am faster.

"Shh. Look quietly." Paian spotted a real bobcat hiding in a hole filled with pine needles, just its ears and twitching tail visible. Everyone watched as the cat scampered after a squirrel that was too fast and disappeared up a tree.

"Slow cat," remarked Ukan.

"Fast squirrel," laughed Maza.

The pine trees ended abruptly at a steep slope of bare rock. The snow peaks of Mount Ida were still far above, but he knew they'd arrived. An ancient altar of roughhewn stones stood in front of the cave, black from burnt offerings, and recently used. A priestess built and lit a fire. The visitors stood around for warmth and prayer.

"Welcome us to your sacred womb, Goddess Jasasara."

"Keep us safe."

Biaja added offerings of boars' meat and pistachio nuts to the pyre. Beside the altar stood a Horns of Consecration, twice as high as a person, smoothly finished, and sparkling white.

Paian looked beyond the altar to the cave entrance, marked with a gold labrys on either side. The size of the opening surprised him. The donkeys could easily enter three or four abreast.

Two novitiates with hair shorter than Biaja emerged to greet them, awkwardly running with their arms raised in salute. "Welcome to Jasasara's sacred place. Greetings and blessing of Jasasara to you. Biaja of Suramarti, you honor us. Maza, welcome, as always."

Biaja and Ukan stepped forward and returned the open palm salutes. "Blessings to you also."

"Why are you here so late? You should have supped and slept at the sanctuary. It is getting cold and will be colder soon."

"The Klawiphoros of Knossos ordered me to urgently bring these items here for safe keeping."

"Surely, tomorrow morning would have been soon enough."

Biaja had no ready reply. Ukan explained, "The priestesses at the sanctuary sent us to speak to the high priestess. They would not let us even rest our animals."

The novitiates exclaimed, "Oh, Jasasara save us," and ran back into the cave.

Biaja turned to Paian. "I must wait here for the high priestess. Take some of those bundles of pine branches for light and drive the donkeys into the cave. We must unload their treasures."

Ukan followed. "Maza and I will accompany him and help."

Maza took the lead. "I know my way through the caves. If we work quickly we can return to the sanctuary before dark. The trail is all downhill and sunset is very late in the summer."

The size of the cave and the darkness both surprised Paian. Once inside, his eyes adjusted to the black. Unexpected rock columns hung from the ceiling and similar cylinders seem to grow from the floor. In the firelight, they appeared shiny and multicolored in reds, oranges, and yellows. He had never seen anything like them.

Their torches encased them in a small circle of dull light. He was grateful for Maza, otherwise, he could have gotten lost. He knew that the novitiates had run into the cavern and were bringing the priestess out, but he never saw another person. He was both awed and frightened by the size and strangeness. *Jasasara must be a powerful goddess to have such a home.*

"We'll cross the stream here and follow that path. It is only wide enough for a single donkey."

He looked where she was pointing, but saw nothing, not even shadows.

"You two can unload and I will lead the donkeys to you."

He followed the first donkey through a long tunnel ending at a small niche. It was dry, a perfect place to store tablets and even papyrus. He left some of his tablets and writings on papyrus and promised himself to make a copy of his history and map and return to store it here.

He and Ukan got to work unloading and carefully stacking their cargo.

SCENE 7 — JURA IN THE WILD
|ᴵ |ᶜ

The shepherd ran her staff through the flowers growing at the side of the road. A few bright yellow buttercups were still in bloom, but most flowers had spread their seeds and were dying in the hot, dry summer. Any seeds not eaten by the birds and mice would bloom again when the rains returned next spring. *Jasasara willing*.

Jura looked across the familiar hills. He spotted his aunt's villa. Even with the sun obscured by the angry clouds of ash, the flat roof of the main house shone. His cousin had bragged that the sparkling roof of white sand brought all the way from the beach kept the rooms cooler in the summer. Jura didn't believe this and wondered if such pride had offended Potidas. His aunt's family was typical of the telestai abandoning the traditions. They were more concerned about comfortable bedrooms than sacred shrines.

In another display of pride, his aunt had abandoned the traditional fresco subjects of dolphins, octopi, and tritons that pleased Potidas. Instead, her frescoes featured her and her husband and their children. Images of his aunt even decorated the sacred rhytons used in the ceremonies honoring Jasasara and Potidas. No surprise that Potidas now brought disaster to the Keftiu and Jasasara no longer deigned to protect them.

From this view, Jura also felt some pride for the accomplishments of the telestai. He admired the orderly organization of the villa, which glistened as the sole beacon of civilization enclosed by the wild. He had to look carefully to recognize the small cultivated patches of vegetables and barley, some in bloom with yellow or white flowers. Craft buildings, homes for the atomai, and stables nestled among orchards. Rows of olive trees flashed green and white as the leaves flapped in the breeze. Smaller patches were fruit orchards, which appeared soft and fluffy like green sheep ready for the shearer. The farmed trees blended into the untamed expanse.

226

As a child, he had played hide-and-seek or tag with his cousins there without realizing how the small villa compared to the enclosing hills, like a boat afloat in a green sea of wild forest delineated by crags and creeks. *How was he to find the atomai camping in that vast expanse? Would a shepherd who idolized Kitane more than Jasasara and Potidas know the way? Telestai following atomai. Potidas attacking Keftiu. Where was Jasasara? Why was the world so upside-down?*

"Here is the trail." The shepherd's staff pushed aside some fern fronds uncovering a track of dirt. The staff moved forward showing a path of bare ground through the forest floor otherwise covered with dead leaves. The little party, now just Jura, his steward, and a few atomai turned downhill and walked into the wild. Jura rarely left the wide paths between the villas, except when he joined tree-harvesting teams to select oak trees for roof beams. Now thinking about those previous excursions into the wild, he realized that he had also been following the atomai then. He had been on their paths, with their guides. But not here, not this forest, these wilds.

He had entered an atomai world. An unknown place of mystery. Deeper into the forest, the temperature dropped and everything became vibrantly green. Vines with large green leaves covered the tree trunks. Ferns and flowers encroached on the already narrow trails. Moss covered the rocks. It almost seemed like the air had turned green.

The shepherd turned to address the small group. "The good trail is ending. It is rough and slippery from here. You should take off your sandals."

Jura looked around. He was the only one wearing sandals. He sat on a moss-covered rock and unlaced his sandals from his calves. He tied them together and hung them over his shoulder. The guide had not waited for him, but a creek had slowed her enough for him to catch up. He watched the atomai walk across balancing on the green rocks, placed there for that purpose.

He stepped on one rock to test it. It was too slippery. He already had his sandals off, so he just walked into the creek and placed his hands on the stepping-stones to maintain his balance as he bent over and waded across. It wasn't elegant, but he didn't want to risk slipping and falling into the cold creek.

On the other side, the only way to get out of the creek channel was for him to climb up a dead tree. Kano had splashed through the creek and leaped from the channel. She looked down at Jura, wagging her tail in encouragement. She had already explored the creek and was eager to move forward. Kano was more prepared for this adventure than Jura. A couple of atomai interlocked their hands to make a step for him and get him started. Once he'd taken that first step, he completed the remaining ascent on his own, feeling a little less awkward, but realizing how much he depended on the atomai in so many small and large ways.

The trail never turned into a proper path, and several times he silently prayed to Jasasara for protection. He knew wild cats might be in the trees, scorpions on the ground, and snakes could be anywhere. He was beyond any chance to turn around and return to the Mount Ida path. He followed and prayed.

As they continued, he got better at fording creeks, climbing dead trees, and sliding down moss-covered crags.

"Blessing of the Goddess."

"Blessing to the Goddess to you."

They left a grove of vine-covered trees and found themselves in a grassy glen. Black clouds still shrouded the sun, but compared to the depth of the wild, it was painfully bright. Jura shaded his eyes with a large leaf and looked around. There were hundreds and hundreds of atomai. Too many to count.

The small valley was close enough to the coast to feel a sea breeze, but still within the fertile hills. He could see two creeks with running water even though it was summer. To no one in particular, he asked, "Does this place have a name?"

A small child pulled on his robe. "Gazi. This is Gazi."

Jura repeated, "Gazi," and marveled at an entire village in the wild, near to Tylissos, but one he'd never known.

Everyone else ignored him. Telestai were not important in Gazi. They were happy to see the shepherd. The woman told them about the bull jumping, mostly Kitane's performance and her successful challenge to save the noble animals. She didn't mention how Jura's bull replaced the trained-animal sacrifice.

Eventually, the storytelling moved on to the battle of Amnisos. The narrative again concentrated on Kitane, as Jura had come to expect.

"She rode Enosidas across the beach, shouting orders and defeating pirates."

When the cheering died down, Jura spoke up, "She sent us here to recruit more fighters."

The crowd noticed him and backed off. Some of those farthest away, turned to walk into the wild, chatting among themselves about their reasons for leaving: the prophecy about buildings falling down and killing atomai.

The talk discouraged volunteers.

"The battle is probably over by now."

A small earthquake shook the camp.

"The prophecy says we need to stay in the wild."

"Forget pirates, Potidas is coming for the Keftiu."

He tried again. "From the Mount Ida path, we saw more pirates sailing to attack Amnisos."

The shepherd dutifully agreed. She tried to help. "Kitane said she didn't trust the pirates and requested help, our help."

By this time, the audience had scattered. Only half the people remained in the open field. Jura knew he needed to do something else, but didn't know what. He prayed to Jasasara for inspiration.

A small group from Tylissos came up to Jura and his steward. They offered to help Kitane defend Amnisos. He thanked them. "Blessings of the Goddess!" But he knew he needed to recruit more than this small group.

The sun had dropped low in the sky, the community had broken into small groups for the evening meal. The central fire heated many saj, mostly simple pottery domes with no decorations. Children lined up to bake bread.

Jura asked his steward why they didn't use bronze saj. "Don't the ceramic domes break a lot?"

His steward replied, "Of course they break, that is the nature of pottery, but atomai cannot afford bronze."

Jura wondered if the telestai could pass older domes to the atomai instead of melting them down. He recalled that Kitane had mentioned something like this and wondered if some of her ideas about villa management might deserve more consideration.

The center of the fire contained a pile of cooking rocks. A wise woman controlled access to the hot stones. Before anyone could add a stone to the collection, she examined it.

Again, Jura had to turn to his steward. "Why are they baking rocks? What is that old woman doing?"

The steward smiled. "Keep watching, you'll see. The grandmother is checking that they are dry and without cracks."

Jura gave him a puzzled look.

"Remember that explosion, many seasons ago, when an atomai house caught fire and two children were burned?"

Jura frowned. "Was that from cooking rocks?"

"Yes. A small child. A big rock. Cracked and wet."

Jura watched pairs of children carry baskets with barley, spices, and vegetables to the creek to fill with water. The tightly woven baskets surprised Jura when they held water without any leaks. The children carried the mixture to the fire where two older children used long sticks to place hot rocks into the water. After an initial rush of steam, the stones settled to the bottom of the basket to cook the soupy stew while the children stirred the mixture with wooden spoons.

Jura understood their choices this time. *The baskets last longer than pottery, since they can drop heavy rocks into them without causing damage.* Here was another opportunity to extend the lifetime of old bronze utensils—the atomai could use some bronze cooking pots. Though the baskets certainly worked well, being able to put pots directly onto the fire would mean cooking more stew, more quickly.

The smell of spicy vegetables and roasted meat filled the air. Everywhere, children ran around bringing water from the nearby creeks and carrying cups and bowls of food to the others. Jura noticed a variety of fruits and vegetables, with a plentiful supply of revithia and barley.

He looked to his steward as if to ask, what do we eat? The steward went over to the atomai from Tylissos and returned with a dinner invitation. Jura joined them, sitting on the ground and sharing their meal. He noticed some of the stolen supplies that he intended for the bull-jumping ceremony at Knossos, but didn't say anything. He was sure Kitane wouldn't have mentioned it. And the foodstuffs hadn't been needed at the ceremony. It was better spent here.

After everyone had eaten, he tossed a meaty boar rib to Kano and turned to his group. "Can you add to the cooking fire to make a bonfire? I'd like to talk to everyone."

Mostly the Tylissos children responded, running in every direction to collect twigs and branches. Soon, the other children joined in the game and the central fire burned high and bright and attracted the adults.

Jura thought about Kitane and the atomai. *Jasasara, what shall I say?* He stood tall and began, "I know your prophecy warned you to stay in the wild until after the earthquakes. That was a good prophecy."

The crowd got quiet, but still he had to shout. The fire crackled; whispers added up to a big noise with so many people gathered around.

He walked around the fire to draw everyone's attention. "But how do we know when the earthquakes are over? Maybe they are already over?"

Jura removed his robe and spun it around his head. The smooth linen shimmered in the firelight.

"The earthquake came for Thera."

He increased the speed of twirling his robe, fanning the flames, and sending a mist of sparks into the air.

"The earthquake took Thera."

The flashes died out.

"Now Thera is gone."

He pointed to the black haze above them.

"That is all that remains."

He looked to the crowd. Every eye stared at him.

"The earthquakes are over. The bull jumpers have appeased Potidas. Kitane has calmed Potidas. You have followed your prophecy."

The tall bonfire collapsed, again splashing sparks into the air.

"The only threat to Keftiu is from pirates. Jasasara protects us, but we must do our part. We will be fighting out in the open, not in the buildings at Knossos!"

The crowd cheered.

"Chase the pirates away."

"Jasasara protects us."

"We must help Kitane."

Jura was proud to hear how many shouted Kitane's name.

With the crowd enthusiasm high, Jura felt the time was right.

"On to Amnisos!"

"On to Amnisos," the crowd repeated.

"Defend Kitane and Keftiu!"

The crowded was on their feet, cheering and waving their arms.

Jura turned to his steward and the shepherd. "We should head out to Amnisos immediately. Is there a trail to Amnisos from here?"

He wrapped his robe back over his shoulders and sat down to remove his sandals again. His steward conversed with the shepherd and a few others. "Follow them, they know the fastest way."

"Creek."

"Creek."

"Creek."

As each obstacle approached, the warning passed down the line of marchers. The leaders carried bundles of burning branches to light the vanguard. Shouting children ran back and forth collecting twigs and scaring away snakes, cats, and anything in their path.

"Climb this tree."

"Climb up here."

"This goes up."

Jura was grateful for his training in the daylight. He climbed dead trees, walked across stepping-stones, and slid down moss-covered rocks with confidence.

He felt sure they would be to Amnisos by daybreak. More importantly, he had recruited the people Kitane needed to win the battle. Telestai were leaders. It didn't matter whether he could find his way in the wild or even fight pirates. After the battle victory—because of these atomai—Kitane would be ready to marry a leader instead of a pirate. They would oversee Suramarti together. Their atomai would cook with bronze.

SCENE 8 — BIAJA AT MT. IDA CAVERNS
𐘂𐘼𐙇

The coolness of the caves helped refresh the workers, but Biaja could still feel time slipping away as they stashed the last of the treasures from Knossos into safety. She stood just inside the entrance, out of the sun, out of the way, hands folded as she waited. Paian raised a quizzical eyebrow as he passed. She shrugged, exasperated.

"Someone's supposed to be meeting with me here about a prophecy. After all that rush to come straight here, it doesn't seem so important after all, since I have been waiting so long."

"Do you believe these Seers, these priestesses who tell the future?" Paian asked.

"They have holy visions, sent by the Goddess. The visions are often warnings sent to protect us. But we must interpret them, and sometimes *we* are not right."

"We do not have such things."

"Jasasara protects Keftiu. Perhaps she does not reach so far as your home, the land of Hellenes." She smiled at the fair-skinned man. "Who is it you worship?"

He smiled back. "Several gods: War, Commerce, Underworld. And Love." His smile turned shy.

Was he flirting with her?

Had he given up on Kitane, who had, in fact, ignored him, or treated his endearing poetry as a sort of joke?

She smiled back, her hand dropping artfully to her throat, hoping to draw his attention more fully to *her*. Then she felt the dragonfly necklace that rested against her skin.

"Oh! Paian, can you please put this in a safe place inside, perhaps with some of the Suramarti pithoi? I forgot to leave it at home, and I cannot keep wearing and forgetting it."

"Of course." He waited while she fished a soft chamois bag out of her carry sack. She emptied the simple and inexpensive jewelry —a seed necklace, one of her seashell rings—out of it. She put the dragonfly necklace gently inside, then rolled up the bag, letting the folds of soft leather enfold the necklace. She tied it shut into a neatly wrapped package and gave it to Paian.

Maza exited the cave and gave Bee an annoyed look as she went to the donkey train for another load. "Could use some help," she muttered. Ukan came out and moved up behind Maza.

"I'm here," he said, obviously thinking Maza had been speaking to him, not Paian.

Paian cleared his throat, then went to the last donkey in line and pulled out a heavy sack of tablets. He cradled the sack in his arms, the wrapped necklace lying safely on top. He nodded to Biaja, gave her a sweet smile, and disappeared back down the cave path.

Bee was left to worry and wonder what the rush-and-wait was about. What prophecy was the priestess going to share? Was it about her mother? Okune was still safe, as far as she knew. Kit was marrying a pirate, but she was now *fighting* pirates—could it be about that?

And no one had heard from Sakusna or Diwoki for an entire season. Was the prophecy about them? Praying her family was safe, Biaja continued to wait, wishing she had a spindle and some wool to keep her hands busy.

The priestess in charge of the caves finally arrived to speak with her. She arrived breathless. It had taken her a very long time to come, and Biaja could not imagine how far down into the caverns she must have been.

"Suramarti," she said in greeting. "I was consulting with our Seer," she said, panting for breath. "Trying to clarify the vision. She has proclaimed an immediate danger to Amnisos and all upon that shore!"

"What? Why?"—and why had it taken so long to get the message up to her after being told to rush up here, then wait?

"We aren't finished unloading," Maza said, back again. Ukan looked from Bee to Maza to the priestess and back.

"You!" the priestess pointed to Biaja. "You should leave immediately to warn Amnisos!" The priestess clutched her chest, still gasping. "These others can go at their own pace."

"What is the danger?" Bee asked, signaling Maza to bring her one of the donkeys for riding.

"This is not known. All that is known is devastation to the north shore. She *saw* Amnisos in ruins, but we believe from her words there is danger to the entire northern edge of Keftiu."

"Well, we already know pirates are attacking Amnisos. Is that what she saw?"

The priestess shook her head. Her already disheveled hair fell out of its loose bun and cascaded down her shoulders. She pushed it back impatiently, reminding Bee of her sister.

"Oh, Goddess, Kitane is there, fighting the pirates."

"Go! Tell them to get to Knossos *now*. Knossos will survive!"

Survive *what?*

It would be good to know this, but Bee knew she must deliver the warning she had received, not expect more details. Often enough the visions never became clear to the priestesses who had them. She just had to trust they had done their best with this one.

Maza led up one of the bigger donkeys, a tall one that already had the narrow strap around its belly for her feet, and reins for her hands. Bee looked around for a stool or pithoi she could stand on to mount, but instead Maza linked her hands together to fashion a step. Bee kicked off her sandals, and Maza boosted her onto the donkey's back.

"We will go down to Tylissos," Ukan said, moving up next to her, "to warn my family."

"Please tell Suramarti as well," Biaja said, kicking the donkey into motion.

"*Run!*" the priestess called. "It is soon! Very soon!"

Biaja sat up tall, looking for a path through the trees in the dark. She had thought the shortcut behind the Suramarti and Tylissos villas would be faster than the winding road, but the darkness beneath the trees was more intense than she had bargained for. The sure-footed donkey still trotted, though it was breathing heavily, and she knew they must stop for a short rest soon. The journey would be even slower—perhaps fatally slow—if she had to abandon the animal and finish the downhill race on foot.

When they came to the creek, she knew they only had a short distance remaining before they rejoined the road to Knossos. And they must drink. She dismounted, sliding down the animal's sweat-soaked side. They both drank from the creek, stomachs complaining about the icy water and no food.

She stood on the fallen log ready to mount when the earth shook. The quaking went for a long time. It was not horribly strong, like some of the ones had been earlier in the spring. But it felt like it lasted forever. The donkey's ear's twitched, and it breathed through wide-open nostrils, foam marking its mouth and muzzle. The shaking stopped. She mounted, kicked the animal into a jagged gait faster than a trot, but not quite a gallop.

They ducked between trees, moving as fast as Bee felt they could. Her mount caught a foot, and she looked down to see what had happened, but it recovered, and she raised her head back up just in time to connect with an enormous low branch. She saw it, she hit it, she was swept off the donkey's back, and she fell into darkness.

Her eyes opened into smoky daylight, a weird sound near her head. She sat up, felt her stomach heave, and she scrambled to vomit as far from herself as she could, a squirrel watching her with beady eyes. It chittered at her, offering helpful advice, no doubt.

Feeling slightly better, she used a sapling to pull herself to her feet.

What was she doing here in the woods?

Then she saw the donkey cropping grass in an open glade between the trees. She was riding to…Amnisos. Yes. To warn…to warn everyone to flee to the safety of Knossos as quickly as possible! Horror chilled her skin. How long had she been unconscious? Was it already too late?

She made her way to the donkey. It looked at her, mouth full of grass, chewing calmly. She led it to a small rock outcrop, managed to mount without vomiting again, though her stomach was very unhappy. They moved off slowly, then back to a trot when they got to the road, her head splitting anew with each thump of hoof onto the pounded dirt of the road. It felt as if some drummer was using her head as his drum pounding with his fists.

Bee could hear an awful silence in the air: no bird calls, no insect sounds, only the clopping of her donkey and a breeze through the leaves of the oak trees nearby. She turned left at the junction to Amnisos, away from the road to Knossos and presumed safety.

Was she too late? Did the strange quiet mean the destruction had already happened? She asked the donkey for a faster pace.

She passed a small camp where some clerics and priestesses tended to Keftiu who looked to have been wounded. Atomai were cooking, huge kettles braced over fires.

"Hello!" she yelled. "The Seer of Mt. Ida has spoken: you must flee to Knossos. *Now!* Everyone go!"

Startled, the people in the camp looked up and called questions, but she was already past them, heading down to the beach and her sister. Praying she was still in time.

SCENE 9 — KITANE AT AMNISOS

ᐱᏟᏆ

A surge of pirates pushed the line of bulls back up the road a dozen cubits before Kitane directed Enosidas to kick the attackers in front of them. Other bull jumpers saw what she and Eno were doing and did likewise, turning the attack back onto the pirates. They managed to push the line further down the hill than they had started, but Kit refused the bait to follow them further. She was quite certain they'd be quickly encircled if they ventured onto the beach.

She sat a moment in the morning sun, trying to get a sense of what was happening. The pirates seemed afraid to bunch up in groups—probably because the bulls just had a better kicking target when they did so. Thus, most of the attackers came at them one at a time. They could hold, if this continued. But Kit suspected once their leader cleared the beach, he would send his entire ragged army up the road. Then her group would be overwhelmed, no matter where they stood.

Zetis had managed to clear a path for some wounded defenders to escape. They went to the campsite where temple healers worked. Zetis told her of pirates who buried themselves in the sand, then attacked Keftiu from the back. Some groups of pirates lurked behind buildings, and when the defenders passed by, attacked—again from the back, like cowards. It seemed they feared the Keftiu, at least to some degree. She could use that.

Other fighters joined Kit's group, extending the line of defenders downhill a ways into the swamp. She took advantage of a pause in the pirate's attack to search the beach and lines of warehouses for her people. Were any surrounded, needing rescue?

Her stomach growled again. She ignored her hunger, but soon she would not be able to ignore Eno's, nor his thirst. Brackish swamp water in the estuary was not going to serve. The animals must have proper care. The temple had promised food and water.

And where were the reinforcements they'd been promised? It felt like Jura had been gone for days.

The pirates pushed again, a wedge driving up the road, trying to split her line of bulls in two. Wishing the road was wide enough that they could simply surround this batch of pirates, Kit used Enosidas' bulk to stop the attackers' progress, standing sideways across the road. She jabbed her hay fork at the raiders' faces and chests. Between the bulls, she could see the king's shielded soldiers also stabbing with their long spears.

Several pirates fell, breaking the shape of their attack wedge. Abruptly they broke off and retreated down the road. Kit felt wetness against her leg. When she looked down, she gasped at blood streaming down Eno's shoulder. During the melee, someone must have struck a blow to Eno that she didn't see. She called two of the other bull riders to take over and retreated. The bleeding had to be stopped. If it was bad enough, she would leave Eno at the camp—he had been valiant and dutiful during this fight, for which he had never been trained.

He trusted her. That was a trust she would not, could not betray.

When Kitane had cleaned the blood away, she could see that a sharp weapon had broken Eno's skin, but had not penetrated deeply. She dipped a clean rag in a pithoi of drinking water and pressed it to the wound.

One of the guasileus' wife's embroidery ladies had been pressed into service as a medic's aid, her fine tools and golden threads replaced with strong bronze needles and waxed linen.

"Do you think you can stitch this closed?" Kit asked her.

The woman glanced at the bull, then at Kit, then back at Eno, obviously unwilling to work on an animal.

"He has been a hero in this fight," Kit said, letting her opinion of the woman show. What had *she* contributed to the greatness of Keftiu? A few ornate gowns? Enosidas was saving Knossos.

"I— Will he bite?"

Oh. She was afraid of Eno, that was all.

"I have asked him to be still," Kit said. "But perhaps we could rub some ground kuzbarah to help numb the skin first...?"

The woman nodded and went to ask one of the Temple healers to help.

Enosidas stood stoically, allowing the medicines, the cleaning, and the stitching. He rolled his eyes to look at Kit at one point, and she used her fingers to comb his forelock. She ran her strong, sure hands along his neck, and stroked his wide forehead and nose, murmuring endearments the whole time. Eno had not asked for all this; he had been trained to run and turn and let her jump at him, dance on his back, compete in tournaments. This was so far beyond his training, Kit could only believe Jasasara had put her hand on the bull—this one, and all of them—to protect Her land, Her people.

Kit gave him grain and plenty of water, while she ate cold cooked revithia, enriched with cheese and fiery spices.

Then she mounted Enosidas and they returned to the fight.

Just as she was returning to the road, she saw a welcome face leading a huge mob of fighters. Jura had brought hundreds of atomai: the reinforcements had arrived!

She laughed and leaned over to put her hands on Jura's shoulders. "I am so glad to see you!"

"What shall we do, then?"

"Let me see what is happening on the beach. We need to be sensible about where to attack."

Jura nodded, his mouth taut, a light of ferocity glowing deep in his eyes.

On the beach, Kit could see the pirates had surrounded a Keftiu contingent. She studied the path they could take from the road to the defenders. It might be a trap, but she thought with so many Keftiu eager to fight, they ought to be able to get down there and rescue their countrymen and get safely back.

Yes, she would use the line of bulls to clear a swath through the attackers, also ensuring there were no pirates hidden in the sand or behind warehouses. If the pirates were a little bit afraid of the sturdy defenders, they were a lot afraid of the big bulls. This should work.

She explained to Jura and the atomai what they were doing. Then she led the attack.

Once on the beach, the bull riders directed their animals to stretch out in a line, with a double spear-length between them. They rode across the sand, the thunder of hooves accompanied by the thud of atomai feet. A few soldiers with double-circle shields were interleaved with the bulls, a few more flanked the mob of atomai defenders.

They reached the entrapped Keftiu with ease, as the pirates fled to either side. The atomai behind Kit kept a file three or four people deep, as she had asked, to help prevent the pirates from encircling her attack group. They absorbed the previously entrapped defenders, and kept going, toward the wall, and the group of adult Keftiu who were still prisoners behind it.

Some bull riders and some atomai fighters darted off to the sides now and then to put down the few pirates brave enough to attack. Like a line of sentinel stones, the atomai behind the attack group formed up along a pathway back to their camp and Knossos, protecting their line of retreat.

A pirate ship exploded into flames on the south side of the peninsula. Kit nodded. That was Zetis and his group, doing their job. Shortly afterward, a pirate vessel on the north went up in smoke as well.

Kit used her rake to shove a pirate away from Jura and his steward. There were fewer and fewer pirates between them and the wall. She saw a group of pirates flee down the beach, and at least one black-flagged ship had pushed off and was running full sails away from the Keftiu shore.

One of the other bull riders shoved through the gate in the wall, a shield-carrying Keftiu warrior right beside him. They pushed the pirates back, who suddenly found themselves trapped between the attacking force and the prisoners.

As if mimicking the rumble of the bulls, the ground shook. It kept on shaking, and then Kit realized it was a quake, not part of her attack. It was a long, slow grinding sort of quake, not terribly strong, but it lasted several moments longer than usual.

Then all the pirates she could see on the peninsula were gone: either dead or in flight to their ships—or anyone's ship, Kit supposed. Had the earthquake scared them, or Kit and Jura?

Jura was on the ground, removing the thongs from around one prisoner's feet. Atomai helped free telestai, telestai freed atomai.

Was it possible they were winning?

Just as she felt they could celebrate, she saw two things: Jura was on the ground, but he wasn't freeing anyone. He was leaning against his steward, a raw bloody wound in his shoulder pouring blood down his chest. Then she looked up to make sure their retreat was still clear and saw her little sister slapping a lathered donkey's sides so it would run faster. Biaja's face was terrified.

Jura was being attended to, so Kit turned Eno and rode back a few paces to meet her sister.

"Go back!" Biaja cried. "You must take all our people back to Knossos!"

Kit waved a hand at the nearly empty beach. "But, we are winning."

"Amnisos is not safe! The Mt. Ida priestess has seen it! You *must* leave now, Kitane. Please."

Kit could see more pirate ships lifting anchor or heading out to sea. Other fighters stood in defensive lines in front of their ships. There were few pirates to defend against at the moment—they were fleeing. Perhaps they knew Amnisos was not safe also, somehow.

Jura's dog was barking her head off, darting toward Jura, then running back up the beach. When its master did not follow, the dog kept barking.

Well, Jura was wounded. She supposed the dog made sense, urging him to retreat.

"Get everyone back to the camp," she yelled out, waving her arms and pointing up the road.

"No, Kit. It's not safe there, either. You have to go all the way to Knossos."

"Why?"

Bee groaned and shrugged her shoulders. "I don't know— She couldn't see— It's not safe here. It's not safe at the camp. Knossos is safe."

Beneath her, Kit could feel Eno's restive feet. He pawed the sand. In fact, all the animals seemed distressed. She had thought it was the smell of blood, but now it seemed to be more than that.

She turned to Jura's steward. "Please help me get him up here. We will go as far as the camp for now, to tend the wounded. Everyone else can go on to Knossos if they like."

It took several men to load Jura up onto Eno's back. He slumped against her. She clasped him with one arm, careful to not touch his wound.

Beside her, Biaja's donkey staggered, then dropped to the sand, Bee rolling off in a graceless heap as the animal collapsed.

"Oh, I have killed the poor thing," she said. She looked up at Kit, face pale, eyes wet. "We *must* leave."

They began moving off the beach, up the road toward the campsite, many atomai running faster than the tired and in some cases injured bulls. Most of the donkeys refused to carry anyone, braying and running in circles, or zig-zagging across the beach. Beside Eno's feet, Jura's dog continued to bark as it trotted along with Biaja and Jura's steward.

Kit glanced back to be sure the pirates hadn't decided to counterattack, but she saw very few of them, those few scurrying onto a boat or wandering aimlessly on the beach. Instead she saw that the choppy waves of the Middle Sea brought small floating stones to shore. Whatever that was, it didn't seem good. She urged Eno to a faster pace.

When they arrived at the campsite, she could see that everyone had already fled. Beside her, Biaja now rode with Jura's steward on one of the Tylissos donkeys they'd managed to capture and calm.

"Kit, we must move on to Knossos!"

"Yes, I see," she said. There was no help for Jura here. But would he survive the rest of the way to the temple?

She murmured a prayer to Jasasara. Jura could not die, not now. She did not know if her furious desire could help convince the Goddess or not. But what good would it do either Jasasara or Potidas to let this devoted man leave the world?

"Please," she murmured and urged Eno to walk faster.

SCENE 10 — TROS AFTER KEFTIU RETREATS

The pirates' shouts of victory overwhelmed the roar of the surf crashing against the fleet of ships docked on the promontory. The Keftiu had abandoned their makeshift weapons and some of their donkeys. They carried off the wounded, but a few dead remained after their hasty retreat.

The orderly battle lines disintegrated without an opponent. Some pirates reverted to looting the warehouses and collecting booty discarded in the sand. A few ships that had retreated now returned, or paused in their positions, as if waiting to see what would happen. Very few fighters chased the Keftiu up the road to Knossos. Tros jumped on a donkey and crashed through the jubilant mob. "Stop. Stop. Don't be fools. Don't follow! It's a trap!"

He pushed aside fighters until he reached the front of the group. "Stop. Look around you." He pointed to the narrow path. "Can you see that cliff on one side and the marsh on the other?"

The pirates paused and became quiet.

"Undoubtedly many Keftiu are up there with missiles to rain down. That marsh might harbor crocodiles and venomous snakes. If we rush into their trap, we will be massacred."

The pirates drifted back to the beach.

"We will conquer the great temple, but not like this. I will meet with the captains and we will plan our assault."

He saw a few more of his allies boarding their ships or in some cases, even sailing away. He shook his fist at them. Cowards.

"Tomorrow, Knossos will be ours!" The pirates cheered and returned to looting the warehouses. "We have won!"

During the night, he woke to a roiling sea.

He could feel his ship heeling over, the waves pushing it. It rolled over steeply onto its side, tossing some of the sleeping crew onto the deck, or overboard into the rough water. Was it going to capsize?

What a time for a storm to strike. Well, there was no need to ride this one out. He shouted, "Quit! Quit! All overboard. Head for high land!"

Only the full cargo of stolen goods kept the ship steady enough to roll back upright. Another enormous wave rocked the ship. Tros reflected on his good fortune to have fully loaded his ship, but bad luck to have docked pointed into the promontory so the onrushing surf pummeled the broad side of the ship. Along with his crew, he splashed through the rising water, up the shrinking beach. They scrambled atop the warehouses.

From their safe vantage point, they watched the headland and the beach disappear in the advancing sea. Water climbed Sail Rock, submerging its base, swamping the peninsula and the wall.

This looked like no storm Tros had ever seen. And the stars had shone in the *Dolphin* constellation at dawn: there were no storms under that sign throughout the Archipelago.

Stragglers swam to the warehouses. A few ships capsized, and the waves swept some men out to sea. Tros looked around. All his crew had made it to the rooftop. The sea tossed his ship, but it did not overturn.

"The gods smile on us! We are safe and our ships also."

The men cheered. Everyone watched the spectacle, waiting for the waves to subside. Tros did his best to hide his concern. The Middle Sea was not behaving right. What was it going to do next?

The rising water stopped, just before splashing into the lowest warehouses. The sea calmed, and the men turned their attention toward Knossos, fantasizing about the treasures of gold, fine garments, and decorated ceramics they would carry to Kmt.

After seeing Potidas destroy Thera, some waves and rough seas did not frighten his sailors. They laughed and bragged to the others.

"On Thera, Potidas threw an entire island at us!"

"This is just water. If it is not aflame, we won't worry."

"Burning rocks as big as bulls dropped from the sky."

Then abruptly the sea turned silent. The water receded. The beach reappeared. The dark wet sand drained and the beach lightened in the rising sun. Then, the bay drained as though a gigantic whale had sucked the sea away. The octopi wriggled in the air. The seals feasted on their helpless prey uncovered as the protecting sea abandoned the shallows. Seabirds feasted on flailing fish and sea urchins.

The ships all rolled over on their sides as the subsiding sea left them on damp land, their oars piled up into jumbles of sticks. The grinding noise as they scraped against sand and rocks made Tros grit his teeth. Pithoi rolled off the ships. Some ships, unfortunately docked above huge rocks, rocked back and forth until they broke in two.

The men watched in silence. Tros had never seen anything like this. He didn't know what to call it or what to expect next. He stationed himself at the edge of the building, curled his fingers to better see in the distance, and stood watch.

For the longest time, nothing happened.

Then Tros spied a wave.

It was not really a wave. It was a wall of water; a wall of water rushing toward the shore. One by one, the others noticed, until all the men were at the edge of the roof watching the Middle Sea rushing at them.

Tros expected the water wall to collapse and crash like a big wave, but the wave did not break. Instinctively, he backed away from the edge.

When the wave reached the beach, he realized he was looking *up* to see it. It towered above them. The wave was taller than the warehouse, taller than them, taller than a ship's mast—and it still hadn't broken.

He thought about running, but he could see it was far too late.

The wave finally broke.

The wall of water descended upon him and his men.

Tros had experienced many waves crashing over his head. The important thing was not to panic. As he watched the foamy water, he took three short breaths and just before it hit him, he took a deep gulp of air and held it. He sealed his mouth and nose with his hands, curled his legs close to his body, and braced for the impact.

The crush of water tumbled him around and around. His shoulder hit the roof. He tensed the joint. It was painful, but not broken. Another spin and his knee hit something hard. This time the leg felt damaged—broken or dislocated.

Then he was in deeper water. He was disoriented, unsure of which way to swim to get air. His lungs felt like they would burst. He knew to keep his mouth closed until he reached the surface.

His arms worked perfectly. A little sore, but capable of pulling him through the water. His legs dragged behind him. He looked around and saw a light. He swam in that direction, confident that he'd find air.

He thought about the riches he'd bring to Kmt and the beautiful women there. With newfound strength, his arms propelled him toward the surface. He had no difficulty holding his breath.

He kept swimming. It seemed a very long way up to reach the light. When he finally reached the light, he took a deep breath.

He realized too late he was still underwater. He was drowning. He struggled again to reach the surface.

After a while, he stopped trying.

SCENE 11 — KITANE AT KNOSSOS

彡[I

Kit kept checking: Jura was still alive, groaning and bleeding, when they finally reach Knossos. His steward and a couple clerics helped get him down off Eno's back. A healer took a quick look at him, instructed one of the clerics to press a clean, dry scrap of linen against the wound, and then moved on to other wounded. Kit took that as a good sign: Jura would survive. She did not stop her prayers, though.

She used her knees to guide Enosidas out to the paddock area, where a few bulls were already eating or being tended to by healers. Eno was quivering, in dire need of water and food and rest.

Exhausted, she slid down off Eno's back. She poured water from a pithos into a huge low bowl for him to drink. She quickly checked him over. There were no further wounds. The stitched cut on his shoulder looked a little red beneath the fur, but it was not swollen or hot, so she felt safe to leave him with a full sack of grain and fresh hay.

She made her way to the roof of the temple, where she saw a crowd of people including the guasileus, his wife and son, and her sister, Qazipatima, among them, along with her cousin and aunt. They were all looking north.

Feeling all the weary weight of the last two days on her body, she shuffled her feet over the cool stone toward the edge.

Indeed, they could see the Middle Sea. They could see Potidas' rage swelling the water, heaving in the shallow bay at Amnisos.

Many of the pirate boats had either returned or never fled: the shore was dotted with shadowy ships. Sunrise lit the sand of the beach at Amnisos a gory red, as though it was bleeding.

Bleeding like so much of Keftiu, she thought. So many people died, atomai and telestai alike. She was too exhausted to feel rage at Tros and his people—it was more like disgust after what the Keftiu had gone through at the hands of these supposed partners.

Clearly the man only cared about gold, completely disregarding the human cost of acquiring it.

The Sea moved strangely, catching her eye.

Then it retreated. It moved faster than any tide, sucking back off the sand, the rocks. Finally, the muddy sand at the bottom of the bay was revealed in the dying light as the water moved away.

As if Potidas took a deep breath, there was a moment of motionless silence.

Then the water came back.

The worst thunder of the worst storm and the strongest rumbling of the biggest earthquake accompanied the huge wave. Kit covered her ears with her hands, but it did not help: the sound was in the air and in the ground and in her bones. Knossos shook as she did.

At Amnisos, Kit thought she recognized Tros' ship being pushed toward the cliffs below Knossos. It disappeared, as did all signs of pirates, or indeed any ships at all. All they could see from the temple's rooftop was heaving water. It came toward them.

It kept coming toward them. She could see the now-shallow front edge of the wave as it flooded up the river, coming halfway up the height of the viaduct that marked the road to Suramarti.

The water kept coming, though it did slow down to a creep. It became shallower. It flooded the South House, the propylaea and processional path. She could see the gleam of water as it slid over the sand and stone of the Central Court.

She became alarmed for the safety of Eno and the other bulls in the paddock by the customs house at the north end of the temple grounds, but by then the water was only a hand's width deep. She saw a pair of guards wading through it from the Grand Staircase toward the customs house. The water was at their ankles.

The animals should be safe, unless Potidas had another wave coming. But the priestess had said Knossos would be safe, hadn't she?

She looked back out at the north edge of their land. Beyond the cliff that dropped off between Knossos and Amnisos beach, there was only roiling water. Sail Rock had disappeared. Water swirled and tumbled, pieces of junk rolling to the surface, too distant to recognize, but larger than seashells and dolphins. Probably boats. Mostly pirate boats, but also Keftiu trading ships, the few that had not been fired into ash by the pirates.

Praying Diwoki was in some safe harbor far away, Kit at last turned to her family. Beside her, Biaja wiped tears from her cheeks and essayed a half-smile at Kit. They hugged, then Kit felt another pair of arms around them, the rich scent of myrrh identifying Qazipatima.

Over Bee's shoulder, Kit was amazed to see her cousin Isari holding hands with—was it?—yes, the son of the guasileus. She couldn't even remember the young man's name, but he was clearly enraptured by Isari. Kit grinned, finding a small bit of pleasure in the day.

That meant she would have Jura all to herself, after all.

"I suppose I needn't say that I have changed my mind," she murmured to her sisters.

They stepped back from each other and Bee and Qazi eyed her warily.

"I will certainly not be marrying Tros!"

For some reason, they all found this funny. Perhaps in relief at surviving Potidas' giant wave, or the pirate attack, or racing down the mountain to give warning. They began to laugh. They laughed and did not stop until the sun fell below the horizon.

Act V — Weddings

Scene 1 — Kitane at Suramarti

⟡ᴸᴉ

As they walked out into the courtyard, Kitane could still see the pall of smoke over Thera, which had drifted to cover Keftiu as well. The volcano threw ashy darkness into the sky, obscuring the sun every day. It did not seem a good omen for planning weddings. Joinings should be joyful, with blue skies and bright sunlight.

"Is Eluwari joining us?" Okune wondered.

"Yes, I expected her before now," Kit said, then stepped far enough into the courtyard to see beyond the wall of the new wing. Sure enough, Jura's sister and mother were even now entering the Suramarti gateway. Kit waved a greeting, then asked one of the atomai gardeners to help Jura's mother. She was much older than Okune; she'd had both Eluwari and Ukan in her later years of childbearing, and now she was an old woman. Her mouth was set in a tight line, her movements stiff and slow. It was all Eluwari could do to keep her upright, it seemed.

Wondering why the Tylissos family had not ridden in a cart or even on donkeys, Kit slowly walked toward Jura's representatives in the wedding planning. She did not want to pressure the elder, or Eluwari, to rush.

"I still do not think there is enough room here to host the wedding celebration," Asije said, sharp tones in her voice.

Exasperated with the woman's criticisms, Kit snapped. "It is not your choice, Aunt."

Okune's eyebrows went up, but after she looked at her sister and then Kit, she said nothing. Perhaps her mother was tired of her own little sister's complaints also. Kit wondered anew why Okune put up with it. Wasn't the elder sister supposed to be the bossy one? Wasn't Okune the one to put Asije in her place?

But her mother was a peacemaker, which was why, no doubt, Asije was even present today. The woman was bored out of her mind without her own villa. Maybe that's why she was so irritable and irritating. Kit just wished Asije hadn't been invited to the wedding planning. The decisions were complicated enough without dealing with an outsider's criticism at every step.

Looking as if she was happy to see her daughter-in-law to be, Jura's mother relaxed her mouth into what might have been a smile, then opened her arms for an embrace with Kit. While Kit gently rubbed the woman's shoulders with her flat palms, she met Elu's gaze.

Jura's sister was worried. About the wedding? Or her mother? It would be impolitic to bluntly ask, so Kit led them to the two small tables she had set up in the shady part of the courtyard, where a rhyton of cool wine was placed. Biaja stepped forward and formally offered wine, which she poured gracefully when the two Tylissos ladies accepted.

"Thank you, Bee," Kit said. She was glad her sister had decided to join the planning, but was still concerned over the young woman's relative quietness since the battle of Amnisos. It was as if a different Biaja had raced down the mountain than had gone up.

"I think the first order of business is to determine the approximate number of guests," Okune said, opening the discussion. "Then we might have a better idea of where it should be held."

Eluwari and Jura's mother sipped her wine, set it down and leaned forward with a grimace, but she said nothing.

"It is the marriage of two great telestai houses," Eluwari said, and her mother nodded.

Kit bit her lip. She had been hoping to keep the ceremony small. She was enjoying a newfound appreciation of Jura. It would have been good to have a more intimate wedding—but of course, Elu was correct. They would have to welcome all the telestai of the land.

"That is a good many people," Kit said.

Both Eluwari and her mother nodded at this, foreheads wrinkled in thought. Kit could not tell if the mother was happy about anything so far or not. Both families would share the wedding expense; were they concerned about that? Or something else? Jura was recovering well from his battle wound, so it would not be about him. If only she could speak to them in private.

The splotched white and tan and orange villa cat wandered up and stropped herself against Kit's ankles. She bent down and petted the animal, which had recently returned from wherever she had hidden her kittens. Kit nodded to the atomai girl who was helping serve food and drink today. The girl filled a small bowl with goat's milk and set it down under the serving table. The mama cat lapped up milk, her purr visible as a tremor in her sides. Sometimes she wished Eno could purr, so she could have verification of his happiness.

Realizing she was avoiding all her guests, she stepped toward the propylaea and nodded at the musicians who were just inside. With the polythyron open, the music would drift softly out to the courtyard, creating the delicate effect she wanted. A sistrum rustled out a pattern, then the forminx joined in followed by sweet blown notes from the auloi. This was the music she and Jura had discussed; this soft gentle sound would help to keep the party from getting too rowdy.

"Oh, that is just going to put everyone to sleep," Asije said with a sneer on her lip.

"Sister," Okune warned. At last, she put a little bridle on Asije's mouth. Asije scowled, but she said nothing further.

"This is what we want," Kitane said, emphasizing the 'we' and not looking at her aunt.

Eluwari's eyes widened. "Do you mean to say Jura helped you pick out music?"

Kit grinned. "He did."

Jura's mother laughed, a ratchetty coughing sort of chuckle, and she smiled too, at last. Kit felt some of the tension leave her chest. This was going to be all right, if just the thought of her big strong son picking out dainty music made the Tylissos elder happy.

It seemed they needed to invite a couple of hundred people, including a few of the atomai leaders, all the bull jumpers from the recent competition, and friends of both Kitane and Jura.

Over the next few days, they kept adding to the list, as they realized all the priestesses from both Knossos and Mt. Ida must come—or at least be invited—as well as the guasileus and his family and important staff members.

Virtually as soon as that decision had been made, the guasileus sent a formal offer for the wedding ceremony and celebration to be held at Knossos. At the "palace," at his expense.

As disturbing as the wording of the invitation was, the reaction from the priestesses was worse.

Qazipatima arrived, simultaneously angry and conciliatory.

"Of course, you will have the support of the priestesses, whether you hold the celebration here, or at the temple in Knossos," she told Kitane. "But I hope you can see that acceding to the guasileus and accepting what he calls his "palace" as a venue are not in the best interests of you, us, or Keftiu at large."

Kit and Okune both looked at her in dismay. Of course, they had considered the guasileus' offer—it was a compliment to Suramarti, as well as an acknowledgment of their part in the defense of Keftiu. The king was honoring both Jura and Zetis as heroes of the battle at Amnisos, and it seemed wrong and foolish to spurn his invitation.

Kit could see how it was a bit of a trap, however. She had already weakened the priestesses' influence by accepting the guasileus' help to save the losing competition bulls—not that she had asked for that help. Of course, Qazi would see this "palace" invitation as a strike at the Temple.

But the real question had become: was Knossos a palace, or a temple? Were the priestesses in charge, or the guasileus?

"He has completely downplayed your part in the defense, Kit, and utterly ignored Biaja's amazing ride to warn of the tsunami."

Kit made a face. "That is true. But I think Jura does deserve recognition for gathering the atomai into an army. He saved the day. And Zetis—while I despise his methods, without him, we would have been lost several times."

"The same is said of you and your defense until Jura arrived. *You* led the soldiers the guasileus sent while he remained safe and tidy in his quarters. *You* guided the fight and made the best use of your resources. And then Biaja used up a fine animal and nearly herself as well, getting the warning to you all in time. The guasileus should not be ignoring these things."

"And still," Okune said softly to her eldest daughter, "still we cannot insult him by refusing his offer outright. Do you have a plan, Qazi?"

Asije's triumphant smile should have been a warning. But Isari seemed transported to the heavens, and Kit smiled to see her cousin so happy. What could this be about?

Asije stepped commandingly between Kit and Isari. She lifted her chin. "Isari will wed the guasileus' son. This will be announced at your wedding," Asije said, "which is why it must be held at Knossos." Her voice echoed in the cross-corridor.

"And what do you think gives you the right to make that decision, Asije?" Okune's voice was harsh with anger, and possibly, with fear. Kit stepped forward and put a hand on her mother's shoulder, offering what support she could. She could feel Okune trembling. Charmingly, Halima appeared from nowhere on Okune's other side, offering her own support.

In the silence that followed, Kit could hear the pair of doves that lived out in the courtyard coo to each other.

Her cousin was going to marry the guasileus' son. Did such a marriage suddenly mean Asije could control Suramarti? That was an ugly thought. And that could be fatal to Keftiu's balance of power. Her heart blazed with anger that her aunt tried to seize power, to elevate herself beyond her station—especially after Suramarti had welcomed them as refugees. What had happened to gratitude, to love?

Kit imagined trampling Asije with Eno, smashing her into the ground. While that was not a kind thought for Enosidas, who had surely earned his retirement, yet it made Kit feel better to think it.

Somehow, she must keep Suramarti strong without offending either the guasileus or the priestesses.

"I see why you say so," Kit offered. *Weak. That was weak.* "And congratulations, Isari." Her cousin's smile seemed to wobble. Did Isari want this at all? It was impossible for Kit to tell. Her mother certainly did.

Kit felt that Asije would not be thwarted by anything. She had to try, though. "This is a *Suramarti and Tylissos* wedding. We must decide."

"There is nothing complicated about it! It is an honor the guasileus has extended to you, and you would be fools to ignore that."

Kit glanced at her mother. Asije somehow seemed to have forgotten that Okune's eldest daughter was a powerful priestess of the Temple. They had more to consider than the favor of the guasileus.

"We must please Qazipatima and Mt. Ida, as well, sister," Okune said mildly. She had stopped trembling. Kit moved her own hand from her mother's shoulder down to clasp her hand. "We will find the best way to please the wife and husband first, and then the others."

Okune the peacemaker. Why had Kit not realized how strong her mother was, before?

SCENE 2 — BIAJA AT KNOSSOS

森丫日

Biaja stood up straight and clasped Nopine's hand. They stood before the Aurochs and the Goddess Incarnation, far in the depths of the temple. They had asked to be released from their training as initiates.

At least Nopine had a good reason: she and Waro had fallen in love. The bull jumper had begun courting, and Nopine had asked for her freedom, to marry.

Biaja, who had decided to leave the Temple weeks ago, still had little reason to offer. Her own sister Qazipatima was aware Bee had been unhappy since the day she arrived. But Qazi was not the priestess standing before them. Suddenly, "I don't like it here," did not seem much of a reason.

The Aurochs' lips were pinched tight. When she met Biaja's gaze, her eyes were cold.

"Biaja of Suramarti, Nopine of the village near Tylissos. You have both asked to formally renounce your initiate training and status and leave Knossos. Nopine wishes to wed." The Goddess Incarnate smiled gently at the atomai girl whose hand clenched Biaja's so tightly. "Of course, your request is granted."

Bee could hear Nopine swallow, then she bowed slightly, released Biaja's hand and stepped back.

"Biaja, I have learned of no reason for your desire to leave. Are you so unhappy here?"

At this, the Aurochs stepped forward. "The girl is not suited to temple work. She has learned all we can teach her."

Bee blinked, trying to understand. Was the Aurochs agreeing to free her?

"As well," the Aurochs stated in her harsh voice, "the Suramarti family has given much to the Temple, and much to Keftiu. If she wishes to depart, I would not object."

The Goddess Incarnate glanced at her klawiphoros, then returned her gaze back to Biaja. Her smile went a bit crooked. "There is not much call for heroines as a profession," she said, both acknowledging Bee's Ride and dismissing it. "What is it you will do now that your house's new leader will wed Tylissos after all?"

How could she say she didn't know? How could she say she wanted to learn...other things? Things she didn't know she wanted to know?

It sounded so much less valid than Nopine's reason for leaving. "Of course, I have no intention of heroing," she murmured with a small smile. She had heard the priestess' gentle warning. "I— " she scowled and looked at the floor. Examining her true feelings was so difficult with the beady eyes of the Aurochs upon her. "I wish to study further, but at the libraries of other nations," she said, feeling suddenly strong in this wish. "Perhaps in Kmt, or Alashiya, or the land of the Hellenes."

The priestess' sober expression was worrying. Surprisingly, the Aurochs had raised an eyebrow as if she seriously considered Biaja's statement.

"It can be very difficult for women to study in those other lands," the Goddess Incarnate said. The Aurochs nodded.

"I believe if anyone can do it, it would be a woman from our land. A woman of Keftiu."

The Aurochs actually smiled. "If anyone can do it, it would be our Biaja from Suramarti," the old woman said. She tilted her head. "But you will need to be very careful around buckets of sudsy water, child."

Did the Aurochs just make a joke?

Did the Aurochs just *compliment* her?

Still blinking in astonishment as the priestess gave her permission to depart, Bee once again clasped hands with her friend, and left the presence of the powerful women. She heard the Aurochs chuckle as they backed out of the room.

In the hallway, they grabbed their sandals and passed quickly into the dormitory to gather their remaining things.

"Buckets of sudsy water?" Nopine burst out. "Did she mean when you splashed her?"

"Yes, I think. I need to be careful because I am often clumsy."

"I cannot believe that was the most instructive thing she thought to say. Foreign studies? You think you can do that?"

"I don't know." Bee felt her shoulders relax after days of tension. "We are free, Nopine. That is what I care about, now. You can marry. I can travel."

The Suramarti wedding plans had been thoroughly confused by the guasileus' offer. Bee was relieved not to have to participate in the many decisions—and disagreements—about her sister and Jura's wedding.

But at the same time, she was sad to be left out. Of course, it was Kitane's time to be honored, but still—it felt like her family was being broken into pieces after years of doing things together.

Bee fought her hurt feelings. She didn't want to be the jealous little sister who whined and insisted on attention. But she also didn't want to be eliminated from the wedding planning.

So, she took it upon herself to organize Nopine and Waro's celebration. Biaja had the perfect plan, but where was Nopine?

Nopine had said something about joining Waro at Gazi, an encampment of atomai, where Jura had gathered his army to turn back the pirates. Jura, or his steward, must know how to find Gazi. Or perhaps the atomai at Tylissos could get a message to Nopine before she and Waro got themselves married.

A few days after she'd left temple service, Biaja walked down the path toward Tylissos. Dusty oak and pine trees lined the path, casting shade she was grateful for in the early afternoon heat. She entered the gateway at Tylissos and saw Paian sitting in the shade at a table with Eluwari. Bee felt an unexpected pang. What was the Hellene doing with Jura's sister? Now that the poet could not be courting Kit, was he trying to win favor with Elu?

She clamped her teeth together so hard her jaw ached. Where were her feelings on this? She had no reason to be angry with her friends. Paian was not hers, and neither was Elu, yet she felt betrayed by their obvious interest in one another.

Elu looked up and smiled at Bee. "We were just talking about you!" she said, standing and reaching to Bee for a hug.

"Nothing bad, I hope."

"Not at all. Your decision to leave the Temple, and go study — Paian, here, is so happy, he dances like a stork!"

Indeed, the Hellene man was standing and grinning, excitement in his eyes as he looked at Biaja. Biaja, not Eluwari. Was Bee just a jealous idiot, then?

He reached for her hand and kissed the back of it when she gave it to him. "It is good to see you, Biaja," he said.

"I— I am surprised to see you here, Paian."

He smiled. "Ukan invited me to stay awhile."

"Come, sit," Elu invited, waving toward a third, empty stool. As if they had expected her.

Biaja sat.

"Paian has finished his map, and is writing a history of his time here on Keftiu!"

"Oh yes, I knew about the map," Bee said. "But a history seems, I don't know, a little grand, don't you think?"

Paian shrugged. "It is just a simple recounting," he said, making little of his work, as usual.

Oh! Map!

"Do you, perhaps, have Gazi marked on your map? Is there a way to follow your map to that place?"

"I do have Gazi. I'm not sure it's detailed enough to lead you there without a guide, if you have never been there. I have not been either."

"Do you need to go to Gazi, Bee?" Eluwari asked.

"My friend Nopine said she was going there. I am planning a small wedding for her and Waro."

"That is kind of you," Nopine said.

Bee said nothing about her mixed feelings about why she wanted to help Nopine and Waro. She just smiled.

"Of course, Jura has been there," Elu said. "And our steward. Perhaps one of them can guide you."

"I would not dare to intrude upon Jura at this busy time. But if your steward could take me there, or even take a message for me, I would appreciate that."

Elu twisted her lips. "Jura is like a little lost pup, Bee. It would be helpful to give him something like this to do. Mother and I are due back at Suramarti for further wedding planning, but he isn't welcome, yet."

"I hear your sister and Jura picked out music together for their celebration," Paian said. "I thought that was sweet."

Eluwari laughed. "Shocking is more like it. But I am glad they did that. It may be the only decision they could freely make together about the event."

"My aunt is interfering."

Elu nodded. "Isari's announcement certainly takes much away from Kitane and Jura's day," she said.

"Why wouldn't the guasileus want to announce this as a special event at Knossos, instead of usurping my sister's wedding," Bee wondered.

"Influence," Paian said.

Both young women looked at him, eyebrows raised.

"In this way, making the announcement at the Suramarti and Tylissos wedding, he is insinuating himself into telestai politics, strengthening his influence, and weakening that of the priestesses." He blinked and blushed. "I think," he added. "Of course, as an outsider I may be reading this wrong— "

"No, I don't think you are," Biaja said. Paian had come to a good understanding of the political tensions on Keftiu in his brief time here. Bee admired that, at the same time she was a bit embarrassed that Keftiu politics were so transparent.

"The guasileus has long been jealous of the Temple's mighty influence over all Keftiu," Eluwari said. "It is something the telestai have played against over the years." She bit her lip. "But now, things are changing." She jumped to her feet, bumping the table so that the tea in their cups quivered and almost spilled. "Jura!"

Her brother emerged from inside the main villa building. He nodded at Biaja and Paian. "Elu? You need something?"

"Can you guide Biaja to Gazi?"

Bee smiled, "Nopine is there, and probably Waro. I have arranged for the priestess at Mt. Ida Sanctuary to make a small wedding ceremony for them. It is peaceful there."

"And far from the chaos of Knossos or Suramarti," Elu chuckled.

Jura smiled. "That sounds nice. Of course, I can try to show you the way to Gazi, but it is complicated. I had a guide myself when I went."

"Oh, your shepherd woman," Elu said.

Jura nodded.

"Did you mean to go now?" Elu wondered.

Biaja compressed her lips, thinking. "How far is it? I mean, how long would it take? Do we have time before dark?"

"Yes, if I don't lead us astray," Jura said.

"Paian's map might help," Elu said, pointing to the document that they'd set aside on the stone ledge.

Jura bent and looked at it, Paian pointing out features and the meaning of his markings.

Jura nodded. "It's almost a straight walk from here, we just have to cross a couple streams and dodge around trees and rocks and such."

"May I join you?" Paian asked. "I could add detail to this," he pointed his chin at the map he was rolling up. "I still need to make more copies, and add other details. I suppose it will never be truly 'finished,'" he said with a wry smile.

Scene 3 — Jura, Future Soldiers

|ⲅ |ⱃ

Jura had mixed emotions as he climbed to the hill to the Tylissos sanctuary—happy to join Suramarti, but sad to leave Tylissos. As a child, he'd imagined this day. Even among the pungent olive trees, he could recall the smell of the wooden chest he kept in his room. The best wood carvers at Tylissos had made it of fine cedar wood from the island of Alashiya.

Growing up, he prepared for his eventual departure from Tylissos by adding and removing things from the box. As a small boy, the box had colorful seashells from excursions to the beach, and a rabbit skeleton he'd found in the wild. Later he replaced these childish treasures with his first donkey halter and a small bronze axe. Now the chest held his best shoes, a linen nightshirt, and his bronze sword.

Soon he would make the journey he'd anticipated for so many years. He turned to Kano, "We're moving! You will have a new home, new places to run and hide." And a new friend, he thought, remembering the times Kano and Kitane's cat chased each other. Kano jumped up and wagged her tail with the appropriate excitement. She ran from olive tree to olive tree marking her territory as if she realized this might be her last chance.

He sat on a bench outside the sanctuary and patted his dog. He bowed his head, displayed his open palms to Jasasara's labrys, and thanked the goddess. Kano barked. He petted her neck and scratched her ears. "We're going to miss Tylissos." He admired the sanctuary where he'd conducted so many morning ceremonies. He kicked a pile of shards from discarded cups. Kano sniffed the heap. "Do you smell all the people?" Kano wagged her tail.

Jura picked up a fragment. "I'll put this in my chest and we'll take it to Suramarti with us. Kano licked his hand and headed downhill back to the villa. He smiled, "You're right. We're ready to go."

"There's the happy groom." His sister Eluwari, closely followed by his brother Ukan, ran to him. Both siblings gave him open palm salutes. "Blessing of Jasasara to you."

He couldn't help smiling when he returned the greeting. This was a joyous occasion.

Kano barked and joined a group of younger atomai boys who had formed two lines and marched around the Tylissos paddock calling out their cadence, "Po-TI-das. PO-ti-DAS." They held long sticks in their hands and jabbed them forward in unison. The older boys shouted encouragement and orders.

"Defenders of Keftiu."

"Straighten your lines."

"Honor Potidas."

From behind the stables, another group of similarly armed boys charged. They sparred with their wooden swords, laughing and shouting. Some boys fell to the ground as if wounded, holding their injured arm, legs, or bellies, shouting in pain, and screaming for help.

"I am the pirate Tros. I am dying."

"The Keftiu soldiers have killed me."

Others waved their weapons in the air, whooping in triumph.

"Potidas and Keftiu! Defeat the invaders."

Soon boys panting in mock pain and victory littered the ground.

Jura ran over to the "wounded" soldiers. "Well done," he said as he offered a hand in congratulations and to help the boys rise to their feet. "You will be ready for the next attack."

The boys gathered around Jura in admiration. "Tell us about the battle."

Jura told them about hiking through the wild in the dark night. He pantomimed holding a burning bundle of branches to light the way.

"Some men tripped on rocks. Other fell into the creek." He fell, struggled back to his feet, and shook off the water. "Nothing slowed us and by sunrise, we arrived at Amnisos harbor."

The boys who had already memorized this now legendary trek responded, "You charged the pirates!"

"We shouted, 'Potidas! Potidas. Death to pirates!' and they ran into the sea with fear."

The boys cheered.

Eluwari took her brother's hand to pull him away from his audience. She chided the children. "This is not the Keftiu way. We are not fighters."

Jura freed his hand. He knew she would marry and take control of Tylissos, but today was Jura's time to celebrate. He responded in a cheerful voice. "Not anymore. Keftiu has changed."

Ukan, the middle sibling, didn't take sides. "They are children. This is just a game to them."

"Ukan is right," Jura agreed with a laugh, but then added, "They have seen victory in battle. The atomai will fight, either for the telestai or for the guasileus."

The children returned to their game and the three siblings retreated to the inner courtyard where two atomai girls brought a basket of fresh pears, still cold and wet. During the warm weather, Tylissos stored ripe fruit in a ceramic jar submerged in the creek, cooled by the snowmelt coming down from the mountains.

Jura wiped one off on his robe, sat in a comfortable chair, leaned back, and took a big bite. With juice spilling down his chin, he mused on the future for Keftiu. "Now that foreigners have attacked Keftiu, soldiers are more important. The guasileus has plans for barracks outside his Knossos palace and garrisons in each villa. We should support our atomai boys and arm them, to be prepared."

"Knife," Eluwari said. One of the atomai girls ran to retrieve a favorite bronze knife with a gold and silver handle in the shape of a dolphin. She cut a slice of pear and examined it. Evidently it had a blemish because she tossed it away. Kano snapped it up, tail wagging. Elu ate the next slice.

She chewed slowly, while her brothers waited. "Tylissos is my responsibility." She swallowed her pear slice. "I can assure you there will not be a garrison here. Keftiu is a land of peace, of craftspeople, farmers, and traders."

"The atomai are now something else." Jura leaned back and knitted his fingers behind his head. "Elu, my sister, you were not at the battle. I saw the change."

She threw away another piece of blemished fruit.

"Since that morning, the atomai are soldiers, victorious, powerful fighters. I saw it in their eyes."

This time Ukan supported his brother, "They imagine more victories and changes. Atomai are thinking of new possibilities."

Eluwari stabbed her knife into the ground and crossed her arms. Jura felt he had said too much. He leaned forward in his chair, put his arm around her shoulder. "My intelligent sister, I am sure you will lead Tylissos to continued prosperity, but even before the battle, some atomai abandoned the safety and stability of villa life. Let's talk instead about my upcoming wedding."

He could feel her relax. She stood up and pulled him with her. She sang a cheerful song of dolphins courting in the warm sea. She held his waist and he her shoulders and they spun around in the traditional wedding dance. Ukan clapped in time to the impromptu music.

She looked at her big brother, "It will be a wonderful wedding."

As he spun around, his mind wandered to thoughts of his garrison at Suramarti, but that was a discussion to have with Kitane, not here with his younger siblings.

The siblings sat back down and rested in the warm sun. Eventually Ukan retreated to his room.

Elu turned to her older brother. "I worry about him. Does he have any marriage prospects? Does he now imagine a life as a soldier?"

Jura worried about him also.

Maza entered the Tylissos gate with two donkeys in tow and walked up to Ukan and Jura. "Could I keep my donkeys in your paddock for the night?"

Ukan smiled and gave her an open-palm salute. "Blessings of Jasasara to you. Certainly. Any servant of the Knossos temple is welcome at Tylissos."

She frowned and turned around.

"Did I say something wrong?"

"I no longer work for the Temple. These are my donkeys and I work for myself."

Ukan took the reins of one donkey and walked toward the stable area. "Let me correct my welcome. You and your donkeys are welcome. Stay as long as you'd like."

Ukan and Maza walked together accompanied by the donkeys.

Jura wondered aloud, "I've never heard of that. The Temple and the villas have their own donkeys. Who will hire you?"

Ukan looked at Maza as she turned toward Jura. "Surely you've heard that the guasileus is building barracks for his army. He has no donkeys. He will have to hire donkeys to bring his supplies."

Ukan moved closer to Maza. "My brother has just been talking about how Keftiu is changing."

She had more to say. "And those new soldiers? They will need help when they move to the Knossos garrison."

Jura admired her logic and ingenuity. However, he had another question. "Where did you get those donkeys?"

"They were wild. I found them wandering the hills after the water receded."

"But they seem to be tame."

Ukan rushed to her defense. "If she found them, they are her donkeys. We are not barbarians like the Kmt. We do not torture our animals by burning our mark into their hide. Tame animals stay close to those who feed them."

Jura marveled at how quickly Keftiu had changed. Atomai were leaving their villas to join the guasileus' army. Atomai now owned donkeys and worked for hire. Between his marriage and the changes, Jura wondered what the future held for him, for Keftiu.

Ukan repeated his welcome. "You and your donkeys are welcome. Stay as long as you'd like."

Jura laughed to himself and added to his list of changes: And telestai are courting atomai.

SCENE 4 — PAIAN THE HISTORIAN
‡ᴟᵼᵼ

The brave Keftiu defended their island. Kitane of Suramarti and Jura of Tylissos bravely fought the Pirate Tros on the beach of Amnisos. The battle was for naught because Potidas, the God of Land and Sea, used the occasion to demonstrate his dominion over all mortals. The Goddess Jasasara sent her messenger Biaja of Suramarti to foil his display. She warned the Keftiu before Potidas could drown them. Biaja's valiant run from Mount Ida saved Keftiu and delivered the victory.

Paian sat on the dirt floor of his small room on the lowest level of Knossos rereading the final paragraph of his history as he copied the Hellene script into Keftiu. In the copy, he put extra care into Biaja's name, scribing it into the tablet slightly larger and with delicate flourishes to reflect her beauty and importance.

He imagined her smiling when she read his words. He admired his tablets, how they told a story. Surely Biaja would recognize his accomplishment. He'd added something new to his tablets, his own innovation: numbers. Each tablet had a number to indicate the order to read it. All other tablets were complete in themselves: inventory lists, poems, or prayers—one tablet each. Bee would understand and approve. She was the one to bring home to meet his parents.

He would accompany Bee to Mount Ida for the wedding of Nopine and Waro. After the wedding, he would share his writings just before he stored them in the sacred caves. That would be the time to suggest their marriage.

"Blessing of Jasasara to you." Biaja interrupted his reverie.

He jumped up and knocked over a stack of completed tablets. "Bee. I mean Biaja. Yes, Biaja." He scrambled to pick up everything and put them in sequence in a wooden box he'd found. "I didn't expect you. Is it time to leave for Mount Ida?"

She laughed. "No. Don't you remember? We leave in the morning. The day after tomorrow."

Of course, he remembered. He could feel his face getting warm and turned away from her, sorting tablets. He was so close. He was ready to show her the tablets and ask her to marry him now, but this was Keftiu and he needed to speak to her parents first. He covered up his excitement. "Will we stop at Suramarti on the way to the sanctuary?"

"Of course," she laughed again. "Let's go. The guasileus' wife has invited us to dinner. We can't be late."

He relaxed. He understood the guasileus, who was like the chief man in his home village. The evening's diversion would clear his mind to consider how to face Biaja's family. He planned to show Bee the saga of her heroism, but how should he approach her parents? His father had successfully married a Keftiu woman, so he remembered that as he built his confidence. He would say the right thing and gain their approval.

The imposing Suramarti gate with its double-axe labrys carved on each side and the horns of consecration displayed above the lintel along with delicately carved grape vines, signaled their arrival. Paian was ready. Okune and Radamitu offered traditional open palm salutes. He automatically raised his hand and replied, "Blessing of Jasasara to you and Suramarti." Keftiu culture was second nature, now.

Biaja and Okune took charge of the arrangements, directing the staff to unload and feed the donkeys, place the travelers' belongings in their assigned sleeping quarters, and prepare for another Suramarti feast. Amid all the activity, Radamitu and Paian stood to the side. The women were in charge.

Paian turned to Biaja's father. "Will you be making the trek to Mount Ida for the wedding?"

Radamitu thought for a while. "I wouldn't miss Kit's wedding. She is the new matriarch of Suramarti. Of course, I will be there."

Paian realized that her father misunderstood the question. He'd meant the ceremony for Nopine and Waro, not Kit and Jura.

Before he could say anything, Radamitu added, "But I didn't hear that Kit decided where to have it. Okune wants it here, but her sister seeks to favor the guasileus with the celebration at

Knossos. Qazi is against that." A long pause and a sly smile. "I suggest you and I stay out of it."

Paian took this advice and changed the subject. "I know am not telestai or even Keftiu, but I would like court Biaja. I think she might be open to joining our paths together."

He considered mentioning that his mother was Keftiu, but decided not to say this. Radamitu might not like the idea of his youngest daughter moving far away as his mother had.

Just then an atomai child ran to the men. "The food is ready."

The musicians were already playing. The rhythm of the sistrum and the harmony of a forminx trio filled the courtyard. Paian recognized the tune, a harvest song about shaking olive trees and gathering the fruit in baskets.

Radamitu led the way to the evening's festivities. As they arrived, and barely loud enough for Paian to hear over the music, he finally answered the question. "Yes, of course you may court her, but you need to also speak with Okune."

Paian confidently thought, *I knew that*, and stood a bit taller ready for the dinner to proceed.

Paian found a bowl and Biaja. Together they sampled the roasted meats, fresh fruits, sour pickles, and revithia flavored with lamb juices. She took a seat and he went to the saj to collect hot pita for them both.

When he handed her the bread, she smiled, and he asked, "Would this be an appropriate time to speak to your mother?"

"After we eat would be better." She folded her pita to pick up a crispy piece of roast lamb.

He was learning to navigate the strange Keftiu customs. His parents would be proud of him when he returned with a Keftiu wife.

After dinner, he walked over to Okune. He stood at a respectful distance while she issued instructions to several atomai. Just when he thought it was his turn, he remembered that he should have a gift. He turned and ran outside to the paddock.

"Where are the packages that the donkeys carried?"

An atomai boy pointed to the stable. He found the pack frames and went through boxes of tablets, wedding presents for Nopine and Waro, and a few more packages the priestesses wanted transported to Mount Ida. He untied wool ropes and spread everything out until he found the papyrus scroll he wanted. He ran back to where Okune stood.

Again, he waited for his turn.

With one palm raised in greeting and the other proffering the scroll, he said, "Jasasara's blessing to you."

Okune did not reach for the scroll.

"Greetings to you," he began again. He moved the scroll closer. "This is for you."

She took the scroll and opened it. She gave it a half smile and looked at him with a puzzled look.

"This is a map of Keftiu." He pointed while she unrolled the scroll."

"This is Suramarti. We are here."

He moved to the right. "Here is Knossos."

He moved to the left. "That is Mount Ida, covered in snow."

She smiled, pointing farther to the right. "Is that Mount Dikti?"

"Yes. I haven't been there, but that is where I've been told it is."

She pointed all the way to the right. "That is Zakros. Someday I would like to go there."

"This is for you. You can use it to plan your adventures."

She rolled the scroll and held it to her chest. "Biaja has told me that you were clever." She unrolled the map to examine it again. "We have maps of the Middle Sea, not of the land. They say your Goddess Athena is a goddess of wisdom. You should thank her for your many talents."

He replied, "I thank Athena and Jasasara as well."

Now is the moment, he thought as he recalled how she had called him clever and wise. "I'd also like to go on some more adventures. With your permission, I'd like to ask Biaja to join me, as my wife."

She hugged the scroll tighter. "You must get her agreement, but you have my blessing to try."

"Thank you."

He raised both palms and backed away.

She gave him a grin. "Biaja is independent. Her agreement might not be as easy as you expect."

He nodded. He had Okune's approval, and he now felt confident Biaja would consent.

The priestesses of the Mount Ida Sanctuary offered them the hospitality of an evening meal and small rooms to spend the night before their final ascent to the sacred cave. The modest evening meal reminded Paian how much had changed since the battle of Amnisos. Fewer pilgrims had brought offerings to the out-of-the-way location. The priestesses were glad for the salt and saffron among the packages from Knossos.

The meal consisted of freshly-baked pita and a thin soup of okra and squash. After the uphill trek from Suramarti, everyone appreciated a warm meal. Nopine and Waro sat together sharing a single bowl. The happy couple did not seem concerned about the menu.

Biaja approached them. "Tomorrow is your wedding day."

Waro took Nopine's hand and she blushed. They looked at Bee and nodded.

"I've been visiting Mount Ida since I was a small girl. You can see how close it is to Suramarti."

"Yes," Nopine replied. "Your stories of the sacred caves convinced me that this would be a wonderful place for our joining."

Waro added, "Thank you for arranging this. Atomai usually marry in one of our small cottages or sometimes outside at a clearing in the wild."

"You two are dear to me and my sister. I wanted your ceremony to be special."

"We thank you," and, "Jasasara's blessings to you," they quickly replied.

"This time of year, the sacred caves get cold in the evening. Snow does not come for a few moons, but the sun sets earlier, and the evenings are not comfortable."

"What should we do?"

"We haven't brought blankets."

"Don't worry. We'll leave early and have the ceremony when the sun is high in the sky. It will be warm enough and we'll return to the sanctuary for your wedding feast."

The following morning, the donkeys and the wedding party headed up to the sacred caves. Paian walked with Waro. "Did you ask Nopine's mother for permission to marry her?"

"No. Her family lives past Malia, halfway to Zakros. I have never been that far."

"How is that allowed?"

"You are thinking about telestai women. They control land and wealth, but must follow many rules. Atomai girls make their own decisions."

Paian puzzled about this. "Where will you live after you are married?"

"I have a patron to continue bull jumping, even after my mediocre performance at the festival. We will live at her villa in the morning shadow of Mount Dikti."

Paian had never heard of a Keftiu couple following the husband, except, he reminded himself, his mother had left Keftiu to live in Athens. Everything had been going so well, but now he wondered if his mother had been telestai or atomai. He worried that only atomai women could follow their husbands.

He prayed to Jasasara, *Guide me through stormy nights*, the best prayer he could recall. He finally fell asleep knowing tomorrow would answer all his questions.

Arriving at the cave early, Biaja led Paian through a long tunnel to a deep chamber where they would store the tablets and scrolls. He marveled at the collection.

"Now I see where my mother got her love for reading and writing. Have I told you she was from Keftiu, but now is head of a school in Athens?"

Bee looked around at the collection of writings. "No. I've never heard of a Keftiu leaving the island. She must be atomai."

"I don't know. She never said anything about that, but she reads and writes very well, both in the style of Hellenes and Keftiu. Of course, both writings are similar."

"A telestai can travel if she wishes. It is possible."

Paian took a deep breath to contain his excitement. "You would like her. She is from Phaistos, I think. She doesn't talk about her time in Keftiu very often, but I believe she refused to follow the path her parents chose. She is very independent."

"I suppose I am also independent. Certainly, now that I am not a novice priestess, nobody tells me what to do."

Paian lit a new bundle of branches and found the tablet with the battle of Amnisos. He handed it to Bee. "Read this." She looked at the tablet. "Please."

He watched her read. Her eyes sparkled with the flames as they moved back and forth. Occasionally she smiled. Once she even laughed. When she put the tablet down, he asked, "Would you like to meet my mother?"

As soon as he asked, he feared that he'd said the wrong thing. Should he have just asked her to marry him? Courting on Keftiu seemed to be a labyrinth with more wrong turns than correct ones. He was learning, but still no expert.

She did not reply, but started walking out of the cave. "We should hurry. It is time for the wedding ceremony."

He followed her. When they approached the entrance, the bright sunlight surrounded Bee with a glow. He could see Nopine and Waro standing between the altar and the labrys, so he walked faster, but just then Bee stopped. She spun around and hugged him. "Your heart is beating so fast. Are you all right?"

He held on to her waist and took a deep breath. He could not calm his heart. "I am fine. I didn't want to be late for the ceremony."

She looked at him. Her green eyes sparkled. She laughed and hugged him again. "Did you just ask me to marry you?"

He couldn't think of anything else to say. "Yes?"

"We'll have to wait to make an announcement until after Kit gets married. It's only fair."

Was that a yes?

SCENE 5 — KITANE AT SURAMARTI, DIWOKI RETURNS

ΫΓI

There was a hubbub in the center courtyard that Kit could hear all the way from her room. The room she was preparing for her and Jura.

She sighed, looking around at the few rearranged furnishings. How much space would Jura need? She guessed not more than she did herself, for clothing and a few personal belongings. Still mulling whether she should add a shelf to his side of the room, she went through the polythyron into the courtyard, to find her family swarming around her elder brother.

Diwoki! He was home, and safe!

She ran up and took her own turn in giving him a welcoming hug. He smelled strange, like the sea and yet also like spices and dry wood. And fish.

He held her at arm's length. "I have heard you are to be wed!"

"Yes," she nodded.

"I am glad you chose Jura and not that arrogant Tros."

"Actually— "

"Tros and all his followers were killed in the tsunami," Biaja said, pushing herself between them to get her own chance at a hug.

"Ah," Diwoki said, a smile on his handsome but weathered face. "I had heard rumors. I know we lost most of our fleet. I had heard there was a pirate attack, before the wave."

"That was Tros," Kit said, "and his many allies."

"Well, I am glad my ships were safe in the south. I added two more ships to my fleet along the way. Suramarti is in an advantageous position now, almost the exclusive traders to the Middle Sea!"

"There is other news, not so good," Kit said, "but that can wait until later."

"Mother has already planned a big dinner for tonight, with guests from Tylissos," Biaja said. "I'm sure there will be plenty to discuss!"

"Now, let us leave you and your own family to a private welcome," Okune said, stepping past Diwoki and sweeping up Bee, Kit, and Isari in her wake.

As Kit went back through the doorway into her room, she saw Diwoki embrace Halima. Their toddler boy clung to his mother's legs, peering up at Diwoki. Had he forgotten his father, then? Diwoki had been gone almost a year, so it was possible.

Kit closed the door to give them as much privacy out in the courtyard as was possible.

She returned to her problem. Part of her dilemma was a result of her own father having his workshop and separate sleeping quarters in the Suramarti compound. He seldom spent time in Okune's quarters nowadays, so she hadn't a good feel for a couple sharing space.

She went through the arch into the indoor colonnade that led to Radamitu's workshop.

He looked up from his workbench, perched on a stool in front of a sunny doorway to the outside of the villa. He smiled at Kit, then looked back down at his work. She felt melancholy rise as she noticed again the silver in his hair, which gleamed in the sun now like the fine wires of one of his creations. How long would she have his wise advice? How long would either of her parents be around to share their experience and support?

She walked up and gave him a silent hug. He set down the tool he held and turned to her, returning the hug.

"Did you see Diwoki?"

"I did. He seems quite prosperous and happy," Radamitu said.

"He added *more* ships to his fleet. We were wrong to worry he had been lost."

She could feel her father's chuckle as she lifted her head from his shoulder and stepped back, letting her arms fall to her sides.

"I have a personal question to ask you."

He raised his bushy eyebrows, looking at her. "Oh?"

Kit saw one of his apprentices rise from the rug on the floor where he'd been working. He quietly stepped out, motioning to the other worker in the room to leave also.

Apparently, they thought it was a *very* personal question, Kit realized. She giggled, sounding like she was ten summers old again. "Oh, not so personal as all that." She looked her father in the eye. "So, when you first came to stay with mother here at Suramarti, how much space did you need?"

"Oh, you are trying to prepare your room?"

She nodded.

"As I recall, I had one small box of tools, which I insisted on keeping beside me. Also, an old linen sail I used as a shade roof across my booth at celebrations, and a few poles to hang it from." He smiled crookedly. "I had no workshop at the time, being a new goldsmith, barely out of apprenticeship and not a master yet.

"Your mother refused to allow my dusty cloth and 'dirty old poles' in the room. Instead, they were laid into a storeroom until my workshop was built. To answer your dilemma, I had very little. I would imagine Jura has even less, not having specific tools of his own."

"I see."

"You might think of where to put his donkey, and his dog."

"Oh, Kano! I forgot about her." She made a face, realizing he was teasing about the donkey. "She should be happy out in the courtyard, unless she chases the cat too much."

"They will learn to live together," Radamitu said, "just as you and Jura will."

**"Potidas has shown his support for Keftiu, through all this,"
Diwoki said.** "The tsunami destroyed Tros' coalition of pirates, yet spared Suramarti's ships and trading partners."

"But he destroyed the port at Amnisos," Asije said, thrusting her point forward like a spear, Kit thought. Her aunt's wealth, rescued from Thera, was paying for the port's rebuilding. Asije wasn't going to let anyone forget it.

"Worse," Jura said, surprising Kit, "Tros' attack showed that Keftiu is vulnerable. We can be attacked. No one dared try an invasion like that before, and if not for the tsunami, it could have been successful."

Diwoki leaned forward sharply. "The perception in Kmt and Alashiya and Arzawa is changing. Keftiu is no longer an untouchable, impregnable island. We will see how that may change when I go on the next round of trade," he said.

"The guasileus is building an army," Asije said. Other conversations around the table went quiet. "He is training soldiers, permanent soldiers he will pay to be always on duty, to protect Knossos, and the port, once Amnisos is rebuilt."

"He will pay them with riches he has stolen from the temples," Qazipatima said, scowling. "This is changing who we are," she added. "This is making us like Kmt and Arzawa, always looking for a fight. And like Alashiya, always defending."

"That is not our way," Okune said. "That is not peaceful, rich Keftiu."

"It may be the only way we can survive," Diwoki said. Kit turned to look at him, feeling betrayed. Okune looked also. Kit saw with a glance that her mother was pale and disturbed. Besides her brother, Halima nodded her own agreement.

"Kmt has long looked at you with a greedy eye," she murmured.

"Are we so weak, then?" Okune wondered.

"We *look* weak, mother. Whether we are or not, it is how we are perceived that will determine what others think to do about Keftiu. Certainly, others are jealous of our prosperity. Which will continue, for a good long time, since we are presently the masters of trade around the entire Middle Sea," Diwoki said, obviously considering his words and their impact with care.

"Are we?" Kit wondered. "What about the Hellenes, the ones Tros came from?"

"I want to put my two new ships in the north, trading there and among the islands of the Archipelago," Diwoki said. "Partly to keep an eye on them, and partly because there is now a gap in trade there." He set down the pita he had stuffed with lamb and revithia. "In fact, I have a proposal." He looked at the farther end of the table, where Ukan sat across from his brother. Ukan and Jura glanced at each other, then back at Diwoki.

"I had hoped to give Sakusna the two new ships," Diwoki said.

"That was my other news. Sakusna sailed with Tros and now she is gone." Kit could feel the sadness drop like a pall over the table. Sakusna's adventurous spirit was indeed a great loss to Suramarti, but even more so to the siblings she had left behind. There was a hole in their family where Sakusna belonged.

Kit sensed that Diwoki had already heard about Sakusna. News traveled fast among traders, especially bad news. She searched for some balancing subject. "We can all rejoice that the prophecy of Okune's death is assuredly rebuked."

Okune had a tear in her eye when she asked, "Do you think that prophecy was transferred to Sakusna? Did she die so I could live?"

Qazi jumped in. "We cannot know Jasasara's plans. Not all prophesies happen as we expect, but we must never ignore them."

"Yes! Yes! Bee saved us from drowning when she brought the prophecy from Mt. Ida," Jura added.

Everyone joined in about how Jasasara saved them while Potidas drowned the pirates. The gloom dissipated.

Diwoki returned to the subject of ships. "I think I have found someone else who might take on the job of trade in the north." Diwoki stared straight into Ukan's eyes. "My new brother-to-be, Ukan."

Ukan blinked and sat frozen in shock. Then a slow smile built on his face.

"I realize you are not acquainted with the details of sailing, so I will put my top captain on your ship to guide you, but I have been told you and your…partner?…Maza? are adept at transport and trade, and that you will drive hard bargains, to Keftiu's benefit. Is this a good plan?"

Kit looked around the table, wondering who had suggested this idea. Jura? No, he looked as dumbfounded as his brother. No one's face told a thing until she got to Okune, who was smiling gently, and then Asije, who looked quite vexed, red rising on her neck and cheeks, an angry glint in her eyes.

Okune had thwarted Asije's ambition, was that it? Clearly Diwoki had no idea of the undercurrents between the Keftiu sister and the one from lost Thera. But it was an elegant solution for both Diwoki and for Jura's little brother as well as a way to help rein in Asije's plotting.

Unknowing of all this, Ukan jumped to his feet and raised his rhyton of wine. "To my powerful brother in trade, Diwoki!"

"Diwoki!" they cried around the table, and the thing was now done; Tylissos and Suramarti linked in another way.

Eluwari met Kit's eyes, and they smiled at one another. It should be a great relief to Tylissos to have Ukan placed so well, and Kit was grateful to her brother for taking their mother's suggestion in this. It was a good plan.

She could see her mother's hand in more than that, for all the guests variously sat, knelt, or lay sprawled around *one* long, low table.

One table to promote the unity of the family, not splinter it into factions or argumentative groups. Okune allowed everyone to choose their own place to sit, so there were still some friendly groupings, and some less friendly. But, indeed, Kit could see everyone was enjoying conversation, sharing food and ideas. It was a brilliant use of space.

Her heart sometimes quailed trying to imagine herself in Okune's place. How could she hope to be so wise with every detail of Suramarti life?

Biaja and Paian were chatting together, and Kit heard her sister's friend—and suitor?—suggest they could travel on his friend Ukan's boat to visit his homeland. "My mother is from Phaistos, you know. She would be delighted to have a visitor from her Keftiu, her original home."

Biaja laughed and bent her head to hear whatever Paian was saying in her ear. *I hope they are courting,* Kit thought. Their behavior was becoming embarrassingly intimate.

"What of your wedding plans, Kitane?" Asije asked, diverting the topic from one she found uncomfortable, to one she still hoped to control, no doubt.

Kit reached for the dish of olives the atomai server was passing around. She took a small handful, put them on her plate and licked the oil from her fingers before answering. "The date is set, fortuitous and pleasing, under the constellation the Swallow."

"At Knossos?" her aunt said, pushing her way back into some sort of leadership in this silent contest that pulsed on. Most of the diners were oblivious, but Isari glanced up at Kit, wide-eyed, then quickly stared back at her own plate again. That told Kit that mother and daughter did not entirely agree on whatever Asije had been working on.

"There are several reasons that Knossos is not favored," Kit said.

"But just as many that make Suramarti a poor choice as well."

"Well, I have the perfect place," Biaja said, mouth full of roasted lamb. She finished chewing, swallowed, and met Kit's eyes. "It meets your requirement for somewhere hallowed and beautiful, it has enough room, and it honors the Goddess."

"Oh, where could this wondrous place be?" Asije said. The acid in her tone did not go unnoticed, even by the usually oblivious Ukan. There were raised eyebrows and querulous expressions around the table.

Biaja smiled. "The Sanctuary at Mount Ida." Bee glanced around at her friends and family. "It honors the Seer who warned us of the great wave in time to save our defenders. And it honors the Goddess who sent the vision to preserve us."

Kit stared at her sister a moment in thought. And then smiled. "That is a wonderful idea, Bee." The more she thought about it, the more splendid it seemed. It would be approved by Qazipatima, who had threatened to not bless the wedding if she had to do it in what the guasileus imagined was his stronghold. It would not offend said king, because it was a holy place. All honored the Goddess Jasasara and thanked her for saving

Knossos. It was not a denial of Knossos so much as a choosing of a better place.

There was plenty of room at the site, and it was lovely, with views of the Middle Sea, blue sky, trees. It was distant enough that only the most determined guests would come. That was good for two reasons: there would be less of a frivolous party atmosphere, yet also more of the people she and Jura truly liked in attendance.

Kit stood and met Jura's eyes, asking if that idea was pleasing to him. She could see by his relief and his smile that he liked that plan. And it was a decision, plucked from a neutral place, that said nothing about their politics, about who was siding with whom.

"To my lovely sister, for finding the perfect solution," she said, raising her glass. "To the Mount Ida Sanctuary, and to Biaja."

"Biaja!" they all said, drinking in honor of her sister. Even Asije seemed impressed. She had been outmaneuvered, and there was nothing she could say against it.

Scene 6 — Biaja at Mt. Ida Sanctuary
太۲日

White clouds dotted the smoke-stained sky, which was almost blue up here so high at the Sanctuary. Biaja looked around, from the west end of Keftiu all the way over to the east, where Mount Dikti mostly blocked the view. The grey smoke from Thera still stained the heavens but at least it was *blue*, pale and ashy, but blue. How long would it take before the sky returned to the deep, open sky color they were accustomed to?

Paian joined her on the low ridge above the wedding preparations.

"Your map cannot show this beauty, alas," she said.

"Keftiu is beautiful. I attempted to make a beautiful map to reflect this, but of course nothing can actually show the beauty except the real thing."

The Athenian dared to reach over and take her hand. Bee grasped it in return and flashed him a quick smile.

"How does our land compare with your Athens?"

"Athens is a small city. It sits among hills on a peninsula surrounded by the Middle Sea."

"So, your view is almost all water."

"Yes. With trees, pine and fir along the rocky slopes, not unlike here. We also grow olives and grapes."

"I see. So Ukan and Maza should not bring those to trade, though I suppose Diwoki will tell them that."

"Your pottery is very appreciated, and good cloth is always welcome."

As the sun rose higher in the sky, scattered sun rays broke through between clouds, their beams lighting up the Sanctuary grounds below.

"I think it's time I went down to help," Biaja said.

"Is there anything I can do?"

"I'm sure if you offer, they will find plenty for you to do, Paian. Thank you."

He nodded. Still clasping hands, they walked down from the ridge toward the storeroom where Okune and Kitane and even Qazipatima were already at work, taking out the gifts that would be given to the guests—some of whom had already arrived and spent the night, and others who were even now walking or riding into the Sanctuary. They bore armloads or donkey-backs of flowers and greens, the traditional gift from guests to the bridal couple.

"Oh, that's what you can do. Find where my mother has put the rhytons for the flowers, and you can accept them from the guests and put them in water, then place the rhytons all around."

Seeming startled, Paian nodded and went to do as she had asked. Maybe, guests did not bring flowers to Athenian weddings, Bee thought. Hellenes certainly would have different customs from Keftiu.

"Oh, good," her mother interrupted her musings of Paian. "Bee, I need you to put a pot of honey at each place." The priestesses were arranging blankets and boards for seating. "Also, have Paian put a rhyton of flowers are each grouping of guests."

"Yes," Bee said, and went into the cool storeroom to collect an armload of honeypots. Jura's people had made many batches of the small pots and filled them with honey from his wonderful beehives and wild nests. They capped each pot with either beeswax, or in fancier cases, with a cork stopper. Cork was another Diwoki find. He'd gotten it at Kmt, but had found a way to trade directly with the people of Magrib who grew it. The cork was cut to fit the top of the pot, and kept the honey fresh.

That was a good find, since Jura ran out of beeswax long before he ran out of honey. He took care not to destroy any bee's nests, merely harvesting from, not taking all the wax and honey. He had recently tried making hives for the bees, using straw and clay as they did in the Hittite Empire and Kmt. He had already set up several rows of these at Suramarti. The honey was a precious gift.

Biaja carefully set a pot at each place, where the priestesses were putting a bowl or small plate, and a cup. These came from the Sanctuary's own storerooms as well as those brought from

Tylissos and Suramarti, along with many borrowed from telestai friends. No one had over a hundred of cups and bowls, which was how many wedding guests Okune and Asije had counted.

Kit arrived with a pile of blankets and cloths to serve as more tables. She and Isari spread them out on the clean-swept stones of the Sanctuary court, trying to leave plenty of room for people to move around between groupings.

While Bee was just finishing setting out the honey, Jura's steward arrived from Tylissos with one last load of gifts, including more honey. Bee enlisted the steward's aid in counting the place settings. Were they even close? It was difficult to judge that many spaces.

"How many?" Okune called, seeing what they were doing.

"We have one hundred forty-five," Bee said. She and her mother contemplated the space left in the court.

"People can sit on the wall on this side," Bee suggested.

"And there is room for more blankets along the pathway to the guest rooms," Okune said. "That will have to do." She showed the priestesses where to lay the last batch of blankets and cloths, while Bee set the last honeypots along the wall edging the court, counting as she went.

"There is no need to be exact, I think," Kit said after staring around the court. "People will move from group to group, and some people will not stay the whole time."

"I have almost enough set out now," Bee said. "I'll put the rest behind the altar, where people can pick them up if they like."

Kit nodded, watching as Paian arranged a batch of bay laurel branches in the center of one blanket. Bee watched also, as the man carefully set a pot of saffron crocus flowers someone had brought in front of the greens.

"Lovely," Kit murmured, and went off to do something else.

"When shall we start?" Bee called.

"When the sun is above the peak," Okune said.

Guests continued to arrive, bringing sunflowers, orkis, cedar branches, cypress, more laurel, and pine. They brought lavender, dittany, myrtle, and mint. Bee helped Paian lay out some rose hips to give color to bracts of fern and strands of mint on the last few boards or cloths; they'd run out of rhytons for flowers; the rest were needed for serving wine or cool water from the sanctuary well. Lavender and greens could survive the day without water. They swapped out some so that late-arriving sea lilies could be in rhytons.

Finished, Bee stood with Paian looking around at the boards, cloths, and flowers. Okune joined them, drying her hands on a worn linen rag. The Suramarti steward and cooks fluttered around the stone ovens and open fires where aurochs and goats roasted. Atomai used wood sticks to flip the many pita baking on saj. They piled up stacks of the bread, ready to serve.

Kitane had disappeared to take her ritual bath and dress in her new wedding clothes. Bee could see Jura heading toward the baths, also.

"Are we ready?" Paian wondered.

"Is this anything like a Hellene wedding?" Bee asked.

Paian's eyes were round with wonder. "No. We don't have weddings or a ceremony, the bride just...moves into the husband's house."

"Hmm," Bee said.

"We should go there! We can go with Ukan and Maza. You can meet my mother, see her school."

"I think we will do that," Bee said. "But I think we will marry here, first," she grinned at him.

He waved an arm at all the place settings, the bustle of the cooks and guests, amazement in his eyes.

"Ours will not be this grand," Bee said. "This is a joining of two important telestai villas. Our wedding will be simpler." Biaja sniffed. "And smaller. But we will have a feast. I cannot deny my mother the opportunity to stage another feast."

Paian nodded, staring at the guests who were wandering around, finding seating with friends, as atomai raced to serve drinks to each group.

"I need to get dressed," Bee said. "We'll start soon."

Paian went over to the blanket he and Bee had selected and sat down next to Ukan and Maza, while she trotted to her guest room.

Wearing her new golden-orange robe, Biaja joined the board with Paian, Maza, and Ukan. Beside them sat Diwoki and his family, Halima's beautiful dark skin tone gleaming beside her husband's tanned coloring. Halima wore a deep green robe that Bee coveted, even knowing the rich color would not flatter her paler complexion like it did the Kmt woman.

Qazipatima sat there also, beautiful and in fancy dress, her hair wound with a strand of gold beads and dainty pearls from the Archipelago. She seemed to be having fun, with no duties until the formal blessing after the games.

Then their mother stood up. Okune shook a sistrum, hit it sharply several times with the palm of her hand, using the noise to attract everyone's attention. "Please be seated, if you are not already. We begin. Every unwed male, please take a pita from our servers."

Kitane sat alone at a small table at the altar end of the court. Her hair was piled up on the back of her head in the loose bun of the married woman, wound with ribbons. She wore the aqua and green robe she had woven herself, her neck graced by a new pendant from their father. Biaja had to admit that her usually plain-looking but feisty sister looked delicate and beautiful today.

Kit also took a pita from the server, who then went on to nearby boards and tables to offer them to guests.

Okune hit the sistrum again, smiling broadly. "Now please tear your pita in half."

Guests began laughing, realizing what the game was.

"Whose bread will match Kitane's? Who will be her true mate?"

Zetis jumped up and approached Kit, weaving between groups of guests. "My beautiful, agile sister cannot marry me, can she?" he asked, trying to fit his pita half to hers. Of course, they did not match, and Zetis pretended to be mightily relieved, to much laughter. Of course, brother and sister would never marry, but he was the perfect person to begin the game.

Other young men came up, first praising Kitane or saying what they could offer as husbands, and then attempting to fit their pitas together with hers.

None fit, of course, until guests called for Jura to try. He came forward from the sidelines where he had been standing, his half-pita in hand.

Biaja was pleased to see he had decided to wear the mint-green linen robe Kit had made for him, rather than the traditional blue a new husband often wore. He could wear the blue—the one his sister had made for him with such care—after the party. Today it was good he did not outshine his bride.

Now he bowed to Kit, and made a surprisingly long speech about joining his agricultural knowledge with her rich lands, and how they fit together as families, as complementary villas, and as friends.

"I am pleased to announce, also," he said, "that yesterday morning when I left Suramarti, I left behind a dog and a cat who slept together in the sun of Jasasara's shrine, beside the holy tree." He smiled at Kit. "They looked happy together in the warm sunlight. In their bare paws."

Kit's lip quirked as he made the last comment.

He reached over, holding his half-pita up. Laughing, Kit held up her half—but they did not match!

Guests began catcalling and making outrageous insults at the couple.

"Oh no!" Kit called out. "Is Jasasara set against us?"

"Will we not marry?" Jura wondered.

At this point, Zetis jumped up and stood on his hands, then turned cartwheels through the crowd. "Over! Turn it over!" he cried.

Laughing, both Jura and Kit turned their pita halves over, and of course, they still did not fit. By now Kit was laughing so hard she could hardly keep hold of her pita.

Jura bowed to her, and to the crowd, then took Kit's piece of bread from her hand, turned it over and matched it against his.

And now the two pieces fit together as one.

All the guests cheered. Many toasts were made, as the feast began. All that remained was the blessing, which Qazipatima would take care of, and the distribution of gifts, which was Kit and Jura's job.

Bee relaxed, and filled her plate with baked, raisin-stuffed pheasant, honey-crusted goat, roasted vegetables, revithia and their various spiced and herbed sauces. She made Paian try the stuffed boiled egg with a spicy filling that was a specialty of the Suramarti cooks. His eyes watered, but he smiled. They drank wine, and fresh juice, and cool water.

Ukan used his bronze knife to slice off some of his roasted fish to share with Maza. Servers brought round baked aurochs on huge platters. The meat had been cooked so long the juicy bits fell off the bones. Minted revithia refreshed them in between more servings of meat—goat, duck, and fish. Fruit began making the rounds, as people became sated. The light, pleasant music Jura and Kitane had chosen seemed to flow over the guests, binding them together in celebration. Biaja leaned against Paian, content, as it seemed her sister and new brother-in-law were also.

SCENE 7 — JURA, WEDDING GIFTS

|ͬ |ᶜ

Jura and Kitane walked around the courtyard followed by the Tylissos steward and flock of atomai children, all delivering personal gifts. Their first visit went to Okune. He greeted her with two open palms and the traditional wedding greeting, "Jasasara's blessings to you. I can never match your gifts of shelter at your villa and the warmth of your daughter's arms." At this point, his steward signaled the children and one by one they handed Jura gifts to present to Okune.

He started with the traditional small gifts that different workers at Tylissos had prepared signifying their well wishes for Jura's new home. These included a small pot of the finest clay to hold ointments, a papyrus basket which held three perfect pears, a carved hand from the whitest limestone to hold rings at night, and a framed page of papyrus with a drawing of the Suramarti gate. The jewelry workers could not imagine any ornament worthy of presentation to the wife of Radamitu, so they gave her a silver soup spoon with a handle shaped like a carrot. When she accepted the carrot spoon, she laughed.

He finished with a carved wooden table carried in by four children. The Tylissos carvers had shaped the legs like papyrus branches. Okune brushed her hand across the smooth surface of the table top where the craftsmen had inlaid a scene of Suramarti trading ships and polished the surface with olive oil. She nodded her approval and many people moved closer to get a better look.

Jura reflected how much had changed since he had approached Okune like a small child whining about how Kitane mistreated and ignored him. Wearing his sandals in the Suramarti sanctuary seemed like such a silly concern now that they had fought the pirates and survived the wrath-of-Potidas waves.

He stood proudly next to Kit as guests filed by to admire the skill of the Tylissos woodworkers who Jura supervised. Today he demonstrated he was a good manager and valuable addition to

Suramarti, but also a partner with Kitane in caring for everyone living at that villa.

Next, Kitane waved her hand at Jura's steward and touched her ears. The happy couple visited the woman relatives with more gifts: Okune, Jura's mother, Bee, Qazi, Eluwari, Asije, Halima, Isari, and others. Each woman graciously accepted a pair of gold earrings and saluted Radamitu who stood beside Okune smiling proudly as expected from the father of such a powerful bride. The artists had shaped the earrings like sea stars and octopuses reflecting popular marine motifs. The final pair went to Maza in recognition of her betrothal to Ukan. The girl proudly put them on, removing the wood and silver ones that had been her best till now.

In the days leading up to the wedding, Jura had seen the conflict between Suramarti and the guasileus grow. Qazipatima rarely missed an opportunity to object to the guasileus' desire to convert Knossos from a Temple of Peace to a Palace of War. Okune's sister Asije exacerbated the dissension at every turn, making large Isari's betrothal to the son of the guasileus.

Being now of Suramarti, Jura of course supported Okune and Kitane and Qazi. Regardless, he understood that he could not ignore the guasileus. He and Kit faced the man with an open palm salute. "Blessings of Jasasara to you and your family."

He returned the greeting. "Protection of Potidas to you and all of Keftiu."

Jura cringed at this break in tradition. He knew that Qazi would object to this introduction of Potidas into the wedding celebration, the domain of Jasasara. Jura gave Kitane's hand a conspiratorial squeeze and signaled for the children. The youngsters brought forward an enormous polished bronze labrys. Four girls held the double-headed ax, and four more supported the shaft, as long as three priestesses were tall.

In a strong voice, Jura announced. "For your rebuilt port of Amnisos, a new labrys to replace the one lost in Potidas' wave."

The guasileus accepted the gift. "Thank you, Tylissos and Suramarti."

As they walked to the next guests, Qazi gave a wink to her new brother-in-law. The gift procession would continue until every guest had received something, if only a salute and a blessing. During this time, the musicians played music and the young people, telestai and atomai alike, danced.

Jura stopped to talk with his brother. "Ukan, I am so glad you've found a partner in Maza."

Ukan pulled Maza close. "Yes, we both have a desire for adventure. We will be traders with Diwoki. Maza will join me on all our voyages."

Jura noticed that when Maza stood tall, she was taller than Ukan.

"I am trading my donkeys for a trading ship, otherwise I will do what I have always done."

Ukan picked up a cup. "To Potidas, god of the land and sea!"

Jura hugged his brother and accidentally, on purpose, spilled Ukan's drink splashing them both. "I think you've had enough to drink tonight. You are to be a husband and an important trader. Your heavy drinking days are over."

Maza laughed. "Brother Jura, your big-brother days are also over. You no longer need to be watching over Ukan, not that you'll be able to when we are out at sea." She then rubbed her finger against the wet spot on Jura's mint-green linen robe. She brought the finger to her nose and took a deep breath. "Pear? Grape? Apple? No, definitely pear." She turned to Jura. You should rinse that pear juice right away before it leaves a stain on your lovely robe.

Ukan was drinking pear juice? Jura smiled and walked away, slightly embarrassed for falsely accusing his brother, but happy to see Ukan had grown up too.

Jura took Kit's hand and they walked to the opposite end of the field from the musicians. There seated in a comfortable chair with several cushions, they found Jura's mother. Even though she was older, she took in all the festivities with her alert eyes jumping from one group to another. Her hand moved up and down in time to the music.

"Mother, I am so glad you could make the long distance to the sanctuary."

"Maza and Ukan organized a donkey cart for me with plenty of blankets and pillows to protect me from the bouncing and cold. I may look frail, but I still have strength of spirit."

Kit handed her a silk robe that Diwoki had brought from Kmt, who had traded for it from far to the east. She didn't wear earrings and bracelets anymore, but Radamitu had made her a special gold pendant of a bird sitting in a nest to honor her as a mother. She accepted these gifts with a sweet smile for Kitane and her son.

Kit gave Jura a sly look and whispered to his mother. "We will make you a grandmother as soon as Jasasara allows."

At this, his mother laughed out loud, a sound from her he had not heard in many years.

Zetis ran by with his boys following, shouting something about the Amnisos battle. Kit reached out and grabbed his arm. The boy spun around and fell to the ground, rolling, writhing, and howling. "Zetis! Stop that right now! You are too old for that foolishness. Besides, it is time for the wedding dance. Can you start it?"

As quickly as he had fallen, he was back on his feet. His group joined hands and snaked through the crowd grabbing others to join the procession. "Wedding dance! Wedding dance!"

Jura and Kitane worked their way to the center, while Zetis led the growing procession in larger circles around them. The musicians increased the tempo of the familiar rhythm and the crowd grew louder and stepped faster.

Finally, with the women ululating and the auloi whistling frantically to a crescendo, the entire wedding went silent. Everyone raised their palms to the center. Jura and Kitane kissed.

Jura raised his hand and spoke softly to the silent party. "Now that we've distributed gifts to all the guests, I have one final gift I want to present. Kit squeezed his hand and squinted at him. He placed his lips on her ear. "I have a little surprise for you, something both familiar and never seen before."

"Suramarti is honoring us with an expansion to the old wing of the villa for Kitane and me as a home and office. The construction is not complete, but I have prepared a special decoration to incorporate into the new wall."

He signaled his steward. Six men appeared carrying something that was obviously heavy. It looked like a tabletop or a door, but heavier. Someone had covered it with a cotton robe and tied it with a red rope.

As the men walked to the center, they stopped several times to set it on the ground and rest. Finally, they placed it on edge in front of Kitane and untied the rope.

Jura said, "I love you Kitane, bull jumper." He removed the cotton covering and revealed a beautiful fresco of Kitane leaping over Enosidas. Tears shone in Kit's eyes, and Jura knew he had succeeded in pleasing her.

The last gift had been given, the last bits of food served and eaten, and now Kit took a deep breath, ready to move on to the next stage of the wedding. Usually the presentation of a telestai bride and groom was done by the parents or the highest-ranking members of the two families, but Kit and Jura had decided to do something a little different.

The tension between her mother and her aunt was already brutal. Of course, Kit wanted her own mother and father to present her, but Asije had insinuated herself into everything having to do with the wedding and Suramarti's status. Instead of arguing down Asije, Kit chose Enosidas to present her. This served several purposes.

She wanted to honor the bull's role in the battle to protect Keftiu—he represented all the bulls and their brave and majestic stand against the pirates. She also wanted to acknowledge that he was the most honorable and consistent of her friends, especially given Isari's apparent defection. And most of all, she wanted to show that Jura's devotion to their animals was as great as her own.

Finally, it removed the awkwardness of Jura's mother being physically unable to walk. Of course, she had come to the Sanctuary for her son's wedding, taking two days in a small hand-pulled cart. But she was unable to stand for any prolonged period. Expecting her to present Jura was cruel, and while his sister certainly could have done it, it highlighted the fact that Eluwari was herself yet unwed.

So, when the time came, Kit signaled the musicians, then she and Jura disappeared behind the nearest guest house where Enosidas stood calmly, swishing his tail as atomai tied on bundles of flowers and draped his withers with garlands. Kit used a small platform to mount his back, and Jura stood on the ground at the bull's shoulder as though he led the bull. When the auloi brayed a discordant call for quiet, Jura stepped forward in time to Eno's big hoofbeats, and without a word being said, the groom and her bull presented the bride and new leader of Suramarti to the assembled guests, who applauded the bull, and the unique presentation, as much as the bride.

Qazipatima stood up, her flounced apron fluttering from the movement as she stepped toward Jasasara's altar.

Jura seemed to lead Eno to the altar, carefully stepping between groups of guests, who moved back as the bull approached and they perceived the full size of the beast.

Jura gave Eno a small branch of his favorite snack bush to eat as Kit dismounted to stand beside him, one hand on Eno's nose, the other on Jura's shoulder.

"Goddess bless and preserve our friends of Suramarti and Tylissos," Qazi said, her trained voice carrying over the Sanctuary grounds. "Bless them with fertility of fields and orchards, stables and vineyards." She placed one hand on Jura's low abdomen, the other on Kitane's. "Bless them with fertility for Suramarti and Keftiu!" The crowd roared at this, and Qazipatima backed away as Kit and Jura turned and faced their guests, hands clasped.

"We thank you for joining us, friends and leaders of all Keftiu. Now, we know there is more to be said, more honor to be given, more news of weddings to come," Kit said, while Jura smiled.

And indeed, there were. While the guasileus made his way forward, Qazipatima thanked the guests for their gifts to the Temple, and reminded them of all the food and bandages used in the defense of Knossos. She asked for increased donations during the sign of the Swallow so that the Temple was once again fully replenished and strong.

The guasileus made a short bow to Kit and Jura, another to Qazi, then stepped forward to make his own announcements. As expected, he told the guests that his son was now courting Isari, daughter of Asije, who was rebuilding Amnisos. This surprised no one.

The smiling couple walked to the front carrying a carved wooden box decorated with the guasileus' seal. Kitane wondered if this was another wedding present, but they passed her and took the box to Qazi. The guasileus stood between the couple and Qazipatima. "These are tablets from Thera we found on the Amnisos beach, returned by Potidas, his blessing for Keftiu." Qazi's lips remained tightly closed as she accepted the unexpected gift.

He also announced changes in the way his guards and Knossos soldiers were being hired, paid to serve, and trained. They would also staff the watchtower at Amnisos as soon as that building was completed. He nodded to Asije at this, who preened like a peacock. Jura's eyes met Kit's and they shared a tiny smile with one another. It would be good to have Isari married; then she and her mother would move to Knossos and be gone from Suramarti. Some of the guests murmured objections at the mention of a standing army, but the guasileus ignored them.

He went on to honor "Those that fought at Amnisos," and said that one young man's skills would be hired by the "Palace at Knossos."

Palace? Kit shook her head slightly. Was he building a palace, too? Or did he plan to take over the temple? Her glance at Qazi revealed no information. Qazi's face looked like a statue in its beauty and stillness.

"Zetis, of house Suramarti, will be in our service henceforth, as an information gatherer," the guasileus pointed toward Kit's brother.

Zetis stood up and struck his chest with a closed fist. Then he did a backflip and pretended to sneak among the guests. "Or spy, if you prefer," the guasileus said to much laughter.

"Finally," the king said, "I thank both Tylissos and Suramarti for this beautiful celebration, for honoring our heroes and each other. I cannot imagine our wonderful Keftiu continuing without the strength, abundance, and generosity of our telestai families. Congratulations on your marriage." He smiled at Jura, then Kit, and moved back toward his board, clasping wrists with friends, and acknowledging bows and open-handed pledges as he went.

"I believe Okune of Suramarti has an announcement," Jura said loudly, to quiet the commotion of the guasileus' passage.

Okune, who had been standing nearby, stepped forward. "My friends, I am pleased to announce that the historian and poet Paian of the Hellenes will court my daughter Biaja." Bee and Paian stood up and bowed at the applause. "They also have an announcement of their own to make."

Kit squeezed Jura's hand as Bee and Paian announced the completion of his "History of the Amnisos battle" and his map and translation tablets, that had been placed in the safety of the caverns at Mt. Ida peak. They also stated they would travel to Athens together to visit the school and library. Then they introduced Diwoki, who had further news.

"Keftiu is the strongest power on the Middle Sea now that the pirates were washed away by Potidas' great strength. We are thankful for the preservation of so many Suramarti ships! Now I present our new partners who will trade in the north." Ukan and Maza walked forward and were cheered by all the telestai who would have goods to trade, and who looked forward to acquiring valuables from Athens and other ports of the Hellenes, as well as all the others around the Middle Sea.

Jura's mother, now sitting in her cart and clutching the frame with one hand while she waved the other, caught Kit's eye. Beside her, Kit could feel Jura's surprise as he started, noticing his mother as well. Eluwari stood up, looking happy as she put her arm around her mother's shoulders.

"Tylissos has an announcement?" Jura asked, curiosity and wonder equally obvious in his tone.

"I wish to tell all that Rendoki of Zakros now courts my daughter, Eluwari of Tylissos!" she said in a surprisingly strong voice. She nodded her head as if to refute any arguments and Eluwari acknowledged the applause.

"Is there any further news from our guests?" Jura asked. When no one responded, "Praise to Potidas!" Jura cried, raising his and Kit's clenched hands.

"Praise to Jasasara!" Kitane said, and Qazipatima stepped forward to give the final blessing to all the guests and the new couple.

When she finished, Ukan, coached in advance, made a step for Jura to mount Enosidas, who had stood patiently, buried in flowers, and chewing his cud. Jura jump-climbed aboard, then leaned back so Kit could land safely as she vaulted—wedding clothes and all—onto Eno's back in front of Jura, just as they'd practiced. She leaned back into her new husband and grinned, to the delight of their guests.

Everyone stood and applauded as Kit directed the great bull through the many people and boards, gifts, dishes, and cups, toward their Sanctuary guest house—the one set well back from the court and the other guest rooms, for privacy.

Jura helped her efficiently strip the flowers from Eno's broad back, then she led the bull to the small enclosure behind their room that had been filled with his favorite treats. Eno whuffed, and sniffed around his treasure trove. "You are now officially off duty, Eno," Kit said. "Eat as much as you like, sleep as long as you want." The bull whuffed again and blinked sleepily, nostrils flaring.

Kit followed Jura into their guest house, where he collapsed on the platform bed. Strewn with bay laurel leaves and lavender sprigs so it smelled and looked like a bower, the bed welcomed Kit as well.

"I am so tired," Jura said. "Who knew a wedding was this much work?"

Kit snuggled up next to him, resting her head on his shoulder. "It was all wonderful, but I'm glad it is done. Now we can begin to live our lives together." It would be rude to suggest all the people who had helped with the wedding were an annoyance, but in fact, that was just what they had become.

"Alone," Jura said.

She giggled, partly from exhaustion, partly from gladness that Jura felt the same. "Yes."

The heavy rains of spring were past, but today it was sprinkling again, as if to squeeze the last bit of water from the sky. Kit, already in the habit of resting her arms on her rounded belly, paused to look down the hill where the brickworks was just beginning its production for the year.

"It is an innovative idea to provide the shade for the workers, but I think we need to find a sturdier cloth for it. The sun rots it faster than a sail at sea," Jura said, watching as the workers unrolled the heavy woolen roll of cloth that had been stored away for the winter. Holes and torn edges made it clear the thing wasn't going to last the season.

"Diwoki spoke of a way of waxing the linen, not with beeswax, but with thick olive oil or certain resins, that helps preserve it from the sea. I don't know if that works against the sun, though."

Jura nodded. Kit stepped closer to him, putting her arm under his and around his waist. He put that arm on her shoulder, still studying the brickworks. "Maybe we should just use wood for it. The atomai don't have a prophecy about wood buildings falling down, just stone ones."

"They still believe that will happen?" She'd thought the disasters surrounding Thera had negated all the prophecies about destruction, but the atomai seemed to have their own seers with their own prophecies, about which the telestai still knew very little. Although Jura was working on it.

Jura nodded. "They are using some of these bricks to build brick-walled huts in the forest at Gazi, but they put wood pole roofs on them, and cover them with branches or sod to keep out the weather. The guasileus is having trouble getting his soldiers to sleep in the palace dormitories. They sleep outside in the court, or in huts they build themselves, of woolen cloth or branches."

They walked along the cart path that was still in the process of becoming a road between the orchards and fields of Suramarti, until they came to the place where a creek crossed the road, cutting ruts through the pounded dirt. "This is where I think a small bridge would be wise," Jura said.

Kit nodded. It was easy to see that if there was much rain, the road would be washed out entirely. "This did not use to be here," she said, looking uphill toward the presumed source of the creek.

"I believe that the last earthquake opened up a new spring," Jura said. "Or closed off the route that an old one took."

They both turned to watch as a small herd of goats exited the forest and trotted toward them. Once they'd reached the middle of the meadow, though, they stopped and ate the tender new grass, as well as some mushrooms that had sprung up in a circle around the remains of a dead tree.

"Biaja is coming soon. She wants to be here for the birth of our child. And also, to brag about Athens, I think." She laughed a bit. "Who would have guessed she was the scholar among us?"

Jura looked down at her face, a gentle smile softening his gaze. "I'm sure Okune is looking forward to that." He looked back up, at the goats, the forest, then upward to the peak of Mount Ida. "We must think of suitable gifts for Isari's wedding."

"Yes," Kit said. "I've already begun weaving the finest linen thread we have. She always admired Bee's blue and green layered gown, so my ladies are embroidering ribbons and panels for the skirt in those colors. My father has a grandiose gold collar-necklace designed and begun. But I think that much of Asije's wealth has gone to Amnisos, and that she isn't all that rich anymore so we needn't be *too* generous."

"As the guasileus likes it, I'm sure."

"Indeed." It still puzzled her how her aunt had played into the king's hands. "I think she still does not realize that he used her."

Jura shrugged. He did not know. He did not care, Kit realized.

She poked him. "I have to say, I am glad he did not offer his son to me." That would have made her choice even more difficult. She still wasn't certain why she had found Tros so attractive, when there was Jura, solid as a Keftiu oak. Tros would have plundered Suramarti's riches, as her aunt had plundered Thera's. Jura built what Tros would have torn down. How had it taken her so long to see that?

She poked him again. "Also, you should know I am glad Jura of Tylissos is my child's father." She smiled, glancing sideways to see his reaction. "I am happy Suramarti and Tylissos still follow the old ways."

"Hmm. Except for all the old ways we don't follow?" Jura teased, waving a hand toward the donkeys the Suramarti steward led past them, down the road toward the village. Their atomai soldiers were beginning to train in mounted exercises, as well as practicing with their weapons in mock battles on foot each day. "I am thinking we should give each soldier his own donkey, to keep, to train, to have for his own."

"Then we will also need to give them grain enough to feed them, for the donkeys' sake."

"And permission to graze in fields left fallow each year."

Kit nodded. "Whichever field Enosidas isn't in," she said.

Jura's eyebrows quirked up. "I think that's a good plan."

They could hear excited voices as the donkeys arrived in the village, which was out of sight from where they stood.

The gentle rain stopped, and the fresh scent of clean bay laurel and olive leaves enriched the breeze that blew downhill. The sun broke through the clouds, lighting the orchards below with a golden glow. Hope seemed to grow on their lands.

They turned and began walking again, back toward the villa. Back toward home.

POSTSCRIPT — DR. MARTIS, MT. IDA

"Well, I certainly hope they get us out of here," Dr. Martis said, setting the last of the boxed tablets aside. "I will be delighted to show Dr. Stone how wrong his ideas are. This was definitely a matriarchal society at the time of the Theran explosion."

Beside her, Jane started to giggle, then laughed until she hiccupped. "And...that's the only reason you hope they get us out?" she managed.

Dr. Martis grinned when she realized what she'd said. "I suppose I have faith we will be rescued; I'm just eager to share this news."

"Of course, we filled in a lot of the blanks in this Paian's story," Jane said, looking at the pile of tablets. "Just the bare bones of this history exist here."

"Yes, it will take many years of examination and authentication to put together a more pure, unimaginative translation. But this is the first real detail about people's daily lives."

"I love the pita game," Jane said.

"I love Miss Kitane and her magical bull."

"Do you think those bulls really could have done all that?"

Dr. Martis rubbed her forehead with gritty fingers. "I'm sure there was a great deal of exaggeration—look at Homer, and the Gilgamesh epic—these were wondrous tales meant to impress their audience. But we have the frescoes that show the bull jumping; everyone agrees that was a real event. And ancient aurochs were a different breed; perhaps it was so."

She examined a pot they'd found earlier, with a bull-jumping scene incised and painted upon it.

"Once again an important find demonstrates the many ways we have consistently underestimated how highly developed Bronze Age culture was."

Jane finished photographing the hard clay tablets and the two women slowly replaced them, in the order first discovered, back into the flimsy wooden boxes they'd been in.

They looked over the find, avoiding piles of what might have once been fabric. Special tools would be used to investigate those, tools that they didn't have with them.

"Oh, look at this," Jane called, holding an extremely intricate gold necklace up in her trembling gloved hands. "The dragonfly necklace from the story?"

"That is just gorgeous. No wonder Radamitu had such a reputation as a master goldsmith."

Dr. Martis' cell phone rang. She put it on speaker and answered.

"You're alive!" the rough dig supervisor's voice was loud in the quiet space.

"Indeed, we both are, alive and safe. Any prognosis on getting us out?"

"We've begun clearing already. It may take a while, though, I'm sorry. Some large ceiling segments came down that may require a crane."

"There's a hole in our ceiling in the back of this space. Our computer's compass says it's at the east end of this cavern. We can see daylight."

"I'll send a crew around to see if we can find you."

"We have a stunningly important find here. We have to get these materials out."

"That we will," the man said. "And you, too." They could hear other voices and machinery behind his words.

"Lunch would be lovely," Jane called. They could hear laughter, and arguments about how to get food and water into them.

"We'll feed you like zoo animals, drop it down on a line. As soon as we find the opening."

"Probably fresh rock exposed around it," Dr. Martis said.

"Yes."

"We'll be waiting." She and Jane exchanged a smile, and simply sat, admiring the dragonfly necklace, which gleamed in the steady light of their work lamps.

EXEUENT — TO THE READER

Please accept the authors' thanks for finding and reading our book.

We are independent authors and appreciate how difficult it is to select our book from the flood of offerings. We are dependent on reader-to-reader recommendations.

If you enjoyed our novel and wish to support independent writers, we would appreciate any posts on social media, and especially an all-important Amazon review.

Thank you.
  J. and D.R.

DRAMATIS PERSONAE

The Aurochs — the klawiphoros, or superintendent of the initiate priestesses at Knossos; Biaja's nemesis; around 40 years old

Asije — ah-SEE-jeh — Okune's younger sister evacuated from Akrotiri; Kitane and Biaja's aunt; Isari is her daughter; her son runs with Zetis; she lost two babies; early 40's

Biaja — bee-AH-jzyah — youngest Suramarti sister; novice priestess; often called Bee; 15

太Ψ日

Diwoki — dee-WOHK-ee — Suramarti trade ship captain; oldest Suramarti brother; married to Halima (from Kmt); 24

Eluwari — eh-LOO-wah-ree — Jura and Ukan's younger sister at Tylissos; Biaja's friend, sometimes called Elu; 16

Enosidas — eh-NOH-see-das — Kitane's bull, often called Eno

the guasileus — the king; head of state for trade and diplomacy purposes, but until now, not governance or religion.

Halima — hah-LEE-mah — Diwoki's wife, from Kmt; now honorarily of Suramarti, 22; two children: a female infant and a toddler boy

Isari — EEHS-ah-ree — Kitane's friend; her cousin from Akrotiri; Asije's daughter; about 17

Jura — JOO-rah — next-door neighbor of Suramarti; one of Kitane's suitors; eldest child from Tylissos villa; 20

𐘇 𐜼

Jura's mother — also Eluwari and Ukan's mother. An old, frail woman, we rarely see. Eluwari took over duties as head of house a long time ago, even though she has not married yet

Kano — KAH-noh — Jura's dog

Kitane — KEEHT-ah-neh — heroine, bull jumper; must marry soon; often called Kit; second youngest Suramarti sister, almost 17

𐛟𐜉𐜢

Maza — MAH-zah — atomai; guide/helper around the temple; good donkey handler; would like to marry a telestai; 15 or 16

Nopine — NOH-pee-neh — Biaja's friend and fellow initiate, atomai; 15

Okune — oh-KOO-neh — mother of Kitane and Biaja, plus two more daughters and two sons; head of Suramarti villa, farms, and trading; mid-40's

Paian — PAH-ee-ahn — scribe from Athens; he wants to marry a Keftiu girl, tries to interest Kitane; 18

𐜡𐜅𐜟

Qazipatima — kah-zee-PAHT-ee-mah — full priestess at Knossos who can be the Goddess Incarnation; beautiful; sometimes called Qazi; eldest Suramarti sister, 27

Radamitu — rah-dah-MEE-too — Kit & Bee's father; renowned goldsmith; late 40's

Sakusna — Sah-KOOS-nah—Suramarti trade ship sister; second eldest Suramarti sister, 21

Tros —TROHS — Hellene trade ship captain; Kitane's first choice of the suitors; 20

𐝁𐜪𐝍

Ukan — OO-kahn — Brother of Jura, sent from Tylissos to Knossos to learn about the Temple, and hopefully find a wife; about 18

Waro — WAH-roh — young atomai bull jumper performing in his first contest and ceremony at Knossos

Zetis — ZEH-tees — Kit & Bee's ambitious, bratty little brother; 12; the youngest of the Suramarti clan

Glossary and Gazetteer

Alashiya: what is now the island of Cyprus.

Akrotiri: the main city of *Thera*.

ammoudha: sandstone valued because of its distinctive color and texture and the ease with which it could be cut and carved.

Amnisos: the coastal city and harbor closest to *Knossos* is *Amnisos*, about 5 km (3 mi) north. 3,500 years later, it is mostly underwater and replaced by Heraklion.

Archipelago: the more than 2000 islands known today as the Cyclades. Traders stop at many of these islands when sailing between the *Hellene territories* and *Keftiu*.

Arzawa: what is now southern Turkey.

auloi: wind instrument, usually carved from bone. Usually two were played at once, one droning, one melodic.

Athens: a small city dedicated to the Goddess Athena in the northern part of the *Hellene territories*, in what is now Greece.

atomai: the *atomai* are the workers of *Keftiu*, both farmers and craftspeople, as opposed to the landowners, who are *telestai*.

aurochs: an ancient type of large cattle.

bronze-gold: the recipe for bronze is nine parts of *bronze-gold* (copper). This mineral is plentiful throughout the region.

bronze-silver: the recipe for bronze requires one part of *bronze-silver* (tin). The mineral is rare and might come from as far away as the land of the *Stone Circles*.

cubit: unit of measurement (length of a man's forearm from the elbow to the tip of the middle finger).

dittany: a medicinal herb native to *Keftiu*.

forminx: an early stringed instrument similar to a lyre; usually seven sheep gut strings on a wood or bone frame. One hand would pluck the melody with a hooked pick made of bone, the other would strum a drone sound. The forminx was usually held between the knees or on the lap.

guasileus: king, headman; there is an honorary king at Knossos, called the guasileus, who meets with foreign dignitaries and maintains trade rights with other rulers around the Middle Sea.

Hellene territories: the mainland of what is now Greece.

Hellenes: the *Hellenes* are the peoples who live in the *Hellene territories* during the time of this story.

Horns of Consecration: the *Horns of Consecration* was an abstract representation of the bull's horns displayed at sacred sites.

Jasasara: the goddess of life, fertility, marriage, and rebirth. Main goddess of *Keftiu*.

Kaimeni: the island volcano in the middle of the lagoon contained by the circular island of *Thera* (what is now Santorini).

Keftiu: *Keftiu* is the island of Crete during the second millennium BCE. *Keftiu* is also the name of the people that live there.

klawiphoros: literally, "key-bearer." A priest or priestesses in charge of initiates, their quarters, and their training.

Kmt: the Black Land, the people of the Black Land (what is now Egypt), from the rich dark soil along the Nile.

Knossos: *Knossos* is the largest temple on *Keftiu*, and possibly the largest in the world. It is dedicated to the Goddess Jasasara and the God Potidas (who are not a couple; rather adversaries, not unlike Ares/Poseidon vs. Demeter/Artemis/Aphrodite).

kuzbarah: seeds which were crushed and used medicinally to numb and clean, and as a flavoring agent; probably coriander.

labrys: the *labrys* is a double-headed ax. This was one of the two main *Keftiu* sacred symbols, usually associated with a goddess.

lustral basin: A sunken room in temples and other sacred spaces which we have imagined was filled with herbs and leaves for religious ceremonies.

Magrib: a trading partner of Kmt and sometimes Keftiu; the coastal plains and hills of what is now Algeria and Tunis; a source of cork.

Malia: a north coast harbor to the east of *Knossos*. There is a temple in *Malia*.

Middle Sea: the Mediterranean, including the Aegean Sea.

Phaistos: a temple south of *Knossos*, on the southern side *of Keftiu*.

pithos: (plural *pithoi*): a large ceramic jar used for storage. It might be as tall as a person. Its capacity is about 900 liters or 250 gallons and can weigh over a tonne/ton.

Potidas: the *Keftiu* god of the earth, sea, and underworld is *Potidas*, who later became the Greek god Poseidon and perhaps also was a precursor to Hades and Ares.

polythyron: "pier and door" construction, where a wall is pierced by several doors on the ground floor, each with a window above. Shutters or doors were opened or closed to control the view and the light in ceremonies.

propylaea: ceremonial entrance.

revithia: chickpea (of which a familiar type is garbanzo beans).

rhyton: a ceremonial pitcher, often in the shape of a bull's head, used to pour wine during religious ceremonies and important meals. Sometimes used as a cup.

saj: a large domed pan (copper or bronze) used for cooking pita (flatbread) over an open fire.

sistrum: percussion musical instrument (a cross between a rattle and tambourine in sound).

stone circle: the stone circles impress the *Keftiu* because they use such large stones. The *stone circles* are in what is now England, which was a source of tin.

talent: a unit of weight used for bulk goods such as ore. *Bronze-gold* and *bronze-silver* were smelted into ingots called talents and weighing approximately 29 kilograms or 64 pounds.

Tanis: port city of Bronze Age *Kmt* (what is now Egypt).

temple, the: generally meant as the priestesses' stronghold at Knossos; also, any *temple*, as distinguished from a guasileus' palace. At the time of this story, there are *temples* at Knossos, Malia, Phaistos, Zakros and a small temple or large sanctuary at Mt. Ida. *The Temple* also figuratively referred to the organization controlled by the priestesses.

telestai: the *telestai* are the landowners of *Keftiu*. They manage large estates where there are workshops, fields of grain and vegetables, olive and fruit orchards, and vineyards. They owe taxes to the temples. Some of their workers are free, others are serfs, bound to the land (collectively the workers are referred to as *atomai*).

Thera: the closest *Archipelago Island* to *Keftiu;* what is now Santorini.

Zakros: *Keftiu* port city on the far eastern shore of the island.

KEFTIU ASTRONOMY

Over the course of a year, the nighttime stars appear to rotate around the earth. Different star configurations, called constellations, become associated with the seasons. For a contemporary example, the astrology signs of Cancer, Leo, and Virgo are the summer constellations.

An exception to this rule is the North Star, Polaris. In recent history, Polaris was fixed. It was believed to be always in the north.

Ancient civilization observed several cycles, from the daily cycle of the Sun to the monthly cycle of the Moon, and the annual cycle of the constellations. The objects that failed to follow these cycles were the planets (named for the Greek word *wanderers*).

In the last century, science has identified several longer cycles, now collectively called Milankovitch cycles. These cycles include orbital eccentricity, obliquity, and precession, with time periods of approximately 100,000 years, 41,000 years, and 25,771.5 years respectively.

For the purposes of formulating astrology for the Keftiu (3,500 years ago), the authors only considered precession.

Figure 1: Precession

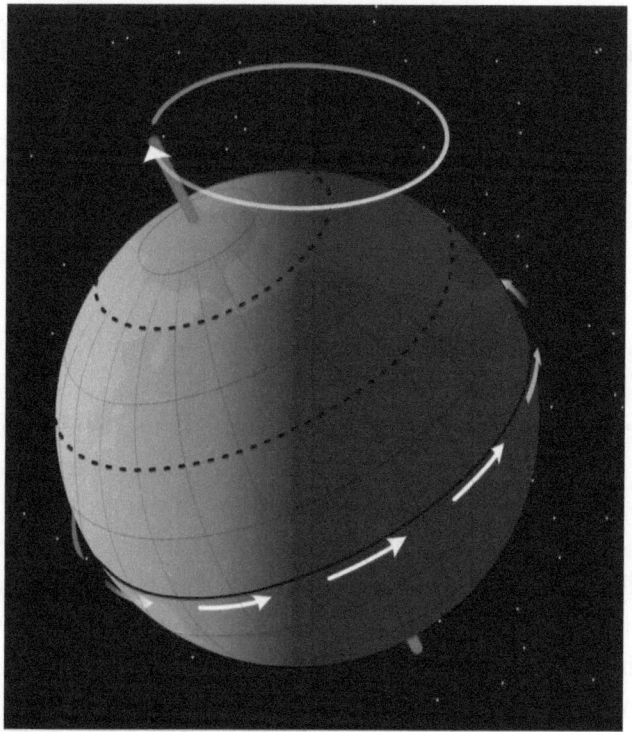

Precession: The rotational axis of the earth slowly moves as shown by the small circle in the figure, completing one circuit approximately every 26,000 years.

The star directly above the rotational axis is the North Star. In the current era, we are fortunate that axis points to Polaris. However, this is not always true. In general, the axis points to empty space. There is no North Star.

Let's just review the current situation. The North Star is located by finding the Big Dipper, aka Big Bear, aka Ursa Major. A couple of stars in this constellation point to Polaris. Polaris is a star at handle-end of the Little Dipper, aka Little Bear, aka Ursa Minor.

During the time of our story, there was no ideal North Star, like Polaris. However, the star closest to the north would have been the chosen North Star of the time.

For the purposes of the Keftiu, the authors renamed these two constellations with Keftiu-appropriate names: Big Double Axe and the Little Double Axe (Labrys). The North Star is on the handle end of the Little Double Axe and is called the Bull Star.

Keftiu sailors would have located the Big Double Axe and followed two stars to locate the Bull Star within the Little Double Axe. This is like the process used in the current era, except that different stars are employed, even though the polar constellations are the same.

The other effect of precession is the movement of the constellations with respect to the seasons. 3,500-years-ago represents a change of one zodiac sign. Thus, while Cancer, Leo, Virgo are summer constellations now, Leo, Virgo, and Libra would have been summer constellations in the past.

Of course, the Keftiu would have had their own names for the constellations. The authors renamed the constellations for the Keftiu as follows:

Spring: Spring Flowers, Initiates, Triton
Summer: Dolphin, Snake Goddess, Swallow
Autumn: Three Women, Octopus, Trading Ship
Winter: Bull Jumper, Papyrus, Bee

KEFTIU LANGUAGE AND WRITING

Historical fiction presents a mixture of opportunities and challenges. The more remote the setting, the more the authors must fill in blanks in the historical record. My co-author and I have chosen a bronze age setting, about 3,500 years ago. The bronze age is on the boundary between history and archeology. Artifacts, pottery, ruins, and middens tend to be more important and plentiful than written records during this time.

While many cultures had developed writing by the bronze age, few of these have been deciphered. One bronze age system has been famously deciphered: Egyptian Hieroglyphics.

Many systems are on the other side of the ledger, including:

- Harappan: Indus Valley from 3500 to 1900 BCE.
- Olmec: Middle America from 1250 to 400 BCE.
- Ba and Shu: Southwestern China 5th and 4th century BCE.
- Linear A: Crete from 2500 to 1450 BCE.

In general, scientists cannot decipher writing systems without a connection to a known language. With the dearth of written evidence, writers take advantage of whatever evidence is available. We set our novel on Minoan Crete during the time when Linear A was in use, thus the written history provided little information.

Fortunately, the Minoan civilization lasted from 2600 to 1400 BCE and left many artifacts, most notably the temple/palace at Knossos. During the time of our novel, an enormous volcanic eruption preserved the Minoan settlement of Akrotiri on Thera (much like Pompeii).

While we included much of the archeological research, we also wanted to credit their written record. While scholars have not deciphered the language of Linear A, they do understand the phonetics of the alphabet. We used this limited syllabary to name our characters with one notable exception.

We took inspiration for this story from Shakespeare's *Taming of the Shrew* where one sister is named Bianca. There is no B sound in the Linear A syllabary, but we compromised in favor of the bard. We chose Biaja for the sister's name and used the Linear A "P" sound to spell it. Keftiu nameplates for Biaja, Kitane, and Jura employ Linear A, while the Hellene names for Tros and Paian use Linear B.

We resolved other vocabulary issues drawing on the written record of other cultures, both historical and current. The Minoans lived during a time where other people were writing history, notably the Myceneans (Greeks) to the north and Egyptians to the south. For example, we don't know what the Minoans called themselves, so we used the names used by the Egyptians (Keftiu)—another word not available with the Linear A alphabet (no "F"). We took the same approach with place names which are only known by the Greek today, such as Phaistos.

In cases where we needed ancient vocabulary, we drew on known lexicons from the area, including Greek, Egyptian, and Middle Eastern languages.

We believe that this attention to details and careful decisions is much of the fun of reading and writing historical fiction. Linear A and Linear B are two similar bronze age writing systems. While archeologists have deciphered Linear B (proto-Greek), they have had no success with Linear A (Minoan). Famously, they have deciphered Egyptian hieroglyphics with the help of the Rosetta Stone. This was an exceptional achievement.

The Phaistos Disc discovered in 1908 is the most famous example of Linear A.

We have used the conceit of an educated historian (Paian) who has knowledge of both Linear A and B, writing a "history" copied into both languages, which provides a "Rosetta Stone" for Dr. Martis to find 3500 years later.

ACKNOWLEDGMENTS AND CREDITS

Many people and organizations (knowingly and not) contributed to this work of fiction. Acknowledgment here does not imply an endorsement, review, or even knowledge, of this book. For further research, check out the reading list below.

Precession graphic: Credit NASA

Middle Sea map: Credit Norman B. Leventhal Map Center at the Boston Public Library

We also want to thank our family: for information, support, and understanding: Jason, Jennie, Matt, and Samantha.

We must acknowledge these two who still believe we set this book in Egypt (Kmt) where people knew how to treat cats properly.

SUGGESTED FURTHER READING

The Aegean Bronze Age, Cynthia W. Shalmerdine, Ed., ISBN 978-0-521-89127-1

Art and Religion in Thera, **Nanno Marinatos, ISBN 960-7310-27-6**

Crete, John Freely, ISBN 0-941533-63-8

The Destruction of Knossos, H.E.L. Mellersh, ISBN 1-56619-194-7

The Dwellers on the Nile, E. A. Wallis Budge, ISBN 0-486-23501-7

The Greek Islands, Eyewitness Travel Guides, ISBN 0-7894-1453-8

Greek People, Robert B. Kebric, ISBN 1-55934-645-0

Knossos, Alexandre Farnoux, ISBN 0-8109-2819-1

Life in Ancient Egypt, Adolf Erman, ISBN 0-486-22632-8

Minoan and Mycenaean Art, **Reynold Higgins, ISBN 0-500-20303-2**

Minoan Kingship and the Solar Goddess, **Nanno Marinatos, ISBN 978-0-252-07967-2**

Minoan Crete, E. Sapouna-Sakellaraki, Muses Publications, ISBN 960-7994-03-5

Minoans, **Rodney Castleden, ISBN 0-415-08833-X**

The Search for Ancient Greece, Roland and Francoise Etienne, ISBN 0-8109-2804-3

Women's Work, Elizabeth Wayland Barber, ISBN 978-0-393-31348-2

Time/Life series Lost Civilizations:
   Anatolia, Cauldron of Cultures ISBN 0-8094-9108-7
   Egypt: Land of the Pharaohs, ISBN 0-8094-9850-2
   Mesopotamia: The Mighty Kings, ISBN 0-8094-9041-2
   Persians: Masters of Empire, ISBN 0-8094-9104-4
   Ramses II: Magnificence on the Nile, ISBN 0-8094-9012-9
   Sumer, Cities of Eden, ISBN 0-8094-9887-1

Wondrous realms of the Aegean, ISBN 0-8094-9875-8

We found the information in the books highlighted in **bold** most helpful to our imagining of ancient Minoan culture. As always, please note this is a work of fiction, thus any errors or fantasies we devised based on this information are our responsibility.

ALSO BY J. OESTREICHER AND D.R. OESTREICHER

Darwin's Paradox: An international science mystery
Pandemic Mysteries #1

Pandemic Mysteries: a series of independent science mysteries

The world is on the verge of a rabies-like pandemic. Using tribal and scientific medicine, can a small group of amateur scientists solve the unsolvable?

Available in all Amazon stores
ISBN: 978-0-9631755-5-6
http://amzn.to/2k8qJgi

Amazon review excerpts

As the best fiction does, this book works to educate as well as to entertain, with true detail about daily life in the novel's various settings, the process of science, challenges of management, ...

There is rich, resonant character development and much curiosity about the nature of the human condition. In its understated way, this novel wonders at the fact that some of the most vibrant humans are nurtured in some of the planet's toughest environments.

Plague of Equals: A science thriller of international disease, politics, and drug discovery.
Pandemic Mysteries #2

Pandemic Mysteries: a series of independent science mysteries

The world is experiencing wide-spread, unexplained miscarriages. Everyone has a piece of the puzzle, but will anyone see the full pattern?

Available in all Amazon stores
ISBN: 978-0-9631755-4-0
http://amzn.to/2jEwdyp

A big, sprawling adventure tale centered on a specific theme, with an almost Chaucerian cast of characters — Goodreads 5-star review

In this story, the scientists do what scientists always do … they find the truth. The truth is surprising to both scientific and non-scientific readers. Enjoy. — review by a research biologist

Amazon reviews

"…it takes you away and brings you back home, a little richer."

"The accuracy and humor of the conversation between scientists were amazing"

"…the tension between scientific discovery and social justice."

"…the science was on point."

"multiple story lines … everything ties in right at the end."

327

ABOUT THE AUTHORS

The authors grew up in San Francisco Bay Area, CA and Long Island, NY before meeting in Salt Lake City. J. raised three wonderful children while making time to publish poems and short stories. D.R. researched Silicon Valley startups. Today they live in Southern California with their two cats. They enjoy international travel, reading, and writing, and gathering unique perspectives from the magical minds of their grandchildren.

They write research-based fiction with an emphasis on international locations and cultures.

BONUS: ORIGINAL COVER ARTWORK

Checkout: https://www.etsy.com/shop/MythMaking

(acrylic on canvas)

www.ingramcontent.com/pod-product-compliance
Lightning Source LLC
Chambersburg PA
CBHW021532250626
47154CB00006BA/2088